THE DEVIL'S HORN

Also by David L. Robbins:

Souls to Keep
War of the Rats
The End of War
Scorched Earth
Last Citadel
Liberation Road
The Assassins Gallery
The Betrayal Game
Broken Jewel

USAF Pararescue Thrillers:
The Devil's Waters
The Empty Quarter

For the stage:
Scorched Earth (an adaptation)
The End of War (an adaptation)
Sam & Carol

For Scott Williams, John McElroy, and Chris Baker.
My very own Guardian Angels.

THE DEVIL'S HORN

DAVID L. ROBBINS

THOMAS & MERCER

Published by Thomas & Mercer, Seattle

www.apub.com

ISBN-13: 9781503945470
ISBN-10: 1503945472

Cover design by Alan Lynch Artists

Printed in the United States of America

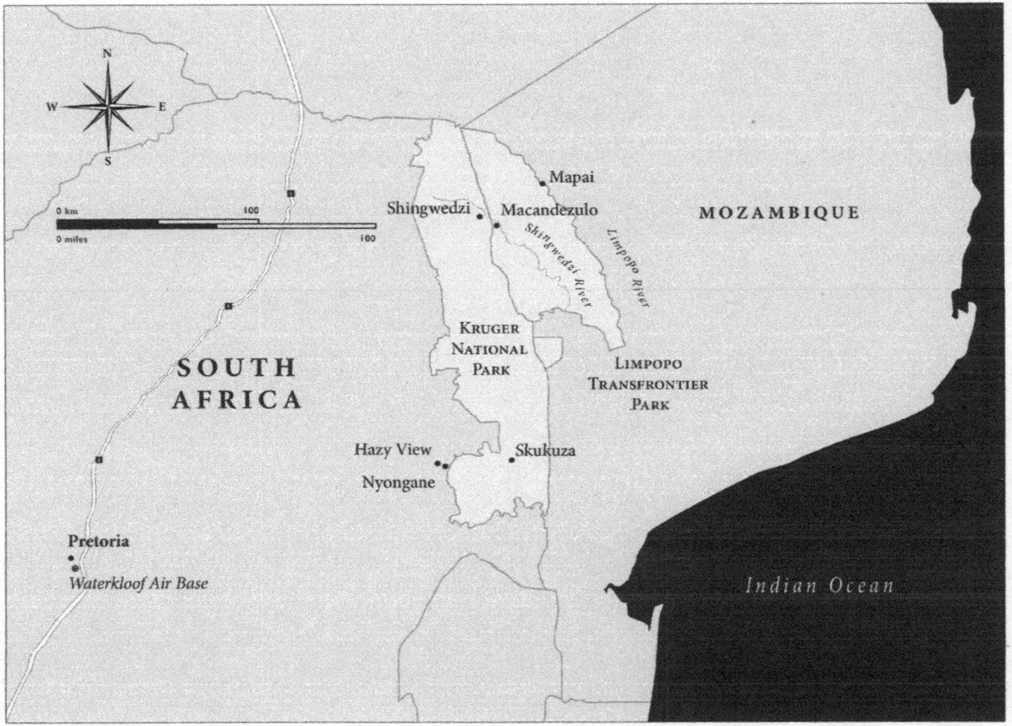
N
W
E
S
0 km
100
0 miles
100
Mapai
Shingwedzi
Macandezulo
MOZAMBIQUE
Shingwedzi River
Limpopo River
KRUGER
NATIONAL
PARK
LIMPOPO
TRANSFRONTIER
PARK
SOUTH
AFRICA
Hazy View
Skukuza
Nyongane
Pretoria
Waterkloof Air Base
Indian Ocean

I am wounded, dangerous,
can bear any pain I feel
less than this.
Zulu poem

He who makes a beast of himself
gets rid of the pain of being a man.
Samuel Johnson

Chapter 1

A poacher's moon rose behind the hills and fever trees east of the border. Promise sat on a granite boulder. Here, not far from the broken fence between her country and theirs, she waited for the Mozambicans.

They arrived as the moon's chin left the earth and the bush became milky. She heard them coming long before they arrived, two men, thin as the light, in sandals, short pants, and American T-shirts, and a rifle.

Promise stood on the rock, taller than the pair until she stepped down. They greeted her in Bantu. She answered in the same, leaving aside her native Zulu.

The first to reach out was the younger, the mule. The hand Promise shook felt boneless, only a shy pressure in the boy's clasp. He looked away quickly, dropping his hand out of hers. He bore on his back a battered pack and gripped a long-handled hatchet. A panga hung from his belt. He gave his name. Hard Life.

The other Mozambican strode forward, the shooter. This one lacked both front teeth in his forced smile. His handshake was even slighter than the boy's, detached and hinting cruelty. A strap cut across his narrow chest; the silenced barrel of a Remington .375 H & H rifle rose above his shoulder. Under the full moon he gave his name, Good Luck.

Promise did not offer her name in return. She wore only a cotton tunic and long pants, both black, and rubber-soled sandals. A machete hung from her belt, and across her own back hung a Belgian R-1 .762 rifle.

"Follow me. Single file."

Good Luck stopped her with a pink palm.

"Wait."

He slid behind Hard Life to open the backpack. The short boy stared straight ahead while Good Luck tugged out a bundle, untied the string that held it, and shook out a leopard skin. He doffed the rifle before putting his head through a hole in the spotted hide to spread it across his shoulders like a poncho. He belted the string at his waist. Good Luck lifted a boar-tusk necklace from the pack, handing this to Hard Life who bowed his head to put it on. These were *muti*, charms given them by their village *sangoma*, a witch doctor, to keep them safe while in the Kruger. The sangoma had probably blessed the rifle and hatchet, too. As a child Promise had worn charms in the bush, but tonight she had none.

Promise set out along a game trail. Good Luck and Hard Life followed in a line as she'd ordered. She did not hear their footsteps and barely heard her own, all of them stepping lightly now on the worn path, making just shallow prints in the pale dirt. The night had lost little of the day's heat, but Promise did not sweat. She'd drunk all her water in the morning, a way to trick thirst.

The moon floated higher behind them, casting long shadows like claw marks on the silver ground. Far off, two lions vocalized. The big cats were not hunting in a full moon but patrolling their territory, letting Promise and the Mozambicans know they were entering it. She glanced back at Hard Life. The boy fingered his tusk necklace but beyond that kept his composure. Behind him, Good Luck flashed his broken grin, unafraid in his leopard pelt.

Piles of dung, large and small, speckled the trail, the scattered pellets of giraffes; grassy, round bricks from elephants; and black beads from antelope. Another path joined the one they walked;

a hundred meters onward another linked up. Game trails always converged as they headed to water and spread apart away from it.

For an hour, Promise led the Mozambicans deeper into the veld, west on their own shadows. She kept the pace fast, never leaving the game trails, not worrying about their own spoor. Her throat began to dry, she put a smooth stone under her tongue to make her mouth water. Hard Life and Good Luck did not speak to her or to one another, they either knew each other very well or not at all. Hiding in the prickly acacias, behind the great baobabs and red bushwillows, among the blooming cacti and shrubs, or grazing in the open fields, the wild children of the bush watched them pass in silence, grunted in the dark to announce themselves, or fled.

The moon had risen a quarter of its way and gone sallow when Promise halted. The poachers, skinny men, took to their knees to rest. Hard Life, burdened with the pack and hatchet, panted. Good Luck spit. He lisped through the gap of his missing front teeth.

"Are we almost there?"

Promise nodded, keeping more words out of the air. She checked the slight breeze. They stood upwind from the water hole, another kilometer away. They could not approach from this direction.

Without waiting for the Mozambicans to stand, Promise left the trail. The two scrabbled to their feet. Good Luck cursed in Bantu. He took the hatchet from Hard Life to hurry the boy.

She led them into a spiny grove, dropping the rifle into her hands to keep it from catching on the stickers while she ducked under them. The moon did not reach here. Promise kept her face to the earth so her cheeks would not be scratched, and left her machete sheathed. The poachers made noise, muttering about the thorns. Ahead of her, something small and fleet spooked and skittered away.

Promise came out on another game trail but did not take it. She'd not yet shifted the wind off her back. Any animal at the water hole had already heard them, though there were too many sounds in the vast bush for her and the Mozambicans to stand out. But their smell to a beast was like a beacon; men were coming. She bent at the waist and led the poachers into more grasping branches and thorns the size of fingers.

A jackal yelped in the near distance. Another replied, pestering some prey. A lion roared again, this time a female. Grasshoppers and crickets chirped.

Promise stayed in the brush and scraggly trees, a slow and grueling passage. Bush rabbits and lizards rattled the leaves around her. She rotated her torso left and right, the way to stop thorns from snagging. After ten long minutes, two hundred meters southward, she pushed out of the scrub into a clearing. She eased her back and tested the wind. The light breeze nipped her ears and throat, well enough in front of them to carry their scent away from the watering hole.

Behind her, the poachers bashed their way through the vegetation. Hard Life had lost patience and begun to hack the underbrush with his panga. Before they emerged, Promise stepped into a clearing where four game trails converged. She knelt to an animal's print, a fat five-pointed star, the spoor of a white rhino. Beside the track, the dirt held the impressions of two boots, faded by a day of wind and sun but clearly deeper at the toes than the heels. These were the marks of someone squatting to look at this same print early this morning. Her.

Hard Life chopped his way out of the last of the brush, perspiring. Good Luck came in his wake. The boy and the man, both scratched by the thorns, joined her in the clearing on the crossroads of the trails. Promise pointed at Hard Life's panga, still sticky with sap and leaves.

"Put that away. Don't touch it again."

The boy wiped the blade before sliding it behind his belt. Good Luck kept smiling, a patch of nothing in the middle of his mouth. Promise raised a hand.

"Have you done this before? Either of you?"

The shooter nodded. The boy shrugged, no.

"Up ahead is a water hole. There will be animals there. There are animals all around us right now. Somewhere in this sector there's also a two-man team of rangers. They are invisible. I don't know where they are. But they know where the water is, too. They have guns. And they have ears."

Hard Life shuffled his feet. He did not look up to speak.

"I'm sorry."

Promise patted the air between them, to forgive and quiet the boy. This young poacher was not important, one of ten thousand unskilled villagers seeking easy money. Hard Life was a little pair of shoulders and legs, a mule. For no more than this, he was recruited to risk his life.

The shooter mattered. Promise would be paid by how well she guided him, not the boy.

"Do you know what you're doing?"

Good Luck unslung the Remington. In the leaden light the weapon was a harsh thing of gray and ebony, without beauty. The man held the long barrel out to Promise.

"Look at the silencer. I made it myself."

Promise examined the tube screwed onto the muzzle. It was a clever piece, cobbled from the baffle of a car muffler. Only someone who knew guns could do this. She pushed the rifle back at him and turned.

"One shot."

At her back, Good Luck repeated, "One shot."

Promise had farther to go to approach the water from the southwest, to send the scent of Hard Life's fresh sweat and Good Luck's leopard pelt wafting over open land. She eased through more brush, switched game trails, and continued to circle. After her reproach, the poachers followed quietly.

Promise chewed on bits of biltong from her pocket, offering some of the dried meat to Hard Life. The moon climbed, shortening the shadows and brightening the path. She eyed the ground for the spoor of men.

She didn't know where they were, no one did. Promise scanned for broken branches and twigs, scuffed dirt, and flattened grass, to catch the passing of the two-man ECP, the extended clandestine patrol, through this sector of the park, Shingwedzi.

She had no idea which team was on patrol tonight, but it made no difference. All the five-day rangers were excellent trackers, born bushmen, hardened like everything left in the sun. They roamed Shingwedzi's water holes and ravines, wide plains, high grasses, and all the gathering places and hunting grounds. Each man knew his terrain intimately, just as he knew the creatures that viewed the Kruger as theirs. The clandestine rangers didn't walk freely but avoided ridgelines, masked their tracks, and dodged tourists, researchers, workers, anyone in the great park who might spot them. The teams camped in hides without open fires, lived on rations, and carried only small tents, camouflage nets and ground sheets, a pot, biofuel stove, radio but no cell phones, Belgian rifles, and ammunition. They washed without soap, buried their waste, moved in day and night. They left little trace of themselves while they hunted poachers.

Promise pressed on until the brush gave way to flat, open ground. The veins of many trails ran together. On all sides, mopane trees had been stripped bare by elephants or knocked over by their passage. Promise stopped on the path. Good Luck sidled beside her, nose in the air.

He whispered, "Water." Good Luck's nostrils flared. "Game."

The faint stink of dung and urine and the moistness of mud drifted on the night air. The poacher tipped his head in the direction of the breeze.

"Go."

Beyond a stand of marula trees and acacia thorns, a hundred meters off, the water hole was painted in the muted palette of moonlight. The noises of animals bathing and drinking mingled with their smell on the gentle wind.

Promise crept forward, keeping behind cover. The water hole was just a depression in the earth, no larger than the yard of a small house. After rains it overflowed, and even in the dry season the bottom stayed a damp pan for wallowing.

She crept into the open to kneel. Hard Life joined her, but Good Luck rose to his feet. He unshouldered his rifle. Promise hissed and made him take a knee.

Together, they watched the water hole. A pair of horned bok came to sip beside three zebras, then ambled away into the dark. A baby elephant stood knee-deep in the water, splashing with its trunk while a big female watched from the muddy shore. Many times Promise had seen lions and leopards lounging beside this little pond, ignoring hyenas drinking greedily on the far bank after gorging on kill. The wildlife who came here kept a truce, it was safer than the river, without crocodiles and the crowding, competing hippos and buffalo. This was Promise's favorite place in Shingwedzi. Tonight she'd brought poachers to it.

Hard Life, still a boy, marveled at the antics of the little elephant. Good Luck sniffed.

"Where is the rhino?"

"Not far."

"It's not here."

"It's been here. Keep quiet. Stay behind me. And put your rifle on your back until I tell you."

Promise led them in a wide arc around the water hole. Now past midnight, the moon had climbed to its highest perch. Granite in the soil twinkled like tinsel. She leaned to the trail but did not read it for the tracks of elephant pads, the careful clawed paws of a cheetah, the half-moon steps of zebras, or the split hooves of eland, kudu, and impala. A giraffe eyed them over a treetop, and a family of bushpigs squealed across their path, surprising Hard Life into dropping his hatchet. Promise walked a full circuit around the water hole and caught no sign of boots.

She led the grumbling poachers on a second loop around the pool. This time she saw the white rhino in the earth. He had gone north from the water. He would not be far, walking his middens, grazing, solitary.

"This way."

Promise put the falling moon to her left, the squawks of the water hole behind her. The land opened into a savanna of dried riverbeds dotted by shrubs, nettles, and grassy patches. During the summer days, this part of Shingwedzi lay empty, the cover too sparse for prey or predator. The African sun made the grasses toxic and unappetizing during the day. But in the cooler nights, large mammals came to eat the sweetened grass and sleep in the open.

Sound and sight carried far on the plain. Six kilometers west, on the other side of the river, the headlamps of a car coursed southward, Kruger tourists on a night drive. From the river a hippo roared, like a belch. Promise shielded her eyes from the glaring moon to scan ahead.

Striding forward, the boy, Hard Life, appeared at her side. The shooter hung back. Hard Life said nothing until Promise spoke first.

"Yes?"

"Why are you doing this?"

"You're a child. Why are you doing this?"

"I'm from a village. Kankomba."

"Don't tell me."

"There's no work. I could go to Maputo or Johannesburg. And make spit for money."

"What about him?"

"Good Luck says he is rich. He has a car and a wife."

"From horn."

"He says."

"And you?"

"I will get rich."

"Not from tonight."

"No. I will have to do this many times."

Promise walked on, Hard Life's shadow spilling across her sandals. The mention of wealth and the rhinos he would butcher for it had beefed up Hard Life's courage to talk. The boy rapped the hatchet against his palm.

"The bosses recruit in the villages on the border. Nothing but poor. What can we do? The bosses say they have money, they have weapons. Go poach for us. There's risk, but there's pay. So we go."

Promise already knew these things, a common story about poachers, but she let the boy talk, it seemed to calm him. She glanced back at Good Luck strolling in his spotted pelt. The high moonlight made caverns of his sockets, and his black eyes did not shine.

"What about him?"

Hard Life shrugged, to say he knew only a little.

"He's from Maputo. I think he was a criminal already. Or a soldier. I don't like him. Can I ask you something?"

"What?"

"Have you done this before?"

"No."

"Who recruited you?"

"No one."

"What do you mean?"

"Stop talking."

"But you want to get rich."

"No."

Promise widened her stride to separate herself from the boy. Hard Life caught the cue and faded behind her, taking his shadow out of her path.

She led the Mozambicans deeper into the open expanse. The world lay the hue and flatness of slate. Far to her left, tracing the horizon, another car trickled down the one paved road. The moon crowded out all but the brightest stars low in the sky. Promise made a wish on those stars, wished away the shooter and the poor boy behind her, but they did not go. The shooter wore his magic leopard skin, the boy his tusks, and she had no charm or magic to counter them. Promise continued to guide the poachers because she, like them, knew of no other way but to the rhino.

In that moment, the earth gave her the animal. Perhaps there was magic in the world, but only for dark uses, for the people like Good Luck. This chilled her on the warm night. Promise turned to the poachers to tell them what she'd found. Good Luck's broken smile and emptied eyes made her shiver. She stopped walking. She could stop everything else. Lie to the shooter and the hatchet boy, tell them the rhino was not on the plain but elsewhere, she did not know where. She would send the Mozambicans back across the border. Tonight, Promise could save the beast and herself. Then tomorrow, she would make the same choice to come back. So she knelt.

The midden had been kicked and spread around. Promise broke open a cool, fist-sized chunk of dung. Under the moon the insides showed green gray, a grazer's stool. She touched the spoor to her lips. The warmth inside told that the rhino had been here within a half hour.

A fresh set of tracks led northeast, away from the river and the road and the moon. She led the poachers toward that darker horizon.

On the scrub-dotted veld, the pearly light made nothing stand out. The bushes and short trees could all be large animals champing grass or asleep on their feet. No birds chirped in the brush, no monkeys howled. The plain lay hushed, starry. Walking fast behind the rhino tracks, Promise clapped her hands. The beast, wherever he was, would not see them coming. A rhino's eyesight was poor, but its hearing was acute.

The savanna did not flinch. Promise sped forward. Hard Life's backpack, Good Luck's rifle, and the gun across her own back all jangled. She clapped again. Passing another midden she clapped a third time.

A shape moved on the veld. To the east, a hundred meters off, the big rhino put his head into a bush, thinking he was hiding.

Again, Good Luck tramped ahead of her. He tugged the long Remington into his hands. Promise stepped in front of him.

"We'll get closer."

"I can shoot him from here."

"Can you kill him from here?"

Promise didn't wait for the hiss of Good Luck's answer. She jammed a finger inside the ring of tusks against Hard Life's chest.

"Stay here. Come fast when you hear the shot."

The boy did not protest but squatted in the patchy grass.

Promise gave the shooter an uncompromising glare. The rhino was hers, in her Shingwedzi, though she only rode a bicycle through it. Good Luck was a trespasser, nothing else; murder and theft gave him no rights here. How many rhinos had this grinning Mozambican killed? After tonight, how many more carcasses would the boy attend to get his riches? After tonight, who would forgive her?

"Follow me."

Good Luck filled the gap in his teeth with a peeking tongue, as if he had a snake in his mouth. The tongue pulled back. Good Luck nodded.

With his lisp, he replied, "As you say."

She pressed ahead, checking that the wind did not carry their scents to the animal. The rhino continued to ignore them, believing he was covered in the brush though his enormous hind end faced Promise and the poacher.

This was not a hunt, though some would call it so. The rhino made no attempt to disguise his spoor in the veld, had no ability to hide behind a bush, and could barely see. Under constellations on this immense plain, he would die from a high-powered bullet fired by a man Promise would lead to within twenty paces. The rhino swung his head out of the brush to look their way. His main horn was over a meter long, the secondary horn a quarter the size, both primitive and beautiful and far more valuable than his life.

Good Luck chambered one magnum round into the silenced Remington. The clack of the bolt made the rhino blink, and nothing more.

Promise did not say, "Shoot," she gave no order or permission. In her heart she clung to the wisp that she had only guided the poachers here, she was not the killer but still, somehow, redeemable. Good Luck smirked at her, darkly pleased.

He raised the rifle to his cheek, turned his night eyes to it. For a motionless moment, Promise and the rhino looked stupidly at Good Luck. The rhino turned his profile. The gun barked, an ugly, muted punch with nothing on the plain to echo it. Promise's hands flew up, whether to her ears or the lie that she was not to blame or to the animal, she did not know.

A rhino with a bullet in its brain will fold to its knees, dead, and remain upright. A mortally wounded rhino will stumble, then collapse on its side. This one ran.

The beast squealed, wheeling away from the sound that had stung him so terribly. He lunged into a copse of brush, lowering his horns to crash ahead as if blind. Good Luck lowered the Remington to gape at his failure.

Promise shoved the shooter in the chest, pushing him almost off his feet. The rhino barreled into a thicket, too large to disappear under the bright moon. His shrieks mingled with the thunder of his clumsy gallop; he'd been hit, surely, and perhaps killed, but would not drop until he'd run out the last of his great terror.

Hard Life skidded to a stop beside Promise.

"What happened?"

Promise grabbed the hatchet from the boy.

"He missed."

She sprinted away with the ax, even as Good Luck advanced on her to answer the shove she'd given him. Promise followed the mewling rhino into the brush. Running flat out, the panga banged against her thigh, and her rifle bounced on her back. Both sandals threatened to fly off, but she gripped them with her toes as she ran. When she burst through a broken line of shrubs, the animal's blood smeared her arm.

When she caught up to the rhino in the open field, he had slowed to a trot. He trudged ahead; driven on by agony, his only understanding was to move. In the moonlight the rhino's head glistened with blood, the bullet had struck behind his eyes, short of the brain. He did not turn to Promise, jogging alongside, but snorted a wet mist. The lumbering beast lowered his horns, sensing an enemy.

Promise could not guess how long the rhino might run. Every step seemed heavier, but the beast was an old bull and had been powerful. If a ranger patrol lurked anywhere near, they'd heard the shot, even with Good Luck's silencer, or the rhino's bellows of agony. Promise could not let him go on. Loping alongside, she laid a palm to his thick, heaving hide.

"Uxholo, umnunzan." (I am sorry, sir.)

Gripping the long-handled hatchet with both hands, she swung high over her head. Promise leaped to bring the blade down as hard as she could into the ridge of the rhino's spine, just behind the head. She'd seen this wound on many carcasses in the Kruger, the brutal way poachers stopped a runaway rhino without firing another shot.

The crunch of meat and bone shot through the handle into her hands. The blow had bit into the rhino's vertebrae but not deep enough to sever the cord. Twisting his head against the hatchet, the rhino shrieked and slashed his long horn her way. Both huge forelegs dragged in the grass, but the beast slogged on, grunting.

Promise hacked at the beast's spine again. The ax only chipped the rhino's backbone. She swung again, missing the spine but chopping into the shoulder, where the blade cut a vessel. Hot blood fountained over her. Promise took aim at the brawny neck and swung one more time, leaving her feet, pounding the ax down with all her strength. The edge broke through the spine; she felt the bones give way. Showering blood, the rhino honked and collapsed to his chest. Spattered and panting for breath, Promise yanked the hatchet free and dropped it.

The blinded rhino sprawled in the grass, legs bent wrong under his massive weight. He could no longer feel his own torso but kept swinging his horns left and right. Promise knelt in his warm breath. Dark mucus drained from the rhino's snorting nostrils. Promise laughed, giddy and confused with nerves strained from the kill, descending toward tears. She choked back the need to weep as Hard Life and Good Luck hurried across the field.

In leopard skin and tusks, gaunt and black in the moonlight, the two Mozambicans seemed phantoms, beasts and men blended, wraiths of the veld rushing to her and the dying animal. Promise watched them come and imagined they brought mercy.

The boy arrived first. His expression fell into awe at bloody Promise and the felled giant. Hard Life's jaw dropped, and he wanted to speak. Good Luck came behind and pushed the boy in the back.

"Get the horns."

Not taking his eyes off the rhino or closing his mouth, Hard Life picked the hatchet up off the grass. He licked his lips and plainly wanted to run away. At the sound of the boy approaching, the crippled rhino shifted his head to fend him off, the only motion he could make. The wound behind his eyes pulsed, gouts of blood reflected the moon like tar.

Promise raised a palm at Good Luck.

"Kill it first."

"Why didn't you shoot it?"

"I can't have one of my bullets found in the carcass."

Promise backed away.

"Kill it."

Good Luck had a round ready in the Remington. He stepped up, but the rhino did not react to him, as though Good Luck were a shade, were death. The rhino lay completely still and closed his ruined eyes when the shooter pressed the silencer against his crown. The beast breathed a long sigh, sinking into the ground even before Good Luck pulled the trigger.

The rifle jerked in the shooter's hands, making only a pop against the skull. The rhino did not shudder.

Good Luck picked up the spent brass casing, then slung the rifle over his shoulder. Promise and the poachers flanked the silent gray mound. The rhino's severed spine rose eye level with little Hard Life. The tip of the long horn stood taller than the boy's waist.

Hard Life eased forward. He shrugged out of his backpack, coming to his knees beside the hushed head. The boy rolled the ax handle in his hands, spinning the blade.

Good Luck waited, then lisped, "Do you know how?"

"I was told."

"Then do it."

Hard Life rolled the hatchet over again, hesitant. He cast a pleading glance at Good Luck, then Promise. Kneeling on the veld, so far from where he ought to be, the boy was easy to pity.

The shooter cursed with his peeking tongue.

"Get out of the way."

Promise stopped him.

"Make the boy do it."

"Why?"

"Because." She squatted beside the boy and spoke gently. "Because you have no other way to your riches."

Hard Life sniveled. Promise slapped him. She left the rhino's blood streaked on the boy's cheek.

"Do it."

Promise stepped away, beside Good Luck. Hard Life ran his bare arm under his nose, sniffling. On his knees, he fingered the tusks around his neck, muttering.

As if the secret words or the muti had given him resolve, the boy raised the ax two-handed. Arching his little body, he hewed hard into the snout at the base of the front horn. The blade bit into solid bone with the sound of grinding rocks. Hard Life struck again, diagonally, the blade digging deep to take flesh with the horn. Good Luck folded his arms, satisfied. Promise did the same, crossing her arms and making herself watch. She did not deserve to look away.

Ten, fifteen more times Hard Life slammed the hatchet down. He wept while he chopped and grew frenzied. The dead rhino's head was so large it barely shook under the little boy's blows. When Hard Life wrenched the horn loose from the mangled face, he climbed to his feet with it held by the tip. He did not raise the horn as a trophy but let it drag in the grass. In his other hand, the gory ax dangled. The boy's face gleamed with tears and blood, and his eyes were as empty as Good Luck's.

The shooter took the horn to admire the heft. In his leopard pelt and rifle, weighing the big, gray spike still jagged with meat, Good Luck looked the role of killer. He tucked the horn into Hard Life's backpack, then pointed.

"Get the other one."

With vacant motions the boy returned to his knees. The ax rose and fell around the shorter horn. The scrape of metal on bone crawled up Promise's back until the boy pried the horn free. Good Luck snatched it to tuck it into the knapsack.

"You know the way back?"

Promise nodded. Good Luck pulled the Remington off his shoulders to make room for the backpack. The gesture said, "I have the horns, and I am in charge now."

"Let's go."

The shooter did not wait for Hard Life to stand but strode into the dimness. Promise did not follow. A dozen steps away Good Luck stopped, annoyed with her and the slender boy.

Promise knelt beside Hard Life and the carcass. Stripped of his horns, shot and cut up, crushing his own legs, the beast looked shamed, nothing like the colossus he had been. On her knees, Promise slid her bloody hand into Hard Life's. His small-boned grip trembled. Good Luck cursed them both and stalked off alone. Promise let him walk off; she could track him.

• • •

She found Good Luck two hundred meters away, pacing over open ground. Promise stomped up to the shooter.

"Give the boy the backpack."

He shook his head. Promise grabbed one of the straps and tugged. Good Luck tried to back away, but she held him fast.

"It's his job. He's afraid you'll try to have him paid less."

Good Luck made his marred smile.

"You're a suspicious woman."

"What I am is not your concern. Take it off."

The poacher sloughed the pack off his shoulders. Promise tossed it to the boy. She addressed both poachers.

"Walk where I walk."

Promise took the lead with Hard Life behind, Good Luck in the rear. She didn't know when the carcass would be discovered.

The ECP might blunder into it tonight; maybe the rangers were on their trail right now. At first light, in four hours, buzzards would circle and mark the dead rhino.

She headed southeast to the busted spot in the fence where the Mozambicans had crossed, following the contours of the land past familiar acacia hedges and fever trees, mopanes and marulas, along game trails and dry creeks. When Promise did not recognize the land, she let the stars lead her. The blood on her skin dried like scabs, her black tunic and pants turned crusty. Promise paid more attention to the tracks and scat on the trail than she did the two poachers behind her. The more she blamed them, the faster she walked, sometimes jogging, and left it to the Mozambicans to keep up.

The trek through the bush took an hour and a half. Without breaking the pace, Promise reached the jumble of boulders near the border where she'd waited earlier. The poachers scrambled to her through the dark. Facing the granite rocks, remembering herself sitting on them with the moon just beginning to climb, Promise recalled a different girl. She wanted to wave her arms and shout at the ghost of herself, drive her away before Hard Life and Good Luck could arrive under the rising moon. But she was too late; the two came huffing up with the severed horns, and the moon had begun to vanish.

Reaching the boulders, Good Luck squatted on his sandals to rest. He spit through his teeth.

"I don't like working with either of you."

Promise and Hard Life stood on either side, looking down on the shooter. The boy poked him with the handle of the ax.

"Let's go."

"When I'm ready."

Promise indicated the backpack.

"Do you have water?"

"Yes."

"Give him some."

Hard Life dropped the pack to dig inside. The long horn stuck out, sharp, accusing, and pointing at Promise.

The shooter grabbed the water bottle from the boy and sucked hard, he was dehydrated.

Hard Life jutted his chin toward the border.

"I know where to go. Come on."

Hard Life shouldered the pack. The shooter made no move to join them but stayed folded and balanced on his sandals in the dirt, finishing the water. The boy took the lead, walking swiftly the way Promise had. On his back, the horn rose above his head.

The border between South Africa and Mozambique was nothing but a decades-old two-meter-high fence, just strands of wire and posts. The barrier lay on its face in as many places as it stood. Every year, thousands of poor Mozambicans snuck across illegally, either to poach in the Kruger or to find work in the cities. Many never returned, prevented by predators in the park, armed and angry rangers, or the urban, even more crushing kind of poverty that awaited them in Johannesburg and Pretoria.

Even with the fence down in so many places, the animals of the Kruger did not stray into Mozambique. They stayed away, as if they knew they would not be cared for there, as if they knew all the rhinos across the border had been killed.

The moon sank in the west while Promise followed Hard Life. East beyond the fence, the terrain climbed softly to a low ridgeline, a dark wave against a star-studded horizon. To the south, the earth fell into a steep ravine, a hidden and favorite crossing spot but not now, in the rainy season, when it was a mire.

A thirty-meter section of barrier lay on the ground, the posts rusty and the strands snapped. A dirt road ran just inside the boundary. Hard Life stepped across into Mozambique, dropped the pack to the road, and withdrew a flashlight. He aimed the beam into the slow-rising hillsides. No answer but winking stars came out of the black. The boy waved the light back and forth.

Good Luck came up and took the light from him with impatience. He blinked it once at the hills, twice, then once again, a signal. On the crest of a knoll a kilometer away, a pair of headlights flicked on and bounced down the slope.

Promise and the poachers waited silently while the pickup wove downhill through the brush. Promise did not cross the borderline but stayed on the verge inside her own country, standing on the links of the downed fence.

The *bakkie* pulled onto the dirt road, squeaking on bad springs to halt in front of Good Luck. The skinny shooter said nothing when he jumped into the truck bed, leaned his back against the cab, and laid the rifle across his bony, crossed ankles. He spit between his teeth a last time, not reaching South Africa or Promise.

Hard Life batted the long lashes of his child's eyes at Promise, as though he might cry again. She only nodded in reply, to say she did not hate him.

Hard Life handed the backpack to the driver, who pulled the horns inside the dark cab. With the bloody hatchet, the boy climbed into the back beside Good Luck and pulled his bare knees to his chest.

The muzzle of an AK-47 appeared on the driver's windowsill, aimed at Promise. Prickles scurried across her skin. Her hands rose from her sides, she retreated a step, not knowing what to do. A low voice issued from inside the bakkie.

"It's alright."

The weapon withdrew. The passenger door of the truck creaked open. The truck seemed to right itself when Juma got out, he was so big.

Juma walked in front of the headlights. In the years since Promise had seen him, his belly had grown, his face had fattened, and his gait had become more roly-poly. Juma's years of wealth were mounting on him.

He spread his long arms and big hands, still strong from his time in the mines. Juma waited on his side of the fence, backlit by the truck's lights. Jewelry sparkled on his wrists. He wore dark, long pants, a white silk pullover shirt, and dress shoes.

"When my sister called, I did not believe her."

"Hello, Granduncle."

"Hello, Nomawethu." He used her family name. It meant *with my ancestors*. "Come give me a hug."

Promise hesitated. Criminals crossed the border like that, on foot, without papers. Juma was a criminal, he should come to her. But Juma had her money.

She stepped over the remains of the fence into Mozambique, into her great-uncle's heavy embrace. Her cheek flattened against his soft chest. Promise did not loop her arms around him, she could not have joined her hands. She rested them on the ledge of his waist.

Juma kissed the top of her head and whispered, "You did well."

Promise dropped her hands, but he did not let her go.

"You have blood on you. Was it hard?"

She nodded into his breast.

"I'm sorry. I would have sent better men with you, not these two baboons. But I didn't believe you would come."

Promise stepped back against his arms. Juma set her loose, looking down on her with the wash of white light from the idling truck behind him. He wiped a broad, warm thumb down her cheek to clean a dot of blood.

"That's why your grandmother calls you Promise. You keep your word."

Juma stepped back, spreading his hands again. He appraised Promise.

"You've become quite a beauty. The bush agrees with you."

Promise wanted to stand here no longer. The lit-up vehicle was a beacon, any patrol for kilometers in every direction could see it. Juma was little more than a stranger to her, a patchwork memory of a gigantic man, a rare visitor to the township bringing expensive gifts. Always her grandfather resented the presents, complaining afterward that Juma was not generous but crowing, showing off his dirty money. Her grandmother clucked her tongue and held out both hands to her brother's visits and gifts.

"Do you have my money?"

Juma cocked his head, mimicking disappointment.

"I wish we had more time to talk, child. Some other time."

Juma pulled from his pocket a roll of bills bound with a rubber band.

"Fifty thousand rand. As agreed."

Promise accepted the cash with one hand. Juma reached to his other pocket for a money clip. He detached another sheaf of bills.

"And ten thousand more, for my family."

Promise took this with her free hand.

Juma clapped meaty fingers around her wrist.

"I want you to know I met you out here on the border because I didn't want you coming to me in Macandezulo. No matter what my sister said. I didn't trust you. You're a Kruger ranger."

Juma laid a white calling card on top of the cash in her open palm.

"I trust you now."

With a squeeze of her arm, Juma released her. He put his broad back to Promise, crossed through the headlights, and left her on the wrong side of the border.

• • •

With Juma, his poachers, and the moon all gone, Promise gazed across a murky vale. She squatted to listen to the far-off lions, the hoots of an owl, and the furtive Kruger. Her eyes readjusted from Juma's headlights to the canopy of stars. She waited ten minutes, immobile on the dirt road in Mozambique, until she was sure she was unseen.

Promise took off her sandals to add a new set of tracks. Keeping to the game trail, she walked backward, careful to lay her bare heels into the dirt first before the pads of her feet to make forward-looking strides. Like this, she backed across the border all the way to the boulders. There she climbed on the rocks, where no prints could be recorded, and hopped from rock to rock until she ran out of granite.

Moving west again, Promise avoided the paths. She moved across open grazing lands that would not remember prints, high stepped through tall grasses to prevent a trail, and avoided sandy soil unless it was to walk backward and barefoot again. She trod through no brush, broke no twigs, stirred no scent from flowers and herbs, the antitracking tricks of the poachers.

With dawn two hours away, she reached the water hole. The animals knew she was coming, heads were up and awaiting. The hyenas were gone; perhaps they'd followed her to the rhino and were the first to feast. The female lions still lounged above the bank. The elephant mother and child had been joined by a great tusked bull who stood with the baby in the shallows. A tall kudu watched Promise with ears straight out, wary and ready to bolt.

Five strides from the water, Promise dropped to her knees. She shrugged the rifle off her back. She tucked Juma's money under the weight of the gun. With the panga she dug a hole in the soft ground. The animals watched, and she watched them.

When the hole was deep enough to reach in up to her elbow, Promise tugged the black tunic over her head and stripped off her pants. She shoved the bloody clothes into the little pit, then covered them. She tamped the earth down, then eased naked into the pool.

In the dark, Promise cupped water over her hips and small breasts. She splashed the shore to blend in the hole she'd dug. The bull elephant took this as play and sprayed the youngster before him. The kudu trotted off.

Promise washed away the dead rhino. She scrubbed her hair and under her nails. The brown water dissolved the flaky blood and cooled her, but saddened her more; with the blood gone, with her clothes buried and tracks disguised, the evidence of what she'd done was left solely in her heart. The burden there seemed greatest.

Promise stood in the water, dripping. On the opposite bank a lioness yawned and eyed her. How could she go back to the rangers with this guilt? She might as well have kept the blood on her face. The lioness stared at her, unmoving. Promise let the big cat's remorseless gaze harden her own heart. The elephants ignored her, playing, and this felt like forgiveness. The stars were distant and small, the night vast, and the untamed bush itself seemed to take no notice.

• • •

For another moonless hour she slipped through the bush, naked but for her sandals, machete, rifle, and money. Though Promise hurried, every step was meant to leave either no trace or a misleading one. Her nakedness made her kin with the animals of the Kruger; she was raw like them, she had killed like them. But no creatures made themselves known to her, no birds chirped, no wild dogs barked along her way. Their absence felt like rejection. Promise nodded to the silence as if to say, *Fine.* She tightened her fingers around Juma's money. In the northern distance, a tumult erupted, a quick skirmish over the fresh rhino carcass, now discovered. The squabble ended with a wounded shriek, then a hush as the beasts settled down to tear the corpse apart. *Fine.* The money in Promise's fist was the piece she had torn off.

With an hour of darkness left, she reached her bicycle and the backpack she'd hidden in a jade bush not far from the paved road and river at dusk. She put on her khaki uniform and boots.

With no traffic, Promise pedaled south in the center of the road, along the river. The breeze felt right again, not against her bare body but only on her face and arms. Her cap and high-laced boots, the bicycle, and the Kruger-ranger patch on her shoulder all signaled her return. Soon she'd be rid of the wad of cash in her backpack.

Promise rode under the rising curtain of night. The first violet stains of sunrise inked the eastern sky as she braked and carried the bike off the road. She stashed it in a hedge of thorns, left the rifle and backpack, too, and took only the panga.

She walked a hundred meters into the bush, into an open space lumpy with rounded mounds of clay, some as tall as she. Promise bent close to the ground, searching in the pallid light. Quickly she found the spoor. Promise knelt to the few sausage-shaped droppings. Breaking one open, she flicked at the insides to reveal the undigested heads of termites and ants. The dung was warm against her lips.

On the edge of the field, a copse of prickly pear cacti twisted out of the ground. Promise squatted near the needles to pluck a fruit. With the machete she carved away the spiny skin to slice the green flesh into quarters, then she swallowed the moisture and pulp. She did not keep watch on the field of termite mounds but shut her eyes and listened.

Sleep lurked close behind her eyelids. The adrenaline, the struggle and blood of the long night, Juma and his poachers had all left her drained. Promise wavered on her heels but caught herself with a hand to the ground. She opened her eyes.

The aardvark snuffled like a pig. Noiselessly, Promise moved from behind the cacti to watch the ungainly creature amble to one of the colonies. The beast stopped at the base, sniffed around it, and with its foreclaws began to dig, flinging dirt past its big hind legs. Promise took her panga in hand but held back to let the aardvark burrow deeper and fix its attention.

The aardvark was an odd-looking beast, with jackrabbit ears, a swinish snout, and the small, dim eyes of a nocturnal feeder; it was muscular but slow, a digging machine with powerful, clawed paws. It scratched in the earth the way a medicine man did for roots, so the tribesmen held the aardvark to be a symbol of healing, even magic, a sangoma.

With amazing speed the grunting creature dug a burrow, then drove in its long snout. It snuffled and inhaled termites by the thousands, chewing lustily. Pale ribbons streaked the eastern sky; the sun would be full up soon, and the aardvark would go to some underground lair. Beyond the schedule of the beast, Promise was in no rush. She could not return to the Shingwedzi ranger station until afternoon, to play out the lie that she'd spent her day in the township with her grandparents.

Promise crept up from behind, moving slowly to raise no alarm. One of the aardvark's ears cocked backward, aware, but the creature kept its nose at the trough. Promise inched closer, crossing into the shower of red dirt the beast heaved behind itself as it raided deeper into the termites' caverns.

Coming alongside, she raised the panga high; the bottom of the handle stuck out from her fist.

Like the dying rhino when Promise was beside him, the aardvark knew only one thing. The rhino ran, and this beast ate. Promise hammered the knob of the machete's handle down on the skull between the long ears. The aardvark, stunned, buckled its back legs and tried to reel its face out of the hole, but Promise banged the panga down again. The beast dropped to its belly, nose still jammed in the earth. Promise clubbed it one more time. She stood erect while the termites, suddenly saved, crawled up and over the beast's inert face.

Chapter 2

The loadmaster shouted, "Door!" He extended his arms together and opened them like an alligator's mouth. When he was sure the pararescuemen saw him, he punched the red button, and the ramp of the HC-130 began to lower.

The ramp's action vibrated in the steel deck under LB's boots. White daylight and humid air flooded around the gate's edges, and the noise in the cargo bay spiked. Blue sky, softened by ten thousand feet of altitude, filled the opening.

Seated by himself in one of the mesh seats across from LB, Wally shouted something into the satellite phone at his lips, a call he'd been on for five minutes. Wally nodded to something he heard, shouted into the mic again, then came out of the seat to drop one knee to the floor.

The big plane shuddered over a rough patch of air. Wally, in full jump gear like the rest of the team, braced against the fuselage. LB glanced away, then back, for lack of anything else to watch in the empty cargo bay except for the loadmaster and the three dozing PJs.

Wally got to his feet. He curled a finger for LB to come over to him. LB mimicked the gesture in return: *No, you come over here.* Wally upped the game, twirling his whole hand to insist LB cross to him.

LB nudged Doc in the seat beside him, making Doc lift his head. LB shrugged, as if to say to Doc, *Why can't he walk over here*? Doc, one of the oldest hands in the unit, along with LB, raised his eyes before closing them again, not amused by yet another match of wills between LB and Wally.

LB barely heard himself say, "Okay."

Standing to give himself room, he rotated his arm in circles as though waving to someone from a great distance.

Tall, slender Wally slid on his sunglasses. He aimed a finger at LB across the cargo bay, then stabbed the digit straight down in front of him. *Come here.*

Covering the short distance across the deck, LB made a show of each shuffling stride. He didn't like standing with the hundred-pound burden of his chute, med ruck, body armor, and weapons; he had a tweaky back, the result of weighing two hundred pounds and standing five nine. He'd never done yoga, never stretched, and hated running. Instead, LB lifted weights and ate as much meat as the air force could provide. He collapsed weightily in a mesh seat. Wally followed every petulant move with the ovals of his reflecting shades.

LB knocked the back of his helmet against the fuselage. He mouthed the word. "What?"

Wally shouted, "I thought you'd like to know." "What?"

"I'm getting married."

LB gagged as much as laughed. He would have doubled over, but the ruck in his lap stopped him.

"Is that what you were doing just now?"

"Yes."

"You asked Torres to marry you on the radio?"

Torres was the director of the PRCC, the Personnel Recovery Coordination Center, at Camp Lemonnier up in Djibouti. She was Latin pretty and air force smart. Torres sent the camp's Guardian Angels—pararescue jumpers, called PJs, including LB—and their combat-rescue officers, or CROs, like Wally, on missions. She and Wally had been doing touch-and-goes for a year now.

"I'll do it again when we get back. But yes."

"On your knee?"

"Alright."

"And she said yes? Not 'Screw you, you're in a plane'?"

Wally tried to wave him off. "Okay."

LB pushed out of the mesh seat, struggling to his feet. He considered motioning to the loadmaster, a tall, lean boy in a green flight suit and headphones, but LB didn't know the airman's name and couldn't be sure he wouldn't be sympathetic to Wally. LB could wake young Jamie, but the kid would only clap Wally on the back because he was nice. Quincy, the giant, didn't care about much except cars, cattle, guns, and rescues; he wouldn't see the humor. Doc had a wife and four daughters back in Vegas. And a female dog. He could go either way depending on what kind of phone call he'd last gotten from home. LB grew almost frantic for an ally.

Before he could decide what play to make, the loadmaster dragged his hand across the lined-up knees of three napping PJs, rousing them. Above the open cargo bay door, the scarlet ready light blazed, the five-minute call. Wally, tall and effortlessly balanced, brushed past LB.

The team formed up, facing the open sky. LB, the jumpmaster, shouldered his way to the front. Digging under Wally's skin would have to wait. LB stashed the urge and concentrated on the job at hand.

Standing before the team, LB bent at the waist, right hand in front, palm up, and rotated his shoulders, the signal that he was giving the team their final report on the wind. He stood to shout over the noise in the bay. "Winds seven!" He held up seven fingers. LB slashed his arm across his body, left to right, the sign for gusts. Again he shouted. "Gusting ten!" He held up all ten fingers.

He fingered the radio tucked in his web vest, made sure it was set to the team freq, depressed the "Push to Talk" button clipped to his chest, then pointed at Wally.

"Juggler, you copy?"

Wally's voice crackled in LB's earpiece.

"Five by five. How me?"

"Five by five."

Each PJ made the same radio check. LB inched forward to peer down past the lowered gate. From this height, the rounded horizon made a gentle world, a green and manicured place.

A new voice sizzled in LB's ear, right on time.

"Mayday, Mayday, Mayday."

The voice stayed under control despite the apparent urgency of the message, a pilot's trained tone.

"F-16 flameout. Ejecting at five thousand feet, bravo one-two sector. Minor injuries. Hostiles on ground. Require immediate evac."

LB revolved to his gathered team. Wally scowled behind his sunglasses. Jamie, Doc, and Quincy all pointed at LB, the unbroken sky at his backside. Showtime.

From the cockpit, the pilot answered the F-16 pilot's distress call.

"F-16, this is Air Rescue HC-130 *Kingsman 1.* We are airborne. Guardian Angels are en route to your location. We are in your sector. Keep your head down."

LB turned to face the whipping air, the plane's huge tail fins overhead, and the roar of four propellers. He lowered his goggles, did one deep squat to shrug all his gear into place, then the green light flicked on. He ran three steps, because there was no fourth.

LB plummeted, arms and legs outstretched, cupped in the palm of rushing air. His cheeks rubberized; the stiff camo uniform flapped. The drop deafened and silenced him, took away his weight, and left LB nothing but velocity and the beauty of falling free.

Far below waited a carnival atmosphere, applause, kids—air shows were a taste of glory, a pat on the back, the best temporary duty a GA team could go on. Looking toward the fast-closing ground, LB saw a pillar of gray smoke billowing from the grassy plain just east of Waterkloof Air Base. By now, the downed pilot would have staggered out of the trees, drawing applause from ten thousand spectators in lawn chairs and on blankets at the edge of the big field. The air show crowd would have heard his Mayday call and *Kingsman 1*'s reply over loudspeakers. Every eye would be scanning the firmament for the plunging dots, the American Guardian Angels jumping to the rescue.

LB's wrist altimeter checked off eight thousand, seven fifty, seven thousand, six fifty. The smoke rising from the fake crash site confirmed that he was coming in downwind. Five miles north of the air base, Pretoria sprawled with pubs and pretty Afrikaans girls for later.

At thirty-five hundred, LB gritted his teeth, crossed his legs to ease the brunt of deceleration, and yanked the pillow grip of his main chute. The canopy fluttered out behind him. The gray silk rectangle filled instantly; the lines went taut and squashed LB together at the midsection as the leg straps yanked his lower body into his upper half. He slowed and snapped back to his squat shape with a grunt, beginning the downward drift to the landing zone.

LB hailed over the team freq: "PJ One up."

Doc, soaring in behind and above, answered, "PJ Two up." Jamie and Quincy responded, then Wally, at the top of the stack, replied last, "Team Leader up."

At eight hundred feet above the open grass, the cheers reached LB. Children pointed skyward, the thousands of folks below clapped and waved American and South African flags, the aromas of steaks and sausages on hundreds of *braai* grills winged up to him. LB worked the left and right toggles beside his head to circle around, coming in downwind to slow his approach.

LB spilled altitude fast. At one hundred feet he released the fifteen-foot tether that lowered his med ruck, doffing that weight before landing, jerking him when the line went taut. He leveled off when the ruck dragged the grass, pulling both toggles to his waist to flare the chute and bleed off the final bit of height. His boots touched down, and with smooth, practiced movements LB released the chest strap and bellyband, then flipped the ejectors on his leg straps, freeing him from the harness. The chute fainted at his back. LB unclipped the tether, dragged the ruck close, and took a knee, weapon up.

Stock to his cheek, eyes down the open sight, LB scanned the open field with his M4. He didn't watch Doc, Jamie, or Quincy drop in a ring around him; his task was to be the first peg down of a protected perimeter. Wally landed fifteen seconds after LB. With the team on the ground, the PJs reeled in their med rucks and left all five chutes collapsed in the grass. Wally, the team's combat-rescue officer, took tactical control.

All his commands, "Move," "Stay tight," "Go, go," "Watch our six," were broadcast over the loudspeakers. Everything was simplified, war-movie dialogue for the whooping and hollering masses. The crowd hit their loudest pitch when the South African pilot stumbled forth from the tree line and his orange marker smoke, waving to the arriving Guardian Angels, shouting, "Thank God you're here."

LB got to him first. He set the pilot on the grass to take a look at his pretend injuries. Jamie, Doc, Quincy, and Wally shielded LB inside a picket of raised rifles facing four directions. Wally got on the ground-to-air freq, again amplified to the thousands of onlookers, to call in the South African Air Force chopper for evac.

LB laid a hand across the pilot's shoulder. To the clapping crowd, this surely looked reassuring.

"I got something for you here, buddy."

LB dug into his ruck, past the ice packs. He handed the pilot a cold beer.

• • •

The pilot, a meaty Afrikaans named Marius, took off one of his boots. For no reason LB could guess, the man dumped a whole Castle Lager into it.

Marius held the boot out for LB to drink. Around the bistro table, Doc, Quincy, and Jamie leaned back in their chairs, away from the offered boot. At tables nearby on the restaurant patio, others paid attention. LB shook his head.

"Dude."

Marius waggled the boot as if the thing itself insisted.

"Drink. It's an honor."

"It's a shoe."

"You're in my country, man. This is for you."

LB pivoted to ask a South African marine seated at his back.

"This a joke? Is he messing with me?"

"No, man. This is shit we do. Go ahead."

LB reached for the boot. He sniffed for the smell of foot, but all he got was the sloshing fizz of beer. Doc, Jamie, and Quincy looked amazed as LB raised the laces and leather tongue to his face, one hand under the rubber heel. Marius seemed pleased, but his pleasure was more about getting his way than imparting a tribute.

LB guzzled the boot. The taste was just beer. The three PJs around him clapped; he'd done it for them, and they had no intention of doing the same. LB handed the wet shoe back to Marius, who wordlessly slipped it over his bare sock. The pilot made a fist bump with LB and a little exploding sound, then looked around for their waitress, impatient. Marius stood and nodded down over LB, bestowing some benediction; LB had passed a test of his.

The big man left the table to fetch the third round from the bar. It wasn't his turn to buy; he refused to take turns. He'd bought all the beers for LB, Doc, Quincy, and Jamie.

LB settled back in his plastic chair, unsure if he'd been initiated or duped. Either way, the patio at Eastwoods sparkled, the tony neighborhood of Pretoria shined. The South Africans on the sidewalks or drinking around LB were a handsome bunch, black and white. Lots of reflecting glass in the modern architecture, green spaces, clean streets, trendy shops, and fashion-conscious people strolling made the place look more like San Francisco than the old home of apartheid.

This trip was LB's third African Aerospace Defense Expo (AADE) in seven years. Wally and Doc had been with him for each, but this was the first for Jamie and Quincy. The annual air show had become a sizeable event. All the big players wanted a piece of South Africa, the leading economy on the continent. China had a major presence at this year's AADE, so did the Russians and French. The United States had brought six aircraft down from Camp Lemonnier in Djibouti—four C-130s and a pair of F-16s—plus a hundred aerospace contractors and the GA team. A dozen nations' militaries held sway at Eastwoods this glistening afternoon, an array of flight suits, camos, berets, and ranks painted the patio. Wally was somewhere in this kaleidoscope, schmoozing.

With Marius gone for a minute, LB swirled a finger around the table to invoke the team's attention.

"Did Wally tell you?"

Quincy flattened his big mitts on the metal table, rattling the dozen empty bottles.

"Yeah. And I think it's sweet."

LB rocked in his seat. The plastic under him threatened to buckle.

"You're kidding."

Quincy made a ridiculous face.

"Fuck yes, I'm kidding."

When Marius returned with beers dangling between his thick fingers, the team stopped sniggering. The pilot asked what the hilarity had been. LB tried to wave it off as nothing, but Jamie told him about Wally on one knee, proposing over the radio in the back of a cargo plane to a major all the way back in Djibouti.

Marius laughed hard, perhaps to be included.

"*Jirre.*" This was the Afrikaans way of saying "wow."

For uncomfortable moments, the laughing Marius remained unaware that no one had joined him. Jamie, who'd told the story, licked his lips and hung his head, a sorry pose. Doc and Quincy drummed their fingers on the metal table. LB worked on his beer, waiting this out. The clueless Marius didn't quit fast enough. LB set down his beer and raised a palm.

"Okay, pal. Let it go."

Marius sniffed away the last of his laughter.

"What?"

"I said just let it go. Wally's getting married. So good for him."

"*Ja*, good for him. But you laughed."

Jamie tried to placate him, leaning across the table.

"I shouldn't have said anything. My fault."

When Marius glared at Jamie, Doc tugged the young PJ upright in his chair, keeping him out of it.

Marius spread his arms to survey the Americans at the table. He could have taken on any of them except Quincy, and he would have been a handful for the big PJ. Though the bar rippled with an international flavor today, Marius had an ample number of South African Army and Air Force members nearby, and as a rule they ran large.

For no reason LB could articulate, because in his way of thinking he'd done nothing to bring this on himself, Marius addressed him.

"I buy you drinks."

"Thank you."

"I let you pretend to rescue me. In front of fucking ten thousand people."

"Like I said . . . Thank you."

"So suddenly I'm an arsehole?"

Why do it? LB had never developed complex answers to simple questions. This was his strength, what he valued most about himself and believed others admired in him: he gave dogged and linear, reliable, repeatable responses to challenges. This was what LB tried to teach young pararescuemen as an instructor at Pararescue Indoctrination, what he tried to give to the wounded in combat when they'd lost almost all their own strength. Never quit. Focus, narrow it down, right here and now. Later will take care of itself. Why jump out of a copter into a raging sea or out of a plane into a boiling desert, into an icy crevasse, into a firefight, into this? Why? Because that was the job.

"Not suddenly."

Marius shot up, the rim of the table in his hands. Bottles cascaded past LB, spilling on the bricks, one of the full ones doused him. With a heave, the big pilot tipped the table into LB's lap; LB fended it off, and the table rolled away to rest upside down. Doc, Jamie, Quincy, and the beer-soaked LB sat in an empty ring where it had been. Marius, standing alone, moved his arms and fists like a flexing gorilla. The rest of the patio's patrons swallowed their tongues; the music in the background was the only sound left, with Marius commanding everyone's attention, awkward and wrong.

"Get up."

Whether through surprise or lack of desire, Doc, Jamie, and Quincy stayed rooted to their seats. LB stayed in his plastic chair for a different reason. He'd been told to stand.

Marius grunted.

"You've got a *snotklap* coming, mate."

The pilot took one stride across crunching glass. His next step was interrupted.

Wally slipped into the circle without making a sound, even without treading on the glass. Taller than Marius, rangy and erect, cropped, tucked, and certain, Wally hoisted both hands to ward off the advancing goonish pilot.

"I don't know what he said or did, but I'm sure you deserve an apology."

Marius pouted, mulling this shift. LB hadn't kept count of the pilot's beers, only his own, and maybe Marius had been further along than he'd known. The big Afrikaner's features dulled the way a drunk's would, sudden and unreasoned.

"Alright."

Without turning his sunglasses away from Marius, Wally reached behind him to snap his fingers.

"First Sergeant."

LB had no urge to fight, but also none to capitulate. He hovered between the two choices, impressed with himself in this moment that he had the presence of mind to wonder what sort of story this would make for later. But the only people to tell it to who might care or understand were the men around him right now.

"Sorry, pal. Didn't mean anything by it."

This defused Marius, but not enough for Wally to walk away. From behind his shades, Wally saw something that kept him rooted between LB and the big pilot. Doc and Jamie set to putting the table on its legs. A waitress with a broom and dustpan wended through the stunned and gawping military men and women from around the globe. Still, Wally faced Marius.

The pilot aimed an arm thick as a post past Wally, at LB.

"Hy's vol kak." This bit of Afrikaans was easy to interpret: "He's full of shit."

Wally nodded. "I agree."

The pilot wavered on his feet and between languages. He growled in a jowly, accented English.

"Just be glad he's one of yours."

"Most days, I'm not." Wally leaned in an inch, just enough. "But understand, friend. He *is* one of mine."

Marius backed a step, not in retreat but to better look Wally up and down, a sort of public dressing-down.

"You're the *moffie* who took the knee on the radio, eh?"

Wally cocked his head.

"I don't know that one."

A British airman at a nearby table provided the translation.

"Pansy."

Wally rubbed the back of his neck with long fingers.

"He told you?"

LB answered before Jamie.

"I thought it was a laugh."

"Was it?"

"Yep."

At this, LB stood. Doc, Quincy, and Jamie, all taller than LB, rose, too. They stacked in a line, ready as ever to jump behind him.

LB closed the distance to Marius, stepping beside Wally to dig a finger into the Afrikaans pilot's burly chest.

"But understand, friend. He's our moffie."

Marius's lips parted, but he had no quick words, stymied just long enough for LB to walk on. Doc tugged Wally by the sleeve to get him moving, too, past the waitress working the broom. The bar, like a tree full of birds when a cat has gone away, began to chirp again.

Chapter 3

When the chopper touched down, a hundred buzzards burst skyward in a dark spiral, a swirling, squealing pillar. On broad, black wings they rode the hard stench into the air, leaving feathers and white droppings over the carcass. The buzzards fluttered into a high, lazy circle to wait for the living to go away.

Neels stepped out of the chopper first, rifle in hand should there be big cats about. He tucked his sunglasses into a pocket, then held up a palm to keep Opu and the photographer in the helicopter until he'd cleared the area.

He did not approach the dead rhino but walked a wide circle around it, to leave the crime scene untouched for Opu. Nothing leaped out of the brush, though tracks were everywhere—of lions, leopards, spotted hyenas, jackals, wild dogs, and men. Neels signaled that it was safe.

Opu approached with his metal detector and knives, the police photographer with his camera and notepad. The pilot finished his shutdown, then emerged in his white bush hat and blue flight suit. The midday heat flooded down, unbroken by wind or shade. Insects kept a constant chatter in the brush, and flies clotted on the carcass.

With no breeze to push the smell of rot away, Neels could find no place to stand out of it. He backed away to lessen it. Opu noticed his grimace and shook his old, black head at Neels, who, even after so many years and carcasses, could stand the sight of fresh death better than its stink.

The rhino lay in a round patch of bare dirt. All the grass had been scrabbled away by the host of animals that had come to eat the carcass, evidence of the great commotion in the bush whenever something big died. The beast's belly had been clawed open, likely by lions. The guts would have been devoured first, then the meat around the ribs, leaving the bones picked clean to bleach in the light. The smaller scavengers would have kept their distance while the big cats and hyenas gorged. Once the body had been stripped of its softer meats and organs, the buzzards swarmed in. They were patient and numerous enough to peck through the tough hide on the back and shoulders. Finally, the sun, rain, and flies would dissolve the flesh and skin into the bush, and the wind and elephants would scatter the skeleton.

Opu stepped onto the orb of raw earth, moving into the choking odor without a flinch. The man was a former poacher. Now an investigator for the Kruger, he rode this chopper to three, four, five murdered rhinos every day of the week.

Neels stood back with the photographer. The cameraman was Zulu, a talkative people, but this one had not spoken in the chopper and did not speak now, only stared. The pilot came alongside Neels. In the heat and reek, all three winced while Opu worked close to the corpse. The young South African National Parks pilot, an Englishman in his first week on the job, pinched his nose. Neels glared at him, and the pilot dropped his hand. Pinching the nose was disrespectful; the dead beast's condition should be witnessed, breathed, recorded, and despised.

Opu waved the head of the metal detector over the rhino's body, guiding it across the white picket of ribs into the emptied torso. Next he scanned the dirt around the body, seeking a casing or a bullet that might have been eaten by a scavenger and spit out or regurgitated. The detector beeped steadily, finding nothing.

The old ex-poacher tugged down the bill of his baseball cap against the sun. He swept the metal detector across the rhino's gray skull. The beeps lengthened into a tinny wail.

Opu set the detector aside and knelt for his kit. He popped open the plastic case he'd brought, removing latex gloves and a long knife. The rhino lay awkwardly on his chest, on his own thick legs without composure. Opu flattened a gloved hand to the top of the beast's great skull to mutter the Xhosa prayer that was his custom, his apology for his past.

The old man waved the photographer forward. Neels walked with him; the young pilot held his ground on the perimeter.

The smell grew grimmer with every step. Neels leaned into the stench to honor the beast and accept his failure to protect it, for it had been killed in his sector, Shingwedzi. Dead men stank but never this badly; they drew buzzards but not in the hundreds. They did not drip with other animals' shit. Forty years ago in the Border War, mates and Angolans alike died in the hot bush, but back then Neels could lift a kerchief over his nose and mouth to pass them without regret. He'd killed many an Angolan and Cuban himself. But those bodies had been soldiers and enemies, they'd died as they saw fit, in uniform and battle, for a cause good or bad. The rhinos of the Kruger were dying to the brink of extinction for no cause but greed.

Neels had never cared how a dead poacher smelled.

He stood behind Opu, with the photographer beside him. Stench pulsed from the carcass like flames. The animal's face had been butchered by an ax, hacked deep into the sinuses to carve out the horns by the roots. Jackals and buzzards had mauled much of the meat away from the snout to reveal how the ax had gashed the bone many times.

Opu fingered a bullet hole behind the rhino's right eye socket. "Entry here."

On the other side, he pointed at a second, larger hole.

"Exit here." The bullet had flattened on entry, then blown away a large piece of the rhino's head on the way out.

"This."

He indicated a deep hack behind the rhino's neck, the cut in the shape of a V as if to fell a tree.

"And this."

Opu touched a finger to a fourth wound, a puncture drilled through the top of the skull. Someone had stood where Neels stood and fired that round.

Neels growled.

"I will *moer* the sons of bitches who did this."

Opu and the police photographer paid no mind, but Neels was glad to hear himself say this. He'd come along on the morning chopper ride to make himself freshly angry. His job was a hard one. Anger eased it.

From his knees, Opu aimed the tip of the knife at him and the policeman.

"Lift the head."

Both men dug hands under the chin. The rhino's skin was coarse, but its bottom lip felt soft, like that of a horse. Short whiskers brushed against Neels's palms. With the photographer he shifted the weighty head to the side so Opu could dig into a small tunnel in the dirt. With his long knife the old man pried out a spent round. He held it up for Neels, then nodded to the photographer. The Zulu cop got busy with his camera, shooting close-ups of the carcass, the holes in the head, the one in the ground, and the wreckage of the rhino's face.

Opu squeezed the bullet between his finger and thumb.

"Three hundred grains. Maybe more."

Neels agreed.

"H & H .375 magnum."

Opu sealed the round in a clear bag from his kit. He carved a small square of skin and flesh off the rhino's neck and tucked that in another bag. The beast's DNA would be recorded and cataloged. Later, if the horns were ever found, they could be typed back to this carcass. The same applied to the bullet; the ballistics would be checked against other poachers' bullets to help spot a trend, a gang, a farmer's stolen rifle, any clue.

Neels reached down to help Opu to his feet. The old man dusted off his knees, then doffed his cap to draw an arm across his brow.

"This one ran."

"Ja."

Opu tapped a finger below his temple.

"They missed the first shot. Caught up with it. Cut the spine. Then."

He tapped a fingertip to the top of his own head to mimic the final shot. Opu puffed out his cheeks.

"One day dead."

He gathered up his kit, knife, and metal detector and strode out of the circle of scoured dirt. The flies overlooked the photographer snapping the body. Opu sprayed green paint on a tree branch, to signal park rangers that this carcass had been spotted and recorded.

Neels walked past the pilot. They'd not met before today. When the ECP called in the coordinates yesterday, this became the first poaching in Neels's sector in three weeks. At two hundred and twenty-five square miles, sixty thousand square hectares, Shingwedzi was one of the smaller of the twenty-two sectors of the Kruger. Higher concentrations of rhinos roamed to the west in Woodlands and Shangoni and south in the Marula region of the park. Usually, the poachers only snuck across Neels's territory on their way to or from the border. Shingwedzi was more passageway than killing ground; it saw more spoor and scurrying poachers than killed rhinos. Because of this, Neels made certain the boys under his command were the best trackers and shots in the Kruger.

The pilot sucked his teeth. "*Bliksems.*" Though he was English, he used the Afrikaans word for bastards. "Can you ever catch them?"

Neels stopped beside the pilot. He glanced back, trying to see the dead rhino through this young man's blue eyes after working one week in the Kruger. Neels couldn't do it, couldn't see the tragedy of only this carcass, couldn't smell just this one.

He noted the word, "ever." If he had that long?

"Ja."

• • •

While Opu and the photographer recorded the carcass, while the pilot folded his arms and shook his head in the unshielded heat, Neels pieced together the story of the poaching.

The rhino had run, just as Opu said. A full day of wind and sun had eroded much of the spoor, but there remained enough blood and tracks to guide Neels along the rhino's path a hundred meters south. The animal's prints showed elongated strides as he rumbled over the veld; dots of blood marked his dying. A pair of sandals, a small-footed and lightweight poacher, ran alongside. The rhino crashed through scrub and thorns trying to escape, always in a straight line. Why?

The bullet holes in the skull behind the eyes. The rhino was likely blinded. Panicked. It could only run straight.

The poacher had dashed up and flailed at the fleeing rhino's spine with a panga or an ax. Once the cord was severed, the beast dropped like a sack.

At the spot where the poacher's sandals joined the rhino's tracks, Neels hung his bush hat on a branch of a scraggly mopane. This saved his place. He returned to the chopper where the others waited.

He grabbed his backpack, rifle, and extra water. The cop buckled himself in, silent as his photographs. Opu reached for his own pack and made to climb out.

"I'll come."

The pilot nodded at Neels.

"Going off to catch them?"

"Going to follow them."

"I see you meant what you said."

"Ja."

"Look. That was the last carcass for the day. I'm headed back to Skukuza." This was the southern sector that housed the central offices for Kruger's rangers and the airport. "I'll wait till sundown for you to radio in."

Opu dropped to the ground. The pilot brought the chopper to life, flipping switches and toggles. He tugged on his helmet as the copter's blades turned.

Neels tossed the young pilot a thumbs-up. He bid no farewell to the stone-faced Zulu cop. With Opu beside him, Neels bent at the waist to hurry out of the chopper's building wind.

Lifting off, the copter whipped up specters of dust and blew away the rotten smell. With Opu, Neels returned to his hat, hanging on the spindly tree, and faced east to the border. The buzzards, in flapping flights of five and ten, descended again on the dead rhino.

• • •

For the first hour, Opu did not speak and Neels only muttered. The poachers had done little to hide their spoor leading away from the carcass. They'd trod single file on game paths, and when they left the bare dirt for grass or rocks, the trail took up again in a line straight for the border. This paltry effort to evade insulted him as the sun climbed and the heat peaked in the buzzing bush.

Neels caught glimpses of three poachers in the earth. One was tall, marked by a longer stride in his sandal prints. The other two were slight, with smaller feet. What were they doing hunting in Shingwedzi? His sector rarely suffered more than a few poachings per year, and these were mostly happenstance and bad luck. In this set of tracks Neels sensed something purposeful, an incautious gait, an unwavering direction. These poachers knew where they were going. The notion nettled Neels more.

The white rhino they'd killed had been great, a solitary giant. Twenty years ago, when Neels was not a baas and had spent more time patrolling Shingwedzi, he'd watched the bull rhinos sharpen their horns against termite mounds and marula trees, witnessed battles between challengers for mates. The ground trembled when these beasts ran near; who would not tremble to feel this? Who had judged Shingwedzi and Neels vulnerable, to sneak here in the night? The image of the Goliath's skeleton laid bare and its blood lapped up drew Neels onward, faster over the tracks, while the sun beat on his shoulders and neck and the rifle across his back. He did not stop because the poachers had not. He could see their feet; walking with them, he vowed he would see their faces.

Skirting a copse of mopane trees, Opu left the path to squat in the shade. He sipped from his canteen and did not ask Neels's permission to stop. Neels halted, remaining in the sun. The instant he stilled, the day became hotter.

Opu asked, "What are you doing?"

Opu was older than Neels, by how many years they'd never discussed. Neels was not certain Opu knew his own age. He'd been born in a township outside Hazy View, into a hovel and all the poverty no one in South Africa needed to describe. Apartheid had not educated Opu, his poorness had. He retained no vestiges of the ways of that time; he was a quiet man, but his was not a servile silence. Opu had seen much and had learned to let each man see his own. He'd been a petty thief in his youth, a jailbird in his middle years, then a poacher in the Kruger, first a mule, then a shooter. He'd earned less in five years of killing than the men who'd shot the Shingwedzi rhino would for that one job. Such was the skyrocketing price of horn. Six years ago on a cold day, Opu had walked into the offices in Skukuza, a rifle across his upright back. He'd laid the gun on the front desk and asked for Neels. Neels came; Opu requested to work for him. When Neels asked why, Opu said that Neels was the only name he'd heard as a poacher. Old Neels was the scout who trained the rangers. Neels asked, "Why are you no longer a poacher?"

Shrugging, Opu asked in return, "Why do you stop them?" Neels did not feel the need to give his reasons, thinking them obvious, and seeing Opu felt the same, Neels hired him.

Opu in the shade and Neels in the sun seemed a silly result. Neels strode under the motionless mopane leaves to sit, checking the ground for ants. Opu handed over his canteen. Neels poured some water in his hand and pressed his palm over the back of his neck to cool his blood.

"You want to ask me something?"

The old man scratched his stubbly chin, making a susurrus like the insects around them, the summer thrum of the bush. Opu capped the canteen and spit between his spread knees.

Neels removed his hat to wipe the band inside with his kerchief. "Go ahead."

Opu ran a crinkled hand across the crackling landscape.

"Why are you out here today? You are a baas."

Neels returned his hat to his head, to signal he would not sit long for this. Opu dropped the long fingers, his yellow nails, to tap Neel's knee.

"How are things at home?"

Neels blinked a long moment at Opu, the uncanny tracker.

"What?"

"You have not been on the chopper in two years. You have not tracked in the bush in five. I know many nights you sleep in your office. We are following armed poachers together, and the sun is going down. So I ask."

"This is my private life."

"Then live it privately. Right now, you are not."

"My wife left."

"When?"

"Two months ago."

The old man nodded sagely. Something fell into place in his head.

"Why have we not spoken of this? We talk every day."

"About dead rhinos. We're not friends, Opu."

Silent Opu looked like a gargoyle squatting on his heels, arms folded in his lap. A bush monkey screeched in a nearby flame tree, flushing a flight of birds. Perhaps the monkey was raiding a nest for eggs. He'd be pecked at for it.

"Then why did you tell me?"

The answer was that Neels had woken on his office sofa this morning, a drained Scotch bottle on the floor. Coffee and a shower had not cleared his head or his growing shame, but at least he'd been a drunkard alone. For the hour of sunrise he'd stood in his office window staring emptily over the parking lot at filthy jeeps and garbage bins. For the next hour he'd lain back down on the sofa under more overwhelming sadness, one arm across his eyes like a compress. He hadn't answered the phone or unlocked his door until late in the morning. When he'd emerged dressed in green camo fatigues, rifle across his back, Neels felt driven out. As Opu said, for the first time in years, he'd stomped to the helipad for the day's carcass ride.

The answer, too, was that Opu was a nobody. Neels could fire the old crook without notice or reason, and Opu knew this. And the answer was the bush, vast and uncaring; this was the place to say it, where it would disappear, as it would with Opu.

Without an answer, with nothing more for Opu to follow, Neels rose from the shade. The sun dazed him until he relocated the poachers' trail.

Opu followed at a distance that let Neels feel alone. Far ahead of the old man, where he wouldn't be heard, Neels argued with her. He did this under his breath at first, then with shouts that he could not control, even if Opu might notice. He told her that she'd abandoned him; she replied that he'd deserted her first, he'd left her for the rhinos. *You knew who I was*, he said in his head. No, she didn't realize that he would rarely come home and that when he did, he could not relax, nor sometimes love. He'd asked her to trust him, he'd made promises, she wanted those promises kept. He'd dented a wall to say she didn't understand, wouldn't listen. Come see for yourself; I'll take you. They're killing four, five rhinos a day in the Kruger, every day. We stop them, only us, no one else. But she didn't want to see murdered animals, snouts half cut off; who would want to look at that? She'd been just one year in his life, a late wife and his only try at it. His voice and hers replayed the argument they'd had beside the wall he'd struck in the house they too rarely shared. When a green mamba slithered across the game trail ten strides in front of him, Neels took his rifle in hand. She ran out of his head as she'd done from his house.

The path afforded no more wildlife. This kind of heat made the animals torpid, left them lounging in mud or shadow until dusk, still an hour away. Neels, too, fought off the languor of the sun. Opu was right, he'd not tracked like this out in the open in a long time. He'd lost some of his stamina behind a desk. But he was still sharp enough to spot the second, fresher set of tracks that crossed the game trail.

"Opu."

Neels took a knee beside the new trace, waiting for the old man to catch up. Opu came saying nothing, his face blank, black as the coming night.

Together they knelt. A sneaker had made this imprint, not the sandals of the poachers they were following, not the boot of an ECP ranger. This mark was from a rubber-soled sport shoe. Opu ran a finger through the dirt next to it, then puckered and blew lightly. He did this until the scuff in the earth turned paler, the soil oxidized by his breath, to match the light-brown color of the shoe print. The wind would have gradually done the same to the track.

Opu nodded when Neels said, "Two, three hours."

They found two more sets of human tracks headed southwest, deeper into the park: another pair of sneakers, one more pair of sandals.

Opu shaded his brow to look in that direction, at the sere landscape and the lowering sun.

"What do you want to do?"

Neels gazed into the Kruger with him.

"Those others have left the park. These bliksems are still in it."

"Yes."

"Go to the ravine south of here. Wait there. Maybe they'll come back that way."

Poachers, refugees, anyone without a ranger's fluency with the land would use natural features to guide their passage in and out of the Kruger. The ravine, a dust bowl in summer, was a prominent landmark in Shingwedzi.

"What will you do?"

"What I said I would do."

Follow the ones who killed yesterday's rhino.

• • •

Neels hurried east to beat the light fading behind him. The poachers' trail waned several times, hiding under dung and the scattered tracks of impalas, zebras, elephants, and giraffes. Each time he lost the spoor, Neels walked in widening circles until the sandal prints resurfaced. The smallest of the poachers was the guide; a second set of tracks lay on top. The tall one came last.

A quarter mile from the border, with the sun touching the western rim of the park, the ground turned hard and rocky. The game trails dissolved because the beasts of the Kruger didn't traffic near the fence. Though the wires and posts were down in many places, the animals stayed away from Mozambique, spooked as if it were a graveyard.

In the gray dregs of daylight over the stony earth, Neels did not lose the track again. He followed straight for the border. He didn't expect to find the killers; surely they were gone. But every bit of evidence was valuable. If he found the spot where they'd crossed, the ECP rangers could keep a closer eye there. The intelligence gatherers at Skukuza would record the place, mark their maps, check the number and locations of crossings against the carcass count and sectors trespassed.

With the sky purpling to the west, Neels approached the border. The tracks had lost their shyness and led him openly over rusting wires and steel poles wasting in the dirt. All three poachers had walked into Mozambique. Neels followed.

He had the authority to do this. A South African National Parks ranger was permitted to cross the international border in pursuit of poachers, while even a policeman could not. He stepped into Mozambique, onto the dirt border road.

The red-brown dust kept a memory of what happened here. A bakkie had stopped, driven from the south. The poachers had climbed in. But someone stepped out of the passenger side. A heavy man who made broad, prominent treads in the road. He wore leather shoes with heels.

The first stars twinkled in a sky that, had it rained or blown during the past twenty hours, would have hidden this part of the story. Neels uttered a thank-you out loud; he took note that he was doing this more recently, talking to no one.

He lowered his face to the new prints to get the best look in the final light. Was this the spoor of one more poacher? No, these marks in the dust might be much more than a poacher. Someone in leather shoes, in a truck driven by another . . . Could this be a moneyman? A boss who ran a network? A big fish? A transporter? Elusive, rare, to see this.

Why had this one come out last night? If he was, in fact, a level up from the miserable, disposable poachers, he'd almost never show himself like this. He'd stay in the background, handling the cash through intermediaries, holding his identity secret. What was it about these three poachers, or the horns they brought him, that made him visible last night? Why did he get out of the truck?

Neels folded to his hands and knees in the road. He crawled beside the great shoe prints that had stepped out of the bakkie. Somewhere in the park, a hyena laughed like a madman, rousing the Kruger now that dusk had ended. Neels found a spot in the road where the leather shoes came toe-to-toe with one of the smaller poachers' sandals.

He sat up on his knees, startled. What had happened here? A disagreement, a fight? An embrace?

Seemingly out of nowhere, a fourth set of tracks appeared in the road, barefoot, small feet.

Neels stood, excited. In the first stains of night, he trailed the bakkie's tire marks southward on the dirt road. Not far from the border crossing point, the truck had clambered down out of the kopje, the small hills on the Mozambican side of the border. The vehicle had been up there waiting for a signal, for a meeting.

Why? Who was among the poachers to merit this kind of attention? Who wore the smallest of the sandals? Who arrived barefoot?

Neels said to the hills, "Who?"

• • •

He pushed off his hat to let it hang behind him, opening his view of the sky. He chose a western star and walked to it with his rifle in hand to keep it quiet. He lay his boots down flat to stop his heels from striking. The bush would know he was here, not the men.

Neels moved quickly, guided not by the game trails or plants; these were just ripples on the veld, seasonal and changing. Elephants would knock down scrub, giraffes and the other big beasts would wear new paths, lightning blasted trees, herds grazed down the grasses. After thirty years, Neels could feel the unchanging parts of Shingwedzi, the rises and plains, watering holes and dry gullies, the river valley, the bones of the place. He knew his sector the way a man understands not a map but a brother. Here, Neels could think like a human or a beast, whichever he chose.

For an hour, he forged southeast toward the streambed where he'd sent Opu. He saw and heard no animals along the way. This was normal soon after the death of something the size of a rhino. The jackals, wild dogs, lions, and hyenas, the night noisemakers of the bush, had gorged their fill over the past day on the carcass. Little hunting was going on. Neels cruised undisturbed through the dark. Anything peering at him did so silently, like the moon rising at his back.

On a flatiron plain dotted with marula trees and dung heaps, Neels stopped for a swallow from his canteen. He spit out the first mouthful, an old soldier's habit, to wash the dust off his tongue. He was only minutes from the ravine and Opu. The southern constellations shone limpid, the moon hadn't yet crowded them out. The stars were the stars of his youth. He was sixty-one now, and his knees ached. He was alone, wifeless, drinking too much. Neels drained the canteen, feeling needy and deserving. Time for something else in his life, but what was there? Since she'd left, he'd asked this question over liquor and water, under sun and moonlight, at work and in dreams. No answer he could give himself was honest. No tracks led Neels inward.

A rifle report rang out of the night, from the direction of the streambed. Neels stowed the canteen, clicked off the safety on his R-1, and bent low.

He sped toward the sound, conscious of moving without revealing himself. Who had fired, one of the poachers?

The reply came fast. Another shot, then another scored the dark, this time a different sound, not the same caliber. One more report and Neels had his answer. This was no poacher taking down a beast. This was combat firing. Either the ECP had made contact or Opu had.

Neels dodged through the scrub, staying concealed as he hurried. The earth sloped downward. He'd entered the dry ravine. The ground turned to sandy clay; the undergrowth thinned. Straight ahead, one more gunshot popped. This was the final bang. The echo faded over the veld. Neels ducked beside a thicket of thorny branches. Here, in the center of the streambed, he caught his breath and saw the dust kicked up by a running poacher.

The man hurtled straight at him, fifty meters off. Neels stood from hiding to put himself in the open, lit by the measly light. He raised the rifle stock against his cheek and swung the sight to the poacher, leading him.

The black man did not see Neels, who, motionless, might have been just a tree in the ravine. The noises of his hard breathing and flapping sandals traveled far ahead of him. In one hand he gripped a rifle. Neels had little trouble following him with his own long barrel. He widened his stance, knowing how this would end.

When the poacher had sprinted within twenty meters, he filled Neels's gun sight. The man wore dark clothes, a shirt flapped unbuttoned over short pants. He was thin; sweat glistened on him.

"Stop! Drop your weapon!"

The poacher skidded, raising more dust around his ankles. Panicking, he scanned the gray ravine, but with the moon low behind Neels, he did not see the ranger quickly enough. He did not drop his gun.

Neels fired once to put him down, not kill him. The round struck where he'd aimed, in the gut. The poacher staggered backward, arms flung wide, then tripped and landed on his rear, sitting up. Neels, F-1 still to his cheek, took long strides. He glared down the barrel as he approached, both eyes open.

"Take your hand off your weapon. Now."

The poacher let the gun clatter from his grasp. He reeled in both skinny arms to press palms against his leaking belly. His shrieks were in Bantu, he was Mozambican. In English, Neels told him to shut up. The poacher whimpered.

Neels lowered the F-1. With a toe, he nudged the poacher's Remington hunting rifle out of reach. A brushy tuft hung from the gun's long barrel, the tail of an eland, a muti. Neels settled to his knees.

"Who sent you?"

The Mozambican pulled his hands from his stomach. The bullet had taken him just above the belly button, in the bowels. His palms dripped, the waistband of his shorts sagged, sopping with his blood. He wore no underwear. His life pulsed out between his shaking legs into the drinking dust. One sandal had fallen off, and the bottom of his foot was almost white with calluses. He muttered in accented English.

"I'm going to die?"

Neels inched closer, into the smell of copper.

"Who sent you?"

The poacher began to rock, holding his stomach again. Neels poked him in the shoulder.

"Hey. Look at me. A big man, right? He sent you."

"Ranger, don't let me die."

"I won't. Who sent you? His name."

The poacher gazed deep into Neels's face to see if he could trust him. Neels poked him again.

"I won't let you die. Now tell me who sent you."

The poacher coughed, and the pain of it wrenched his thin features.

"Juma."

Neels leaned closer now that he had a name, to let the poacher see in his eyes that he would not find there what he was looking for.

Covering his belly once more, the poacher lay back in the dust. He moaned. Neels stood over him.

"How many have you killed? *Jou poes.*" (You cunt.)

The poacher shook his head in the dirt, denying, eyes shut.

His blood coursed down the furrows of his ribs, soaking his black shirttail. The moon gleamed in his tears and sweat. *Daai bleerie fokken ding* (This bloody fucking thing), this poacher, looked shiny dying in the dirt.

Neels rested the muzzle of his F-1 over the Mozambican's heart. The racing beat throbbed through the gun into his hand.

"You sneak into my park. Shoot my animals. Hack them to pieces."

The poacher opened his eyes. He gazed not at Neels but beyond him, to the ageless stars.

Neels spit onto the man's heaving chest. The gob landed beside the muzzle of the F-1.

"You ruin my life."

Neels pulled the trigger. Again, somewhere, the mad hyena cackled.

• • •

Neels dumped the body off his shoulder. The poacher landed on his back, arms splayed, bloody palms turned up as if to show what

Neels had done to him. Old Opu sat beside a corpse of his own, another skinny bastard. Opu looked unhurt, so Neels did not ask how he was. Opu pointed into the dark east.

"One got away."

Neels handed Opu the poacher's Remington. The rifle's ballistics would be compared to bullets pried from rhino carcasses going back two years, searching for matches. The gun itself was most likely stolen, and that record, too, would help the computers at Skukuza create their mosaic of evidence. Opu checked the chamber to see that the gun was unloaded. He fingered the eland-tail muti, then tossed the rifle across the poacher's bare legs.

Neels leaned down to Opu's kill to see the story. Two rounds to the chest. This one died fast. No weapon lay near him in the dirt; he'd been unarmed. A flat, empty knapsack hinted that this team of poachers hadn't found a rhino before they'd stumbled on Opu in the dark.

Opu did the same to Neels's corpse, reading the death there. One bullet in the gut, one clean in the heart. Opu would have heard Neels's two shots, the pause between them.

The old man's white teeth split his black features in a grimace. Both he and Neels had put down men they could have taken alive. Neither poacher had been a threat at the moment he was killed. It remained unsaid between Opu and Neels, and among all the Kruger rangers, chopper pilots, police, prosecutors, sector bosses, intel teams, and office staff, that this was the same bad deal the rhinos got.

Opu jerked a thumb at Neels's dead poacher.

"What did he tell you?"

"A name. Juma."

"Juma?" Opu shook his head at the dark veld.

"You know him?"

"No. Did you follow the tracks?"

Squatting beside the dead men in the dust, Neels told the old man what he'd found in the road on the Mozambican side.

A bakkie had waited in the dark hills, then rolled down to meet yesterday's poachers. A big man, Juma, got out of the passenger side, in heeled leather shoes. There'd been an odd closeness with the smallest pair of sandals. And another unexplained set of barefoot tracks had disappeared into the boulders near the crossing, back into the park.

Neels sat cross-legged in the dirt, turned away from Opu and the bodies. He swirled his canteen, forgetting that he'd emptied it. From his backpack he ate a few bites of biltong, offering some to Opu, taking a swig from the old man's water in return. They couldn't leave the dead poachers overnight in the bush; animals would strip the bodies to the bone before dawn. They needed to be identified. Tomorrow morning, Neels would call in the choppers to evacuate them all, living and dead.

He put on his hat against the creeping chill. Neels was done with the stars for tonight. The lowered brim narrowed the bush to those bits of the world that would concern him until sunup: the dim ravine where he sat, the rifle across his lap, and Opu. Neels's shoulder and knees twinged from carrying the poacher. A throb nagged in his head, the withdrawal after so much adrenaline.

Opu pulled a slim *dagga* cigarette from his shirt pocket. He waggled it at Neels to ask if this was a problem. Neels looked away. The ground flickered orange while Opu lit up. Neels smelled nothing, the smoke blew elsewhere. He spoke over his shoulder.

"You sleep first. Three hours."

Minutes later, Opu rolled onto his side in the cooling dust, old hands joined under his cheek as his only pillow. Neels peered off into the silent bush, keen with his ears. Scrub and fever trees circled the open ravine in gray shapes that seemed to stare back as the poacher had done, to see if Neels could be relied on. Out in the dark flats, unseen beasts padded wide, careful paths around him, wondering if they might get at the scent of fresh death.

Neels, the protector of Shingwedzi, spoke out the name so the land could hear it, too, and be warned of him.

"Juma."

The animals kept their distance, and the brim of his hat blocked the moon. Even so, she crossed his mind. It pleased him to wave Juma at her, to feel a new passion grow.

Chapter 4

The blasts barely shook the tunnel. One dangling lightbulb swayed while dust sifted through its glow. The safety people kept Allyn far from the detonation. Even as the mine's owner, he couldn't insist on being closer.

Allyn pressed a palm to the cool wall to sense the shuddering stone better, the power of the dynamite in the rocks, the rubble and thrill. Slowly, the rumbles faded under his hand. Long ago, when he'd been the one lighting the fuses, the spots on the back of his small hand were not there. So much time had gone by, and the changes were in him, heavy like collected calendars.

He lowered his hand from the wall. A woman beside him scribbled something competently onto a clipboard; a young engineer walked away over the loose stones of the shaft floor. Three grimy miners stood listlessly around him, assigned to answer questions should Allyn have any. All were taller than him, and the roof of the tunnel ran only centimeters from the tops of their heads. All wore the same white coveralls and hard hats branded with the illustrated head of a leopard, the logo of Allyn's company, Ingwe. This was the Xhosa word for the big, spotted cat. The eyes of his company's symbol were drawn wide and alert, lips parted, teeth bared, a predator's face.

With the blast done, the always-moving conveyor belt shivered and bounced under the first chunks of rubble. A flurry of vehicles headed off to clear the debris, modern oddities of oversized tires and short profiles designed to operate in the low-slung dimensions of a mine. All the engines were plug-in electric to avoid emissions and ignition sparks; each vehicle trailed a great black cord. The motors were quiet but potent, strong enough to clear tons of fallen rock or scrape raw ore out of earth that had been hidden since creation.

Allyn's three miners shuffled their boots on the pebbly floor, unaccustomed to standing so near the big boss while idle. They waited on his curiosity, but he had none because he knew their jobs. He'd done them all at one time or another, mining copper in Zambia, gold in Zimbabwe, diamonds here in South Africa. The underground bore no discomfort for Allyn. The immense depths, dark halls, occasional terror, grueling work, he brightened it all in the sunny recollections of his youth. He liked the subterranean chill, the surprising breezes near the ventilation shafts, the blasting and loose rocks; none of it had changed. Allyn had made himself a frequent visitor to his mine for the eleven years since he'd bought the Ingwe operation.

Today was the first time he'd come down in nine months. Labor negotiations had ended yesterday in Jo'burg, the strike was over. He was here to give his support, see the mine up and running, show the men there were no hard feelings though he'd made concessions for their new contract. The shutdown had become costly enough to everyone.

The woman kept her attention on her notes. The overalls made her shapeless, but she seemed trim, judging from her hands and profile. Allyn had not seen her before.

He offered his hand to the three miners around him. He asked their names but did not recall them as the men were saying them. Allyn didn't introduce himself. He indicated one of the low trucks humming past, burdened with stones.

"I used to be a lasher. You boys know what that is?"

All three appeared young but might not have been. This was a trick of the mines, the dust filled the crevices and wrinkles of the face, smoothing the lines. Allyn had been in coal shafts in America where there had been no one with gray or blond hair, no black men or whites, just dirty miners. The smallest of the three before him, a little taller than Allyn, and wiry, said he did know.

"A shoveler."

Allyn popped the man on the upper arm, pleased to find it solid.

"Damn right I was. I started when I was seventeen. We didn't have those machines to do it for us. Just shovels and these."

Allyn displayed his hands.

"Did it for a year straight. I got promoted to trammer. Pushed *cocopans* loaded with rock over the rails. Once we'd pushed twenty cars, a little locomotive took them up to the surface."

The men nodded, unsure what Allyn wanted from them. When the lull lasted too long and Allyn gazed away, the mine calling him further into memory, the largest of the three asked, "How'd you make miner, then?"

Allyn did not return fully to the moment, a bit of him lingered in the old tunnels.

"Back then, the men were from Mozambique and Nyasaland. Blacks mostly, good blokes. I got promoted before all of them. Not fair, but that's how it was. I made learner miner. Spent six months training how to blast. We were measured, how many pounds of dynamite we used to get how many tons of ore. Three-man drilling crews. Two-minute fuses."

The woman lifted her blue eyes from the clipboard, listening now. The middle miner laughed as he spoke.

"I bet you were good, right?"

"That I was, lad. I had the touch. Especially gold." Allyn raised one arm parallel to the ground. "The reef runs like a river, through granite and greenstone for miles until it hits a spot, some jumble in the rock, some complex structure. Right there it pools." He made a fist, tapped the knuckles with the other hand. "This is where you look. This is the find. Where the gold bunches up."

The woman had sidled into their small circle. She smiled, and she was young, perhaps in her late forties. Maybe she was a lawyer. Her tone was level and straight. Like the ore, a shine lurked inside it.

"Mr. Pickston. How did you come up to own your own mines?"

Was she one of his lawyers, or the union's?

"You know, it does beat the living a poor bastard lasher can make in the bottom of a mine."

"True. But how did you do it?"

"Two answers. First, I played cricket for the company team."

"I assume you were quite good at that, as well."

"My dear, I was very good. It got me the attention of the mine's managers. They sent me to engineering school in Cornwall."

"And?"

"And when I returned, I married the boss's daughter."

The woman's smile registered that she rather liked this answer.

Allyn addressed the three miners.

"Thank you, gentlemen, I can see myself out."

The men walked off without ceremony, back to their tasks for the rich man who'd dismissed them. The woman removed her hard hat. Her hair was a gentle brown shade, streaked with gold by the light of the lone bulb. She ran a jeweled hand across her crown, an act of display, before covering it with the hard hat.

"You're one of my attorneys, aren't you?"

She nodded, the leopard on her helmet dipped at Allyn.

"I am."

"Were you on the negotiating team?"

"I was."

"Then you did excellent work. It feels good to be back."

Allyn flattened a hand to usher her before him.

"We should celebrate."

• • •

He knotted his tie in the mirror and straightened his silver hair with her brush. Allyn was conscious of being quiet but not furtive. He wasn't sneaking away, just letting her sleep.

He left five thousand rand from his money clip on the dresser. On hotel stationery he penned a note to leave with the money: *You didn't ask for this, so please accept it.* This would help define their relationship if they encountered each other again, in the office or socially in Pretoria. Allyn slipped out the door. In the lobby, the concierge arranged for a taxi.

• • •

Yesterday's mail included a note of condolence from the wife of Zimbabwe's president, sent two weeks after the funeral. Allyn carried the letter onto the veranda, where Centurion Lake reflected the late day's amber light. The president's wife had been a great friend to Eva during Allyn's affluent years in Zimbabwe. Her note was handwritten and short, not really heartfelt, the sort of message that said, "I have done what was proper and now good-bye." Allyn dropped the note in a bin. The president himself had done better; he'd called Allyn personally. They spoke warmly for ten minutes with no enmity of the past, like two old pirates plying different waters.

Allyn sat outside for the hour of sundown with nothing in his hands, not a gin or newspaper, no one to bring these to him. The maid had been in the house the days while he'd been gone to the office, then the mine. Funny about maids, how they left no evidence of themselves but the absolute lack of evidence.

The big house would begin to feel empty soon. Eva's clothes needed to be given away, her papers arranged and sent to her sisters, some memento photos to their boy who'd gone back to London a day after the funeral. Not much else needed doing.

Below the veranda, fireflies blinked. The other mansions of Centurion Lake began to glow, homey and gilded. Though they were clustered around the water with him, they felt remote, houses he'd not been in, neighbors he didn't know well. Eva had. His own home remained lightless. He did not go inside to turn on lamps or the television; he cooked nothing. Allyn did no chore Eva would have done, and the result was darkness.

When the doorbell rang he did not at first discern it from the big chiming clock in the stairwell. The bells sounded again, and when he could not call for his wife to get the door, Allyn decided that he would find live-in help.

He stepped inside from the veranda, clicking on a table lamp beside the expansive leather sofa Eva never liked. She said it held onto too much temperature, either cool or warm, and sitting on it was like sitting on a living thing. Allyn walked far from the lamp's throw, without turning on more lights, into the dimness of the foyer. Without asking who was at his front door, he turned the knob and tugged. When the door was halfway open, he realized he might have inquired and stopped opening it, not sure if he could close it again and start over.

A deep voice, familiar, curled around the open door from above Allyn's head.

"*Kanjani wena, shamwari?*" (How are you, my friend?)

Fanagolo. The old pidgin tongue of the mines.

Allyn pulled the door fully open. The great figure blocked most of the doorway.

"*Ndara kano wrarawo.*" (I am well if you are well.)

Juma, so large, could not spread his arms until Allyn had stepped back to let him in.

They embraced. Juma bent his cheek to the top of Allyn's head. He spoke in English without letting Allyn loose.

"I am sorry I did not come to the funeral."

"I understand."

Juma backed away, keeping Allyn's shoulders under his heavy palms.

"She was a good woman."

"They don't make them like her anymore."

"And if they do, I hope the men who find them treat them as well as you. Eh? Let's drink."

Allyn led Juma into the vaulted den. He cut on a few lamps, Juma should not see him in a dour house. A breeze arose from the veranda as Allyn poured brandy. He said they ought to go sit outside, but Juma accepted the tumbler and folded his girth onto the leather sofa. Under him, the thing did appear to be an animal, one Juma had killed.

Juma raised his glass. Allyn, on his feet, did the same, and they sipped.

"I wasn't expecting you."

"Should I go?"

"No, of course not. Are you hungry? I don't know what there is, but I can scare something up."

"I'll only be a little while."

"Juma?"

"Yes, *shamwari*?"

Allyn carried the brandy decanter to the sofa. Juma offered his emptied glass.

"Stay a bit."

• • •

Nine months ago, in the first week of the mine strike, Allyn had called Juma to come see him. They'd not been in each other's company in twelve years, not since Allyn had left Zimbabwe for

South Africa to buy the mine outside Pretoria. In those dozen years, they'd spoken on the phone for holiday wishes and birthdays, but few other occasions. Allyn and Juma had both become rich, Allyn very much so. When they talked, Allyn described for Juma the growing mine operation and the rising market for platinum; many times he asked Juma to come work for him, but Juma would not. Juma never spoke of how he'd made his own money. Eva, who'd known Juma as long as Allyn, suspected him, believed an old black man from the mines could not have made proper wealth; she meant legal. Privately, Allyn sensed this might be so but would not admit it to her and would not say anything to Juma. Besides, it made no difference; whatever Juma was doing—and he must have been very good at it—he did it far away in Mozambique. Eva, with the cancer in its first stages, would not have liked to know Allyn was meeting Juma after so many years. Allyn had asked Juma to come to Jo'burg, to a small restaurant downtown where few whites ate. Juma agreed and did not ask why.

That evening they'd filled a patio table with stout beers. Allyn brought cigars. For the first hour they made no mention of business or money. Instead, they skipped backward across their current lives for the stronger clasp of their past. They reminisced about being teenagers in the mines, Allyn a fatherless boy, Juma his big Zulu mentor. How Allyn had become a full-fledged miner while Juma stayed a trammer. How Allyn, on his return from school in England, made certain that Juma was promoted.

On the patio of the little Jo'burg restaurant, Allyn was the only white face. This and the Fanagolo helped him feel safe from prying ears. When they'd had their fill of recollections and found their bond still strong, Juma gave a long sigh. He rested his big arms on the table, clearly happy to have been called.

He asked only, "Ja?"

No black man on the patio or passing in the dim street was the size of Juma. Allyn stubbed out his cigar, finished the last beer, and placed his own arms on the table. He was dwarfed by his old friend, as he'd always been, and this was a comfort. It gave him the sense that nothing had changed and Juma would still help him.

"*Meena kona maningi endaba.*" (I have a big problem.)

Juma reached across the table. He clapped a broad, dark hand over Allyn's forearm.

"I am well if you are well."

• • •

"Come on the veranda. The fireflies are out."

Juma rose from the cushions to follow Allyn outdoors. Under the first stars and open air, Allyn wouldn't feel such unfaithfulness to Eva as he might inside, talking to Juma about things that would have upset her, with Juma on the sofa she disliked. Allyn carried out the brandy decanter.

They settled in chaise lounges overlooking the lake; the decanter stood on the table between them. They did not face each other, both watched the blinking fireflies.

"Why are you here?"

"Several things. First, to tell you how sorry I am."

"You've done that. I'll be alright."

"This I know."

"What else?"

"I need two hundred thousand rand. Cash."

"For what?"

"Two of our poachers were killed a few days ago. From Tchonguene village. It's for the families."

"It's generous."

"Perhaps."

"Alright. What else?"

"I shipped off some very good horn yesterday. I have a new connection in the Kruger. Very promising."

"Tell me."

Juma reached for the decanter to refresh his brandy.

"No, shamwari."

Juma poured for himself and sipped. The brandy glass in his hand seemed no larger than a thimble. Allyn pursed his lips and nodded. Many years back, in the tunnels, he'd learned that the darker and deeper the world became, the more he should trust Juma.

"I'll go get the money."

Allyn left Juma on the veranda. He moved through the house without turning on more lights, and from his office safe removed four banded packets of bills. Outside, he stood before Juma; the man's width spread past the confines of the chaise lounge. Allyn handed over the money and remained standing.

"All this could have been done on the phone."

"True."

"I could have couriered the money to you."

"Yes."

"So why did you come all this way?"

"Sit, Allyn."

He did, elbows on knees, facing Juma. The big man kept his gaze fixed on the lake and the glittering bugs.

"You have a beautiful home."

"Thank you."

"The strike is over."

"It is. And you know how much I appreciate your help. The mine would not have survived without it."

"Of course."

"Juma. What do you want?"

"I came to ask if you want to continue."

"What are you saying?"

Juma set the brandy glass down with a lovely delicacy, something Allyn had noted in the massive Zulu boy almost fifty years ago. A drill, a stone, a woman, a glass, all seemed to soften in his great hands. Juma gave every movement such focus, so careful of his strength that he became gentle.

Juma pivoted on the chaise lounge to face Allyn. He mirrored Allyn's posture, black elbows on his own knees.

"I am saying you do not need me now. Your mine is operating again. The price for platinum is high. The crisis has passed."

Above the lake, something darker than the night cut through the fireflies, a bat feeding on them. Allyn was watching this when Juma asked, "Do you want to stop, shamwari?"

Allyn didn't need to save the mine anymore, that was done. During the strike, Ingwe had lost almost two thousand ounces a day of production. While Allyn's miners sat idle, the world market for platinum continued to grow as the demand for cleaner automobile emissions kept rising. The mine would take a few months until it was fully ramped up again, but Ingwe was a secondary seam to the Merensky Reef, shallower and less expensive to work. Even with the increased salaries and benefits that came out of the negotiations, Ingwe would return to profitability soon. Allyn's investors had been kept in the fold by the money Juma sent, five million rand—half a million American dollars—every month, sometimes much more.

With Juma's help, Allyn had set up a complex web of corporations and accounts, some offshore, one in China, two in Vietnam. He'd bought a small shipping company based in Harare where Juma could make deliveries. Juma was an officer of the firm and received his share of the horn sales as salary. Allyn knew only one name below him, Juma, above, he dealt only with a shadowy Mr. Phuong in Hanoi, who received the intact horns and paid an agreed-upon rate per US pound into a shell corporation in the Philippines. The price for one pound of rhino horn hovered just above $50,000, twice the cost of platinum, almost three times that of gold.

"You're right, Juma."

"I often am. What am I right about in this instance?"

"What you're not saying."

"That is?"

"From this point on, it's just about the money. Greed, I suppose."

"Yes."

"It is easy money."

"It must seem that way to you." Juma hefted the banded packets of rand for Allyn to see. "I promise you it is not."

Juma stood from the chaise lounge, towering over Allyn.

"I will be going."

Allyn stood as well, near enough to feel a damp warmth radiating off Juma's chest.

"I haven't given you my answer."

"I've changed my mind."

"Why?"

"Because you are my friend."

"I know that. But I'd like us to speak as partners. Don't go, Juma. Tell me."

"You will not like it, Allyn. You may, I think, like me less."

"That can't happen, shamwari."

"You have lost your wife. You almost lost your company. I should have waited to come. This is not a good time for you to decide things."

"Juma, you know me."

"Very well."

"With Eva gone, I haven't much else except business. I've no other interests, to tell you the truth. The last nine months frightened me. I thought I might lose everything. I did lose my wife, but because of you I kept the mine. What I'm saying is, if I had to choose between the two, I would have chosen this. I loved Eva, you know it. But I won't let Ingwe be at risk again. Ever. So please. Sit, friend."

Juma considered, looking down his dark cheeks to eye Allyn. He nodded like a tree in a breeze, solemnly, slowly.

"I started trading in horn only to help you. It was the fastest way to raise your cash."

"I know. Thank you."

"I don't tell you this for thanks."

"I understand."

"The horn money is good. But it's dangerous. People die, Allyn."

"They died in the mines, too."

"They did. For much less. I tell you so you will know. If you do business with me from this point forward, it's more than horn."

"What is it?"

"Weapons. Some drugs. And women."

Heavily, Juma sat. Allyn joined him. On the chaise lounges, they turned again to the lake, the fireflies, and the devouring, swooping bat.

Chapter 5

Promise stepped off the morning bus into Nyongane. The clear, early light made the many-colored garb of the women in the paved street electric. They wore sky-blue cotton wraps, orange and yellow shawls, and green sandals. They carried white baskets on their shoulders or balanced on their heads. The women were on their way to the well with laundry or bearing vegetables to sell in the township market. A few women knew Promise and greeted her: fat Blessed, Righteous, and one-eyed Bakabaka, whose name meant "pretty woman." Stepping to them in her olive drab uniform, Promise felt bland, no more vivid than the bare dirt beside the road. But the ladies were loud in their welcome, like all the Zulu women in the street who never whispered in public for fear they would be seen as plotting by other women.

"*Heita*, Promise. Come here, girl."

"Look at her."

"Ha, give us some sugar, *isingane*."

Promise hugged all three, leaning across their large bosoms to peck them on the cheeks. Righteous gestured at the small, white cooler Promise carried.

"You bring your lunch to the Kruger? I thought you ate leaves, girl."

The women jiggled and picked up their baskets to continue on their way. Blessed, her basket hefted high onto her head, pointed a pendulous arm up the road.

"I seen your *gogo*. She's in."

The women walked away, off the pavement, headed on a bare path downhill into the jumble of pastel shanties, tin roofs, and teetering lean-tos that jostled for space on this poor patch of land. Promise moved on, waving to an old woman who'd helped care for her in the AIDS orphanage and two teen girls she'd cared for years later. Both girls wore jean shorts cut short to show their whole dark thighs, and the women in the street clucked while boys watched them go by.

The morning threatened to be hot. Today's patrol started at one o'clock, in the scorching stretch of the afternoon. The Kruger held no shouting women or squalid homes or poverty, only the wildness of the world, the breeze of the bicycles, the open air, the hiding animals, trees, monkeys, birds. Promise liked the Kruger best. She would be on the next bus out of Nyongane.

Twenty thousand lived in the township, and not many owned cars. The few that did had jobs in Hazy View. They began to roll for the gate out to the main road. Each vehicle was packed with four in the rear seats, three in the front, some with loads roped to the roof, items to sell or barter in the city. The men in the cars touched their caps when they passed Promise, the township girl who'd become a ranger.

She stopped first in the co-op machine shop to see her *khulu*. She found him behind a big diesel engine that had been pulled by chains out of a tractor. Shirtless, he gleamed with sweat in the stuffy garage, his muscles shone like wet pebbles. Khulu's hair had only started to gray this year. He waved and called out.

"Will you stay for lunch?"

"No. I have to be at the park."

Khulu waved again, with a wrench in his dark hand. He lowered his head to the motor. Promise did not leave with the dismissal but rounded the large engine to plant a kiss on her grandfather's ear. He showed white teeth. His almond eyes crinkled in the merry way Promise imagined Khulu's daughter's, her own mother, might have done. She left, careful not to track through the grease on the concrete floor.

In the busy street again, under the climbing heat, Promise turned down an alley. Barefoot children scuffled after a ball, not playing a game but just sharing kicks back and forth. Promise wanted to kick with them, but she was older and wore boots and did not fit in their fun.

The structures here were huts of scavenged materials, some wood, some plastic corrugation, cinder blocks, salvaged bricks; the roofs were canted to make the rain run off behind them into the ditch where some urinated or shit. Many huts were rickety and leaned against a neighbor. Each was oddly tidy, because the women ran this alley, swept it and ordered the life of it. None of the people who lived in these shelters called them homes.

Promise stopped outside Gogo's red door, swung wide open for ventilation. Inside, the rooms were dim, the electricity was spotty on this alley. The blue water cistern beside the door had been filled; the truck came twice weekly. Gogo's wood-slat walls were not ramshackle but painted, straight, and sound, as were the walls of the shanties to the left and right. Gogo harangued her neighbors to keep their premises up.

Above the alley, above Gogo's shanty, on the green hillside overlooking the township, the claps of hammering filtered down to Promise. A concrete truck worked its way up a gravel road to the new development, to pour pads and sidewalks for the first houses going up. The government was doing this for Nyongane. The houses on the hill would be tiny, not much bigger than the huts below, but solid and real. They wouldn't leak or fall down, they'd catch the breezes and see far beyond the township; they would not shame their occupants. The homes' first owners would be those township people who could put down a deposit of fifty thousand rand, then pay the rest, almost half a million rand.

Only a few in Nyongane could do this, and it would be their life savings. Some families pooled their money with others. They would continue living crowded, but they would live up there.

Promise stepped inside Gogo's open door. She did not announce herself but spent a moment without her grandmother knowing she was visiting. Gogo moved about in the second room, humming while changing bedsheets. Promise set the cooler on the floorboards; this floor was one of the prides of the alley. A decade ago, Khulu had scavenged the wood from an abandoned railroad cattle car. He'd planed the boards by hand to remove splinters and painted them dusky rose, then set them on tarred timbers to lift his wife above the dirt.

Promise tiptoed through the sitting room to the kitchen, the smallest room of the shanty. A kettle simmered, still hot on the gas burner. She poured herself a china cup and dropped in the next-to-last tea bag. Promise eased toward the sounds of Gogo snapping linens and humming in her lovely voice. In nooks and crannies, on the tabletops, stood Gogo's collection of black glass sculptures, all of African women. Some were bottles, some lamps. Gogo decorated with these figurines and artwork of female warriors, black as the points of their spears, and with photos of her dead children and Promise.

Promise stepped into the little bedroom. Gogo stopped tucking a pillow into a clean case and put her hands to her tiny hips. She raised an eyebrow to ask, *You do not announce yourself in my house*? Promise offered her the fresh cup of tea. Gogo reached knobby hands for it and sat on the made bed, patting for Promise to sit with her.

Gogo's sandals did not reach the floorboards. She was a short woman, narrow from face to feet, winnowed by a life of labor and loss. She held an energy that seemed to consume her as she aged. Gogo was a black Zulu with nothing brown about her, not even her eyes. Gogo, like Khulu, had all her teeth; her tongue was her strength, the way Khulu's arms were his.

When Promise sat next to her grandmother, the mattress was so high that Promise's own feet barely met the floor. Ever since her own childhood in the township, Gogo had raised her beds on stacks of cinder blocks, to guard against the black ghost, the spirit that seeped out of the ground in the night to take sleepers and not let them wake. Though it was understood long ago that the deaths were from the fumes of tires burned in the camp for warmth, even after the practice was stopped Gogo and the other *anties* in Nyongane continued to do what their mothers did and raised their beds.

Gogo blew across the teacup, puffing her black cheeks. When she sipped, her cheeks sank deep. She swallowed and blinked into the cup.

"Up on the hill, there will be no black ghosts."

"No, Gogo. There won't."

"My first night there, I will sleep on the ground. Just to show it."

"I want to see that."

"I walked up there yesterday by myself. I sat under a tree. You can look a long way. Even with the men working, it felt quiet. Strange."

How unlikely that this small woman was huge Juma's sister. Promise had no siblings; her parents died before that could happen. But if she'd had a brother, he would have been seven feet tall if the difference had stayed the same as it was between Juma and Gogo. Sitting on the bed, just the toes of her boots touching the red floor Khulu had made, Promise took Gogo's hand. She held it for a long, silent moment before she put the money in it, so Gogo would not have to ask.

• • •

Promise passed the orphanage, named *Isipho*, for hope. The building was the largest in the township, built of brick, supported by many world charities who put their names on the sign facing Nyongane's one paved street. The morning was still early, and the children would be making their cots or lining up for breakfast in the courtyard with tin plates in hand and a cook spooning out oatmeal or powdered eggs. The milk, too, was powdered. Promise carried the cooler into the orphanage's weedy front yard, to the old swing set.

She set down the cooler before settling into one of the wooden seats. Grabbing the chains, she pushed off. Promise had to lift her legs to fly above the dirt, and in her boots and green uniform, she made the swing set squeak and sway. A white nun she did not know came to ask if Promise could be helped in some way. Promise dragged her feet to stop, but the nun said she could go on, but please be careful. The swings were rusty, there was no money to repair them if something broke. Promise had enough money in her pocket to buy a new playground. She thanked the nun, lifted the cooler, and walked on.

The busyness of the township had waned. Most of the women stayed inside with their chores, the men at work or indolent on plastic chairs. Promise was one of only a few left in the street. She greeted no one and lengthened her strides to be done and on the bus back to the Kruger.

The quick walk, the blocked and breezeless air in Nyongane, these made Promise anxious in a way the bush did not. She didn't pause outside the door to Bongani's store but rode the momentum of her nerves across his threshold.

His shop was the third-biggest building in the township, after the orphanage and the school. It was, in fact, several huts fixed together. As Bongani had expanded his *spaza*, his small convenience store, over the years, he'd swallowed his neighbors. At the scrape of Promise's heels on the clean concrete floor, Bongani turned from his shelves; from his cans, cheap toys, open bins of beets, potatoes, carrots, and roots; from a barrel of beans, a crate of rice with a scoop in it, an old scale. His dark face was smooth and pleasant, creased beside the eyes. Old Bongani was a shopkeeper, never a man to sling a tool or carry a burden. He'd long been the richest man in the township. He was unmarried, but no one questioned him in this. Before Promise was born, Bongani had killed a man who'd publicly doubted him, or so her grandmother had said.

"Look who is here. My ranger."

"*Sawubona*, Bongani."

"Go outside and come in again."

"That's foolish."

"No, I want to see you come into my store."

"I'm sorry I haven't visited."

"Then go outside. Come in. I will consider forgiving you the years you have not come."

Promise sighed and did as she was asked. Bongani stood tall behind the counter, hands on hips, pleased with her entrance. Promise rested the cooler on the counter between them.

"Welcome, Nomawethu. You're grown up."

Bongani had barely changed in the five years since Promise had left the township. He looked well kept and pleased, as if he'd just finished a meal. Perhaps Gogo might have looked like this, full and smooth in her gathering years, if Bongani had won her. Bongani did not have Khulu's muscles, but seemed to have everything else.

"Thank you."

"I must tell you. Those are words I should have heard a while ago. I thought you would have come before now. I see you, you know, when you visit. You walk right past my shop. Like I've done nothing. Like you owe nothing."

The gentleness of Bongani's features faded. His wide eyes narrowed, his lips tucked in. Promise had not come to upset him, but with the opposite intent. She didn't know what she'd done wrong. She tried to keep her voice soft, but she was an orphan and a ranger and could only do so much.

"What do I owe you?"

"This is a joke, yes?"

"No."

"Did your Gogo not tell you?"

"I don't know what you're talking about."

"I can't believe I have to tell you. After all these years."

"The years are gone, Bongani. I am here. Tell me now."

"You owe me that uniform."

"That's . . ." Promise could not complete the sentence, confounded.

"Of course." Bongani slapped the countertop, not hard but enough to toll the suddenness of his change in manner. "I know why she kept it from you."

"Kept what?"

"She wanted you to believe it was him."

"Bongani."

"It was me. I made the call to SANParks. I got you into the game-ranger program. One slot in twenty, that's what it was. I paid money to get you on the list. I even bought your first bus ticket. He couldn't do that for you. I did." Bongani snorted, an ugly spitting noise.

Promise snatched the cooler off the counter and whirled for the shop door. She halted on the edge of the sunlight, did not step into it. Up on the green hill, trucks and men cobbled together the first new homes, every house to be solid and straight, high above everything that held the township down. In the doorway, Promise turned back to Bongani, who'd said nothing more and would have let her go. Again, she rested the cooler on the counter.

"I'm sorry. I didn't know."

"You did nothing wrong, child. You made me proud, that's all. I'll talk with her about this."

"Please don't."

"And why should I not? I will tell you this. She asked me to do it. And she turned my kindness into a lie."

Promise slid the cooler toward him.

"This is for you."

"For me?"

Bongani took from one wall a toy, a plastic water pistol. He put it down next to the cooler.

"A gift for a gift."

It was a silly gesture, and Bongani made a forgiving smile. She took the toy off the counter.

"You have a real gun in the bush?" Bongani asked.

"Yes."

"Do you shoot people with it? Poachers?"

"Others have. I haven't."

"Could you?"

"Yes."

Bongani covered his mouth in mock shock. He surveyed the cooler and reached for it.

"What have you brought me?"

"Muti."

Bongani's hands stalled on the cooler.

"That is a powerful gift, Nomawethu."

"I know you're working with the government. For the new houses on the hill."

Old Bongani cocked his head. He drew out the word as he replied. "Yes."

"You're in charge of the names and applications from the township."

Bongani tapped his fingertips on the cooler. He seemed wary.

"And I will be the first to move up there. Trust that."

Promise touched the back of Bongani's hand, and with the touch cast to Bongani her hope.

"Open it."

Wide-eyed in wonder, Bongani slid aside the cooler's top. He tapped on the iced packet Promise had wrapped in foil from the kitchen of her ranger station.

"What have we here?"

Bongani laid the crinkled package on the counter. He plucked at the foil to peel it back. When the first black nail emerged, he paused to nod gravely, marveling.

"A sangoma."

Bongani uncovered the rest of the severed front feet of the aardvark. The beast's cold paws had been neatly cut, bone and meat even. The claws curled as though still digging.

The old man spread apart all the foil, then flattened his hands on the counter. He spoke without looking up.

"You are trying to heal."

Promise rolled the plastic water gun in her hands. She set it on the countertop to return it, to ask for a far greater gift.

"Yes."

Bongani picked up one of the claws. He scraped the hard, dead tips against his open palm.

"Forty years."

"Gogo has told me."

"He took her from me. He lied."

"I cannot say, Bongani."

"I loved her. She chose me first."

"I know. It's been a very long time."

Bongani put down the claw.

"Has it?"

From a pocket, Promise pulled the last of Juma's cash, ten thousand rand rolled in a rubber band. She set this on the opened foil. Louder than the muti, the money spoke out for healing.

Promise rested a hand on his wrist.

"Please, Bongani. Let them have a house on the hill. Don't stop them."

Bongani lingered under her hand, moving his eyes between the claws and the bills.

He straightened. Promise reeled back her touch. Bongani stowed the cash in a drawer. He folded the foil over the claws;

he would put them in a mesh cage to keep away the birds and rodents, then hang them on his roof to dry. He might sell them, or he might wear them. A sangoma had power.

Bongani reached across the counter to caress Promise's cheek.

"Did she ask you to do this, too?"

"Yes."

"Your grandmother." Bongani blinked at some memory or a tear or both. He lowered his hand. "And if I consider this? Where will they get the money? The mechanic can't buy her a house."

Promise took the toy gun off the counter. She'd give it to a child at the orphanage on her way out of Nyongane. She turned for the shop door and the sun, speaking over her shoulder.

"I'll buy it."

Chapter 6

Opu rode in the back of the chopper with the bodies. Both poachers had fouled themselves in their dying, and at sunrise Opu cleaned them as well as he could, using the last of his canteen. The poachers' blood had dried in the cool night and no longer stank, but even so the pilot and Neels left their window vents open in the copter for the thirty-minute flight to Skukuza.

A bakkie met them at the airport, come for the bodies. Neels and Opu caught a ride in the pickup bed, along with the corpses, to the main headquarters. There, the poachers were locked in cold storage with a dozen more dead Mozambicans awaiting postmortems and identification. Neels and Opu entered the air-conditioning of the offices with rifles strapped across their backs. They stepped into the intelligence room to make their report.

Karskie, a young man Neels barely knew, did not stand when he and Opu walked into the drab room, an office made brown by cheap furniture and wood paneling. Karskie faced many computer screens, and when he looked up, his grin was sporty, his hair combed to a centered ridge. Neels had only spoken to Karskie once before; at the golf course a few evenings back, they'd been at the same table with a dozen others from the main office. Karskie was not a ranger but a contractor, a numbers genius brought in by SANParks last month just before he was let go by a Jo'burg university. Neels recalled being satisfied with how the big boy handled his share of the drinking. That evening, a lion had roared out of the darkness from far across the lake, maybe three kilometers away, but the throaty chuffs filled the night, rising above the cicadas and monkey screams. Karskie had left the table alone to go sit beside the lake and listen.

Neels sat in front of him. Opu remained standing. Karskie pointed.

"Is that blood on your shoulders?"

"Someone else's."

"Ah. Well." The boy lowered plump hands to one of his keyboards. "So you had contact. What happened?"

Karskie typed at an impressive speed while Neels related how he and Opu had followed a set of tracks east, away from the carcass, and what he'd found in the road at the border. Opu had shot one poacher in the dry ravine, Neels shot another, one got away. Neels made no mention of interrogating the poacher. To do so would be to admit the poacher had been alive. Karskie was new. Neels didn't know where the boy stood on this.

Karskie entered data as he asked questions. Where did the poachers cross into the park? Exactly where had they been spotted and engaged? What time? Was there a description of the one who escaped?

The big boy typed blithely, dispassionate.

"How many firearms were recovered?"

"One."

Karskie stopped his fingers.

"One."

"That's what I said."

"Two corpses were brought in."

"That's how many *moers* we shot."

Karskie tucked his tongue behind his lower lip, not disengaging from Neels's hard gaze.

"The nature of the contact?"

Neels had never been asked this, and did not like it. Behind him, Opu shuffled his feet.

"Beg pardon?" Neels asked.

"When you encountered the poachers, what transpired?"

"Transpired."

"What did they do? What did you do? What was said?"

"Why?"

Karskie flattened his hands on the desk, away from his keys, the equivalent of a man from a different generation setting down a pen. Karskie drummed both index fingers, unafraid of Neels.

"Because you are in the tenth month of the year. So far, you've lost close to a thousand white rhinos out of a population in the Kruger of nine thousand. You're on the same pace as last year, which, if you understand, was a record. At this rate, your rhinos are, for all intents and purposes, already extinct. Your kill rate exceeds the birthrate."

"You think you're telling me something I don't know?"

"The point is that I know. You've got no statistical stability to your data. That's what I was brought in to do. What month, day, what phase of the moon? What weather, temperature, what time, what location, how many and what sort of weapons? I've been here a month, and so far what I've seen is a primitive response to a primitive problem. Poachers sneak in, butcher a rhino, then walk out. You follow their tracks. And if somehow you manage to bump into them in a park the size of Israel, you kill them, for the most part."

"We do the fucking best we can."

"And the result of that is your rhinos are being wiped out. It's not enough. We're trying to change that. We can spot tendencies. Be more efficient. We can bring some fucking twenty-first-century technology to bear."

Karskie flicked one finger onto the keyboard to make some facts march.

"Let's see, shall we? Alright."

Karskie pecked one key repeatedly. The gesture agitated Neels, as if the boy were nicking at him.

"Over the last two years, Kruger's lost an average of three rhinos per day. Out of ten to fifteen border crossings daily, your rangers find and follow just one set of tracks. Every day and night, somewhere in the park, where hundreds of thousands of tourists visit year-round, there are shots fired. So, let's just figure, for shits and giggles, that, on any given day, you have twenty to thirty armed and illegally present men creeping over the Kruger. That's six hundred poachers a month. Out of that number, just twenty are neutralized. Sixteen of those are shot dead outright. So, in effect, you're stopping one poacher for every five rhinos killed. Please, tell me, how's the tracking thing working out for you?"

Karskie sat back from his tattletale computer screen. He folded his arms and tilted his head at Neels.

Opu said, "Fuck you," and walked out of the room.

The big boy waited until the old Zulu was gone before speaking again.

"You think I'm judging you. I'm not."

Karskie said this with a lowered voice, to keep his words from carrying out the door Opu had left open behind him.

It seemed acceptable for Neels, the bush warrior, to talk this way, to be critical of their slipping hold on the last rhinos. But in this cool office, away from the bloodletting, with only pictures of half-devoured carcasses and dead black men on his desk, young and new Karskie could not.

The boy leaned forward to speak to Neels above his computer screens, as though cutting them out of the conversation. He almost whispered.

"Look. No one cares if you shoot every bastard you find out there."

"I intend to."

"Good. And along the way, keep me up to speed. We're building intelligence nets in Mozambique. I've got informants in a few of the poaching gangs. Give me what you get in the field. I'll give you back gold. I promise."

Neels got to his feet, shouldering his rifle.

"Alright. Here's your first."

"Give it to me."

"Juma."

• • •

Neels waited past noon at the airport for the chopper pilot to give him a ride north to Shingwedzi. Opu had disappeared and would find his own way.

The first half of the flight back was silent and seething for Neels, grinding his teeth above the vast expanse of the Kruger. Every ranger was aware of the boy Karskie's bleak numbers, but that didn't keep the numbers from being jarring when balled up and thrown in one's face. Karskie was not liked. Neels had given him Juma's name to see what he could do with it.

The pilot, Ian, flew level and straight for thirty minutes. Neels closed his eyes. Before long his gone wife entered through the dark space there and walked on. His heart called out and ached. Neels opened his eyes just as the chopper banked.

Ian had spotted a big herd of bok filling the khaki plain. The pilot nudged the stick to drop down, get a closer, lower look, and to make them run.

A thousand horned antelope leaped away from the zooming helicopter, across the grassless ground, crowded and rippling like troubled water. Ian flew fifty feet over the boks' sprinting, bobbing backs. Neels pressed his forehead to the plexiglass window to see the dashing animals and the rushing earth. When Ian pulled up into the blue afternoon sky, Neels clapped the pilot on the knee.

The rest of the flight north to Shingwedzi was made twice as long; Ian took the two of them on a safari. He circled elephants in a clutch of marula trees, buffalo in the brown river with alligators sunning near them, a hundred zebra and ostriches milling together on an emerald hillside. The day was sunny, and tourists stopped their cars on the road to let grazing giraffes cross.

Neels's mood swung sharply like the chopper; he became joyful, bouncing and pointing in his seat, his own voice a buzz in the headphones. Ian indulged him, finding and flushing out more wildlife. Neels's excitement grew with every sighting of a beast caught in the open or frightened out of hiding. Neels laughed hard, and harder, until a tear slipped down his cheek. Then he asked Ian to head for Shingwedzi.

Neels's small ranger station was set in a copse of trees in the center of a wide, flat plain, broken only by scrub and one dusty road leading to the park byway. In the middle of that plain, only a kilometer from the ranger station, a lone, massive, black rhino stood on its shadow, which made it seem even grander. The animal surveyed the dry and unwelcoming land. Ian, flying up from behind, slowed to hover in midair. The rhino's ears twitched; it stood rock still for moments that to Neels felt ancient and stunning. The rhino began to dance in place, hopping side to side, keeping its tail facing the chopper.

At once the rhino turned to face the chopper, its magnificent horns tipped up at the floating machine. The animal pawed the plain once, again, then bent its anvil head and long horn to the ground to scoop up dirt, casting a cloud in the air. Ian held the copter in place. The rhino pawed a third time, challenging, then charged. Ian let the beast rumble at them, muscle, horns, girth, and rage, not too close but enough for him and Neels to have the thrill of it. When Ian flicked the chopper away and the rhino rampaged beneath them, both men whooped into the microphones bent to their lips. Neels glanced back. The rhino had not pivoted to watch them go but slowed its gait and kept its broad rump to them, in disdain and majesty.

• • •

Neels shook Ian's hand, then slammed the copter's door. He ducked beneath the spinning blades while the chopper lifted off. A stinging dust whipped up, turning Neels away to the ranger station.

He reached the small blockhouse in time to see the pair of day rangers push off on their bicycles. A boy and a girl. She was called Promise, her partner Wophule. The boy was still a teen, the youngest of all the Kruger rangers. His name was a Xhosa joke: Wophule meant *broken*, for broken promise. Bad enough he pedaled Shingwedzi; he did so with a woman.

But he was no less a joke than the girl.

In two decades of training rangers, Neels had yet to see a female up to the job. They needed time off for babies, couldn't carry a full five-day pack, couldn't keep their pants on; one issue or another always needed to be dealt with for the women. Few lasted more than a year in the bush, stuck out in the stations, isolated with the men. None had ever been promoted to the extended patrols, the ECP teams. This young one pedaling away, Promise, had joined the Kruger rangers two years ago, at age twenty. Like the rest of the trainees, the girl came to Neels after completing twelve months of study in tracking, weapons, nature conservancy, and bush survival. She'd been given to Neels, and he'd had no say in that. Promise had proven a good tracker, knew the veld well enough, kept her mouth shut, made no problems. That didn't mean something wasn't going to go wrong; it just hadn't yet. He assigned her to routine daytime patrols on a bicycle. A year later, he gave her the boy, Wophule, to ride with.

She and her little partner wheeled out of sight, rifles on their backs, in the direction of the black rhino. Neels had no faith she could protect that giant if the hard work came her way. She rode a bike, and that's where she would stay. And the boy who rode with her, what kind of ranger rides with a woman?

Neels went inside. Two other rangers were there, lean, quiet Zulus, one with a towel around his waist, fresh out of the shower.

The other, in uniform and black beret, rose from a kitchen chair to give Neels a gentle fist in the shoulder as he walked past. "We heard. Good shooting, baas."

In his small office, Neels cut on the oscillating fan. His desk was clean save for a VHF radio and a daybook that said he was to pick up the Shingwedzi ECP team at six o'clock and drop off the next one, these two in the station. He set his cell phone next to the radio. Together, the two devices could reach almost anyone in the world.

Neels fingered the cell phone, still warm from his pocket. He lifted the radio's microphone to his mouth, the plastic cool at his lips. He replaced the mic to its hook. The radio and phone were a rebuke. Who was there to talk to?

But he wanted to talk. Not about the night before or the man he'd killed; that was just one of hundreds he'd put a bullet into between the Border War and twenty years in the Kruger. He wasn't concerned about consequences from the killings; no ranger was. In a winter meeting, in Pretoria, between the twenty-three Kruger section chiefs and the top federal prosecutor for South Africa, Neels and the rest had been informed privately, in terms not to be repeated, that on her watch, no SANParks ranger would ever be prosecuted for murdering a poacher.

Neels wanted to talk about anything else. The cell phone and the radio on the desk offered themselves. He had only to dial, and he could talk about a garden, a game, some news or memory, cars, food, any topic, anything but the bush and the corpses of animals and men. Neels envisioned himself speaking to someone; he didn't need to recognize the face or voice in his imagination —just a person who knew nothing about him. What came out was a conversation about love and hatred and how to stand them both. He closed his office door on the two rangers readying for their five-day disappearance into the park beginning at sundown. He sat by himself with only the radio, the phone, and the calendar on his desk.

For an hour, the two Zulus made very little noise on the other side of Neels's door. The rangers packed and armed themselves; they gathered food and shelter as Neels had taught them. Neels heard only the scrape of a chair, a closet closing, a murmur. It was not enough. Like Karskie had said, it was not enough. He wished to throw open his door, to see and hear more, not two dark men readying themselves to vanish. Neels looked in his lap at his hard and aging hands, and he wanted. A party, a Christmas, a braai, a family, perhaps joy. He envisioned a ham to carve on the desk in front of him. He considered what he might say to his friends for the occasion. The cell phone rang, and he was surprised to find himself on his feet. He wondered if he'd conjured the ring, too, until it rang again. The ham before him did not dissolve. The phone rang a third time, and Neels blinked himself back to the empty room in the station deep in the Kruger. The fan oscillated past him, beyond him, and he answered.

"Ja."

"It's Karskie."

"What do you have?"

"The name you gave me. Juma. I found some things."

"Ja?"

"He's an old, black Rhodesian. Moved into Mozambique about ten years ago. Lives in Mapai, in a mansion. He's untouchable there, local hero. Got his own syndicate. He's drugs, some guns. Human trafficking. Rotten piece of work."

"What about horn?"

"No word Juma's ever traded horn."

"Find word."

"I'll keep digging."

Karskie hung up. The ranger station's timbers and tin roof crackled from the rising heat. The Zulu trackers had gone to their bunks to rest before dusk. Chubby Professor Karskie considered what he was doing digging. Neels, thinking of war and the Kruger, laughed at how different their two notions of that word must be.

The silence around him, the heaviness of it all, abated. For these moments, Neels's laughter was the loudest sound in the ranger station, perhaps in Shingwedzi.

Chapter 7

The battle raged over the grassy field beside the air base's main runway. A hundred South African troops and a dozen war machines surged forward by air and land; their advance was loud and fiery. Nearby, close enough to feel the thumps of the explosions, today's twenty thousand awed people, half with children on their shoulders, stood in a half-mile-long line, clapping, while an announcer narrated the fight over loudspeakers.

LB watched from a lawn chair on the east-west runway, binoculars up. He cheered each blast, shouted out the spectacle to the lounging team behind him and for Wally, who was not watching, either, but working. Over and again, LB called out, "You gotta see this!"

The infantry company on the ground moved in fine formation toward their pretend target, a hangar. At their rear a pair of choppers swooped in, hovering eighty feet off the ground to discharge two dozen more troops, Special Forces on fast ropes. The South Africans were good. They slid down the ropes smoothly, raised weapons, and moved in a neat firing line. Preset charges blew on their left and right, and none of the soldiers flinched. Behind them, more armored transports charged into place, more men leaped out. Another pair of choppers crept just above them, aerial protectors. Out of nowhere in all the noise and show, a big helicopter gunship howled past, low and lethal; the announcer called out, "Here come the big guns!" A detonation far ahead of the troops sent a gasp through the big crowd as if the gunship had fired. A lone tank rumbled forward, too, painted in desert camouflage, spinning its turret, looking for enemies. The tank's commander rode in the open cupola, hamming it up with one arm out to point the way.

A South African Air Force Gripen, sharp-nosed like a dagger, flashed across the scene next. The jet tore a marvelous rent through the afternoon, so fast its own roar trailed it. Thousands of hands in the crowd, big and little, black and white, reached up to the streak. LB followed the Gripen in the binoculars, watched it snap into a barrel roll just above the earth, then climb straight up on a tail of blue flame.

Satisfied, LB folded the lawn chair and strolled over to his team. War, from the remove of safety, was an epic thing to witness. The endless boy in him thrilled at the thunder of guns, at the thrum of engines, at trained soldiers and dangerous machines moving in concert. LB couldn't understand why anyone who did this stuff for a living, given the chance to see it without the adrenaline and risk, wouldn't watch and enjoy it. That was why he'd called out all the highlights of the exhibition to the rest of the team, to shame them a bit and remind them that what they did in real life was fucking exciting.

He walked under the great wing of *Kingsman 1*, the first of two waiting US Air Force HC-130s. Quincy, Doc, and Jamie lay on the tarmac in the wing's shadow. Dressed in ABUs (airman battle uniforms), they rested their heads on their parachutes, all eyes closed. The military taught this lesson early on: never stand when you can sit, never sit when you can lie down, and never just lie down when you can sleep. Wally didn't recline with the team but stood apart, overseeing the loadmasters while they secured one of the two Guardian Angel Air-Deployable Recovery Vehicles, the PJs' muscular, all-terrain, souped-up buggies. They would toss these GAARVs out of the planes at two thousand feet as the air show's final performance.

LB approached. Wally had little to do mother-henning the loading of the GAARVs. The vehicles were tubular steel, armor plated, and gunned up, with fat tires and powerful engines designed to climb, dash, and fight in and out of trouble. Because America's military and allies operated in every environment on the planet, the GAARVs, like the GAs, had to be prepared to go anywhere to execute their mission of CSAR (combat search and rescue).

A forklift had set one of the vehicles at the foot of the cargo plane's lowered gate; straps held the GAARV tight to a cardboard crush pallet that would absorb the impact of the parachute landing. The loading crew had hooked the pallet to a winch to hoist it up the gate's rollers into the bay. Of all the world's militaries, the United States' pararescuemen were famed for jumping out of planes onto any kind of environment—ice, mountain, jungle, or sea—in any weather, with anything: zodiac inflatable rafts, wave runners, motorcycles, ATVs, all sorts of heavy equipment, weapons, Jaws of Life, cars.

LB watched Wally from behind. The man was doing the same thing LB had done from his lawn chair, making a statement. LB believed the team should have some fun, hoot and holler at things blowing up, support their South African hosts, not lie about and snooze. Likewise, Wally stood here in the sun with his fists on his hips while the loadmasters did their jobs, just to show the team that no detail was too small not to be checked and rechecked.

LB strolled past Wally to the GAARV, jumping up on the plane's ramp while the buggy was hauled over the rollers. He poked at the cardboard fenders and cushions, tugged on the restraining straps, and pretended to take an interest. Wally nodded and did not catch that he was being lampooned. LB shot the loadmasters a thumbs-up, and they, too, got no sense of the joke. He clomped down the metal ramp to Wally, who did not turn his sunglass-covered gaze away from the GAARV fading into the cargo hold. LB put his own hands on his hips, a shorter, much thicker version of Wally.

"So."

Out on the air base's sunny, trampled field, the last fireball erupted as the mini war wound down. Over the loudspeakers, the announcer declared victory.

Wally hooked a thumb across his shoulder at the second HC-130, *Kingsman 2*, thirty yards away. Its GAARV had already been loaded and stowed. Wally, LB, and Doc would ride on that plane, Jamie and Quincy here on *Kingsman 1*.

"All loaded. We spin up in five."

LB rubbed his hands together. "I'll get the boys moving."

He tucked two fingers into his mouth to loose an earsplitting whistle. Under the wing, Doc sat up in the shade. LB twirled a finger beside his head. Doc rose to his boots and began to rouse the team.

Wally peered down on LB from behind his opaque lenses.

"What do you need, LB?"

"Are you pissed at me?"

"Why do you ask?"

"You haven't said two words to me since yesterday."

"Busy."

"Or pissed. I figure you're pissed."

Wally exhaled through his nose, stuttering, a private chuckle.

"No more than usual."

"Good. Sorry about yesterday. That guy was a dick."

"He didn't start out that way."

"Fair enough."

The team clambered upright. Lugging their jump containers, Quincy and Jamie lumbered over the tarmac to climb the lowered ramp of *Kingsman 1*. Doc shouldered both his chute and LB's. Today's jump would be without weapons or med rucks; the

PJs would simply follow the twin GAARVs down to the ground, cut them loose from their chutes and straps, rev them up, then tear up more of the air base's infield, all to cheers.

Kingsman 1's engines whined, caught, and coughed greasy puffs. The propellers turned, the prop noise mounted. LB had to shout.

"You and Torres set a date yet?"

Wally shrugged. He hefted his own container over his shoulder.

"We're waiting."

"For what?"

"Got some decisions to make."

"Like what?"

Wally raised his free arm and slapped it down against his hip.

"First you give me a hard time. Now you're pushing me."

LB raised his volume higher, increasing it more than enough to be heard over the rising engines.

"I'm just saying. If you're gonna do it, do it."

"And what do you know?"

LB lifted his hands with his voice.

"Whoa. What does that mean?"

"It means you got no idea about marriage and a family. As in none. Okay? LB?"

"I?" LB rammed a finger into his own burly chest. "I have no idea about family?"

Then what was all this? What was every scar he bore; every nightmare; every story, laugh, and worry; every person and thing he loved? Who were these men around him?

Before LB could answer, Doc joined them. Wally and LB both froze with hands up, pausing their gesticulating and punctuating.

Doc looked from one to the other, then dropped LB's chute on the runway.

"No. Not doing it."

That was all Doc said. In the swelling pitch of the spinning propellers, he climbed the ramp into *Kingsman 1*, to jump instead with Quincy and Jamie.

• • •

LB and Wally sat opposite each other in the thrumming cargo bay of *Kingsman 2*. Over in his mesh seat, Wally leaned his helmet back against the fuselage, reflective sunglasses down. LB couldn't tell if Wally's eyes were shut or if the man was staring at him. It didn't matter which; stared at or ignored, both bothered LB. He wanted to chat, he always got keyed up before a jump. They could find other things to talk about than Torres and marriage. They could act like friends. Sitting here, bumping along with stoic, quiet Wally made LB uneasy.

They had the big cargo bay to themselves; the loadmaster had disappeared into the cockpit. Deep in the rear of the hold, the GAARV hunkered in yellow tie-downs and cardboard cuffs, looking ready to leap out of its restraints. LB was itchy to go, too.

They were coming up on fifteen years, him and Wally. LB's first sight of Wally Bloom had been Wally as a bony boy at the Air Force Academy. The third-year cadet had been assigned to jumpmaster for LB's eight-man Ranger team for a high-altitude, high-opening training jump, a HAHO. Wally was the leader of the Academy's competitive parachute team. To be on the team, cadet jumpers had to cover a three-inch dot with their boots ten times in a row from different altitudes. To run the team, a cadet had to do it twenty times. Wally was that good. All that summer at the Academy, whether young Wally Bloom stepped out at twenty-five thousand feet or eight hundred, LB leaped into thin air behind him without hesitation. The kid was so thorough and locked down that LB requested him for some dark ops in South America later that autumn. Because all air force cadets were on active duty, Wally Bloom spent much of his fourth year studying by flashlight in the back of a cargo plane or dangling in the air over one jungle or another with LB and his team drifting down at his backside.

After graduating the Academy, Wally followed LB into the Rangers, just as LB was giving up his captain's commission to become a PJ. LB had seen enough of combat from the search-and-destroy side. He'd done his share, a bit more, and wanted—needed—the pararescue mission to save lives instead of take them. By the time Wally Bloom followed him again, LB was a master sergeant and a pararescue jumper. Wally stayed a captain and became a combat-rescue officer, LB's CRO.

That flip in roles had not been healthy for their relationship.

Ten years later, here Captain Wally Bloom sat in the back of another cargo plane, either staring at LB or asleep.

Didn't matter which.

Wally folded his arms over his chest and crossed his long legs at the ankles. So he was awake behind those opaque shades. LB mirrored him, crossing his own arms and feet.

The two sat like this, a Mexican standoff of silence and mimicry. The loadmaster came down the steps from the cockpit. With the punch of a button, he lowered the HC-130's gate; air and white light gushed in around the widening edges. LB and Wally did not move for another minute, until LB surrendered, because it was his job. He tapped his own ear and shouted across to his captain over the propeller noise.

"Hey! Radio check."

Wally stirred but slowly. The two hailed each other over the team freq, answering five by five. Doc, Quincy, and Jamie checked in from *Kingsman 1*. Wally tested his ground-to-air radio with the pilots of both planes, while the loadmaster started to blade away the webbing around the GAARV on its cardboard crush pallet. Only one nylon restraint was left to hold back the big package.

The ramp dropped all the way, yawning into the bright afternoon. Rolling green plains, black ribbon roads, and patchwork hills carved into hamlets and farmland slid by three thousand feet below. The jumpmaster waited with his knife behind the GAARV, ready to shove the pallet over the casters in the deck. Above the open portal, the red ready light came on; this marked the final minutes before the jump.

LB covered the short distance to Wally, who got to his feet. The man was eight inches taller than LB, lean and lithe, more things the two of them did not have in common. LB circled Wally, checking his straps and chute container, then came to a standstill so Wally could tug and prod at him. When they were done, both pounded fists on the other's shoulders to say, *You're good.*

The GAARV would go out first. One good shove and a slice from the loadmaster and the rollers would do the rest. Wally and LB would dive out behind it. The massive crowd below was going to be amazed at the American pararescuemen leaping and landing with a pair of truck-sized GAARVs. On the ground, the team would free the badass, cutting-edge rescue buggies from their pallets in under a minute, fire them up, and roar off to the make-believe rescue.

LB shrugged his equipment into place. Waiting for the green light, Wally ignored him. LB shrugged at this, too. In these moments before the jump, anticipating the drop and popping chute, the thrill and action and cheers, all for being a PJ, Wally's snit was petty. LB would deal with it later.

LB fixed his eyes on the red bulb, waiting for it to extinguish and the green to flick on. He stood to the right of the loadmaster and the big GAARV, Wally to the left. The roar of the plane's twin engines, the whoosh of rushing wind, the blue and green world all flooded in the opened ramp. LB tapped his toe, impatient. He loved the first moments of the drop, the sudden stark silence, the focus and freedom of having his whole life on his back and in a handle in his fist.

The crimson light blinked out.

The green one glowed.

The loadmaster snipped the lone yellow strap. Lowering his shoulder, he heaved two short strides, rolling the GAARV to the lip of the ramp and out. Instantly, the package was snatched away by the wind. Two round, white cargo chutes blossomed.

A hundred yards behind and off to one side, *Kingsman 1* spat its own GAARV out into the African sky. Doc, Quincy, and Jamie followed. They jumped as one, plunging with arms and legs wide.

LB took a step.

Wally's balled fist, the symbol for stop, appeared right in front of LB's goggled eyes.

The GAARV fell fast behind the speeding cargo plane, plummeting from sight. The open gate, rushing air, falling package, all of it drew LB to the leap and the job. But Wally's fist did not move from in front of his face.

LB whirled, expecting to yell something he should not. Even the loadmaster, in his emptied bay, turned to stare.

Wally lowered his hand to press it over his earpiece, to better hear one of his radios. He gave the loadmaster an officer's scowl and pointed at the ramp. *Raise it.*

The loadmaster did as he was told. Even before the button was punched to lift the ramp, before LB could fling up his arms at Wally or insist on an explanation, big *Kingsman 2* banked sharply away from the air show and the crowd below. The cargo bay tilted, but Wally was rangy enough to grab a piece of the superstructure and hold his ground. He kept one hand to his ear. The tilting deck spilled LB back into his seat, without an answer.

Chapter 8

Wophule pedaled ahead of Promise, gaining distance on her up the two-lane road. The boy was happy today and showed it. Before setting out, he'd told Promise about a girl he'd met over the weekend, a waitress at the Shingwedzi tourist station. Wophule had watched her chase a begging monkey away from the restaurant's deck. He liked the way she did it, scolding like an *unina*, a mama. The girl wore an apron and a dark dress, like all the waitresses, in a uniform like him. The monkey hung around in the low trees, charming the tourists, still begging. The girl relented and tossed it a tidbit. Wophule thought that was kind and told her so. She answered him gently. Her name tag read "Treasure." They talked not long, as she was working, but he learned she was Xhosa, too, and a few years older than him, in her twenties.

Promise did not pedal harder to catch up to him. She let him be playful and go. Besides, the midday temperature was scorching. The tarmac road sucked up the heat and breathed it out beneath Promise's spinning tires. Wophule would slow in a little while. A tourist car whisked past, over the speed limit, but on a bicycle there was nothing she could do.

Around a bend she caught up with Wophule, who had stopped alongside the tourist car. A small pack of elephants—a bull, three females, and a pair of calves—grazed in marula trees beside the road. Wophule straddled the crossbar of his bike, explaining to the white tourists how elephants could get drunk on marula fruit if it became overripe and fermented. Promise had never seen this and did not believe it, but said nothing to correct Wophule, who was enjoying himself. Before the car pulled away, he asked the driver to observe the speed limit in the park.

They pedaled deeper into Shingwedzi and the sun. Wophule told her more of the girl. He'd not asked to see her outside her job, but he planned to soon. He wondered if Promise might go with him to the restaurant when Treasure was on duty, to advise him. This was the first girl Wophule had ever mentioned. Promise agreed to go. She'd been with a few men, all from the township. She had gotten away from there, but they had not, so Promise waited. The right man would come, though she'd not yet seen his tracks.

"How do you know she likes you?"

Wophule scrunched his brow, as if the answer was obvious. "She kept her eyes down while we talked."

The older rangers could tell the roar of a hunting lion from a warning, a frightened elephant's trumpet from an angry one. They knew where a leopard might sleep, when a warthog might charge, how to creep up on a herd of antelope without spooking them. The boy Wophule had a quiet sweetness about him. He could read animals as well as the old hands, and the children of the bush seemed to take to him as if they could smell his sweetness, like lavender or honeysuckle. It pleased Wophule to believe he could read Treasure, too. Promise poked him.

"She was looking at her watch."

Wophule answered the jibe by riding away again. This time Promise pedaled after him, and the wind they made cooled them both.

They cycled side by side down a long straightaway, with no cars coming or going, until the road entered a pan of scrub and ocherous earth. Promise pulled off the highway, Wophule followed. Together they stashed their bikes inside an acacia bush and locked them. Promise checked her radio, cell phone, extra ammunition, rations, and flashlight. When Wophule had done the same, she slid her panga inside her belt. They headed into the bush on foot, where they would stay until sundown.

Insects chittered in the tall brush as Promise led the way into Shingwedzi, moving eastward along a game trail. On every side, spindly trees had been knocked over by elephants grazing, playing, fighting. Roots and branches withered in the sun, their green baked to gray, making them look like tumbleweeds scattered over the plain. Before long, sweat trickled down Promise's bare legs into her green kneesocks. She scanned the orange dust of the trail for prints, pausing to challenge Wophule to identify the animals, the bushbuck, cape mongoose, kudu, and hyena.

They left the paved road behind and walked six, seven kilometers. As day rangers they patrolled their sector to mingle with the beasts, report on births, spot sickness before it could spread, track the movements of herds, and watch for the spoor of poachers. This last duty seemed unfair. Promise and Wophule, like all the Kruger rangers, hadn't signed on to be soldiers but to care for the wildland and preserve its creatures. They'd arrived trained in conservation; Neels trained them further, teaching them to track and shoot. Neels taught them that only a few years ago, the ranger's job was 80 percent conservation, 20 percent antipoaching. Now, because of the waves of criminals flooding over the border, the work had become 100 percent and 100 percent.

Behind her, Wophule took to whistling, merry and very young. Sweating down her back beneath the rifle, gradually Promise began to begrudge the boy his ignorance and happiness. On foot, the Kruger could be a dangerous place, and they needed their senses alert. Their purpose was to enter and disturb the vast park as little as possible. The Kruger, the duties of a ranger, love, these were not things to skip over with a whistle. All had teeth.

Promise spoke across her shoulder.

"She won't love you, you know."

Wophule stopped whistling.

"She doesn't know me yet. She might."

"Even if she does, you'll just be poor together."

"Why are you being so mean?"

Promise walked on. Wophule quit whistling. The dust and thirst of the day, which normally did not bother her, caked in her throat.

What would Wophule do if she told him of the blood on her hands, the carcass she'd made, her disloyalty to her duty? She was leading him far from the remains of the great rhino; she didn't want to see the beast with its organs eaten, blood drunk, in a patch of dirt worn bare by the eaters. What would Wophule say if she told him her reasons for killing it? If she said the Kruger was losing over a thousand rhinos a year; a few more would make no difference. A few more, that was all. In return, she could get enough money from Juma to lift her grandparents out of the slop of the township, up the green hill to a home with a breeze and a blue view. There, her gogo would not need to raise her bed high off the ground, because the black ghost would not follow. Khulu could stop working and let his hardness soften. Only a few more rhinos for Promise, and those would have died anyway, because the poachers could not be stopped.

Step after step, Promise planted her heels, meaning to whirl on foolish Wophule, scream at him what she had done and learn how'd he'd answer. He would yell back and turn her over to angry Neels. Or he would be meek, keep her secret, and beg her to stop poaching.

Either way, she would not stop. Stopping made no difference. She'd already taken one rhino. Two, three more would make no difference, would be no worse.

Promise halted on the path. She didn't know why, perhaps to say these things to Wophule and see.

She turned to face him. Wophule stopped, too. When Promise said nothing, he raised his hands from his sides, seeming a little frustrated with her mood, to prompt her.

"What?"

To confess that she was a poacher was not something she could do. That burden could not be set down or lightened, only carried further. Promise fixed the only wrong she could right now.

"I'm sorry. She will love you. I'm sure she will."

Promise walked on before Wophule could reply. She didn't care for his thanks or forgiveness, these things were too small to help her.

• • •

They took a northern route, away from the water holes, into the drier plains of Shingwedzi. Promise let Wophule take the lead while she recorded notes on the number and locations of animals in their path. They came across small herds of kudu, skittish giraffes, scuttling bushpigs, ambling elephants, and a rotting eland carcass that showed the presence of lions. Their training had taught them to tread lightly, disturb nothing, alarm nothing, for on foot Promise and Wophule moved through the bush as equals with the beasts.

They crossed in and out of the brush, walking for a kilometer or two on game trails out in the open, then ducking for passages through branches and scrub. Wophule was not wary of the animals so much as he wanted to surprise a poacher. This, he believed, was how he would be promoted off his bicycle.

With two hours left until nightfall, Wophule turned them west, a return to the road and their bicycles. They shared little conversation, and their patrol today had not been a pleasant one. Promise took the blame for this, Wophule had started out in a sunny frame of mind, and she had rained on it. She'd not been ready for the constant gnawing of guilt.

She concentrated instead on imagining the crisp green of the township hill, the freshness of the houses, new wood and concrete; she saw her gogo up there, free and pleased. Promise walked close behind Wophule, ignoring the flat, brown land. When the boy stopped on the game trail to gaze into the brush, she almost bumped into him.

Wophule pointed.

"What's that?"

A corridor had been bashed through a hedge of thornbushes and spindly marula. At first it seemed nothing more than the path of galloping or clashing elephants that had knocked aside everything in front of them, a common sight. Upended roots, loose leaves and twigs lay scattered. But a long gash had been cut in the earth, running straight through the hedge. Debris that was not of the bush lay strewn in it. Chunks of gray metal, a wheel.

Promise took the lead, the boy at her back. Two more black rubber wheels lay still attached to struts that had been snapped off something. Promise pushed through the shreds of the hedge.

The groove hewn in the dirt ran another fifty meters past the line of scrub. At the end of the rut, in a small clearing, lay the thing that had fallen out of the sky.

Wophule burst away from Promise, dashing ahead. She ran as swiftly as him.

Both halted at what seemed a safe distance. Broken wings, a propeller, an intact fuselage, wheels, all said this was an airplane. It had fallen into the Kruger like a shot arrow, with twin tail fins jutting in the air, the crumpled nose cone rammed into a mound of scooped dirt. The thing recalled the way the aardvark had fallen with its snout crammed in the hole it had dug. The plane's right wing pressed into the ground to hold the whole thing up like an arm; the left one clung only by struts and cables.

The plane made no hisses or mechanical gasps. No human voice, no moan, came from it. Promise couldn't tell how long ago it had crashed, but in the surrounding bush, every animal held its breath; no guano stained the wings, no paw prints in the surrounding dirt showed the approach of a curious creature. Her guess was it had crashed within the last few hours.

Wophule took a step forward. He shrugged away Promise's reaching hand.

"This is no plane. It's a drone."

Promise crept behind the boy. On instinct she took her machete in hand.

Smaller than an airplane, with a wingspan of ten meters, the thing had no windows, was solid gray without insignia. The impact had bent the propeller like wilted petals. A metal ball clung to its sleek belly, and from it a round glass eye gazed darkly at them.

Under the right wing, the one dug into the ground, a long, rectangular box hung from a sleek metal arm, gray like the rest of the machine. Beneath the ruined left wing, a matching box lay dented in the dirt. Both containers were divided into four sections, like packing cartons. What were they?

Bold Wophule inched forward to inspect closer. While he moved in, Promise circled more. She tingled at the wreckage of secrets that lay before her. Big secrets, too, for who had drones like this but nations? Whose was it? What had made it crash? Why was it flying over the Kruger? Promise tightened her circle, drawn by curiosity. This was something she and Wophule were not supposed to see. It was exciting and rare, and in Shingwedzi.

She continued her circuit while Wophule ran a hand over the fuselage. Promise scanned the horizon, wondering who else might have seen it come down. Had the sector EC patrol been near enough? Judging by the furrow in the ground, the drone had flown in from the east, across the Mozambican border. Like all the Kruger's sectors, Shingwedzi was immense. Perhaps only she and Wophule and some hiding animals knew the thing had plummeted here.

Promise put away the panga; her fears eased as she grew more inquisitive. She crept past the nose of the drone, knelt to get a good look inside the box, then jumped to her feet.

"Wophule! Get away!"

The boy froze beside the fuselage.

"I said get back. Now!"

Wophule stumbled while getting clear of the drone. Promise backed away, too, until the boy jogged beside her.

The two stood at a distance that might not have been enough if the missile inside the box, a rocket launcher, were to go off.

• • •

Wophule and Promise sat on their haunches in the slanting sun, trying to decide what to do. All around them, the bush kept its uneasy silence. Wophule concluded they should do nothing. The drone was definitely military. Whoever lost it would know what had happened. Someone would come looking for it. The rocket appeared undamaged and was nothing to fool with. Best to leave it alone, walk away and let it disappear on its own, like a carcass.

Promise listened to Wophule's logic, convinced that he was right. Someone would come. She could only guess at when . . . soon, after dusk. But she had different thoughts about walking away.

Promise got to her feet.

"Stay here."

The boy straightened his legs to stand in her way.

"What are you doing?"

Promise answered only with a palm in his young face, telling him to stay, and stepped around him.

She moved closer to the drone on tiptoes without reason to believe this was a safer way to advance, only going by her habit with animals. The glass eye under the drone took no note of her. She moved near enough to enter the shadow of the broken wing.

Promise ducked under it, sliding her fingers over the metal as if to pet it, soothe it as she approached. The hard skin felt warmed; it had lain in the sun for at least a few hours. The drone let her come, for everything about it seemed dead, except the missile.

Promise kept her hand on the drone instinctively; should it leap suddenly to life she would know. Inching forward, she ducked under the fuselage to the right side where the missile sat in its square nest.

She took a knee beside the battered box on the ground, inspected it, and found it empty. She moved to the launcher still attached to the wing, sliding a gentling hand along the fuselage as she moved. Everything about the drone was frightening. Both launchers were two meters long, narrow, and the most lethal things she had ever touched. Promise ran fluttering fingers over the smooth tip of the missile, touching its thick tinted-glass face.

She backed away, unsure what to do next. The pair of launchers and the drone lacked markings. Did they come from her own South Africa? The drone had crashed only ten kilometers from the Mozambican border, one hundred kilometers south of Zimbabwe, three hundred from Botswana. Whose was it? Where had it been? What hushed job did it do? Plainly, forces far beyond her and Wophule were in play here. The drone and rocket were missing, and somebody's clock was ticking. How valuable were they? How dangerous? How much time until someone showed up?

Her gut roiled, and the boy, as if sensing this, spoke out.

"Leave it."

Promise kept her back to him. She pulled out her cell phone.

"I'm going to call it in."

Promise dialed. She walked away from the crash and young, trusting Wophule, so the boy would not hear her calling Juma.

Chapter 9

Kingsman 2 leveled out of its sharp bank, flying away from the sun.

Why were they headed east? Why hadn't they jumped out behind the GAARV? What about the air show? Doc, Quincy, and Jamie were on the ground with both vehicles, watching LB and Wally zoom off without them. What the hell?

LB unbuckled his chute container and pack. Dropping the fifty-pound burden put a spring in his step. Wally still stood in his jump gear. One hand steadied him against the fuselage; the other pressed on his radio earpiece.

Arms spread, LB moved in front of Wally. He couldn't read Wally's face behind the opaque sunglasses. He reached up to snatch them away. Wally slapped down LB's hand, then raised an index finger, the shut up finger, in the air between them.

The loadmaster had disappeared into the cockpit, probably for a briefing from the air crew. The GAARV was gone. The big, thundering cargo bay held only Wally and LB. LB's patience boiled quickly, since he appeared to be the only one on the plane who didn't know what was going on.

He sat close, where he could see Wally's face to read his lips. Wally turned away, peeved; LB resat, if that was how Wally wanted to play it. This time Wally aimed the silent finger dead into LB's face, very stern. Wally collapsed into a fabric seat, produced a pen and small pad, and started scribbling furious notes.

He shot LB a mirrored glance over thinned lips. Something was going down, and Wally wasn't liking it.

LB went back to the window seat to watch South Africa slide below, and with it the air show, applause, beers on a patio, and his team all faded. Sunset lay two hours off. *Kingsman 2* leaned back, gaining altitude.

Finally, Wally pulled his finger from his ear and stowed his pen. LB kept his seat. Wally shucked his own chute and pack, then plopped into the seat beside him. Wally doffed his helmet to run a hand through his cropped hair, as if trying to rattle his thoughts into an order that made sense. Wally took off his sunglasses. LB laughed, made a little nervous by this.

"Okay. Now you're scaring me."

"You won't believe this."

"Sadly, I will."

Wally tapped the notepad to indicate he wasn't making any of this up.

"That was Torres."

"You stayed off your knees, so I figure this is business."

"LB, not now."

"Check."

"About three hours ago, the CIA chief of station at our embassy in Pretoria got a call. He met with his senior defense officer. The SDO called AFRICOM—"

LB swirled a hand between them.

"Swear to God, I don't care who called who. Where are we going?"

Wally waited LB out, letting him settle down like a curtain in a breeze. Insofar as every man has some genius, this was Wally's. He did nothing before its time, never reacted in anger or frustration. Wally jumped out of planes this way, shot a rifle and led men this way, on target. That was why proposing to Torres in Djibouti, three thousand miles away, over the radio was so precious, out of character, and perfect for razzing.

"I'm telling you so you'll know how far up this has gone."

And it's going to go up further, LB considered, shifting his butt in his seat.

"Whatever."

"The embassy asked AFRICOM what assets were available in South Africa."

"Us? We're on temporary duty, at a fucking air show."

"We're on a plane, we're in chutes. We're ninety minutes out. Nobody else close."

"I'm not going to like this."

"Nope."

"Close to what?"

"The Kruger."

The Kruger? The big game park on the Mozambican border. The place was huge, and full of animals. Big, wild animals.

"We're jumping into the Kruger. Just you and me."

"Correct."

"Why?"

Wally opened his mouth to answer, but LB stopped him with a raised finger of his own.

"And let me add. Why are we jumping into the Kruger with no provisions, no med rucks, no weapons, and no team? Dying to hear."

"The decision was made to go ahead with the show jump. It'll hold down the attention at us turning around. The guys can handle it."

PJs jumped into missions prepared as well as any Spec Ops teams in the world. They were experts at getting in and out of isolated, tough areas: any terrain and weather, any rescue or combat situation, covert or on the record, they had the best training and the right tools. LB patted his pockets for Wally in a show of poverty; for this mission, he had nothing.

"And the rest of it?"

Wally eased a palm down; the gesture said, *No worries, we got this.*

There lay the opposite of Wally's genius. His unyielding optimism.

"A drone's gone down in the Kruger. Torres says she needs eyes on it."

"What? Why are we flying drones over South Africa? We don't have clearance."

For three decades, the United States had treated South Africa as a pariah because of apartheid. The South Africans were working hard to change their society. But they hadn't dropped all their grudges against America. That was the purpose of hands-across-the-water displays like air shows, to rebuild some bridges—and the reason why the United States could not get caught flying a drone over South Africa without permission. That was no small thing.

Wally hedged, almost reluctant to give the answer.

"This is the hard-to-believe part."

He clapped his hands and rubbed his palms together. Then Wally opened them like a magician who'd just made something really unlikely appear.

"It's not our drone."

"Whose is it?"

"South African. It's a Denel."

"Then why are we going after it?"

"Like I said. CIA."

"Wally, just tell me."

"It's our missile."

LB's jaw slacked. Like a gulping fish, he formed the start of several words, all with a *W*: why, where, who, what, when. He finished none of them and collapsed back against the trembling wall of the climbing cargo plane.

Wally referred to his notes and told LB the story of the mission.

For the past few years, Al Shabaab, an Al Qaeda offshoot based in Somalia, had been looking to expand into southern Africa. The Somalian government, with plenty of international pressure and help, had finally begun to get its act together regarding not just piracy in its waters but Al Qaeda in its mountains. Al Shabaab needed new digs.

Tanzania, with a Muslim population of 50 percent and its own share of African poverty, was the next promising step along the continent's east coast. Recently, Al Shabaab had gained a toehold in Tanzania, blowing up a few mosques, gunning down some priests and religious moderates. But an earmark of Al Qaeda was their ability to adapt, and being run out of Somalia wasn't something they meant to repeat. So, while they were dropping roots in Tanzania, they'd also begun to probe the next domino to the south.

The ideal candidate was Mozambique, sparsely populated in its hilly, dry wastelands, plenty of room for clandestine training camps near the northern border with Tanzania, where the Muslim population was concentrated. The long Indian Ocean shoreline was impossible to secure. And the next potential domino, just three hundred miles off the coast, Madagascar.

After watching the debacle in Somalia and the rising violence inside Tanzania, the government in Maputo, Mozambique's capital, had no intention of letting Al Shabaab metastasize in its country.

So Maputo did what many poor, disorganized, and distraught nations did when they wanted somebody killed quietly. Once they got reliable word of a high-level Al Shabaab meeting on their turf, they passed it on to the CIA.

Wally paused while LB tamped all the puzzle pieces into place. LB ventured a few guesses, starting with the obvious.

"So we sent a drone to do the job."

"Yep."

"A South African drone."

"Yep."

"And I assume the bad guys got a knock on the roof."

Wally made an explosion sound and spread his fingers to mimic the blast.

"Okay. Then we're working with the South Africans on this."

"Nope."

"Wait. What?"

LB had hit a dead end faster than he'd expected. How had a US missile gotten on a South African Denel drone without their cooperation? LB slapped both his thighs, then held out one flat palm to Wally, like an usher, motioning for Wally to show him the way.

Wally, who knew the answer, began to give it, but after a few words burst into laughter instead. He tried to restrain himself to finish his report, but whatever he was about to tell LB was plainly so implausible, so wicked or Machiavellian, that it cracked him up. LB couldn't share in the laughter, so he crossed his arms and waited.

Wally wiped a palm across his mouth to plug his mirth. He winced with the effort of keeping himself from guffawing again.

"Okay. The Kruger's a wide-open place. A lot of illegals cross from Mozambique. Security risk. Once in a while the South African military flies drones over the park."

"Alright."

"Well."

Wally bit his quivering lower lip. LB prodded.

"Yeah. Well?"

"Do the math. CIA hacked one."

LB went rock still while this struck him.

"No, they didn't."

Wally had only to nod before LB doubled over, leaning almost out of the cloth chair. LB flicked his gaze around the empty cargo bay, as if looking for something to help him digest this plot, to fathom it. He had to gape down at the steel deck because he couldn't bear to look at Wally, who was chuckling again and trying to wipe it off his face.

LB coughed, but this turned into a snicker. That reignited Wally; both of them gave in, letting the laughter shake itself out of their systems.

When they were done, LB spit on the floor as though to clear his palette and start over.

"You're shitting me."

Wally couldn't do it. He said only, "No," then motioned for LB to give him a second. He composed himself, cleared his throat, then repeated, "No."

"We can actually do that? Hack someone else's drone?"

"Looks like it."

Wally filled in the rest of the operation's odd details. The CIA had determined Al Shabaab's mud-hut meeting in the Mozambican hills a sufficient threat to American interests and agreed to Maputo's request to drop in. Once the target intel was confirmed, the challenge for the CIA came in finding assets for the operation. The US Air Force had no air bases in southern Africa and no drones with sufficient range to make the round-trip from the base in Djibouti to Mozambique.

So they hijacked a South African drone out of the sky, over the Kruger.

The CIA had sent false avionics to the South African controllers to make it look like the Denel had simply stopped transmitting, not an uncommon phenomenon; around 10 percent of all UAVs in every military went off-line at some point during their missions. They usually flickered back to life at some point on their own; some crashed.

While the South African remote pilots were scrambling to figure out what was happening—had their Denel gone down, was it flying blindly somewhere over the park—the drone was winging east with new hands on the stick, soaring high over the Mozambique Channel to a waiting US Navy aircraft carrier.

The navy had been experimenting with drones taking off from carriers. Once flattops became mobile UAV bases, the reach of unmanned military flight would be, for all intents, global.

"Navy landed a drone," LB said.

"They did."

"Oh, man."

LB was of mixed opinion about unmanned warfare. On the one hand, battle by remote control limited the casualties on the field. For a combat-rescue special operator, this was a good thing. But man's abhorrence for bloodletting was usually what stopped the fighting in the end. LB and all professional warriors feared the day when war was taken away from the men and women on the battlefield and handed over to geeks in a bunker a thousand safe miles away. What would stop them? Not what they could see, hear, and smell up close. Certainly not their own peril.

Now drones were combining with sea power. That meant the planet had just become smaller and a little less safe. Taking lives was doing a booming business. Not for the first time, LB was glad to be among the ones saving them.

After the Denel was safely on the carrier's deck, the navy's armorers had gone to work. They'd bolted pylons beneath both wings. Secured to each pylon was a rocket launcher loaded with two Hellfire AGM 114 missiles apiece. All four air-to-ground missiles had been armed by the carrier's munitions men with tritonol charges wired near the warheads. This self-destruct capability was typically reserved for training, not live-fire combat ops. But this was a covert, high-priority mission, and all fingerprints had to be wiped. No one on board the carrier knew the destination for the drone or the missiles.

With its new payload secured, the flight crew wheeled the Denel to the catapult and slingshot it back into the sky. The drone was flown at ten thousand feet for five hundred miles, taking it into Mozambique's northern highlands.

A local tribesman—paid off by the CIA or Maputo—was there on the ground with a laser pointer, waiting to paint Al Shabaab's remote meeting place with the lethal dot. The plan was to fire three Hellfires, make the kill, then turn the Denel back out over the ocean with one Hellfire still on board.

Once the drone reached deep water, the carrier was to beam a coded radio signal into the tritonol charge, detonating the Hellfire's warhead, splashing the Denel. Evidence gone, case closed, mystery unsolved.

The strike went off exactly as drawn up. The Denel arrived high above the Al Shabaab meeting in Mozambique, right on time. The laser tag was confirmed, the fire order issued, and someone somewhere pushed a button.

One, two, three Hellfires streaked down out of the blue.

The mud hut disintegrated, all direct hits.

The remote pilots aimed the drone away, turning east for the Mozambique Channel.

LB had seen this part of the story coming.

"But she didn't turn."

"Nope."

"Malfunction."

"Yep."

This was all part and parcel of unmanned combat. Ghosts in the machine. What caused them was anybody's guess. More than likely in this case, the South African drone wasn't designed to land on a carrier, then be slung back into the air by the ship's huge catapult. A Denel wasn't built to be a launching platform for Hellfire missiles, either. Or maybe this was just crap luck. Regardless, there'd been a short in the Denel's guidance. One small flash from a loose wire caused another in a second wire, then a third; the controls burned out, then the comm; and next the CIA had a blind, dumb, and deaf South African drone with an American missile fixed to it flying by its stupid self. LB pictured a crew of remote pilots, somewhere in the States or Djibouti, seated at a computerized cockpit, hitting buttons and switches, flipping furiously through manuals, calling supervisors, saying, "shit, shit, shit," many times.

Wally continued.

"Apparently, the one thing that kept working in the drone was the GPS. After everything went blank, all the Denel had the sense to do was go back to the spot where it got hijacked."

"Over the Kruger."

"CIA has a fix on where it went down. They've got it pinpointed in a clearing in the northern part of the park."

"Did the missile blow?"

Wally shook his head. "CIA thinks it didn't. The GPS is still transmitting. That last Hellfire has an incendiary warhead. If it had blown, there'd be nothing left but hot dust."

A South African drone with an American missile attached to it was a major diplomatic breach. South Africa was going to scream bloody murder if this got out, and so would probably a dozen more Muslim countries on the continent. Mozambique would be humiliated, America tarnished again.

LB counted the violations on his fingers: "We hacked another country's drone, put our missiles on it, flew it into a third country to blow up nationals from a fourth country, then tried to splash the drone to get rid of the evidence."

"That's what Torres told me. I assume with a straight face."

"Now you and I got to go clean it up."

"Not the first time."

It wasn't. The ruses, gamesmanship, sleight of hand politics, these were always the handiwork of people far from the explosive reality of their schemes. Politicians, ambassadors, spies, sometimes even top military brass, like the drone operators, they stayed far out of harm's way. At least the UAV pilots had their hands on a trigger. A senator, a general, or an intel analyst couldn't even say that.

"Who else knows the drone's on the ground? Who are we racing?"

"No way to know. The Kruger's pretty huge. Probably no one. Maybe someone."

"Threat level? Hostiles?"

"Don't know. Lions."

The urgency on this job was high, the intel lousy. Drop into a massive African game preserve, locate the downed drone and destroy it, then get out. With no weapons, provisions, transportation, maps, the list of what they lacked for this op was just shy of everything. They had parachutes.

"Assets on the ground?"

Wally hedged again, this time with no hint of laughter behind the pause. LB knew him well enough to spot the signs of bad news.

"Really?"

"Torres says a park ranger will pick us up."

"A park ranger. Like a Smokey-the-Bear kind of ranger? Has this guy got clearance?"

"I assume so."

"When?"

"Don't know. Tonight, maybe morning. We stay out of sight and wait by the drone."

"We got a cover story for everyone else?"

"We did a SERE training exercise in the bush."

SERE meant survive, evade, resist, escape, a standard exercise for all Special Operators.

"That works. I assume Smokey's bringing a picnic basket."

"LB, quit. I'm not thrilled with this, either. You know everything I do, which isn't much. I get it. We'll jump in, put eyes on, then wait for the ranger. Torres will send us the radio code to blow the warhead. After we do it, Smokey drives us back to Waterkloof. That's the plan."

"That's it. That's the best we got."

"LB."

"Get on the horn and tell Torres this is fucked up."

"I don't tell Major Torres anything."

"Sure you don't."

"LB."

"Fine. Rules of engagement? In case we bump into someone."

"Evade."

"And what if someone's got big teeth?"

"I just need to outrun you."

"You would, too."

"Without question. Okay. We got two hours' flight time. We jump from twelve thousand nine."

That altitude was one hundred feet below the level where they'd need to be on oxygen, why the HC-130 had been climbing so steeply. LB had figured they'd fly nap of the earth, below radar, then he and Wally would bail at eight hundred over the Kruger. But it seemed getting down fast was being set aside for secrecy. At that great height, no one on the ground would hear the cargo plane coming. Just a blip on the South African radar, *Kingsman 2* was going to sneak in on a commercial airline route, hiding among the eastbound traffic out of Johannesburg and Pretoria.

Wally got to his feet.

LB stayed seated. "I hate this part."

This was going to be a covert mission with political ramifications, and he and Wally couldn't be ID'd as Americans if something went sideways on the ground. Every warrior shared this fear of dying in a forgotten field, an unclaimed body, nameless.

Wally began. He ripped the Velcro-attached American flag off his breast, the first step in cleansing his uniform and himself. Next came his unit patches and name tape. He dropped them all on the cloth seat, along with his wallet. Finally, he left behind his Air Force Academy ring.

LB followed suit. Every bit of identity he tore away dug a shovelful out of his anonymous grave. He lay down all his patches, his name, his papers, all except the Guardian Angel patch. This he wore last and longest before taking it off.

Finished, Wally set a hand on LB's shoulder. The gesture said, *We know who we are.*

"I don't like it, either. Okay?"

Wally shot LB an encouraging smile, which LB did not feel or return. Wally sighed, having done his best, then took in the emptiness of the cargo bay.

"Let's scavenge."

While Wally climbed the steps up to the cockpit, LB dug through the HC-130's few cabinets. He grabbed the plane's small first aid kit, designed more for household scrapes than a mission in the bush. Wally returned with the flight engineer, loadmaster, and copilot. The three airmen combed through their own day bags. From the loadmaster, LB and Wally took a book of matches and an empty canteen, but turned down magazines and wool sweaters. The copilot handed over a satellite phone. The flight engineer gave up a pair of NVGs, light-amplifying night-vision goggles. Then he produced a black Pelican case. The engineer opened it in an unenthusiastic way that said this contained his pet—a Beretta M9 pistol with an extra loaded magazine.

The engineer offered them up, but not without a reluctant tug. LB made a sheepish face and took them.

"Sorry. Lions."

Chapter 10

Allyn's phone fluted during the squash game. His opponent, a fat Pretoria banker, put his hands on his hips and waited, red faced and jowly. Allyn left the court for the vestibule to open his gym bag, find the phone, and silence it. He apologized for his carelessness, then three points later drilled the man in the leg with a forehand.

In his day, the banker had been a nationally ranked player. Now he wore the anchors of his success and years in his waist and chin; Allyn won the best-of-five match three games to one, and the thousand-rand bet with it. This he spent at the bar on the banker.

On the club veranda, in the shade of an umbrella, Allyn checked his calls. His son had rung from London, one time zone behind Pretoria. The boy worked for an English mining firm; Allyn had used his connections to set him up. The long-term hope, a father's wish, was that the son would come back a man, an engineer, and take over Ingwe from Allyn. The call from London, in the late afternoon, would be business. The boy likely needed money, advice, or both. In the rare times he called at night, he was drunk. Allyn set the phone on the tablecloth. It rang under his fingers. The number came up private.

"Hello?"

"Mwanganani, shamwari."

"*Ndara*, Juma."

"Where are you?"

"The club."

"Can you talk?"

Allyn made sure no one was in range of his conversation.

"Ja. Is something wrong?"

"No. Something has fallen into our hands. Actually fallen."

Allyn motioned for a waiter to freshen his seltzer. He palmed one of his damp wristbands. The sweat in the cloth came from play, not a pick or a pushcart of coal. A blond and shapely woman walked past the picture window, off for a game of racquetball in whites.

"Tell me."

Juma described a drone that had crashed in the Kruger. One of his lookouts in the park had called him ten minutes ago to tell him the location, a northern sector of Shingwedzi, eight kilometers west of the Mozambican border.

Allyn sipped his seltzer and, though no one was close enough to hear him, asked only generic, careful questions.

"Whose is it?"

"The contact cannot say."

"Do you think it has value?"

"The drone, no. It's a wreck. Maybe some of the electronics. But there's something else."

"Yes?"

"A missile."

Allyn nodded but had no notion of what a missile might sell for on the black market. His expertise was world markets for ore and diamonds; with Juma he'd only traded in horn. But after their meeting at Allyn's house days ago, they both had agreed to bring Allyn in deeper—a little more risk for a lot more profit.

"What will that bring?"

"Eighty to a hundred thousand American."

"Where are you?"

"In Macandezulo."

"How fast can you get there?"

"One hour."

Allyn swiped some of the dew from the cold glass at his hand. He touched the chill of the glass to his forehead to cool his brow.

"What do you need me to do?"

"Nothing. But we agreed to expand your role, yes?"

"Ja."

"I'll need to transport it. I didn't want to put a missile on one of your ships without telling you."

Allyn needed to do nothing, only get a little richer. Perhaps play some racquetball.

"Alright."

"One more thing. My contact in the Kruger, the one who called. I've told the contact to stay with the drone until I get there."

Allyn couldn't fathom why this was important.

"Why are you telling me?"

"The contact is not alone."

As if the phone had snapped at him, Allyn yanked it from his ear and held it at arm's length.

"Stop talking."

Slowly, Allyn brought the phone back to his ear. Juma loosed a long breath, letting Allyn be the one to speak next, or not.

Here was the boundary. The gate that would lock behind him. Juma had already warned him the money was not easy or bloodless, no matter if it seemed to be. But until now the blood was at a remove. Poachers were shot by rangers, eaten by beasts, these were the natural risks of going into the bush for horn. Fair enough, they were paid to go. But this? The contact was not alone. By telling him, by seeking his permission, Juma bound Allyn in blood.

Allyn peered at a shining, tall, bustling Pretoria. East, over the government buildings and office high-rises, far beyond the green horizon to the bush where life and death were the lone currency, Juma would go on his word.

What did Allyn have left but life and death? Life handed you a bill, it needed to be paid. Life required money. Death was free.

"Juma."

"Allyn."

"I understand."

"Do you?"

"We said we would share."

"So we did. Good-bye."

Chapter 11

The drone had crashed in a dry and dusty spot. The few stunted trees nearby, either withered or picked clean by giraffes and elephants, offered no shade, just sticks against the sun. The only shadow lay beneath the wings of the wrecked drone, and neither Wophule nor Promise would sit so close to the thing and its rocket. The glassy eye under the drone's belly stared blankly, but the two sat where it could not see them, should they be wrong about it being dead.

Wophule squatted on his haunches in the way of a villager; Promise rested her rear on the ground, a township girl. Her rifle lay across her folded knees; Wophule's gun remained across his back. The bush buzzed with bugs and the crackling of heat. The metal drone baked in the brightness. The air above it shimmied.

Juma had told her to wait there. She said she had her partner with her. Juma told her to make up whatever lies she needed, but the partner must stay. Promise didn't like this, but Juma was her great-uncle and a rich man, and she could not earn Gogo's house without him. Juma said he would bring money. She asked how much? He replied only that he would be there in an hour, then hung up. When Wophule asked what was happening, she told him she'd spoken to Shingwedzi headquarters and they knew about the crash. She said the drone and missile were from Mozambique and someone was coming to claim them. That way when Juma showed up, he'd at least look the part. Juma would pay them both as a reward. Wophule listened, then pointed east; the drone had come from that way, from Mozambique. She countered that the drone had gone crazy; that was why it crashed. Then Promise spit, beginning the vigil and ending the boy's questions.

Wophule tried to be quiet. He could not for long, so he began to chat by himself about the waitress Treasure, the day's heat, how much he wanted to become one of the extended patrol rangers, how good he would be at disappearing into the bush, how much he hated poachers and wanted to shoot one.

Promise kept an eye out for anyone approaching. What if a tourist had seen the drone zoom in over the road and phoned it in? Or what if the sector ECP was in the area and headed this way right now? Promise couldn't keep track of the scenarios in her head—rangers and Juma and her and Wophule, the drone and rocket, all in one place—she couldn't concoct enough lies.

Wophule chattered on, circling back to the drone. He speculated where it had been, what it had been sent to do. The first animal came within sight; a warthog scuttled out of the thorns into a thicket of prickly pear. Disappearing, it gave an indignant grunt.

Promise lifted her gaze to the immensity of the sky, sorry that the drone had fallen out of it, sorry for her choices, and frightened. Perhaps it would be better to leave, as Wophule had asked an hour ago.

"Do you know what I think?"

Wophule faced her to answer. Then a whisk cut the air, the sound of a knife slicing cloth. It ended in Wophule with a meaty thud as a muted pop came from the brush. The boy flew backward off his haunches; one of his hands reared up and knocked Promise on the cheek. He landed on his back, spread-eagled. Promise tumbled sideways, shaken and scrabbling in the dirt, away from the convulsing boy. Wophule's belly thrust off the ground, arching his back, then he collapsed. He coughed a red geyser. The blood rained back to his face, ringing his mouth, spattering his neck. His eyelids fluttered; his pink palms turned up, fingers curled. His head struggled once to come up off the dirt, to see what had happened, to ask Promise. Then he sagged, and his eyelids stopped.

Promise climbed to her knees, hands stuffing her open mouth. She waited, fighting panic, expecting her own bullet. She didn't scan the scrub for the shooter and had no notion of running; if she was under crosshairs, she was dead. Seconds passed with no bullet; Promise suspected she might live. Terror clouded her relief as she crawled closer to Wophule, pushing at his boot in a pale hope of rousing him. The boy's boot, high olive sock, and bare black thigh rolled in the dust, but it was a terrible, perished weight. She stopped shaking his boot, and Wophule came to rest. A dark puddle glistened in the center of his tunic, framing a rip between the pockets.

Fifty meters away, Good Luck emerged from the bush. He carried his rifle like a soldier, the homemade silencer high above his shoulder. Even at a distance, the empty space in his teeth blackened his grin. He came without hurry, wearing his leopard pelt.

Frantic, Promise reached for her own rifle. She'd dropped it beside Wophule's body. Without breaking stride, Good Luck leveled his long gun at her, shaking his narrow head.

"No, girl. I'm not here for you. But see if I don't."

Promise raised both hands. Good Luck advanced in long strides. When he stood over Wophule, he bent to admire his shot, dead center, pleased with the murder.

Good Luck kicked Promise's rifle farther from her reach. He motioned for her to toss away her panga. When Promise did, he relaxed the muzzle of his gun down from her.

She breathed fast through her nose, clamped her lips, fighting tears. Promise climbed off her knees. Good Luck showed no fear of her, not with his gun and muti.

"Why?"

Good Luck was a rag of a man. Spare and shabby, he had only his trigger finger to offer the world. He shrugged, and the spotted pelt rose and fell on his skinny shoulders.

"I do not ask Juma why. Only how much. Just like you."

This damned Promise, but was not a surprise. She'd known it the instant Good Luck stepped out of the thorns. When she'd called Juma, she'd killed Wophule.

Her great-uncle appeared from the brush. Juma could not have heard Good Luck invoking his name, or Promise thinking it, but he came as though summoned. In one hand Juma carried a toolbox; against his size it seemed no more than a lunch pail. In his other hand, he walked with a staff taller than his head.

Promise had knelt beside death before. First as a child, beside her father in the AIDS clinic, a young man devastating to look at. Then, four months later, Promise cut down her mother, who'd hung herself and left a note that she'd learned she was infected. A decade after that, a nun at the township orphanage suffered a heart attack in the night. Promise was sent to the sister's room to find her after the woman missed the evening meal. Those times Promise had prayed to the Christian god for the passage of their souls. But kneeling in the dirt under the yellow eyes of Good Luck, waiting for ponderous Juma to approach, Promise did not mutter to Jesus; he seemed to lack the power to hurt anyone. In her seething heart she called on the older gods, the ones who answered offerings of blood and dance, who rewarded meat and great fires. Over Wophule's body, Promise begged the jackal for cunning, the tortoise for patience, the lion for strength.

When Juma's big leather shoes stopped and the wooden rod rapped the dirt below her lowered eyes, Promise spit. She raised her gaze to Good Luck and silently swore she would kill him.

Juma lowered a massive hand to her.

"Get up, Nomawethu."

Promise stiffened her legs to rise without shaking. She took Juma's hand, but her eyes lingered on Good Luck, sending the message that if the old gods answered her, she would use their gifts on him.

The skinny shooter lofted his eyebrows as if to say he understood and welcomed her curse. He patted the leopard pelt over his chest, in the place where he'd shot Wophule. The gesture said, *You cannot do it, girl. But I can.*

Juma blocked the sun. He wore black cotton pants and a sleeveless T, his big arms thick with flab and strength. He set down the tool kit and tree branch. With fingers under her chin, Juma dragged her attention to him.

"He did what I told him to do. If you're going to stare, stare at me."

This she did. Could she kill her gogo's brother? If she swore to it, she must commit to it. Or the old gods would not help.

Juma held out a rubber-banded roll of rands as fat as his wrist. The roll balanced in his immense palm.

Promise cut her eyes at Good Luck before she asked:

"How much?"

The question made her no better than him, just as he'd said. This made no matter, because when she killed Good Luck, she would be better than him.

"One hundred thousand rand."

Promise snatched it off the platter of Juma's hand.

"You are getting closer to your gogo's house all the time."

Promise pocketed the bills. She promised the old gods she would kill Juma, too, after she had enough money.

Good Luck slung his long rifle across his back but kept his sandaled feet between Promise and her own gun on the ground.

Now that she'd been paid, Juma relaxed his posture, so large he slumped like a mudslide. "I am sorry, girl. You know I am. But how was I to explain to your partner why I am here?"

"I told him the drone was from Mozambique. You could have been from there."

Juma held out his empty hands, never with blood on them.

"And what happens when you go back to your headquarters? You report that Mozambique came for their fallen drone and missile. Do we look like soldiers? Your partner there would describe me in detail. Then, when it turns out the drone is not from Mozambique—and believe me, it is not—it becomes clear that a poacher has taken it. They begin to look for me. Me, Nomawethu. I cannot allow that."

Juma indicated the roll of cash bulging in her pocket.

"You cannot allow that."

He lifted the tool kit, humming to himself. Juma turned to the drone.

"Now, what do we have here?" He curled a finger at Promise. "Let's take a look."

Promise held her ground. To step farther away from Wophule's body was to begin to deny him. Big Juma disliked being denied, as well.

"I said come here, child."

With a fast glance at Good Luck, Promise imagined the killer lying in the dirt beside Wophule, his hands cut off by her machete.

Juma ducked under the drone's raised wing. He did as Promise had done, drawing a hand down its gray skin to keep it mild and asleep.

He kept his hand on the fuselage, running fingers over the orb underneath. Juma gazed into its tinted-glass face like the miner he'd been, a dark man peering into darkness, looking for riches. Juma nodded into the glass. From his toolbox he retrieved a hacksaw and a screwdriver. With Promise at his elbow, Juma punched holes in the thin metal skin until he could bring the saw into play. In quick fashion, he ripped the electronic eye out of the drone's belly. He rolled it in his hands like a chopped-off head to examine the opened electronic neck. Juma poked inside with his meaty fingers, then brought his face close, as if to sip from it.

Juma set the orb down gingerly, then set himself to examining the busted, squared-off firing rack lying on the ground. He nudged it with the tip of his shoe, branding it too broken for salvage. He peeked into the second launcher hanging just below his waist and stroked the tip of the lone rocket tucked inside.

"Ah, this." He tapped the warhead. "This is a good one."

He smiled at Promise with the greed of a child. With the screwdriver, Juma loosened the access panel in the sleek pylon connecting the square rack to the underside of the wing. Lifting away the panel door, Juma examined a hive of little levers and wheels, all threaded by red, black, and white wires. He rummaged carefully, so as not to incite anything. Juma rolled several colored wires over in his big fingers, until he saw what he was looking for.

He held out a hand for Promise, as if to dance. She did not take it.

"Come look."

Promise knelt beside the missile launcher. Juma plucked at the wire to separate it from the jumble inside the pylon. He teased it out.

"Can you read that?"

Tiny white lettering on the black wire read *Lockheed Martin USA*.

Juma beamed.

"Nomawethu, you are owed more money, I think."

He tucked the wire back in place, then secured the access panel.

"Go stand over there." Juma snapped his fingers for Good Luck to come in her place.

The Mozambican grabbed Promise's rifle to keep it near him. Wophule lay on his gun, still strapped to his back. Promise could not get to it without drawing attention.

Her great-uncle took several pictures of the downed drone from every angle with his cell phone. When he was done, he explored the ways the missile launcher was harnessed to the wing. He trailed fingertips over all of it, searching for how to free the missile. Quickly, he found the weak place; this was Juma's talent. He pulled a ratchet from his tool kit, then tried several sockets over four bolts that fixed the pylon to a rail attached to the wing. After several misfits, Juma measured one more socket. This one snugged over the bolt.

He laughed at himself.

"I'm stupid. It's not metric. It's half inch. American."

Juma showed Good Luck where to lift to take pressure off the launcher and pylon so he could loosen the bolts. The first fought him off. Then Juma displayed how powerful he was. He leaned into the wrench, groaning, making no progress. He did not back off, straining longer than Promise believed he could. The wrench moved a fraction, the bolt creaked, then broke loose. Juma undid three more the same way, with great exertion. Exhausted but taking no rest, he and Good Luck lowered the freed mechanism gradually, respecting the unfired missile. The thin shooter seemed of little help; Juma bore most of the burden.

The big man folded to the ground beside the launcher. Juma mopped his brow against his bare arm.

"Something . . ." Juma paused to catch his breath. He gathered in the evidence of the crash: the long gash in the earth, a single American missile on an unidentified drone, a pair of rocket launchers, one of them empty. "Something does not match here. Strange."

Juma spoke not to Good Luck but to Promise, as though she were his partner.

Good Luck shot a silent snarl at Promise, sensing the slight. His tongue peeked through the gap in his teeth, making Promise think of the blood around Wophule's mouth, the boy's last red breath only minutes ago. Promise blocked the surge in her breast to leap at Good Luck.

Juma struggled to get his girth off the ground. He pointed at the tree branch. While Good Luck fetched the staff, Juma took three leather straps out of the toolbox. These he tossed beside the launcher.

Juma stood beside Promise, dwarfing her, hands on hips. He continued to survey the scene, calculating. Good Luck lapped the leather bands around the contraption, then slipped the rod through them. When he was finished, he lifted Promise's rifle off the ground and slung it across his back. He pushed Wophule to a sitting position—a horrible thing to see the slack boy yanked upright, empty like a puppet. Good Luck slipped the boy's rifle off him.

Juma turned fully to Promise. He pulled her into his chest and hard gut; she let her arms dangle. Through the heavy layers of the man, she heard no heart.

He whispered, "Give us time to get across the border. Then call your rangers. Tell them you stumbled on the drone. Tell them while you were inspecting the crash, poachers came out of the bush. You exchanged fire, your partner was killed. You surrendered, there were too many. The poachers took your guns and what they wanted from the drone, then left. Do not describe me. But if you like, tell them of Good Luck. I give him to you."

Promise spoke into Juma's chest.

"I'll kill him."

"Leave that for another time, Nomawethu. I need him to help me carry this."

Promise stepped back against Juma's embrace. He let her loose, trailing his hands across her arms as she stepped away.

"Tell your gogo we do good business, you and me. I will expect it to continue. *Yebo*?"

Juma gestured at dead Wophule.

"You should know. I came personally to be sure you would be safe."

With that warning, Juma took her rifle from Good Luck. Aiming it high, he fired one round, paused, then fired two more. The cracks raced away across the open savanna, chasing birds out of a dried bushwillow tree. Juma strapped her rifle across his broad back.

He lifted the electronic eye from the dust to take it with him. Then he and Good Luck hefted the staff onto their shoulders, Juma at the rear. Good Luck hardly managed his end. The two men, great and thin, put the low sun to their backs and walked east into the veld, the American missile slung like a trophy between them.

When they had gone out of sight, Promise drank from the water bottle in her pack. Chewing the last of her biltong, she squatted close to Wophule, with nothing to defend him. She considered picking up a stick or a rock, but she would win no fight with a beast who came to the smell of a man's death.

So Promise waited beside Wophule, watching the slowly pinking sky, the green and gray bush, the rusty earth, for anything, anyone coming.

Chapter 12

At just under thirteen thousand feet, the leap into thin air was frigid. LB's face stung from the razor wind rushing past, below freezing. Wally, the best skydiver in the Guardian Angels, plummeted beside him, and even he, without the proper gear for this high-altitude jump, grimaced against the cold.

Free fall hurtled them into warmth quickly; LB stopped shivering. Miles below, the Kruger sprawled as far as he could see. It was a desolate place, lusterless but for patches of green; pale paths in the reddish earth spread everywhere like capillaries. Dried streambeds and low hills gave the land some texture, but for the most part it looked as drab and scoured as any battlefield. From his descending height, LB scanned for animals and believed he did see something big gallop across the plain.

At three thousand feet, Wally maneuvered away from LB. Facing each other, both reached to their backs to grip the pillow handles on their containers. Two seconds later, at two thousand feet, Wally yanked his cord, LB followed, and both threw out their pilot chutes.

Gray silk and cord unraveled furiously behind them. With a suddenness that LB never grew used to, his chute bloomed, pinning him in midair, snatching away his speed and breath. In that instant he felt every bit of him collapse like an accordion, skin, muscles, eyes, and organs, then jerk back to the right size when the chute slowed his fall. The silence was immediate; three miles overhead, unheard, the cargo plane banked away. LB reached left and right beside his head for the dangling toggles and pulled to circle in behind Wally.

The team freq sizzled in LB's earpiece, Wally sounding off. "One up."

LB responded, "Two up."

A breeze cooled the dusk over the vast Kruger. Sundown was an ideal time for a clandestine daylight jump. The earth was darker than the sky, and the different shades made for tough viewing from the ground. Wally circled downwind above a long slash in the red dirt; there at the end of it, after smashing a hole through a hedge, lay the South African drone. Clearly the missile hadn't exploded on impact, or the Denel would be a scorched crater and nothing else.

Wally turned into the wind to slow his descent, dumping the last of his altitude. LB whooshed behind him. He searched the landing zone for flat ground, ready to touch down running. The drone stood on its nose like a lawn dart, resting on one wing with the other snapped away and clinging by cables. The wheels had been clipped off and lay in the trough. Other than that, the damage looked minimal. Without active avionics, lost, short-circuited, and sightless, the thing simply flew into the ground. Wally aimed for a spot thirty meters from the Denel. LB wondered if this was enough distance from a live Hellfire.

Wally yanked on his toggles, flaring the chute to bleed off the last of his airspeed. He set his boots down perfectly, as if standing out of a chair. LB pulled on the toggles to do the same. But with just fifteen feet of air left, his eye snagged on a dark patch near the drone. From higher up he'd figured this for a low shrub or debris from the crash. With the last of his fading altitude, he made out a human figure.

LB hauled both toggles down to his waist to flare the chute. The instant his boots touched down, he quickly released the chest strap and bellyband, leaving him attached to the container and chute only by the crotch straps. He flipped the ejectors and freed himself.

Before the chute could collapse at his back, LB skidded to a knee, the Beretta in two hands and trained at the drone.

"Wally, down!"

The man on the ground didn't stir.

In a flash, Wally stopped reeling in his silk and dove to his belly. Over the barrel of the pistol, LB searched for movement in the bush and failing light.

"What is it?" Wally's head swiveled.

"Dead guy next to the drone. Move."

LB pivoted a fast circle, covering every direction with the pistol, feeling vulnerable in the open. Wally sprinted for the hedgerow. Once he was out of sight, LB bent low and ran to join him. He dashed through the opening in the brush made by the drone's crash landing. Beside Wally, he tucked himself in close to the leaves and branches.

A thorn snicked LB's battle dress tunic, then his neck.

He groused. "Is there anything, *anything*, about this op I'm not going to hate?"

They waited, bating their breaths to listen to the living land around them. The wildness of the place hushed itself; LB half expected to hear monkeys and elephants, roars like a zoo. But the Kruger did nothing to welcome or frighten them. And it probably wasn't the Kruger that had killed the man lying next to the drone.

For long, tense minutes, LB and Wally crouched side by side. LB kept watch on everything down the short length of the nine millimeter's barrel: the drone, the corpse, the savanna, and the spiny bushes where he hid.

Night fell slowly. With the falling light, the animals of the bush began their calls, grunts, and shrieks. The land was flat, made up of expansive wastes and low vegetation with little to slow the sounds. LB couldn't gauge the distance of any of it; a howl could be unnervingly close or a mile away. To make matters worse, a body lay close by. LB had no idea how long it would take for something with sizeable teeth and claws to get a whiff and head this way. He handed the Beretta off to Wally, his hands tired of squeezing it.

Wally kept vigil with the gun while LB clipped the NVGs to both their helmets.

Wally whispered, "You think it's clear?"

"Dunno. Clear of what?"

Wally shifted his boots under him to rise with the Beretta. "Okay. Stay here."

LB clapped a hand on his shoulder.

"Whoa. Where're you going?"

"Torres wants a report. Time's up."

LB pulled down hard enough to buckle Wally's effort to stand.

"We go together. You check the drone. I'll do the corpse."

Wally dipped his head at that. LB climbed to his knees, muttering.

"Torres'll kill me if I come back without you."

Wally jabbed him with an elbow, then slid the light-amplifying goggles down over his eyes. Behind the pistol, he eased away from the bush.

LB's first steps into the open, unarmed, were disconcerting.

"If something comes to eat me, shoot it."

"I'll just shoot you and keep it busy."

LB brought down his own NVGs. The lenses used the poor light from the emerging stars and the last shreds of sunlight to turn the world emerald and black. Every waving leaf, the twinkling sky, if anything moved in his field of vision, the sharp relief in the goggles would let LB see it.

He and Wally moved cautiously from behind cover. If whoever killed the man was waiting for them, the killer was ready, hidden, and had the first shot. If there were animals about, LB had no clue what to do about that.

Wally split off to the wreckage. LB approached the corpse.

The man lay on his back. A single bullet in the chest had knocked him backward. LB whirled to look in all directions through the NVGs a last time, then lifted them.

The body was that of a young black man, a Kruger ranger in an olive drab uniform, shorts, boots, and high green socks. Blood ringed his mouth. The chest shot was clean, center cut between the lungs, likely through the pulmonary artery. LB didn't bother checking for a pulse.

One round, no other marks. The kid had no weapon near him. Maybe an execution up close. Maybe a long shot from a high-powered rifle. The ranger's eyes were shut; his stained mouth hung open. LB had nothing to drape over him. He disliked leaving a body uncovered. It lacked finality. This mission, like so many over the years, was not ending with a death but just starting.

The young ranger had found the downed drone. It looked like someone had killed him for that. Why?

LB joined Wally beside the wreck. Wally didn't lift his NVGs to talk.

"What have you got?"

LB related his facts, guesses, and questions about the ranger. "What's up with the drone?"

Like LB, Wally swept the wan landscape one last time with the NVGs before lifting them.

"Obviously we're not the first ones here."

"Nope."

"I mean it's worse."

"Than a dead guy?"

"The missile's gone."

The news sent LB staggering, not backward but toward the drone. He stooped under the wing jammed into the dirt to see for himself. One launcher lay on the ground, badly dinged and empty. The pylon on the intact wing ended without a launcher, just a rail and four half-inch bolts in the dirt.

A jagged hole in the drone's belly showed where the Denel's electronic eye had been plucked out.

Without his sunglasses, the concern on Wally's features was plain. His sockets crinkled at the edges, flexing in thought. The ebbing light drained the blue of his eyes to slate gray. Wally looked worried, something rare for his sunny, can-do disposition. That was why he wore the shades, to mask these gloomier moments.

LB shook his head at the night. The darkened Kruger seemed steeped in all kinds of natural dangers. The two of them had jumped into the vast turf of thousands of wild and uncaged animals. Suddenly, the beasts of the Kruger finally let the pair hear them. A wail drifted in from far away, then a screech, a trumpeting bark, and then one roar, a deep thunder from a big throat that couldn't be reduced to a point on the compass but seemed to come from half the black world. Could the animals smell Wally and LB's presence? Had the scent of the ranger's corpse started to make the rounds; was that roar the dinner bell?

"Wally?"

"Yeah."

"What's the new plan? We got no missile, no way to blow this thing. And no idea where it went."

Wally squatted down to his haunches, elbows on his knees, to think as team leader and map out the next step.

"Well?"

"Not a clue. You?"

"What's less than not a clue?"

"You."

LB squatted next to him.

"Good. I'm glad you packed your grudge. 'Cause, you know, I left mine on the plane. Don't want to be out here in the fucking wilderness without a grudge. Now you want to be a pro and figure out what we do next? Or you want to chew me out again?"

Wally scooped some dirt from between his boots. He jiggled it in his fist, then tossed it away like dice.

"You and I been together a long time. Almost twenty years."

"And?"

"The first time I ever saw you at the Academy, you were everything I wanted to be. Smart, tough, a leader."

"You were a better jumper."

"Still am. But I patterned my career after you. Rangers, then the Guardian Angels. You were my hero."

"Still am."

"No. You need to get this. You're not anymore. Torres is. She's everything I want to be now. Loving, kind, strong. We're still a team, you and me, and the guys. We're still brothers. But not like it used to be. You're not my only team. I've come to understand something. It's hard to say, but I'm sad for you. We're all you've got."

LB sat with this, respecting Wally's need to express it, the way a good teammate ought to. Then he rose to walk away and not hear any more. Before he did, he patted Wally's shoulder. Wally hadn't said a word LB didn't know. Long ago he'd accepted it as the price of twenty-two years in the military—much of that spent with lives in his hands, men he'd led, killed, or rescued—and he wanted to ask Wally where to find the ability, the will, the dedication, the time to do something else? How do you bring a woman close and do your best by her, when your best has already been spent on those lives?

Wally gazed up at him with his often-hidden eyes. Wally seemed firm and sorry about what he'd said. But Wally never gave less than his best. Lucky Torres.

Wally got to his feet. Taller, leaner, younger, happier Officer Wally.

"I'm going to get on the sat phone, call it in. See what they want us to do."

LB let the page turn back to the job. There'd be time later, when they weren't surrounded by a mission, to talk more. Or not.

"Get a fix on where Smokey is. He needs to get here fast and bring a lot of shit. Explosives. I want a weapon."

LB patted his stomach.

"And make sure he's got that picnic basket. I'm starving."

The missing missile changed everything. LB and Wally had no way to destroy the evidence of the drone, no way to track the stolen Hellfire. Smokey or somebody had to bring them the tools and intel to do the job. Or Wally and LB had to leave. And they had no way to do that, either.

Wally dug the sat phone out of his jump ruck.

"What are you going to do?"

LB turned toward the corpse. "Figure out some way to cover up the body. Rocks or something."

Wally kept the Beretta. He faced the darkness away from LB, as if the sat call to Torres was somehow private. This was LB's fault—he'd made Wally think that way.

LB knelt beside the dead ranger. He pushed the boy's mouth closed to keep it from filling with grit or stones. The ranger hadn't stiffened, he'd only been dead an hour or two.

The voices of the Kruger's animals made the darkness lush. LB lowered his NVGs to better see the ground and search for stones. He'd build a small tomb of stacked stones around the body, then fill it in with dirt. Without a shovel that was the best he could do until the body was reclaimed. He couldn't use a chute, their orders were to stay out of sight; a big piece of silk would be a dead giveaway.

LB found the first rock, the size of his foot. He lifted with his legs and turned back to the dead ranger.

Fifty feet away, emerald against the ebony air, motionless as a tree but unmistakable, stood a person, a long blade hanging from the figure's waist.

"Leave him alone." The voice belonged to a girl.

LB dropped the rock. He lifted the NVGs.

"Hey. Hi. Who are you?"

"Leave him alone."

She was small, like the dead boy, but in the dark that was all LB could tell. He took a step toward her. She retreated to keep her distance.

"Okay, okay. Wally."

Waiting for the signal to come up, Wally's face glowed from the buttons on the sat phone, making his head look eerie and suspended. He turned at LB's call. Spotting the girl, he lowered the phone then advanced a few steps. She recoiled. Wally held up a hand.

"Whoa. Hey. We're Americans. It's alright."

She stopped backing away.

"It was your missile."

Wally spoke too fast; he took more strides her way.

"How do you know that? Who are you? Stay right there."

She said only, "No."

"We want to ask you some questions."

LB raised both arms to draw her attention from Wally.

"Look, it's okay. We're not going to hurt you. Just . . ."

She took off.

LB lowered his NVGs and lit out after her. Wally followed. The girl's green image dashed for the hole in the hedge.

Vexed and sprinting, LB shouted over his shoulder, "Where'd you learn to talk to women?"

He outran Wally's jumbled curse.

LB reached the gap in the scrub and rushed through. Wally followed, gaining, a faster, long-legged runner. Twenty yards ahead, the girl zigzagged through the brush and low-hanging trees. LB worried if they chased her too far into the night, they'd lose their way back to the drone, even with NVGs. The girl slowed to look back at her pursuers. Rather than dodging the next thick hedge in front of her, she dove straight into it. She disappeared among the branches and leaves shivering in her wake.

LB sped up, figuring to catch her now. He lowered his shoulder to thrust through the hedge and gain on her. Wally, running flat out beside him, crossed his arms to ram into the hedge hard and fast, too.

LB curled an elbow around his face to protect himself. He hit the hedge at the same spot the girl did.

He crashed forward just two more strides before he was stopped in his tracks. His uniform and skin were snared on the longest, sharpest thorns LB had ever seen or imagined. Wally hung next to him, dangling in the spines like a marionette.

The girl had vanished.

Chapter 13

Promise crossed both forearms to protect her face, turned sideways, then hit the acacia hedge at full speed.

Driving through the barbs, she swung her shoulders and torso to keep the thorns from gripping her clothes. A hundred sharp points nicked her bare arms and knees, but she pushed deeper through the nipping branches until she broke free.

Without breaking stride, Promise ran ten more meters, then jumped feetfirst into the shoulders-wide mouth of an aardvark hole. She'd found the hiding place after spotting the strangers' parachutes descending from high in the pink dusk. The anteater that dug the hole wasn't home, or the tunnel would have been closed behind him. Promise had thrown in pebbles to be sure no leopard or mamba, lion, or python was napping inside. Skidding on her rump, she slid down the tunnel into the larger den. In the cool dirt darkness she held her breath, smarting over her many small stabs and cuts.

Above, the two Americans crashed into the hedge. The barbs held them fast; she knew this by their curses.

Promise listened to them thrash against the branches and thorns, and when she was sure they'd been snagged, she crawled out of the aardvark hole.

She approached the hedge warily. Spreading the branches apart, she poked her head inside. In the dim light, without an early moon and with only the first stars, she made out the two figures snared in the acacia like flies on a web. The Americans' every move added to the bush's grasp on them and the volume of their complaints. Promise watched them struggle. One of them, the stouter of the two, took this as a taunt.

"You think this is funny? It fucking hurts."

The other man, tall and lanky, held a pistol. He made a show of forcing his gun-bearing hand through the prickles to tuck the weapon inside his belt. He showed her, with a grunt from more pierced skin, his empty hands.

"Ma'am, I'm sorry if we scared you."

"Alright."

"We need to talk to you."

"Go ahead."

The heavyset one ran out of patience and in a temper raged against the thorns. He planted his feet and leaned forward, as if into a gale, trying to bull through. He did nothing but impale himself more.

Promise made shushing sounds, the way she might calm a calf. The soldier stopped fighting.

"It's a buffalo-hook thorn. The Afrikaaners call it *wag-n-bietjie*. It means *the wait-a-bit*."

The fighter exhaled and sagged. "No shit."

The tall one spoke, a less frantic man.

"The way you moved through this stuff. It was amazing. You're a Kruger ranger."

"Yes."

The stout one interrupted. "Can we talk outside the shrubbery?"

"You want to get out?"

"Fucking yes!"

"I have questions."

The tall soldier told his comrade to be quiet, while still looking at Promise through the thorns and darkness.

"We've got questions, too. I swear, we won't hurt you. I need you to believe me."

"I can see that."

"Please, ma'am. How do we get out of this bush?"

"If you chase me, I will run again. You won't catch me."

"Not a problem."

Promise explained how to break the hold of the thorns by twisting away, not barging straight into them. The tall one turned his body as she showed him; he slipped through with better results than the other. That one was too broad shouldered and thick in the legs, impatient and agitated. The tall American emerged first from the acacia; his face bore scratches, but no blood had been drawn. Standing before Promise, he made no move for the gun. The second man fought his way out of the bush, kicking and growling. Promise stole a few backward steps, should the Americans be liars.

Both were big-boned and powerful-looking men. In the night, their uniforms were gray and white camouflage. They wore helmets with goggles attached and vests stuffed with radios. Snapped branches and leaves clung to the shorter one, the thorns had dug deep into his uniform. While the tall soldier spoke to Promise, the short one plucked himself clean.

"I'm Captain Bloom, United States Air Force. This is Master Sergeant DiNardo. You are?"

"Promise."

DiNardo looked up from shedding the detritus of the bush. The captain smiled, a handsome face.

"That's a pretty name. Can you tell me what happened? I mean to the other ranger?"

"We need to go back to him. We'll talk there."

Promise walked past the Americans, leading them around the hedge to the drone and Wophule and all the questions and answers.

Howls floated over their heads.

"We are not alone in the bush, Captain. Put your hand on your weapon."

The Americans followed her to the crash site. The captain tried to speak at her back, while the short one muttered he was hungry, but Promise walked on. The bush in darkness was no place to be distracted. She focused on the trail and the night sounds. The two Americans seemed out of place, a little lost and defenseless, an unlikely sense for soldiers. Why would they parachute into such a foreign and severe place, so secret and urgent, with one small weapon, no tools, and no food?

Heading back to the drone and Wophule's corpse, Promise's guilt returned and mounted. She'd not realized how good it felt to run away into the bush, even chased by soldiers, until she saw the wreckage again and the boy gray against the earth. She imagined turning away right now, disappearing into another hole; she would live in the veld until she was devoured or forgotten. But she had killed Wophule, and that would run faster than Promise.

Wordless, she walked through the broken hedge, following along the trough dug in the ground by the downed drone. She did this with familiarity, as if it all belonged to her; she had seen it first, had made this crash the worst thing in her life. It was hers more than anyone's.

Promise walked past the drone to squat beside Wophule. This might have been gruesome for the Americans, but she did not concern herself with that. Wophule was hers, too, and though Promise would not admit to the soldiers what she had done, she sat beside the boy to claim his death.

"I speak first." Promise could tell her lies best if she started.

The captain mirrored her posture, folding his long legs under him in the dirt. He took off his helmet to rub a hand over his crew cut. He looked at Wophule with noticeable sadness; this man seemed more than a soldier and a killer. The other one she could not guess at. He set himself to gathering in the ghostly parachutes they'd left on the ground.

"Go ahead, ma'am," the captain prompted.

"Wophule and I found the drone. While we were looking it over, poachers came. They shot Wophule before we knew they were there. I fired back, but they surrounded me. I surrendered. They took our rifles."

"How many were there?"

"Two."

"How long ago?"

"Two hours."

"Alright."

"The drone had a missile under one wing. It was inside a box, a launcher, I think. The poachers pulled it off and took it with them. They said it was an American missile."

She held out a hand to the captain as proof that this was right.

"Why was your missile on this drone?"

"I can't answer that."

His evasion made Promise feel better as a liar. She and the Americans were going to be equals, they would tell each other less than the truth.

Promise moved her hand to her pocket. "I have to phone it in now."

"You haven't done that yet?"

"No."

The captain held up a pale palm in the dark veld.

"I have to ask you not to call anything in just yet."

"Why?"

The captain considered what denial or half-truth to say next.

"My country doesn't just leave things like this lying around. The two of us jumped in to get a handle on the situation. I've got to ask you to let us deal with it."

"Why should I do that? You have your job. I have mine."

The American rubbed a hand across his mouth. He seemed reluctant to say what he had in mind. Promise supposed this would be the first full truth between them, and it would be painful.

"You don't need me to tell you that you and your partner stumbled onto some of my country's secrets. I'm not going to apologize for them, not my place to do that. But the sergeant and me, we've been sent in to clean them up. That's all. If you call this drone in, it'll get out of our hands. The damage that'll do is more than I can describe to you, but believe me, this needs to stay secret."

The captain's hand drifted to the grip of the pistol jammed in his belt.

"If you run, I know we can't catch you. So I will shoot you. I'll do everything I can to shoot you in the leg. But I will fire. Now I'll have your phone, please."

Nothing about the captain said this was a bluff. Promise handed over the phone. The captain left the gun in his belt to accept. She'd called Juma with that phone. This was the first bit of her to fall away, like a comet over the bush. More pieces would tear off before long, lies and murder, and Promise wondered what would be left.

The stout sergeant finished stowing the parachutes and came to stand over her, hands on hips. These men had come to clean up America's secrets; that's what the captain had said. Promise felt an urge, fleeting but powerful, to tell them all of hers: Juma and toothless Good Luck, the rhino she'd cut down, Bongani and the aardvark, Wophule. She might ask the Americans if they could clean away her secrets, too. Promise said nothing. She and the captain exchanged lonesome looks in the starlight, as if he knew and could do nothing for her.

The captain said, "I'm sorry."

No, he'd not protect her.

The sergeant took a knee close to Promise, as if inspecting her. The nearness of Wophule's body did not appear to bother this one.

"What are we going to do with you?"

The captain touched Promise's wrist, sincere.

"Are you going to run? I don't want to tie you up."

"I won't run, Captain. I'll stay with Wophule."

"Can we trust you?"

Promise almost wept at the question; for so much of her life the answer to that question was always yes. She wanted to say it again, to mean it, cherish it.

"Yes." This felt like another secret.

Both Americans got to their feet. Promise stayed seated because she did not know what to do next. Neither did the standing soldiers; they glanced into the dark, and once more the bush reminded them with screeches and roars that their presence was known.

The captain seemed to percolate, rubbing his chin and the top of his head for a plan. The sergeant rubbed only his belly.

"Where's Smokey?"

Promise asked, "Who is that?"

The sergeant scowled. "Never you mind." He seemed to be nursing hurt feelings from being hung up in the thorns.

A dome of pearly light rose in the east over Mozambique, the half-moon would be up soon. The drone, broken and skewed, finally appeared at peace in the milky light, no more tangled than anything else in the dark Kruger. Wophule had been right, they should have left the thing alone. The bush would take it to itself, wind and sun, rain and claws, grinding it down to bits and rust. But the drone had fallen from the hands of man, and man did not let go so easily.

Just so. She could not let go of Wophule. Guilt was another thing only man brought into the Kruger.

"LB, I'm going to call Torres on the sat phone. You get started covering the boy."

Promise would not let him be called "the boy."

"Wophule."

"I apologize. Wophule."

The sergeant turned to his chore. With an easy strength, he lifted the big rock he'd dropped on first sight of Promise and set it beside Wophule's boot.

The captain laid a gentle touch on her again.

"Go help him."

• • •

First, they laid an outline of stones around Wophule. Once he was encircled, Promise and the sergeant paused to rest. Wophule looked peaceful, even handsome inside his palisade. Promise looked on him with a taint of envy that he'd died unmarred by her sins and had died thinking of love.

The sergeant blew out his cheeks. He was less winded than Promise would have guessed a man who looked like him would be. His body was a teakettle, neck as wide as his head. He shook his head, not at the work but at the killing of Wophule.

"Why did the captain call you LB?"

"Why do you call yourself Promise?"

"For Zulu, it is rude to call a person you do not know well by his proper name. So we are given other names, and our real names are kept for family."

"That's actually a good answer."

"Now you."

"You won't like it."

"I already do not like you."

The sergeant laughed at this. He nodded, accepting a sort of fairness in what she'd said.

"It means 'Little Bastard.'"

"It suits."

The sergeant, LB, shrugged.

"Your partner?" he asked.

"Yes. For two years. This is Shingwedzi. Our sector."

LB took off his helmet, an automatic and respectful act.

"That's rough. I'm sorry."

LB had donned a new tone and a new light under the stars. For long moments he did not lift his eyes from the stones and cool body. He seemed to be seeing many more dead on the ground than Wophule.

"Let's get him covered up, okay?"

They returned to work. LB lowered his night goggles to find larger stones off the paths, while Promise collected armfuls of smaller rocks. Together, they did not drop their loads on Wophule but placed the stones one at a time, assembling the mound with an unspoken, shared care.

The captain stood well away, near the drone. He circled the wreck, describing what he saw into the phone at his ear. When he finished his conversation, he came to Promise and LB, adding his hands to the job of covering Wophule.

Quickly, the boy faded beneath a lattice of stones. The rocks were of many sizes, weights, shapes and were shot through with quartz, spotted or solid, as if Wophule had been laid under a collection of his days. Promise stood aside to let the Americans close the last gaps. Finally, with their helmets, the two scooped dirt to pour over the stones, enclosing Wophule's life and the smell of his death.

When they were done, the soldiers stepped back, leaving Promise closest to Wophule. Both men mopped their brows. LB gestured to the mound.

"Go ahead."

Promise did not speak to God or Wophule, but to the Americans.

"He cannot be left here. Wophule is Xhosa. He cannot be away from his village. His ancestors."

The captain replied.

"It's just until we get this sorted out."

"How long will that be?"

The man opened and closed his mouth. Promise answered for him.

"You cannot tell me. I know."

The Americans crossed their hands at their waists, waiting for Promise to conclude. She thought of words but could say none of them, they were all admissions. Wophule's killing was one blade of her grief, but she had many stabbing her. She could drop to her knees and confess all to his spirit, but Wophule would become restless, he would grieve her, not go into the afterlife. And the Americans would hear. She had no muti to give to help him rest. So Promise danced.

She lifted her knees and arms, waved her wrists at the stars. She asked the dark sky to call Wophule's ancestors here to the heart of the Kruger so they might comfort him until he could come home. She promised to kill a beast for them later, an ox or whatever she could afford. She danced to lessen the evil of Wophule's murder, to give him light feet to travel onward, and mostly to make him go away from this life and not haunt her.

Promise lost sight of Wophule, the Americans, and the Kruger. She fixed her eyes upward, pleading into the darkness. She skipped circles around the rock mound, twisting her own spirit into the dance. She rounded Wophule many times, until sweat fell in her eyes. But she sensed nothing from the sky and night. Wophule had died unnaturally, wrongfully. His ancestors would not answer her call; she was responsible for his murder. They waited and wanted more from Promise than secrets and a dance. She was left in life with Wophule, and he with her.

Promise stumbled against the stones. Her knees buckled, and she tumbled to the ground where she belonged.

Before she could collapse, the sergeant caught her by the arm.

"Whoa, okay. Come on, girl."

Promise made herself limp to crumble the rest of the way, but LB held her up. His strength was remarkable.

"Hey, that's enough. Here we go, take a seat."

Somehow the sergeant seemed on all sides of her, like the night. She let him ease her away from Wophule. He sat her down with her back to the mound of stones.

Chapter 14

One scotch glass held two ice cubes. The other, neat, Allyn handed over.

Leaning against the headboard, the whore sipped and closed her eyes to make a show over the quality of the liquor.

She surveyed the big bedroom. Oddly, as her eyes flitted about, she clucked her tongue as though tasting the sculptures, oil paintings, fabrics, appreciating more than their beauty—perhaps their cost. This made Allyn think he'd insist on a better class of prostitute if he did this again.

He sank into his leather reading chair; the cushions cooled his bare bottom, feeling wrong. In all the years he'd lived here, he'd never once sat in this chair naked. Allyn turned on the gooseneck lamp for the whore to see better, but the light shined on his nakedness and age, so he snapped it off. She paid no notice.

"You got a beautiful house."

"Thank you."

"How long ago did your wife pass?"

"Weeks."

"So sorry."

"Of course."

"You don't mind. May I look around?"

Allyn had arrived home with the whore at dusk, and had done nothing to lighten the gloom of the large house. The master bedroom, lit by a small china lamp Eva had bought at a flea market in Rome, was the only glowing spot in the mansion. The woman would have to turn on lights. He had no qualm about that, and rather liked the notion of the place warming up for the whore to wander. Many rooms he'd not entered in years and could not now picture in his mind's eye. Just the kitchen, the den and dining room, his office, and the bedroom. He could not conjure his son's old room or the guest rooms, his wife's sewing room, the servants' quarters; he barely knew the yard beyond the deck umbrellas and chaises. This had been Eva's home far more than his, what Allyn had given his wife and child in the bargain.

"Go ahead."

The whore scooted off the bed, careful not to spill the scotch. She began to pull up the sheets.

"That's alright. Leave it."

She flipped a casual hand to say, *Whatever.* She reached for her dress and underthings lapped over the back of an upholstered wing chair bought in Hong Kong.

"Leave them, too."

Facing him, she swirled the scotch glass, elbow tucked into her bare waist, and shifted her weight to one leg. The woman was shapely, ample in the bottom, with spectacular golden eyes that were likely contact lenses.

"You want me to go around your house like this?"

"Yes."

"Alright."

The whore left the bedroom with the highball in hand. Allyn didn't care where she went in the house or what she saw, and if she was naked, what could she steal? But that wasn't why the notion had come to him to send her off that way. He couldn't be sure why he'd told her to leave her clothes behind. The idea of a naked hooker flowing through the house, admiring and touching Eva's things, seemed somehow cleansing. There was a benefit to that, but he couldn't wrap his thoughts around what that would be. Like a mine, the value lay at the end, in the rock, dark as the woman.

Allyn sat alone, with her in the veins of the house. An hour ago he'd forgotten her name when she told it to him, it sounded as fake as her eyes, so he'd let it slide off him with his pants and shirt. The house was too large to listen out for her; he'd need to stand outside the bedroom and look over the rail, down into the gallery, to get any sense of where she was. She didn't rattle about but, barefoot, glided through the place. Naked in the leather chair, Allyn turned on the gooseneck lamp again. He examined his small hands, their creased palms and spotted backs.

The whore's laugh came from somewhere on the first floor. Her voice was surprised. She'd come upon something expensive and marveled aloud, feeling free to do so in the great expanses of the house. Perhaps she'd intended for Allyn to hear, meant her outburst as flattery. But she came off as vulgar, and Allyn realized why he'd brought her home, and why he'd let her loose.

The whore fouled what she touched, stained what she saw. All of it was Eva's. The whore was helping to bury the last of his wife, helping Allyn say good-bye. The whore was a shame, like Juma and the money he made. Eva, in her lifetime, did nothing shameful. She would not approve, so Allyn was taking away her voice.

He stared at the bedroom's open door for the whore to return. He was not impatient. He waited while she toured, blank of mind the way a man stands a long time in a hot shower, under a good scouring.

When his cell phone lit up, it showed Juma calling. Allyn drew a sharp breath, awakened. He didn't answer Juma but gathered the whore's clothes and shoes, carried them out to the landing, and dumped everything over the rail. At the clatter on the oriental carpet below, she emerged from the recesses of the house. Her breasts jiggled while she collected her things.

"Why did you do that?"

"Take something and go. Something small."

High above her, bare and dangling like the whore, Allyn indicated a table beside a sofa. He pointed at a marble carving of a leaping dolphin, from Florida.

"That."

The whore shook her head up at him, confounded but keeping her mouth shut. She did as instructed. Allyn watched her step into her panties, wiggle into her dress. He felt no distaste or drive for her, only finished. She snatched the statue off the table and flounced out the front door.

Allyn dressed. Downstairs, he turned off all the lights the whore had left burning. Eva had made a bright home, she liked candles and music fluting throughout. She'd not been an overly smart woman but had a full heart, a filling way, even as a girl. Eva gave gift baskets and visited sick friends, threw theme parties, hugged everyone hello and good-bye. Over the decades, as Allyn got rich, she didn't change, not a whit. Maybe this was because she'd been born wealthy, and he had not. The struggle for money claimed him, hardened him more than Eva could soften him. But he'd done much of it for her, to protect her and their son. He'd won that contest. Eva's life was a cushioned thing, so was the boy's. She was gone now, and the boy was on his own. Allyn had been abandoned to be the wealthy man he'd become.

He followed the whore and Eva around the first floor. One room and light switch at a time, he sank the empty house into dimness. When the only glow was again from the upstairs bedroom, Allyn took the phone outside.

• • •

The black lake made an upside-down reflected world. Stars glittered beneath the windows of the lit-up homes on the opposite shore. Doors and porches were flipped. One neighbor came home and walked in on his ceiling. Allyn wished for a pebble to throw into the lake to break the surface and the quiet, separate world on it. He had nothing on hand but the cell phone. He considered throwing it, but the man who could do that, who could not call Juma back, was long gone, if he'd ever existed.

Juma answered on the first ring. He'd been waiting.

"Hello, shamwari."

"Juma. What is it?"

"Are you alright? You sound tired."

"It's difficult sometimes. That's all."

"I understand. I've lost, too. Many times over. It's a sad thing. Not the loss of the loved one alone but the hardening, the killing of your own heart to get through it. A sensitive man like you can't survive if you don't die a little."

This was always Juma. In the mines, in the early days, it was, "This is how you swing a shovel, young Allyn. Turn at the hips, spare your back. Push the tram with short strides, spare your knees. Fuses, drills, the boss's daughter . . . Here is how you survive, young Allyn."

"Thank you. I'll be fine. Why did you call? Did something go wrong in the park?"

Juma laughed, knowing what he would say but savoring it first, letting Allyn know this was going to be good.

"No. I have the rocket."

"Intact?"

"Perfect. It's American. A Hellfire. Very powerful. It will sell."

"Good. What about the drone?"

"Wrecked. There's something about it I wanted you to know. That is why I called."

"Alright."

"This may be outside my abilities, Allyn."

Again, this was the man Allyn had known for so long. Big Juma did not go beyond his scope. He would never have been promoted to engineer in Rhodesia, no matter what he could do in the mines. Allyn had been the one to go onward. Juma never begrudged him that.

"What are you saying?"

"I brought a piece of it back with me, and I took pictures. I've identified it. It's a Denel. South African."

Allyn lowered the phone without intending to. His gaze locked on the spangled lake, a dark slate for him to figure out the stunning implications of what Juma had just told him.

A South African drone had been armed with an American missile.

How could this be?

When did the Americans and South Africans start collaborating on covert strikes? Had the two countries, old antagonists, new but cautious allies, made some secret pact? That would be an incredible event. Allyn had spent thirty years selling platinum, coal, and gems on global markets, he knew the relations and trade treaties of the entire developed world. The United States did not sell advanced tech missiles but to a handful of countries, only their closest cronies, and South Africa was not one of them, nor likely to be. America was the world's most prolific remote control killer, and if South Africa was now involved in drone warfare alongside them, this was being done utterly out of the light of public scrutiny. It seemed inexplicable. Dodgy at best.

The Denel had flown off to do some nasty job somewhere out of sight, and for whatever reason—bad luck, most likely—one American rocket was still attached when it pranged into the Kruger.

Juma wasn't just talking about the black market sale of a rocket that, as he'd said, had literally fallen into their hands in the bush. No. Their customer wasn't going to be some shadowy nonstate actor with enough cash and bitterness to want this American-made weapon.

"Juma."

"Yes, shamwari."

"You're talking about blackmail here. Aren't you?"

"Perhaps. And."

Allyn knew the next words but wanted Juma to say them. That way he could keep believing these were Juma's schemes, not his own.

"And what?"

"A great deal of money."

Without question. Governments spent untold millions making sure that what they meant to be hidden remained that way. A few million more would be nothing.

For that matter, so would a two-dollar bullet.

But there might be millions.

Should they do this? Could they?

Would it be blackmail to simply notify the South African government that their Yank missile and wrecked drone had been found in the middle of the Kruger and carried off for safekeeping? Why was this not a good thing, removing a dangerous item such as a live rocket lying about? Allyn assumed some violence had been done in the taking of the missile, but that could always be blamed on poachers, wild, untamable men. The rocket had been rescued from them and was in good hands; so was the secret. No need to stir up public mistrust over the incident, nothing to be gained from an international furor. A reward would be in order.

Allyn overlaid his thoughts on the dark, flat lake, assembling, machining, engineering the next moves.

He'd need lawyers, a fleet of them, to insulate him. Corporate shells and veils, maybe a high-priced former government official or retired general to play spokesman; he could buy either as required. His relationship with Juma might have to change, perhaps come to an end if enough scrutiny came their way. No problem there, with sufficient payment to ease the separation.

"This has to be handled very carefully. You know that."

"Of course. That is why I called."

"We're going to kick a hornet's nest."

"Understood. What shall I do?"

"Nothing, Juma. Nothing. I will call you soon."

"Alright, shamwari. Good-bye."

Allyn opened his mouth to reply in kind. But the good-bye stuck on his tongue. He said instead, "Wait."

Doubt checked him. Not over whether he could do this; he could, a hundred times over. He was canny enough, rich enough already. Allyn was a businessman, and this was, after all, a transaction, dicey and a bit treacherous but little else, and well worth the risk. No different than drilling a new shaft.

His hesitation rose from Juma's question: What to do next? Who should Allyn call, hire, bribe? Who would he delegate? Who would handle this for him?

Juma held his end of the silence while Allyn measured and weighed. Allyn turned away from the quiet lake to carry the phone off the deck into his unlit house.

Standing in the vaulted great room, he lowered the phone to his side. Allyn felt the whore in his house more than Eva.

What would be his tools? Phones, cash, wariness.

As a young man, how well he could swing a pickax and a cricket bat had pleased him and made others proud. Those had been his tools then, and his tickets out. Those and Eva. From that young, marvelous time, he'd grown away from being an engineer into a corporate boss whom others would not even allow near the explosions in his own mines, explosions he'd set a thousand times. Over the decades—the years fell on a man so quickly, like a cave-in—he'd become ensconced, a boardroom miner. He'd embraced his work and held himself at arm's length from his wife and child, who probably loved him.

This drone could be the richest strike of his life. For that, would he send someone else?

He turned a palm up to his face. He had not lost all his calluses.

Allyn brought the phone to his lips.

"Juma."

"Yes."

"I'm coming."

Chapter 15

LB squatted beside the ranger girl, fingers knit, and let her have a good cry. He didn't pat her shoulder or mutter platitudes. The girl wept with anger, strength threaded through her grief, with fists balled.

Wally approached before she was done. He began to speak; LB waved the back of his hand. *Let it wait a few seconds. Let her finish.*

Promise snuffled into her wrist, swallowed hard, and brought her intense, black eyes up. She cleared her throat.

"Sorry."

LB stood. He reached down a mitt to pull her up.

"Nothing to be sorry about."

She gritted her bright teeth in the starlight. Wally waited no more. He curled a finger for LB to follow, away from Promise. She took the cue and walked off into the dark to give them privacy.

"I talked with Torres."

"Okay."

"I gave her the sit rep. Told her we got nothing out here but a pistol. No explosives, no supplies, no transport. No Smokey."

"What did she say?"

"They're working out a plan."

"Maybe they should've done that before we jumped."

"She'll get back to us."

"What about Smokey?"

"They're sending him. He's on the way with explosives, weapons, and food. We stay put."

"That means CIA had to fess up."

"That's my guess. I reckon the South Africans figured it was better to play ball and help us keep this quiet than make a stink."

LB could only guess at the millions, billions of dollars that were going to be secretly appropriated, squirreled away into some US defense bill, to pay off the South Africans for keeping this snafu quiet. Far more games were played under the table between nations than on top of it.

"So Charley Mike."

"Charley Mike."

"And you didn't talk her out of it?"

"You mean *Major* Torres?"

LB opened his mouth, but Wally cut him short.

"Don't say it. No. I did not talk the major out of her orders."

Wally spread his hands, the gesture asking, *What do you want me to do*?

LB mirrored Wally's extended, frustrated arms.

"And how exactly are we supposed to do that? We got no idea who took the damn missile or where it went."

"Torres says we hold in place until Smokey gets here."

"Why? Who's this guy?"

"At this point, you know what I know, LB."

"Okay. Fine. We're stuck out here. But you understand, I thought I'd been to the middle of nowhere before. I was wrong. That wasn't it. This is."

LB turned his back on Wally to survey their surroundings with a new disdain. He imagined fangs in every shadow, behind every shrub, sailing overhead, growling and snorting to each other.

He spoke into a deep night, which only appeared empty but was surely full and would just as certainly be long.

"I'm hungry."

The girl ranger moved. If it was possible to be darker than the bush, she was. She'd been standing close and unseen. She made no sound but her voice.

"What does that mean? 'Charley Mike'?"

LB turned to Wally.

"What do you think? Bring her in?"

Wally chewed his lip.

"She's the only asset we got right now."

"I agree." LB addressed the girl, though it felt like speaking to a specter. "It means 'continue mission.'"

"What is your mission?"

"Right now, we wait."

"For what?"

"Someone's coming."

"Who?"

"We'll find out."

"What about the rocket? The men who took it?"

"Again, we've got to wait."

"Will you go after them?"

"We'll see. That's enough for now, okay?"

LB turned on Wally for a moment's acknowledgment. Wally shrugged, the best he could offer.

Promise floated closer, halting beside Wophule's mound. She lowered her gaze, and the two white gleams of her eyes snuffed out.

When she spoke to LB, she seemed to have consulted her dead partner.

"I can feed you."

LB took a step toward her, eager.

"You can? Hey, thank you."

"It depends on your desire to eat."

He thumped his stomach.

"I got desire."

Wally piped up. "And water?"

"Yes."

Wally nodded, resolved to obey their orders, obviously with no more than a sketch in mind of how to follow them.

"You're a ranger. You know the area pretty well."

"Better than pretty well."

Wally walked to the drone. Opening his pack, he tossed the empty canteen to LB. Then he bent for his helmet and the night goggles.

"You take LB first. I'll wait here."

"And do what, Captain?"

Wally started to answer, but Promise cut him off.

"Guard the drone from more poachers? With your pistol, from desperate men? Or will you protect Wophule from animals?"

"That was my intention."

"We will all go. There's nothing you can do if the bush wants your drone or my partner." The girl ranger pointed to the brightening east. "You won't need your goggles. The moon is rising. It will be light enough soon."

LB didn't like the notion of leaving his NVGs behind.

"What if we run into something big?"

Promise shook her dark head, while LB tucked the night goggles into his pack.

"No matter how well you see the animals, they are far more aware of you."

She indicated the pistol tucked in Wally's belt.

"And that will stop nothing but me. Come."

• • •

Promise led them far from the crash. For the first minutes of striding into the night, LB worried they might lose their way. But she made turns on and off paths that she seemed to know like highways, and it grew plain she was taking them somewhere. He followed, with Wally and the pistol in the rear.

Promise spoke over her shoulder, describing what she saw and heard, what LB was missing. She kept her voice hushed and seemed to savor playing guide. Either that or she was keeping LB distracted. Was he that plainly unnerved?

Many times they disturbed birds in the dark. Promise turned to murmur:

"That is a nightjar. Listen to his song. 'Good Lord, deliver us.'"

She murmured later: "Hear him? A water thick-knee. He has a pleading, mournful chirp. Listen."

The breeze wafted through a line of shrubs, making an unsettling rattle. The girl explained these were bushwillows, what in Afrikaans were called *raasblaars*, or noisy leaves, for the sound the leaves made when the wind shook them. She paused over dung heaps in the trails, big piles and black pellets. Quietly she explained how to tell giraffe dung from antelope, similar in appearance, both like brown pebbles, but the giraffe's leavings came from higher and so were more scattered over the ground. She whispered the ways to tell a jackal's howl from a wild dog's yelp, a lion's roar from a leopard's bark. A stench of decay crossed their path; Promise described a springbok killed by cheetahs just two days ago a hundred meters north from where they trod.

"They still around? The cheetahs?"

Promise grinned, enjoying herself.

They left the game path, striding over a flat reach bordered on one side by elephant grass taller than LB's head. Without glancing back, the girl pushed into the grass and disappeared. This was the second time she'd vanished, and she seemed able to do it anytime she wanted. LB sucked a deep, reluctant breath and parted the moon-gray wall of reeds. Wordlessly, Wally stepped in after him.

LB could not see the girl ahead or hear her for the grasses brushing against him. He only followed where she'd passed, in her wake of crushed and bent stalks. He assumed Wally was doing the same on his six.

LB trudged onward, invisible, unarmed, and uncomfortable. Just as he was about to say something, to call out, the blinding grasses thinned and ended. He emerged into a flat plain stretching beneath the pearly light. Twenty yards out, Promise made straight for the black cutout of a great, spreading tree. Near the fat trunk, stars and the low-slung moon reflected in frets off a pond.

Promise waited in the shaded sward beneath the tree. LB and Wally caught up. When they stepped into the deeper darkness, she was gone again. LB flapped his arms.

"How the fuck does she do that?"

Wally only laughed.

Promise reappeared, literally stepping out of the tree's trunk, a great hollow LB had not seen. He poked her in the arm.

"Stop that."

The girl ranger feigned ignorance, still reveling in treating LB and Wally, the Americans who'd dropped from the sky, like helpless orphans in the bush.

"This is a baobab tree. They are often hollow. I had to make sure nothing was inside."

"Like what?"

"There's no need to scare you further."

Promise put a finger into LB's burly chest in a challenging way, returning the poke he'd given her.

"So you are hungry?"

"Yeah?" His reply was a question.

"We will see."

With that, Promise walked from under the tree. At the pond's edge, she pulled her ranger's tunic over her head to dip it into the water like a rag. She came back to the baobab naked from the waist up, unselfconscious, muscled, and small breasted. She plopped the sodden jersey on the grass and turned to LB.

"Give me a boost."

LB hesitated, unsure where this was going, until she prodded him into linking his hands. The girl raised her boot into his mitts, and LB heaved her up to the lowest branch. The knobs of her spine, the dimples in her back, showed as she shinnied easily up into the tree. Sitting on the branch, Promise pointed.

"Go stand in the water."

LB sensed that the girl was measuring him. Maybe she'd met no Americans before, maybe she was showing off, or maybe she was just bossy. He held his ground beneath her hanging boots and bare breasts. She jabbed her naked arm again at the pond.

"Do you want to get stung?"

Wally moved first. LB lingered, just long enough to shake a finger at her. She turned from him, pleased, and ascended the old tree. LB hustled the twenty yards to the rim of the water where Wally was already up to his knees. At first LB did not wade in; he imagined shadows withdrawing around the shore of the pond.

Slowly, Wally backed in until he was up to his waist.

"You know, these are called killer bees."

"Jesus. Even the fucking bees in this place."

LB almost slipped in the mud, then splashed into the pond. Warm water sloshed over his boots, above his knees, until he settled beside Wally. LB scanned the shore and the pond's surface, he didn't know for what.

"Piece of work, this girl."

Wally nodded. "She'd make a good PJ."

High in the dense, dark baobab, a branch shook. Leaves hissed as though a wind scissored through them. A papery thud hit the ground. LB bent at the knees to lower himself into the water, letting it rise past his belt. Wally had already ducked up to his neck.

A hum swirled at the base of the tree, surprisingly loud, then swelled to an angry buzz. LB dropped his knees into the muck, chin to the water, and had time to curse before the mad swarm, sounding like a sawmill in the air, tore across the water at him and Wally. LB dove under, eyes open. Wally thrashed, a bee had nailed him on the back before he could get down all the way. LB swam for deeper water, and with every stroke worried what he might meet.

He held his breath as long as he could before coming up. Wally surfaced, too. He sucked his teeth and muttered, sore, but LB listened for the bees, ready to gasp and go down again. The night stayed quiet, the bees were gone, but he turned a circle to check on all sides.

On shore, under the baobab, Promise stood, not waving her arms to ward anything off, but calmly peering out to where LB's and Wally's heads bobbed like hippos. She waved for them to come back.

Dripping, they returned to the tree. Promise stood over her wet ranger shirt, which had been thrown across a lump on the ground, the hive.

She wrapped it, the size of a rugby ball, in her shirt, then smacked the hive against the ground.

Inside the tunic, the hive crunched. She left the shirt in place, dampening and confusing any bees left in residence, as well as hiding it from angry returnees. Promise reached in for broken bits. She handed the first to Wally, another to LB, and kept one for herself. Each waxy shard drizzled honey.

Promise, still all skin from the waist up, bit into the honeycomb first, eyes on LB. He sucked away as much honey as he could, catching the dribbles in his free palm, then nibbled off a corner of the honeycomb. The texture was stiff, with a bland flavor, but he chewed and swallowed. Wally did the same, while Promise finished her chunk of the hive with relish. LB wadded the rest into a ball and stuffed it into his mouth. The comb collapsed slowly between his teeth, but made it to his stomach.

The girl handed them more bits of the hive; they lapped the rest of the honey away, but LB ate no more of the wax. He was hungry but not enough to eat a candle.

While Wally and LB finished, Promise surveyed the dark bush, tuning her senses to it. Finding everything in order, she nodded to herself the way an animal might. Pulling her damp jersey over her shoulders, the ranger put away her nakedness.

"More?"

Wally gave her a thumbs-up, but she'd addressed the question to LB, plainly testing him. He put his fists on his hips.

"What've you got?"

"Come on, then."

Promise led the way from under the baobab, leading them northeast toward the moon. In the dimness, she walked differently from Wally and LB. Her tread fell lighter. Her boots didn't strike the ground like theirs, she didn't roll heel to toe but planted her soles flat, a glide as much as a gait. Nothing on her jangled. Years ago, in jungles with the Rangers, LB had seen people move like this. They'd been insurgents or friendlies, soundless and sometimes invisible because they were natives to the lands where LB was a stranger. They were powerful because the part of the earth where he'd come to fight was their homeland. Walking behind Promise in the bush made him feel even more out of place, more exposed and unfit to be here.

She guided them along a game trail, around more prickly hedges and the rustles of small creatures scurrying out of their path. The brush gave way to wide-open ground. A hundred yards across the gray plain, what LB thought were just more bushes got to their feet and pranced off, a herd of something with horns and pale backsides disturbed from grazing and sleeping. Promise whispered these were hartebeests. LB heard nothing from their mass movement. Silence in the Kruger seemed the norm, broken once in a while by roars, trumpets, and screeches that carried for miles.

Promise halted near a tall mound of dirt built like a small watchtower and bigger around than the baobab's trunk. It stood level with LB's eyes. With no hesitation, Promise plunged her hand through the crusty exterior, up to her elbow.

She withdrew her clenched fist and opened her fingers under LB's nose. Her palm crawled. Before LB could gape or recoil, she shoved the contents of her hand into her mouth. With a darting tongue and fast fingers, Promise nabbed tiny escapees on her chin and shoved them past her lips. The munching sound she made put a grimace on Wally's face. But she was gauging LB, and he stayed stoic, only clearing his throat.

"What was that?"

Promise wrung her hands to rub off any clinging survivors.

"Termites."

LB peered into the hole she'd punched in the mound.

"You're eating bugs. Really."

"Termites have seven times the protein of steak."

LB made no move to reach in for his own fistful of insects; the girl turned instead to Wally.

"Captain?"

Wally sighed.

"I like a good steak. Fuck it."

He strode to the mound and rammed in a fist to make his own hole. Groping around, Wally grunted in revulsion at keeping his arm in. When he pulled out his hand, he stared at it as if it were not his own before flinging the contents into his mouth. Wally bit down once, stopped chewing, closed his eyes, and forced himself to swallow.

"What do they taste like?"

Wally brushed his chin and cheeks clean of termites fleeing his teeth. He wagged a finger.

"Oh, no. You do it. Then we'll talk."

A little proudly, Wally stepped beside Promise, both termite eaters now. LB's reluctance showed in his sluggish turn to the mound. He searched for his bravado, that surge that made him jump from planes, ships, choppers; drove him onward under gunfire and exhaustion; let him ignore the odds in the remotest parts of the planet. LB rummaged in himself for the thing that made him a PJ. He couldn't find it.

"No thanks."

Promise and Wally snapped at him together. "Do it."

Humiliation did the trick. LB screwed up his face and stuck his hand deep into the opening Wally had made.

Instantly his wrist was encased by a creeping, itching, pinching horde, like living grains of sand. LB shook his fingers to dislodge them before remembering that he was supposed to grab them. He closed his fist around a shifting, squirming mass. LB yanked out his arm. Termites spilled off his sleeve and began to march under his cuffs, up his arm. He had to let them go or eat them.

LB shut his eyes to remove at least one of his senses from what he was about to do. He rushed his hand to his mouth to cram in the shifting ball of bugs. He wanted to spit them out. LB tried to swallow but couldn't do it with his teeth so far apart, he came close to gagging. Focusing on his pride while trying to shut down his tongue the way he'd his eyes, LB closed his jaws on the termites.

They crackled and released juices. If taste could have a color, this was brown, oddly like wood. LB bit down again and gained confidence that he would not retch. Though the idea of eating living things was revolting, their flavor was not. He opened his lids to face the girl ranger and Wally, then swiped a few termites off his cheeks before brushing out the ones headed up his sleeve. LB focused inward to feel if insects were teeming in his gut.

He put his hand back into the hole, grabbed one more wriggling ball of bugs, and gobbled them. LB walked away from the mound and crossed his arms over his barrel chest, standing alone.

"They're better the second time."

Wally raised his hands, surrendering this round of whatever little competition they always had between them. Promise gave LB a tight-lipped smile.

The girl ranger turned on her heels. Wally and LB followed to the pond.

"You can't drink this water. But . . ."

A few strides from the water's edge, Promise dropped to her knees. She clawed at the soft ground, digging a tunnel straight down. A handful at a time, she excavated until she hauled out mud dripping between her fingers. When the hole was elbow deep, Promise withdrew a cupped palm of clear water. This she drank.

"The earth filters it. Go ahead. It's clean."

Wally tried first, reaching down, then lapping the water out of his hand. He nodded at LB, who found the water cool and sweet.

LB widened the hole enough to dip in the empty canteen. This was the first time the Kruger had cooperated without a barb or a bite.

When they'd drunk their fill, Promise led them into the night. They stopped at a prickly pear plant and a sour-plum tree to suck on the fruits for moisture. The moon had risen enough for LB to walk behind the girl ranger and let his mind wander, thinking about what it must be like to have this harsh, vast place as an office. To know the bush so well, to love it as much as she plainly did, even though it fought her, fought everything of man. This wasn't so different from what LB did. His workplace had tried to kill him plenty of times.

Approaching the drone, Promise slowed on the game trail, holding a hand behind her, signaling for LB and Wally to stop and be silent. Alone she walked the groove in the ground from the drone's crash, disappearing through the broken, thorny hedge. Wally drew the pistol from his waistband.

"What's she doing?" he whispered.

Before LB could figure a reply, Promise whistled for them. Wally held the gun ready as they moved toward the drone.

In the clearing, the wrecked UAV cast a strange, scarecrow-like silhouette. Promise stood beside her partner's rocky grave. She'd spread both arms wide, facing the open bush and the stars beyond. In the dim, silver light, something dark, something on four legs, walked away.

Wally and LB both held their ground. Wally raised the Beretta only a little.

"What was that?"

Promise made no answer other than to gaze into the night after whatever she'd convinced to leave. She turned not to Wally and LB, but to her partner. The girl ranger folded her legs to sit beside the stacked-stone grave. She hung her head. Now that she'd returned to her partner, something had left her, had gone out into the bush, too. LB sat with Promise. He laid a hand on the rocks above Wophule.

"It wasn't your fault. Poachers did this. The Kruger did this."

The girl ranger hid her face behind both hands. LB wrapped an arm around her shoulders, and she leaned against him.

Chapter 16

Neels did not play golf. He drank. The nearest and best place to do that was the outdoor bar at the Skukuza golf course.

He sat alone with a beer, at a plastic table in a plastic chair. The other rangers who came to while away the last daylight hours left him that way. Neels had no reputation as a chatty man. He kept the untruth of that to himself; he would have talked if invited. He'd trained most of the younger rangers. And though none had been in Angola or any war outside the Kruger, there was plenty else they could converse about. They all had women, they could speak of that. But they left Neels to himself, and by doing so, made him begrudge his empty table.

A lion's roar rolled across the big lake as if it were a foghorn. Deep, hungry, pompous, the lion lay claim to everything in earshot and this included the golf course. All eighteen holes were inside the park without fences to separate it from the bush. So the animals wandered it, too, free ranging with the players over greens and fairways. Golfers in carts routinely chased away warthogs, kudu, and antelope. A half dozen hippos lived in the water between the eighteenth tee box and the green; they snorted at shots that fell short on them and came out to roll in the bunker. Croc attacks near the water holes were not uncommon. The Skukuza golf course rated as the eighth most dangerous in the world. The other seven were all beside active volcanoes or in minefields. For Neels, this meant that there might only be seven better places in the world to have a beer.

He sipped his third while two empty cans dripped on the table, still cold. In the dusk the lion bellowed and Neels wished he could go find him. He'd do nothing but stand in the lion's voice, let it shake him, he could bask in something so resolute. The rangers at other tables gabbed, giving the lion no due. Neels grunted privately, offended on the lion's behalf and swallowed his next sip in toast of the shouting king out there.

Karskie sat, unexpected. The big boy plopped a fresh beer in front of Neels, and set down two for himself. Neels finished the last of his can then opened the new one.

"How'd you find me?"

"How many places are there to look?"

The lion moaned; even this was audible from a distance. Neels waited until he was done, as if in conversation with the lion, not Karskie.

"What do you want?"

Without Neels noticing, the analyst had finished his first beer and popped the top on the second with a fizz.

"I got a very strange phone call."

"What's that to do with me?"

Karskie ignored the question.

"About two hours ago, the general himself called me."

Former two-star General de Haven, the man in charge of the Kruger. Everyone's *baas*.

"What did he want with you?"

"He told me to gather up food and water and drive to Shingwedzi to pick up two American airmen. Apparently they were in the Kruger doing some survivalist training or something. The general said to wait until I heard back from him before leaving."

Neels took a swig, slowing the pace of his reply to show disdain.

"Shingwedzi's my sector. No one told me about two Americans."

Karskie brushed the complaint out of the air between them. "Can't help you with that."

"Did he call back?"

"Twenty minutes ago. And things had changed."

"How so?"

"We talked about you."

Neels drummed his fingers on the flimsy table.

"Why's the general calling you about me?"

In the cheap chair, Neels straightened out of his slouch. Karskie waved his hand again.

"Keep your seat. He's a friend of my father. He got me this job."

Neels slid back into the chair slowly.

"Plucked you off the scrap heap, you mean."

"Absolutely. Would you like me to wait for more cutting wit, or do you want to know what he wanted?"

"So you're de Haven's rat inside Kruger. I figured you for a shit."

"He did me a favor, that's all. I told him you were a capable chap and not the soulless prick you are."

Neels answered with a cock of his head. They'd swapped insults, so he could leave it at even for the moment. Besides, if Karskie was the general's boy, it made no sense to spar with him openly. In the deepening night outside the bar's lights, far beyond the limp flag of the eighteenth green, the lion had gone quiet. Karskie waited for Neels's response to see how the conversation would turn.

"If I'm capable, what did you get me involved in?"

Karskie seemed glad that Neels did not fire back but asked a question.

"The general told me about a phone call he got. From the director of SSA."

SSA, the State Security Agency. South Africa's spies. Neels flattened both palms on the plastic tablecloth to keep them from balling. Long ago, doing counterintel and surveillance in Angola, he'd learned to have no love for spies, for lies. The butcher's bill rarely landed in the laps of the liars.

"What did that twit want?"

"He gave de Haven a new shopping list. Clothes and food, but a lot more. The general gave the list to me. And I bring it to you."

"Let's see it."

Karskie tapped his temple.

"All up here, mate. Nothing written down. But wait till I tell you. This is black-ops stuff. Something's going on in Shingwedzi."

The large boy leaned back in his plastic chair, which bent under his girth. With a soft smile and pale cheeks untanned from the light of a computer, he finished his second beer, guzzling like an experienced hand. But then, he'd been a druggie.

"And what do I do with your list?"

"Take it into the bush. To the Americans."

"What for?"

"The general didn't say. Just gave me the coordinates in Shingwedzi. And he said we should get there as fast as we can."

"We?"

Karskie put the empty can on the table with a smack, intending it to be some sort of starting signal.

• • •

"Then you should have said no."

Neels didn't pull his eyes from the narrow road. Animals were not careful of cars.

"And watch someone else *kak* it up? I don't care if you wash the general's ball sack for him, it's my sector. It'll be me answering for it."

Karskie sagged in the passenger seat of the speeding Land Cruiser.

"Then quit your bitching."

Neels slowed to turn off the paved surface. The Land Cruiser bumped onto the rutted dirt road leading through the bush to the shooting range.

"And just why are you tagging along?"

Karskie reached for the dashboard handle as the vehicle hit a pothole. He muttered, "Jesus," and kept both hands on the grip.

"Like I said already. The general asked me to go."

"That was a lie the first time you said it. Tell me straight or get left. And before you answer, I may leave you anyway."

Karskie seemed reluctant to tell the truth. This set Neels's teeth on edge, and he resolved to let the big boy walk back to Skukuza. The Land Cruiser rattled into the yard of the shooting range before Karskie spoke up.

"I want . . ." He stopped himself. Neels pulled up, set the parking brake, and shut down the ignition.

"You want what?"

Karskie licked his lips and lowered his eyes. This was going to be some kind of confession.

"Speak up, boy, or it's a long stroll back."

Karskie remained tight-lipped. Neels finished the boy's sentence for him.

"*Jou ma.*" (Your mother.) "You want to be a ranger."

Karskie shifted in the seat. Neels's first shot had hit close to the mark.

"Not a ranger, no."

"Good. Because you're not. You're a computer."

Karskie stiffened at this. Without facing Neels, shamed for no good reason, he snapped, "Do you even have a fucking heart?"

Neels got out of the car. He stomped under the corrugated roof of the firing range, fishing in his pockets for the key to the armory closet. Behind him, the passenger door to the Land Cruiser closed.

Neels opened the padlock to the gun closet. Karskie appeared at his side.

"Let me go with you."

Neels stepped inside the large steel enclosure. He snared two R-1s off the racks; his own weapon lay on the backseat of the car. He handed the two rifles to Karskie, then grabbed boxes of .762 ammo. He tucked a sheathed, long-bladed knife into his boot.

Neels shut the armory door, then muttered, "*Fok.*" He flung the steel door open and grabbed a third rifle.

• • •

Steelpoort lay a two-hour drive southeast from Skukuza. The chromium operation there was the closest mine to the Kruger; the roads all wound through the backcountry. Neels had never liked driving into this sparse, denuded landscape outside Pretoria, where much of South Africa's wealth lay deep below the ground. Mining was hard and honest work, but what it made of the land was a disgrace.

Karskie talked for the entire drive. He interpreted Neels's silence for attention, but Neels was quietly heartened by the boy's vivacity. Karskie filled the dark cabin of the Land Cruiser with stories of his upbringing in the Seychelles; wicked tales of excess in university; his family's landed wealth, something he had little interest in; his opinions about the corruption in African politics; and poaching trends he'd spotted in the park after just a month of harvesting numbers. He asked Neels questions about himself, seeming to be genuinely interested, and when Neels gave those inquiries short shrift, Karskie filled the gaps with more about himself.

During a lull, with only ten kilometers left to the Assmang chrome mine in Dwarsrivier, Neels caught the boy staring at him.

"What?"

"Thank you, Neels."

"For what?"

"Bringing me along. I can tell you why."

"You don't have to. I got it figured."

"Yeah?"

"You and me are pretty much fokken opposites. You talk, you're educated and rich, you're fat."

"Am I supposed to say thank you?"

"But we got things in common. The Kruger, poachers. You might wind up having some good ideas."

"I might."

"That's not why you're here. You've got things you want to leave behind. I understand that. You want to be a man. So."

Karskie faced the road and hushed. A passing car whitened his face briefly and showed him blinking. Neels looked away to let the boy settle himself.

In the near distance, the night-lights of the Dwarsrivier mine rose above the bare hills. Neels had called the mine's engineering office in advance; someone would be waiting for them with the dynamite.

• • •

Dwarsrivier's chief engineer took a look at their SANParks credentials, then sold them a crate holding twenty sticks. Neels asked if the explosives were fresh; old dynamite was more volatile. The engineer, a chap as old and craggy as Neels, assured them everything was up-and-up, but urged them to be careful anyway. He included a reel of thirty-seconds-per-foot fuse, two rolls of duct tape, and two cigarette lighters. With the tape, Neels secured the thirty-pound wooden box in the rear of the Land Cruiser, alongside the rifles, ammo, food, and water. The old miner didn't ask questions; he kept his business to himself and let them do the same. By the man's manner, Neels supposed that he'd been in the wars, too. Without being asked to, Karskie paid for the crate and fuse with a credit card, one thousand rand.

Headed back into the night, east to the Kruger, Karskie rubbed his hands.

"My father will be very curious when he gets that bill."

Neels asked nothing, not curious about the dynamics of a wealthy family. His own father had been military, fighting Mussolini in the East African Campaign, his mother a soldier's wife. They wound up on a small farm in Southern Rhodesia. Both died long ago from alcohol, hard work, and the poverty that had chased Neels into the army.

The dynamite strapped in the back gave the return drive to the Kruger a gravity that the ride out to the mine had lacked. The danger seemed to weigh on Karskie. It underscored that he was on an adventure, with his own rifle, requiring him to be a man like Neels had said. Apparently, a man was quiet; Karskie rode along in relative silence. Neels even tried to get him to talk some, but Karskie gave curt answers and nods, as if Neels had become his model.

They stopped for a cold six-pack. Neels and the boy each drank two quickly. Karskie tried to ease the mood by turning on the radio, but the tunes were nothing but love songs, and Neels cut them off. Karskie gazed straight ahead at the stars and sparse traffic as they motored out of the mining hills into vast, unlit tracts of farmland. He rubbed his hands. Karskie was trying to gird himself, anxious, like a boy going to war.

"You want to know the first time I ever saw a rhino?"

Karskie started, surprised; his thoughts had taken him far away.

"Sure."

"In Rhodesia. I was younger than you. On patrol one morning. I was by myself, a stupid thing but I was still proving myself back then."

Karskie smiled, and Neels did not have to say, "Like you are."

"The big bastard burst out of the bush, straight at me. He rumbled like a train, I can tell you. I tried to climb a tree, but, fok, the thorns cut me up. So I jumped up on a termite mound. Fell right through the top of the damn thing. Standing in termites up to my chin. The rhino stopped right in front of me, eyeing me. So I couldn't break out of the termites. Had to stand there itching, getting bit and crawled all over, until the great bastard walked off. I heard him laughing."

Karskie laughed, and the dark air in the Land Cruiser lightened.

"I heard you were Special Forces. That true?"

"Selous Scouts."

The boy must have known some history, for he gawped.

"You were with the Scouts."

During the Rhodesian War, the Selous Scouts became legendary counterinsurgents, bush fighters, and relentless man trackers. Famously harsh training gave the Scouts the ability to operate and live in the worst of the bush. The British touted them as the hardiest of men, the Angolans and Cubans thought they were mad—both were close to the truth.

Karskie curled fingers at Neels, beckoning a story.

"Give me the worst."

"The worst, eh?"

Was Karskie looking to hear about killing? No. The rich boy wanted a piece of Neels's wealth, a story of manhood.

"I'll tell you about the baboon."

Karskie stopped Neels long enough to open the final two beers. Neels tipped his can toward him, and they tapped rims before swallowing.

"When I was just a recruit, we were taken out in the bush to a cabin. We had to sleep outside, make our own shelters. They didn't feed us for three days. A dead baboon had been nailed to a fence with a cigarette in his mouth. The carcass started to rot, and he stank to hell. Finally, a sergeant came out of the cabin to ask if we were hungry. He said, 'Your dinner's been hanging on that fence for three days.' We skinned the bastard, cooked him. I have never eaten anything that tasted so terrible. And I have never since been hungry again."

Karskie drained the last of his beer.

"I couldn't have done that."

"Neither could I until I did."

"There's the lesson, yeah?"

"Ja."

Karskie crushed the beer can and tossed it over his shoulder to the rear of the vehicle, back where the crate of dynamite rode. He cringed as soon as he let the can go, realizing what he'd done. Both had a laugh.

"I didn't tell you everything the general said to me."

"That's not good, boy. We're in this together."

"I know. He told me to tell you after we got there. Security, he said."

"Like I can't be trusted."

"You drink, Neels."

This was fair. Karskie had a right to say that. When Neels nodded and let it pass, they were, indeed, in it together.

"Go on."

Karskie described the situation in Shingwedzi. A South African drone had crashed with a live American missile attached.

"How the hell did a Yank missile get on one of our drones?"

Karskie tapped the air with one finger, as if dinging a bell.

"Exactly."

Hours ago, the United States had dropped a two-man Spec Ops team into the bush to eliminate the evidence. Obviously, something nefarious and highly secret was going on, and the Americans had been caught red-handed. The South African government was briefed and agreed to cooperate with the United States to avoid an international incident, despite the fact that this was a major violation of security, sovereignty, and trust between nations trying to find a way to be allies again.

Karskie snickered.

"In other words, the Americans wrote a big check."

Yet for some reason, the team they'd dropped into the Kruger lacked the supplies to blow the drone. So the general got a call. Then Karskie.

Neels raised a middle finger.

"A Spec Ops team without guns, supplies, or explosives. Great. Who are these clumsy bastards?"

Karskie grew more breathless as the story unfolded. The general had offered no explanations about why a South African drone had been armed with a US missile, where the drone had been, or what it had done. He'd left Karskie to speculate on his own. De Haven had said only that this was deeply classified. Then he'd asked who was the best tracker in the rangers.

"Why does he need a tracker?"

"Before the Yanks got there, the drone was found by poachers. Neels, they stole the fucking missile."

Neels could do little but shake his head at the plans of big shots.

"You told the general I was the tracker he wanted."

"Of course. Listen, this is big. Americans parachuting in. The general on the phone. Dynamite, poachers, rockets. Secrets, man, everywhere."

If Karskie had told Neels all this at the outset, he wouldn't have let the boy come. This was going to be much more than the adventure Karskie thought he was tagging along on.

The general had asked for the best tracker in the rangers for one reason.

They were going after the missile. And the poachers.

Chapter 17

Allyn told Juma he would be in Mozambique inside two hours, 250 miles from Pretoria. When he heard this, Juma laughed. He recalled something Allyn had told him long ago, something Eva had said back when they were all young. "You have delusions of grandeur, Allyn. The difference between you and others is you go out and do them." She had not meant it as a compliment. It was the sort of thing an uppity girl said to a hardscrabble boy.

"Do not come to me in Macandezulo. Wait at the border directly west of it, inside the park. I'll come for you."

"Alright."

"In two hours." Juma hung up, still chuckling.

Allyn ran into more expense than trouble chartering a helicopter pilot to take him into the park at night. An honest man could always be bought, he simply had a higher price than a thief. Allyn asked what the fine would be for getting caught flying illicitly into the Kruger. The pilot guessed five thousand rand, roughly five hundred US dollars. Allyn tripled it on top of the exorbitant cost of the flight, another twenty thousand rand, paid in cash. The pilot asked no more questions. Allyn arranged to meet him in twenty minutes at Waterkloof Heliport five miles away.

• • •

The flight northeast from Pretoria crossed over twinkling villages of golden light and white headlamps on the few roads, all set against broad swaths of darkness. The glows did little but pock the black land, reminders of how small a portion of the country was settled, how enormous the emptiness. The helicopter whisked Allyn above it for a smooth hour, muffled by earphones, unbroken by chat because the pilot had sold Allyn his silence as well as his flying.

When the beaded lights petered out and the horizon ahead showed nothing but night, the pilot eased the stick forward to shed altitude. He uttered his first words since leaving Waterkloof.

"The Kruger."

They flew into the park fifty meters off the ground, enough to clear the dim treetops. The pilot shut down all his lights, and the chopper brought nothing across the border but Allyn and the sound of beating props. Allyn focused on the veld, hoping to spot something taking flight, some dark, running dot. But the bush gave him nothing special for stealing in like this. The Kruger showed no surprise at his arrival.

The helicopter zoomed low and fast, chasing its own shadow cast by the westward setting moon. Ahead, silver ripples reflected off a stripe of river. Allyn prepared himself to disembark. He'd brought no bag with spare clothes, no water bottle or even a jacket. He'd thought of none of this before phoning the heliport, then rushing out the door. It struck him freshly that Eva was dead, she'd always packed for his trips. His own lack of preparation annoyed him, felt like a missed chore. An urge to scold Eva arose; when it fell away it left him sad and feeling hapless. Allyn resolved again to get a live-in maid.

Minutes after passing the river, the chopper leaned back on its cushion of air to slow. The pilot touched down in a clear swath not far from a moonlit mound of boulders. The man reached across himself to shake Allyn's hand, then opened the door for him. Allyn doffed the big headphones and stepped down.

The pilot did not hesitate to leave him behind. He whipped up dust, bounding into the air before Allyn was out of range. The copter remained blacked out, the fading thrum of its rotors its only evidence in the night sky.

Allyn took in his surroundings. He'd expected the Kruger to abound with sound, but it stayed quiet after the chopper was gone. The grinding of insects seemed no different from the bugs around the lake at home. The sky shone brilliantly, far from man's works. His solitude, without luggage or another soul nearby, tilted his chin to the stars. He waited and adjusted to the dark; in minutes he sensed himself dissolving into it just a little. Allyn couldn't put his finger on the last time he'd been this isolated. A businessman was rarely by himself, too many people made their money by him. Husband, father, miner, boss, every role in his life had been determined by how others viewed him. Allyn never denied them, never thought to do it, and so over the years had become defined by them. But not here, now, not in the bush like this. Bit by bit, he began to believe he could see farther into this void, hear the silence of the Kruger more sharply, smell the earth and the need for rain. He put his hands to his hips and filled his lungs like a man breathing in sea air.

When a bakkie rumbled up the dirt road nearby, Allyn felt a little torn from the night. The headlamps bouncing on the rutted track seemed indecent against the perfect distances and black openness of the Kruger. The pickup truck stopped, and for the first time Allyn noticed he'd been standing near a downed fence. He walked over it, careless that he crossed the border illegally.

Juma waited for him in the road beside the pickup. In the small truck's bed, a silent black man rode with his spine against the cabin, an automatic rifle across his knees. Juma spread his great arms.

"Shamwari. Under two hours. You are a man of your word."

Allyn accepted a quick embrace. He climbed into the passenger side without speaking to Juma or the figure in the back, a bit sorry that they'd shown up as quickly as they did. The Kruger was about to tell him something, and it had been interrupted. Allyn promised to come back by himself some other time and listen.

Chapter 18

Promise would not let the Americans light a fire. The squat one, LB, carped as he did over many things. At the same time, he was compassionate, gentle though in a brick-like way, hardened and protective. She moved them away from Wophule and the drone, closer to the broken hedge, where they sat out of the wind and their smell would not travel so far.

The moon had almost set; the captain's watch said the time approached midnight. She was not hungry, nor were they, and they had water in their canteen. Promise and Wophule should have reported back at the Shingwedzi ranger station hours ago. Her phone had buzzed several times in the captain's pocket.

She could leave them at any minute. Neither of the Yanks was attentive enough, the pistol was not frightening. She could use the bush against them like before and be gone. Gone where? To more lies. To losing her partner, to leaving Wophule unavenged, because despite her oath and anger, she could not ever kill Good Luck. Promise hugged her knees to her chest and stayed with the Americans because they'd said someone was coming. They might go after the stolen rocket. If they did that, she would go, too, take them to Juma and have Good Luck killed that way. Maybe Juma, as well, though then the house on the hill for Gogo would have to wait.

The temperature in the Kruger had fallen. The ground leeched out the last of its warmth from the day. Promise was not dressed for midnight in the park; she wore khaki shorts and her short-sleeved tunic had not dried from being soaked. Both Americans were damp also from their swim away from the bees, but they didn't appear to mind, and their uniforms were long and thick. LB dug into his pack and pulled out part of a parachute. He draped this around Promise's shoulders. When LB sat again, he believed this allowed him to ask her questions.

"Where are you from?"

Promise considered giving him back the parachute and ending this claim on her. Talking about herself would mean more lies, because so much of the truth could not be said. And what she could say honestly would sound ugly to an American. *I am an AIDS orphan from a poor township. I am a woman in a man's job. I am not valued or trusted.* But she was warm and wanted to keep the silk, so she asked him instead.

"Where are you from?"

LB looked surprised. He chewed on this tactic, hadn't expected the switch. He'd been trying to be kind, but Promise read this as the arrogance of a man, thinking a woman needed his kindness.

"Okay. I'm from Las Vegas."

"I know Las Vegas. It's an Elvis song."

"No way. You know Elvis?"

Promise screwed up her features. These Americans, the first Promise had ever met, seemed unaware of what their country gave the world: missiles, drones, and music.

"I'm from a township near the park. Now, why are you both here?"

The captain answered. "Like we said. To get rid of the drone. It's supposed to be a secret."

"How do you feel about your country's secrets?"

"We don't judge. That stops when the uniform goes on." The captain indicated Promise's olive khakis beneath the silk, the ranger patch on her shoulder. "It's the same for you, I guess."

In the dark, Promise shook her head at the games God played, how he nicked and goaded and dared her with her own lies. Or was it the old gods, the jackal prancing, the hyena laughing? She deflected again.

"But why are you here? What are you?"

The captain explained that they were part of a special unit in the United States Air Force called Guardian Angels. LB was a pararescue jumper, or a PJ for short. The captain was a tactical officer. Their unit was called on for combat-rescue missions whenever an American warrior or ally was isolated and in trouble on hostile territory. The GAs were paramedics and officers trained to operate in every kind of environment, because the US military and its allies covered all the earth's terrains. They were Special Forces, and because of the demands of combat search and rescue, the range of skills needed, there were not very many Guardian Angels.

"What are you rescuing in the Kruger?"

"We don't just do rescue missions. We do recovery, too. Like this one. When a US drone goes down in a remote place, sometimes we get called in to clean it up."

"To remove the proof."

"Yes, ma'am. But let's not be naive."

"About what, Captain?"

"About power. Force. And how hard it is to use it for good."

"Whose good, Captain? Mine, or yours? Who decides?"

He hesitated. Promise gestured to the night veld.

"It's the same in the Kruger. It's easy to be a lion. It must be easy to be an American."

The captain's eyes crinkled above a handsome grin. He dipped his head, accepting. Promise prodded again.

"What kind of missile was it?"

"A Hellfire."

"Such a name. What can it do?"

"It's made to destroy reinforced ground targets. Like tanks, bunkers."

"So it is powerful."

"Very."

"But you have no supplies, one little gun, no food. Waiting. How did this happen?"

The captain told how he and LB had been at an international air show in Pretoria, ready to jump, when their plane was diverted. They had to parachute into the park with only what they could scrounge on the plane.

"We were lucky to meet you. LB here isn't pretty. Believe me, he's worse when he's hungry."

LB licked his lips comedically.

"I'm thinking grasshoppers next."

Promise gave him the laugh he sought.

"You still haven't answered my question. Why were you sent here? I think the drone is not yours."

The captain nodded, unwilling to pursue or explain this further. He'd come to the boundary where he must lie or say nothing. He shrugged, and his silence expressed itself as uprightness.

"I admire you, Captain." Like him, Promise did not explain herself.

Thick LB leaned across his folded legs, his demeanor suddenly stern. He hoisted a finger between them.

"Why do you think that?"

"Think what?"

"There are no markings on that drone. You said it's not American."

The truth shot to her tongue: because her great-uncle Juma did not think so. Speaking his name would be a release, like a breath held too long. The words squeezed into her throat: Juma; the rhino; her grandmother; Wophule; the money; her reasons, which were innocent; her guilt, which had gone far beyond what she'd expected. Promise didn't know where she found the strength to hold the truth in longer. She mouthed half of it.

"I heard the poachers say it."

LB leaned back, lowering the finger. Plainly her answer did not sit well with him. Promise, a tracker, would soon lose her way down this path of deceits. LB had more questions, as he ought. The truth wanted out of her chest, like a gasp.

She had no more tales. The captain eyed her, keyed into LB's suspicion. LB nodded, plotting the next question that would trap her. Promise thought again of running.

One more time LB lifted his finger.

Promise raised her own. Again, was God the trickster or Gogo's old spirits of the bush? One or the other had come to rescue her from these rescuers.

"Shhh."

LB opened his hand, letting one query go for another. He whispered, "What is it?"

Promise could describe a rustling leaf, a shuffling hoof, a voice, but not the tensing of the Kruger at the coming of men.

Chapter 19

Neels loved the bush at night. His fighting youth had been spent in it, then he'd spent time in it as a tracker and a teacher of trackers.

He trained his rangers to love the dark Kruger as well, to respect and fear it. The veld fed at night, it roamed and rested. The land and sky were eternal, they were endless and black together. Though the dangers did not go away, the twisted, sun-beat bush became more mysterious and artful in moonlight, starlight. The mystery and art of the place—that was what Neels taught his rangers to blend with. The poachers who came here did not love or understand the Kruger. They would stand out because of it, and could be caught.

He parked the Land Cruiser off the pavement, just far enough to be hidden. Vehicles were not allowed off-road in the park's natural habitat. Karskie waited in the car while Neels did a quick walk around. He'd seen a female honey badger in the area recently. She was not a creature to surprise if she had cubs.

He opened the boot. When Karskie got out, Neels let the last chance to tell the boy to stay in the car, drive it back, and go home to sleep slip away.

Though doughy, Karskie was a broad lad and could carry plenty. Neels slung both packs of food and water on his own back and two rifles. In one hand Karskie carried boxes of ammo, in the other the tape and reel of fuse. Neels hoisted the crate of dynamite onto one shoulder, then grabbed his own rifle.

"Stay far behind me."

Karskie bulged like a pack mule.

"Why?"

"Because I might trip and blow myself up. Sure you want to come?"

"And miss that?"

Neels grunted, turning for the bush. Karskie had pointed on a map to the coordinates the general had given him. Neels knew the spot where the drone had crashed, an open patch of scrub and marulas, elephant-grazing ground. The ten-kilometer walk due east should take two hours under their burdens, if the boy could keep the pace and Neels did not, indeed, blow up.

He headed out under the crate, a hundred meters on a game trail, then looked back. Karskie was not yet following.

Neels called out, "I'm not carrying a fucking nuke."

Karskie rounded a corner of brush; he came into sight grumbling that he didn't know about things like dynamite.

"Time to learn, boyo."

Neels did not let them rest for the first trudging hour. They covered more than half the distance, and when Karskie collapsed next to Neels, he looked done in. Neels offered to switch loads; the boy demurred.

The boy panted louder than the insects. When his breathing leveled out, Neels let him have another few minutes, to be sure they could make it the rest of the way. His own shoulders were slumped and sore from the crate.

"So what did you do to get thrown out of the university?"

"I didn't get thrown out."

"You quit first. What did you do?"

Karskie leaned back on his elbows, crossed his ankles, a leisurely pose, a pampered man. Neels almost began disliking him again.

"There was a girl. There frequently is, you know."

Neels didn't.

"Go on."

"One of my students. She knew my family had some money. She let me spend it on her. And so it goes."

"No. How does it go?"

"Not so different from you, really. We both trained to do something. Mine was numbers and teaching. Yours was tracking and killing men. You and I got very good at what we did. Both young and invincible. Took risks, did things we marveled at later. You ate a baboon off a fence. I slept with a young girl and did drugs."

Karskie stood first, looking down on Neels.

"Want to swap loads?"

Neels climbed to his own feet.

"If I could."

Karskie held his ground, not laughing.

"I'm not the general's boy. Frankly, there's nothing he can buy me with. I want you to know I'm actually happy to be working in the Kruger. It's cruel and stupid shit, what the poachers do. I've been on the chopper, I've seen the carcasses. It feels good to be in the fight. I can help, I can do things. But I need the rangers to believe in me. To bring me the facts, the numbers. I need to be trusted. So I'm here. Tracking poachers."

"You mean again."

"What?"

"You need to be trusted again."

"Yeah. If we're being honest. Yeah."

Neels held out a hand; they shook. Not so different, as the boy had said.

Karskie donned his burden. He swept a hand before him for Neels to do the same and lead the way, far out in front.

For the remainder of the trek, Karskie held up better than Neels. The big boy didn't complain or fall behind, while Neels's knees and back griped from the crate carried high on one shoulder. His mood tumbled into his discomfort. Still, he held no conversations with his gone wife. Neels had tried to pull his heart from the bush for her, his memory from carcasses and the war, and put it elsewhere. He'd failed, but there was no need for the boy following him to hear or know that. Besides, carrying dynamite was no time to let the woman make him crazy.

Neels let the land guide him. They crossed into an open plain where predators prowled in the daylight and in the spring the hedges bloomed. Herds grazed here, impala, bushbuck, and kudu, feeling safer on the flatlands with great distances to run. Elephants grazed on the scrub and trees; giraffes plucked the highest branches. There might have been animals there now, but the night cloaked them.

Neels shifted the crate to his other shoulder, also worn down. He forged across the grassland, nearing the crash site at its far edge. He cleared himself of curiosity, what he would find ahead, what the Americans would need him to do. He put his mind on his tiring legs and could not recall what it was like to be young.

• • •

Neels didn't trust himself to lower the crate carefully from a standing position. He folded to his knees before hefting it from his shoulder, shifting the weight into both hands. He eased the dynamite to the ground and stayed down with it, waiting for Karskie.

The boy galumphed up the trail, jangling his load, dragging his boots. He said nothing when he arrived but assumed they were resting again and began to unburden himself. Neels stopped him by reaching a hand for help off the ground.

"Stay quiet."

"What's up?"

"That hedge ahead. The drone will be on the other side of it. I'll be back."

"No. We go together."

"I said stay here."

"They're Americans."

"They say they're Americans."

"Is that a little paranoid?"

"Yes. Until something goes wrong. Then it's not."

"Look, if something does go wrong, I'm useless by myself anyway. They'd find me wandering the park next Tuesday. So I'm going with you."

Too tuckered to argue more and not sure he should, Neels nodded.

"Leave it all here but the rifles. Walk where I walk. Don't talk."

Karskie dropped everything quietly but kept one rifle. With Karskie striding behind, Neels led the way toward the hedge. He followed evidence of the crash, a furrow in the earth, the landing rig of an aircraft, warped metal and rubber wheels. The groove ran through a ragged opening in the hedge; Neels paused there, hidden. Big Karskie slipped in beside him.

After decades in the bush, Neels knew its shapes and motions intimately. Man was unnatural here; his works and movements, his spoor, did not belong. Even in the dark at fifty paces, the wreckage of the drone stood out, looked like nothing wild.

Neels also had a keen sense of what and who belonged in his park. Two American Special Operators, if that was what they were, did not. Not without his knowledge or permission, regardless of what the general had to say.

Neels didn't see them. But he would if they moved. Behind the hedge, he brought his rifle stock to his cheek. Neels whispered to Karskie.

"Do nothing."

"What? What are you going to do?"

Neels shouted across the open ground.

"Put your hands where I can see them."

Immediately two figures, lumps in the dark near the wreck, grew in height. Neels centered his gun barrel on one of the silhouettes. A man's voice answered.

"Who are you?"

"I'm the one with a rifle aimed at your heart, lad. So first, who are you?"

"Captain Wally Bloom. US Air Force."

"Drop your weapons, Captain."

The figure with the voice folded at the waist, setting a gun down. Neels firmed his finger on the trigger as he moved from behind cover. He whispered again for Karskie to stay behind him and shut up.

Neels approached in combat mode, weapon tucked to his cheek, scanning. He strode only far enough to get a clear look at the two men before halting to scrutinize them down the barrel of his FN. They wore the same stiff camo uniforms, military web vests. One stood tall and lean, the other short and burly. Both held their arms from their sides to show open hands. A handgun lay in the dirt between them.

Nearby, the tangled wreck of the drone rose, one wing intact, the other ripped off and hanging. The fuselage had dug its nose into the earth. Not far away, stones had been stacked into a long, low mound. Was somebody dead? That upped the ante.

Neels moved the muzzle to the shorter man.

"Who's this then?"

"Master Sergeant Gus DiNardo. US Air Force."

"Fine. Let's see some ID, boys."

Both dropped their hands at that. The squat one made a deflating sound. The tall shadow kept talking for them both.

"That's going to be a problem."

"Is it? Then get your hands back up."

Behind Neels, out of the darkness, another voice answered.

"They're Americans."

Karskie pivoted at the sound. Neels did not, keeping his barrel trained on the two unknown men.

"That you, Promise?"

"I saw them parachute in."

"What are you doing here, girl?"

"I stayed to help them."

"Step out here."

"Lower the gun first. They're not armed."

"Are you?"

Chirping bugs filled the seconds until Promise spoke.

"No."

Neels tamped down the urge to wheel on her, shouting. Why was one of his rangers unarmed in the park? Why hadn't she called any of this in? Whose goddamn side was the girl on? Was she a Kruger ranger or a fucking American?

"Where's the boy, Promise?"

"Dead. The poachers shot him."

"That him under the rocks?"

"Yes."

"Yissus."

Neels sucked his teeth. The boy had been young, immature, and small. Neels blamed himself for teaming him up with this girl.

The two Americans had not lifted their hands as he'd ordered. Promise was not in sight. Karskie, behind him, radiated nervousness, restive and shifting. Neels lowered the rifle.

"Alright."

The gun went down, but the tension hardly lessened. The Americans held their ground, Neels as well. Karskie turned a full circle, jittery and unsure where to look. Promise formed out of the night, closer to the Americans than to Neels, as if she'd chosen a side. The squat American jabbed a finger at her as the girl appeared out of nothing.

"Did you teach her to do that? It's just weird."

The captain moved next, plucking the pistol off the ground. He shoved it inside his belt before walking to Neels with a hand extended. Neels shouldered the rifle strap and met the American's handshake. Closer now, the captain's battle uniform lacked insignia and patches; this sort of cleansing had been standard for covert ops in the Scouts; apparently the Yanks did the same. The captain repeated his name, Bloom. Quietly Neels compared himself to this more modern warrior, gave the man's hand a press, and got one back. Bloom had proper bearing, a rod up his arse like a good officer. But Neels stood in the Kruger, his park and his sector, with one of his rangers dead and another one disobedient. Neels knew nothing of these Americans except that they needed dynamite, food, water, and him. He did not release the captain's hand but squeezed harder.

"What are you doing here?"

"You have a name, sir?"

"I do. What are you doing here?"

The captain increased the pressure in his own clasp.

"I'll tell when you let go of my hand. Or we can do this for a while, if you like."

Neels held long enough to imply that he could, indeed, go on for a bit more, and on another day, around some beers, he and this captain might.

Both let go.

"Neels Boing. Sector chief of Shingwedzi."

"Are we in Shingwedzi?"

"We are."

"Who's this with you?"

Karskie stepped forward, one hand out. He held his rifle so it pointed straight up over his shoulder, carrying it like a toy soldier.

"Donald Karskie. I work in intel."

Neels had not known Karskie's first name. It suited the boy.

"Captain, before we settle in, I have to ask you and your sergeant to move away from this area. Go sit over there." Neels pointed to the broken hedge.

"Why?"

"This is a crime scene. A ranger's been killed. A missile's stolen. Your missile, if I understand it right. Every step you take makes my job harder."

"You're a tracker."

"I'm a lot of things, Captain. Donald there will give you the supplies we brought. Got plenty of food and water."

"Explosives?"

"More than enough."

"We need to blow the drone."

"You'll do it in the morning."

"Sir—"

Neels cut him off. "I'm not going to make a crater until I've examined the site."

Neels raised a palm to stop more objections from the American officer.

"You're in my park. One of my boys was murdered because your fucking missile was more important than his life. Now go sit where I showed you. I want a private word with my ranger."

Neels didn't give Bloom time to respond. He turned sharply away.

"Promise."

Karskie led the Americans to the backpacks and dynamite he'd left at the hedge. The girl came to Neels but kept a notable distance.

"What happened here?"

In the dark, Neels kept an eye on her hands and feet, an ear fixed to her tones, watchful for hesitation, a misstep, a falsehood while she related the events of the crashed drone: She and Wophule stumbled on the wreck late in the day; then, while they were investigating, two poachers showed up; they shot Wophule right off and made her surrender. The poachers dislodged the missile from the aircraft and left, taking it and both ranger rifles. Promise sat with Wophule as he died. Before she could think to call in a report, the Americans dropped out of the dusk. They demanded her phone, saying the crash was a big secret. She could have run from them but would not leave Wophule. Neels had taught his rangers to sit with the bodies of men, even poachers, until they could be recovered.

Neels would not have trusted the tale from any of his rangers but her. The surrender to poachers, not reporting the crash, handing over the phone to the Americans, helping them. He was inclined to believe the girl, all the failures fit her. Promise, too, was aware of her breakdowns, she inched away from Neels as she described them.

"Go sit with your new friends."

The girl stopped her slow retreat, she did not go at his order. None of her timidity showed when she spoke.

"What are you going to do?"

"Stay with the boy. Make sure nothing bothers him. Dawn's in four hours."

"I'll do it. He was my partner."

Neels took a seat beside the pile of rocks, crossing his boots beneath him. The girl sat on the other side.

They did not speak, the rocks separated them like a wall. Neels knew very little about Wophule; the Xhosa boy's death did nothing to increase his interest. That wasn't required for loyalty, to keep a vigil for a ranger against the bush.

Neels lowered the brim on his hat and faced the wreckage. Soon, at sunup, he would see for himself what happened.

• • •

The girl's chin slumped to her chest, she dozed sitting upright. Promise shivered in the night, and Neels, cursing under his breath, unbuttoned his khaki tunic to mantle it around her. She awoke enough to look up, wordless, blinking black eyes at him. In his T-shirt, Neels awaited and greeted the sunrise.

The Americans slept curled on the ground beneath the hedge, Karskie, too. PowerBar wrappers and empty water bottles lay around them. The sleepers looked uncomfortable and homeless. This was good, because the Kruger was not their home. Neels, the only one awake, didn't move until the sun had cleared the horizon. Shadows raked the ground, and the golden light put the tracks all around him into crisp relief. Neels rolled to his cranky knees and stood. He went first to the drone.

The wrecked vehicle was an eerie contraption, guided but untouched by men. Neels expected to hate it as he closed in but did not, patting the broken wing as he passed. The drone was a technological marvel that did no more than what Neels could do: track, find, and kill. The machine was a validation of him, a colleague of sorts.

When the drone had plowed into the earth, it sprayed loose soil and sand on every side. The ground around it was a confusion of fresh tracks. The big Americans' knobby soles bit deep into the soil. Neels knew well the prints made by ranger boots, lightweight Promise and small Wophule. Surprisingly, the paws of a big cat had crept close. With care, Neels ducked under the drone's one intact wing. He bent low, eyes to the earth, searching for tracks he did not recognize.

A set of sandal prints emerged. This wasn't unusual for poachers. It was incredible how they traveled so far over hard land in such cheap thongs, sometimes barefoot. Neels gleaned nothing from the sandals except that they supported Promise's story.

Neels shifted his focus closer to the fuselage, imagining the taking of the missile. The Americans had stood here, Wophule and Promise, too. Neels leaned lower to the dirt.

His jaw went slack at what the ground gave him, what rose like flotsam out of the crisscrossing tracks. He dropped to his knees to be sure. In awe and anger, Neels touched a fingertip to a flat expanse of impressed dirt—not the spoor of a stranger but a broad, large print he knew and had sworn to find again and follow.

The leather dress shoe of an outsized man.

The baas, Juma.

What was he doing here? For the second time in a week, he'd made himself visible. Juma had appeared out of the Mozambican hills to meet a rhino-horn crew at the border. Now he'd come personally into the Kruger to steal an American rocket off a downed South African drone, a dangerous thing to do. Why? What drew Juma to the two places? What was the connection? How did he even know the drone was here?

Neels inspected the hole gutted in the vehicle's fuselage where something had been ripped out. He searched for more tracks in the tossed-up dirt around the wreck: Juma's flat soles and the single pair of sandals left the marks of poachers, mingled with four sets of boots, the Americans and rangers. Neels moved to the open ground where the earth was weedy and dry. What few tracks he could spot in the clean morning light covered and scuffed each other, including his own. No patterns emerged, no story in the dirt, just the players.

No one had stirred. Karskie and the Americans lay beside the acacia hedge next to their trash. Promise sat upright in Neels's tunic beside Wophule. Neels took a knee beside the stones. He rolled the first, the biggest, aside. Promise jerked awake.

"What are you doing?"

"Help me, or go back to sleep."

Neels scrabbled at the rock pile. He worked to clear only the top half of the mound, leaving the body's waist and legs covered. The girl was of little use, halfheartedly brushing at the sand covering the boy.

When the black, bloody chest appeared, then the shoulders and head, Neels pushed away Promise's hands. He paused to rest, to gaze down on the ranger boy's dark features. Neels had no illusion that Wophule looked restful. He'd died coughing blood; grit mottled the rusty crust around his lips. Terror had left its trail on his face.

With a pocketknife, Neels snipped the buttons from Wophule's jersey. He peeled back the shirt, exposing the dark skin.

A single round in the center of the chest, an expert shot, had done him in. The mouth of the wound was collapsed, pouty, but it had been lethal. Neels tucked both hands under the boy's torso to lift him into a sitting posture. Wophule had been small, but death made him heavy, as if the soul was what made a man light. One quick glance at the back told Neels the bullet had not gone through. He eased Wophule down in the dirt.

The commotion of moving the rocks had awakened the Americans and Karskie. All three stood; Neels told them to stay on the perimeter. They called back no questions. Promise kept her place beside her partner.

Neels spread the entry wound to hold the channel open. He inserted the pocketknife's blade to dig past ragged bone and rigid tissue, pressing down until the tip scraped metal. Withdrawing the knife, he patted the dead boy's shoulder in case the black Africans were right, the souls of the dead did linger until they were sent on. Neels sliced the wound wider, making an X cut, to make room for his hand.

He wormed into the hole. The meat of the boy felt chillier than the morning. Just under the skin, ribs barred his wriggling fingers; Neels forced his way past the bones until they bent and he could shove in his hand to the knuckles. Over his thirty years in the park, he'd gouged bullets out of uncounted rhinos, elephants, lions, antelope, all killed as wrongly as this, but never a man. Neels stilled his breathing, focused only on the crime as he delved deeper, reaching out his middle finger to root for the bullet.

Down in the hole his wife waited; she sprang, another ambush, to tell him she could not love a man who could do such sordid things. Neels dug in harder, probing for the bastards who'd stolen his life as surely as they'd taken Wophule's. She was right, he could not be loved, and if he did not catch Juma, he'd be left with nothing in the end. The gaping wound sucked at his wrist. Sinew and vessels, the boy's dry heart and cool lungs, his stiffening muscles crowded Neels's fingertips as if to clutch the bullet to themselves, their last relic of living. Neels sensed Wophule's strength in this dead struggle against him and considered that perhaps he'd thought too little of the boy. Neels groped deeper, then touched the round. His wife did not understand why that was so important.

When he plucked it out, she was quick to leave.

Neels got to his feet. His hand dripped jellied blood. Promise stayed beside the body, hands covering her mouth. Neels hefted the round. Three hundred grains. Holland & Holland magnum .375.

"Karskie, come here. Bring the Yanks."

Neels walked to meet them. He held out the bullet to Karskie. The big lad was slow to offer his palm, then did so with disgust. The Americans seemed somber, peering past Neels's gory fingers to the boy's exposed and spoiled body, the tunneled chest.

"I think this will match the round Opu and I dug out of the Shingwedzi rhino this week. Put it in your pocket."

Karskie looked about for something to wipe the bullet clean before pocketing it. He used his pant leg.

Neels turned on Promise. The girl had gotten to her feet. Her stance was wide, hands out from her sides. She looked ready to jump left or right, like someone caught in a searchlight. Her breathing came quick and shallow, a rising panic.

Near her boots lay Neels's rifle.

He spun on the Americans faster than they could react. With one hand shoving the captain backward, he snared the pistol from the man's belt. Whirling again on Promise, Neels raised the gun. She had not moved.

He stomped toward her, paying no attention to the noises behind him, the Yanks objecting, questioning, chasing him. Promise did not back away when he stuck the pistol's muzzle into the center of her chest, exactly where Wophule had been shot.

Neels called over his shoulder.

"Captain."

"Neels, what are you doing?"

"If I pull the trigger, how long will this girl live?"

"Put it down. She's one of your rangers."

Promise stood at the end of Neels's arm. He saw no ranger there.

"Answer me, Captain."

The American did not comprehend. Karskie prodded him.

"Go ahead. Tell him."

"Not long."

"An hour?"

The captain paused to figure.

"Probably not, no."

"Did you see the boy's wound?"

"Neels."

"Did you see it?"

"No. The sergeant did."

"Sergeant, how long did that boy live?"

"Minutes, man. Less."

Neels lowered the pistol. With the back of his bloodied hand, he clouted Promise across the face. The blow turned her shoulders, but she did not stagger. She came erect, her cheek stained red but without tears.

Neels whispered.

"Run."

She wagged her head, slow, sad, and knowing.

With cautious treads, the Americans approached. Karskie stayed back.

The captain held out both hands, palms down.

"Stay calm. What's going on?"

"She said she didn't report the drone because she was sitting with the boy while he died. That's a lie. He was dead when he hit the ground. You know it."

Promise had gone wooden. The blood smeared on her face and the accusations hardened her.

"She says poachers showed up, shot the boy, and took the missile. But one of the bastards Karskie and I know. I've seen his tracks before. He's a syndicate boss named Juma. He would never have been in the park poaching. Others do that for him."

Neels returned the captain's pistol and moved around Promise to snatch his FN off the ground. He was done speaking to the girl. He addressed the Americans.

"He had to get rid of witnesses, but why not shoot her, too? Why did Juma come himself, why risk being seen by a ranger? How did he even know the drone and the missile were in the Kruger?"

The sergeant indulged him.

"How?"

"He wasn't in the park poaching. No, Juma didn't just happen on your missile like she says. The bastard was called here. Called by someone who works for him. Someone he could trust not to tell. Maybe someone he wanted to protect."

Neels raised the scarlet hand that had struck Promise.

"Her."

Chapter 20

Neels bored in on Promise. She turned her back even as he barked questions. The girl knelt beside her partner and lifted the first rock to cover him again; Neels surged to spin her around to face him, to answer him. She snarled and slapped at him, coiling against the corpse. LB slid a hand inside Neels's elbow to tug him back. Neels fought him off but stepped away, boiling mad.

LB knelt with the girl. As before, they stacked stones over Wophule. LB closed the boy's tunic across the grisly hole where Neels had reached into his chest. Wally and Karskie stayed back. Neels walked a growling circle.

LB set a heavy stone in place.

"Did you do it?"

Without breaking her labor, the girl nodded.

The mound over Wophule grew. The boy faded once more beneath dirt and rock, his pained face the last to disappear under cupped handfuls of dirt. LB struggled to stay silent, to not ask in whispers, *Why? What about your oath, to the rangers, your partner, the Kruger? How could you break it? For what? Money*? LB could imagine but could not understand. Since becoming a pararescueman he'd poured his own life into the Guardian Angels' oath, "That others may live," the last patch he'd removed for this mission. He'd hardened in the mold of that vow; without it he'd be formless. Wally, the team, all the men and women who served alongside them, the isolated and endangered warriors they rescued, the wounded they saved and the dead they could not, all those who risked or gave their lives for duty, mission, mates, and country . . . What would it mean for him to turn his back on them? Who would he be then? The man he was before the GAs, a soldier with bloody dreams. LB watched Promise lay the last stones over her partner and didn't believe he could ever do what she had done. His oath was specific on this point. Never quit. Die first.

Wally'd said that LB had nothing left but the Guardian Angels; he'd made it an accusation. To live without ever feeling what Promise was going through, to never know that anything in the world might be stronger than his oath, LB would admit Wally was right.

Once Wophule was enclosed, Promise turned to face Neels. She stood in the immensity of the Kruger and under the blue of the early morning sky, having done for her partner what she could. The girl squared her shoulders at Neels, who came at her like a boxer. The old ranger shouted into her face.

"Who is Juma?"

She would not answer, uncringing, almost nose to nose with his fury, until he pulled back.

"My grandmother's brother."

"That's why the boy was shot, not you."

"Yes."

"Do you work for him?"

"Only once."

"The rhino in Shingwedzi."

"Yes."

Neels pivoted on LB and Wally like they were his jury, dishing both hands back at Promise as if to say, *See? See this?*

LB didn't know what this meant, "The rhino in Shingwedzi." But her admission made Neels shake fists at her, enraged over this even more than the death of the boy. Here was the breaking of her oath, the rangers' pledge to safeguard the Kruger animals. Neels bared his teeth, fighting for the control to continue.

He raised one finger between himself and Promise, breathing hard. He wanted one answer. So did LB.

"Why?"

Promise did not wither but drew back her shoulders.

"My family."

Neels leaned forward as if he might charge the girl. He bellowed, and the vast Kruger did not flinch.

"Your fucking family?"

The two rangers, boss and traitor, glared their hatred. To LB, it did not seem new.

Like Neels had done, Promise appealed to him and Wally with her arms extended at Neels. *Do you see?*

Wally only shrugged. LB spoke.

"What about your family?"

Neels threw up a white palm to tell him to stay quiet. LB ignored it.

"Go ahead."

"My grandparents raised me in a poverty you would not tolerate. My grandmother wants a house, on a hill. Do you know how much money there is in rhino horn?" The girl pointed behind LB and Wally to the downed drone. "How much your rocket is worth?"

Again, LB could picture the crippling poverty she was talking about; he had seen it firsthand around the world, but he'd always been in uniform, passing through it. He could shower it off later, bear his own hunger because the pangs wouldn't last, never feel the depths of that kind of lack and need beyond curiosity and sympathy.

"My grandmother went to Juma for help. He said he would, but I had to do something for him. I would guide his poachers into the park. He said there was so much money in horn there would only need to be three or four rhinos. After that, I would have the money."

Promise turned back to Neels. The rest of her story seemed to be for him.

"They're dying. Two and three a day. We can't save them. I only wanted a house for my grandmother."

The old ranger's knuckles whitened on his rifle, and he ground his teeth, wanting to scream back. Promise pressed on.

"I led two of Juma's men to the rhino in Shingwedzi. I had to kill it myself, with a machete. It was terrible, and I said I was done, I could not bear that again. But I had to keep my word to my grandparents. They have no hope without me. When Wophule and I found the drone, I hoped it might be worth enough for me to stop poaching. I called Juma. He came, and Wophule was shot dead. Juma lied to me. I swear to you, I did not know that would happen."

Neels spit.

"This is your family. Your bliksem family."

His curse cast a stalemate over them. Not far outside their circle, the gray drone lay tilted in the dirt, leaning as if listening for a decision on its fate. The bush simmered, the shadows had begun to shorten. Wally's hands worked at his sides while he searched for what to say. LB stayed quiet, unable to defend Promise.

Big Karskie stepped forward, easing between Neels and the girl. He glanced left and right at them, making sure they were in separate corners.

• • •

During the night, before they fell asleep under the acacia bush, the big boy had talked a lot. He wanted to know about pararescue, the Guardian Angels, if the South African military had anything like it, what were the qualifications? He claimed to be a fit athlete not long ago, a strong swimmer. Wally encouraged him to look into it. LB, who every year spent a month at Indoc eliminating nine out of ten candidates, did not.

Karskie asked Promise, "Did Juma shoot Wophule?"

"No."

"Do you know the one who did?"

Promise's face clouded more. "His name is Good Luck."

"But you say Juma has the missile?"

"He took it."

"Do you know where?"

At this question, Wally inched away from LB's side. This information was what he needed to hear.

"Yes."

"Tell us."

"On one condition. I go with you."

Neels waved this off with a sweeping gesture, as if warning Wally away.

"Nooit."

He pushed Karskie aside, lunging at Promise.

"You don't make conditions. I'll kill you. I'll leave you for the jackals. You understand?"

Neels hoisted the rifle to his shoulder. For the second time, he trained a weapon at Promise. The girl seemed to consider letting Neels just end it.

LB moved, expecting Wally to stop him, but he did not. LB stepped beside Neels, reaching a hand to the raised weapon without touching it. The old ranger's cheeks flushed, his eyes bulged behind the barrel. Neels would shoot the girl, LB had no doubt.

"Man, come on. That's not going to settle anything."

"Shut your mouth, Sergeant. Go blow up the drone."

"We will. But lower the gun. Let's talk it out."

"You have no jurisdiction here. The girl's a poacher."

"She knows where the missile is."

"No worries, I'll get it out of her. Now mind your business."

LB opened a hand at Wally, who returned the gesture, both stymied. LB puffed his cheeks.

"I fucking hate this."

He sidestepped between Neels and Promise, blocking her from the black eye of Neels's rifle.

"We really don't do the jurisdiction thing."

Neels did not lower the gun. At that, with LB threatened, Wally had no choice. Two-handed, he raised the Beretta, snapping an order.

"Back it off, Neels. Right now."

"You siding with her?"

"We don't stand around while people get shot."

Promise moved from behind LB. She would not hide. Neels swung the gun at her. LB didn't react, letting her face Neels. Seething, jutting his jaw with an eye on Wally's combat stance and raised pistol, the old ranger lowered the rifle.

"You're finished, girl. Now or later. Doesn't matter."

Promise nodded, accepting.

Neels spun on Wally, who'd tucked the Beretta into his belt.

"If she runs. If she screws us up. I'll kill her. You try to stop me again, it's you and me. Right?"

Wally unfolded the sunglasses from his vest to slide them on. He answered by letting Neels see his own glowering reflection before he motioned to the girl.

"Promise. Where's the missile?"

"Juma said Macandezulo."

"Is that far from here?"

Karskie had kept himself at bay while anger and weapons were raised. He stepped forward, patting the air at Neels to calm him.

"Across the border in Mozambique. Eight kilometers. It's in the Limpopo."

"What's that?"

"A transfrontier park. Mozambique, Zimbabwe, and South Africa are trying to create a giant wildlife preserve. They're taking down fences, relocating the locals, turning it over to the animals. It's a good idea, except for one thing."

"That is?"

"Poaching in Mozambique is just a misdemeanor. Not even enforced. There's almost no wildlife left on that side of the border. That's why the poachers come into the Kruger."

Neels growled across his turned shoulder.

"With fokken rangers guiding them."

Karskie grimaced, apologizing but not ashamed for Neels. Wally pressed on. The morning warmed, and Torres was expecting a report.

"What's Macandezulo?"

"An abandoned village. If Juma's moved in there, it makes sense. No one around. Close to the border. A few generators and he's in business. A poaching haven."

Big Karskie didn't lack for answers, with a quick wit. He seemed protective of Neels. LB couldn't guess where the boy stood on what to do with Promise.

LB asked, "Can we find it?"

Neels treated the question as an insult.

"Of course we can bloody find it."

Promise had not left LB's side. He needed to walk away, to figure out with Wally what the next steps would be. LB faced her, reluctant to judge but needing to. She'd gotten her partner murdered. She'd taken down a rhino with a knife and her bare hands, for money. She'd dishonored her oath, lied to her superiors. Yet she could have run off at any point in the night and did not. She'd stayed with him and Wally, helping them when she didn't have to. She sat until daybreak next to Wophule's corpse, beside Neels who might ruin, even execute her outright. She insisted on going to Macandezulo, to do what? Promise couldn't make everything right; her partner's body and the carcass of a rhino somewhere in the bush saw to that. Promise was guilty as hell, and she was going to stay that way.

She probably owed LB her life; Neels was going to gun her down. And still could. But nothing in the girl's posture or face hinted she was even grateful, or that she would try to escape.

Promise was going to Macandezulo to keep some other oath.

Chapter 21

Allyn awoke on a grass-filled mattress tick. Dawn gilded a window frame. The small room was empty of all but the bedding, a jug of water, Allyn, and a black woman asleep beside him. He sat up, naked and cold. The bed lay sheetless, the woman slight and without warmth. Allyn shook his head at himself. His clothes lay in a jumble on the floor. He rose gingerly to avoid disturbing the woman, a habit from life with Eva, a late riser.

He grabbed the gallon jug of water, gathered his clothes, and stepped outside. The dead village had not awakened, but a generator rumbled somewhere up the weedy street. Allyn moved into the slanting light, warming up, and poured half the water over his head, brisk and reviving. He scrubbed with his bare hands, then poured the rest. Allyn stood in the dirt street, in the sun, stripped and dripping until he felt dry enough to dress. He checked in pockets for his phone and wallet, found them both unmolested, and walked into Macandezulo.

The village had been deserted by its former owners but not by the bush. In two years of abandonment, the one-story shacks had begun to lose their balance; only a few stood straight. Sag and rot pecked at the place, while the bush laid a green claim everywhere, in kitchens and parlors, pushing up through floorboards, flowering on the roofs of homes, the small school, the rain gutters of a motor shop, under the dusty porch of a store. A single unpaved lane cut through the center of the village, flanked by smaller paths, all connected by alleyways. The stench of human piss and bowels fouled the alleys. Windblown trash cartwheeled down them. The garbage and stink and the hum of the generator belonged to Macandezulo's new residents.

Allyn walked down the center of the road, wishing he'd brought a hat and sunglasses. He headed toward the rumble of the generator, the power of Juma. Macandezulo had been partitioned into quarters; Juma assigned his Mozambican workers their housing by profession and desperation. In the tumbledown hovels on the eastern outskirts lived the poachers, twelve poor men accustomed to squalor. On the north side of the main street, four drug dealers lived in pastel houses closest to the well. Juma kept his four guards south of the road, in a dwelling of tin walls. Beside them, in the two-room schoolhouse, a pair of cooks lived and worked barbecue pits in the rusting playground. To the west, on the ground floor of a two-story cinder block structure with working windows and doors, once the village town hall, Juma made his lodging. The generator was for him to run his computer and modem, charge his phones, cool his beer. Juma stored weapons in the basement, with a henchman always stationed outside the building. Juma allowed only himself and his guards to be armed in Macandezulo. Those few officials in local governments who might cause him concern were on his payroll, and because he was fair and generous, rival gangs did not attack him. Any *impimpi* (informant) in the villages was rooted out and sometimes necklaced—murdered by being forced to wear a petrol-filled burning rubber tire around the neck. Eight young women from the border towns occupied the second floor of his blockhouse while they became addicted to drugs and turned into whores. Macandezulo had belonged to no one, and the animals did not want it, so Juma had taken it. Everything he brought here, and everyone, was for sale.

Several pickup trucks were parked haphazardly about the village. Each appeared ready to fall apart at the rivets from dents and hard use. A large machine gun had been welded to a pivot in the bed of the bakkie outside Juma's building. In the throb of the generator, Allyn rapped on the building's door, then sat in the lawn chair he'd gotten drunk in last night. A dozen cans lay about. Allyn took a swallow from one half-full can but spit out the flat beer. He spit again to erase the taste. Hunger and a rancid thirst made him knock again.

Behind the door, Juma's big, bare feet padded. He opened up wearing a shimmery, blue silk housecoat, holding a mug of water. Allyn sent him back inside for another.

Juma returned and joined Allyn outside, taking the second lawn chair. They sat as they had until midnight last night, except this morning Allyn was dressed in the clothes he'd arrived in, while big Juma sipped in silk as if he were at the Savoy. Last night, Allyn had been a little manic about being in Macandęzulo among cutthroats, poachers, and whores. He wasn't accustomed to beer, did not respect it, and drank too many too fast. Allyn wanted to know about everything around him, Juma's syndicate, how it worked, who the shadowy people were. He felt entitled because he'd financed much of this. Juma told him as much as he could until Allyn began to lean. He sent Allyn off to a house with one of the girls. Allyn had staggered once in the street, she'd caught him, and he did not recall her letting go.

Juma scratched his chest beneath the silk, leaving his hand to rest on the platter of his great belly.

"I despair, Allyn. What we have made of you."

"Do I look that rough?"

"Yes."

"Is there a change of clothes?"

"Yes. In Maputo, where I will send you after we finish our business."

A willowy girl in white pants and a pink bra drifted out of the building. Her black skin held no luster. Her eyes buttery, she stood behind Juma with a hand on his meaty shoulder. She asked nothing, needing silently. He patted her hand and nodded. The girl left without acknowledging Allyn, heading for the pastel houses in the sunrise.

Juma finished his water.

"I'll have the cooks roused. We have meat. I make it a practice not to ask what it is."

Allyn asked if he might see a rhino horn. Juma had none at the moment, but he intended to send a team into the Kruger tonight. Allyn wanted to stay another night, he had no one in Jo'burg waiting for him. Juma hedged.

"We'll see, shamwari."

Allyn was not used to this Juma, either, the one who may or may not grant his requests. The man commanded here, a king among thieves in Macandezulo. Juma's people had only what rights and protection he allotted. Allyn wondered if this was how Eva had felt.

While he and Juma waited in the lawn chairs to be fed, the main street of Macandezulo took on a shambling morning activity. Dark, tattered men in short pants, unbuttoned shirts, and sandals shuffled for the well or to relieve themselves in the alleys. Juma gave Allyn the names of the men he did not last night, their home villages, their crimes. "This one sells heroin, this one dagga and stolen pharmaceuticals. That one is blind in one eye but has a big family and will do anything. That one likes boys. This one is shy. That one is a killer."

More girls filtered down out of the block building. In the sharp morning they seemed unsure on their ebony feet, floating like wraiths. They wore sheer nightclothes, some immodest. Juma uttered each name as the girls trailed past: Marvelous, Beauty, Light, a tall one named Angel. Some touched Juma, and none, like the first, noticed Allyn.

"How do you find them? Where do they come from?"

Big Juma shrugged, as if to say where the women had been before Macandezulo was of no importance.

"They find me. These girls, the men"—Juma swept an arm across the street scene, his resurrected place—"they are all the same. The girls can't hunt, and no one would pay these men to fuck. They have no work in their villages, no skills. You and I were poor boys, too, we were born in shacks like them. But we were fortunate, we had the mines and each other. I pay the men better than they can earn doing anything else. Drugs, horn, doesn't matter. I could cheat them if I cared to. But I don't, so they stay. The women can't afford the drugs I make available to them. They stay until I place them into a village to work for me. If there are deaths, I pay the families. I provide for them all, no one goes wanting. I treat everyone well."

Breakfast arrived served on fan-shaped fronds, the leaves of a lala palm. Antelope meat had been browned and spiced, chapati bread served to scoop it up. The boy who brought the food was the one Juma had called shy, named Hard Life.

"Is it?" Allyn asked the boy before he turned away.

The boy stopped, not looking up from his dusky, bare feet.

"What, sir?"

"Is it hard? Your life?"

Hard Life would not reply, holding still until Juma gestured for him to speak.

"No, sir."

Allyn held out the palm leaf and breakfast to the boy.

"Take this. I can get some later."

The boy looked around, as though he'd heard someone calling him away. Eyes downcast, he left.

"Did I say something wrong?"

Juma motioned for Allyn to bring his offering back to his lap. Hard Life, just as the young women had, seemed to blow away like the refuse in the alleys.

"You misunderstand. These people do not take charity. They are poor, but only to you and me. They do not see themselves that way. They are poachers, whores, and dealers. But they work. This is their mine, shamwari."

The meat was strongly seasoned, smoky with cumin and nutmeg. The chapati tore easily, freshly baked. Eating, Allyn pondered what his name might be if he were one of Juma's people. Lush Life. Or maybe Alone.

The girls trailed back to the blockhouse, including the one Allyn had awakened next to. He didn't ask Juma her name. Before she passed he took from his wallet a thousand-rand note. He held it between fingers for her to pluck. She did, then, following the girls inside, dropped the bill into Juma's lap. Juma returned it to Allyn.

"I'm confused."

Juma stood, belting his long silk jacket.

"Which is why you should not have come. We'll go into the basement. You'll see our missile. We'll decide what to do. Then I will have you driven to Maputo and a hotel. You may fly home when you like."

Allyn rose, too. Down the street, one of the men in the pastel houses cranked a bakkie to life and drove away south, an early start to the day. Cook smoke curled from behind the schoolhouse, and several poachers shambled that way.

"No."

Juma had already turned on his slippers for the house. He didn't register Allyn's answer.

"I said no."

Juma halted with his broad, shiny back still to Allyn. He drew in a large breath, swelling with it, before rotating back to Allyn.

"What, shamwari?"

"I'll stay. Another day."

"Why would you do that? Even I don't want to stay here."

Because there was a great, empty house with more echoes than sound, more shadows than light, and an unchanging, starry lake. A mine that did not need him.

"I slept well last night. It's been a while."

"You were drunk. And with a whore."

Allyn would give Juma more money, for a guesthouse here in Macandezulo.

• • •

Allyn waited outside in the lawn chair while Juma washed and dressed. Morning insects in the scrub and weeds chirruped even louder than Juma's grumbling generator. Along the main street, black, glistening men came out to sit on stoops, set elbows to knees, and puff cigarettes or dagga. No one approached Allyn, though he was plainly Juma's important guest. Like the bugs, the men went through their routines and prepared for their daily tasks. Inside the blockhouse, the women waited to be used, sold, or further addicted to cocaine or crystal meth, called *tik* because of the sound it made burning in a pipe. Juma's people did have a hard life, a shell they had no means to break out of.

Juma emerged in a fresh linen tunic, cool cotton trousers, and leather brogans. He presented himself like the parent of the new children of Macandezulo. Four years older than Allyn, one and a half times his size, Juma thrived like a great tree, spread wide and rooted, luxuriant.

"Shall we go down to see our missile?"

Allyn followed him inside, down wooden steps to a steel door. Juma pushed into a large, dark expanse. He tugged the chain on a bulb to light a room of hard, gray, windowless walls.

Guns lay everywhere, on the concrete floor, leaning against every wall, stacked in piles. The mounds and rows of rifles and pistols, some long-barreled hunters with scope sights, and the machetes all looked like scrap to Allyn. He'd rarely been around firearms; they'd not been part of his youth in the mines or in business later. Nothing in this room called to his hands, none of the dark metal intrigued him. Nothing, except, there in the center of the room, alone on a scarred wooden table as if guarded by all the other weapons, the Hellfire missile.

A path had been cleared to it. Juma motioned Allyn forward.

The Hellfire seemed a model of efficient lethality. Allyn had grown up with explosives, trained as an engineer, and this rocket was designed to a sleek perfection. Four small fins forward, four larger ones framing the propulsion port in the rear, hard, green steel casing, glass face for guidance electronics and camera; the assembly probably weighed a hundred pounds. He'd seen on the news what this hundred pounds could do, such massive destruction with pinpoint accuracy.

Allyn placed both hands on the chilly cylinder. He chose not to speak his initial thought. It would sound silly, and it surprised him that on first seeing the rocket he considered buying it himself. He'd pay a fair price to Juma and sneak it home to Jo'burg to put in his own basement. Allyn had never been this close to anything more powerful. No machine or number in a bank, no ship or structure, he'd been near nothing the Hellfire could not ruin. But it wasn't ruin that attracted him; Allyn was not a destroyer. He walked his fingers down the missile like a spider. This was a thing of great worth and purpose. Owning it would be purposeless and valueless. Perhaps that was the appeal, doing something special and perverse, like keeping a tiger. Juma was the master of wicked Macandezulo. It would feel like that.

Juma loomed closer, impinging on him.

"What can we get for it, shamwari?"

Allyn bit back a rebuke. Juma had no romance for the missile or what it could do for them, or to them. The Hellfire was just another item to be sold.

Allyn patted the rocket, wishing it good-bye with regret. He turned for the door, looking past the heaps of niggling guns, little things any man could possess.

"I'll make a call."

Chapter 22

Neels and Karskie hauled the wheels and landing struts from the long crash rut. Promise was left aside to watch, as if she couldn't be trusted even to drag things. The Americans used all twenty sticks of dynamite, coating the drone with tape and explosives, stuffing one stick each into their parachute containers. When they were done the busted vehicle and collected bits looked pitiful and sorry, naively caught up in something beyond themselves, sentenced to die for it.

Neels helped the captain and LB with the fuses, using a big knife from his boot to cut matching lengths, then securing them to the sticks. He seemed to know what he was doing to make them detonate at the same time. Karskie stood to the side like Promise but not near her.

A band of curious eland appeared through the brush fifty meters off, eyeing the scene with a swishing detachment. Promise thought to warn them away, what a ranger would do, but she did not.

The Americans and Neels webbed the drone in gray strands of fuse that funneled down to one igniting piece. Promise grew thirsty, she'd not had water since the night. She called to Karskie, but the big boy said she'd have to ask Neels. Promise imagined Neels shooting her in the back if she wandered into the bush to find a drink.

She could run, lose herself easily in the Kruger. The old man wouldn't catch her, she had a dozen ways to vanish before he could get her in his sights. Even a superb tracker like Neels would lose ground to her. Promise could survive for days on her own.

Then what? After she'd escaped? She couldn't go home to Hazy View and Gogo or curl in her cot at the ranger station. She would never again ride with Wophule. Everything she'd ever held close or hoped for had fled when Neels walked out of the dark last night. No, when the drone crashed in Shingwedzi. No, not then. Before, when Gogo asked Juma for money.

No. No. Nothing and no one else. Only Promise. She'd made the choices. Others were poor, had families and dreams, had love like Wophule, but they didn't take the horn, didn't call the devil, didn't call Juma. Promise had left the path of her old life for a terrible and dark trail. It was leading to the one place she'd never wanted to be. On her own.

She saw herself standing inside the web of fuses, all lit and sparking around her, closing in to remove all evidence of her, too.

Chapter 23

Neels huddled with the Americans and Karskie. The girl was left alone. Neels pointed into the bush to make his point.

"As soon as it blows, we leave. I've got a two-man patrol out here somewhere in Shingwedzi. When they hear the blast, they'll come straightaway. I assume you don't want them to find two Americans standing next to a dead ranger's grave and a bloody great hole in the ground."

The captain took a satellite phone from his vest.

"Okay. Give me a few minutes."

He walked off. The thick, little sergeant indicated the girl.

"What about her?"

"She can't go with us."

The sergeant, as if by instinct, slid sideways, blocking Neel's path to Promise.

"No."

"If I was going to shoot the little moer, I would have done it. But understand me, Sergeant. I've shot men for less. Karskie's going to take her back."

The big boy tossed up his hands, defeated before he started.

"No, I'm not."

Karskie launched into his reasons. Sending her with him would be the same as turning her loose. He could never chase her down, couldn't shoot her if she made a break. Even if Neels bound her hands, Karskie couldn't do it.

Neels crossed his arms at the sergeant.

"You want to tell me your opinion?"

"I don't know. Maybe tie her up, leave her here. When your team shows up, have them take her back."

"They'll see Wophule's grave, and bits of the blasted drone all over the place. She'll have to lie. If my boys believe her, maybe. She's a shitty liar. I wouldn't bet on her chances, they don't like poachers any more than me. They don't like dead rangers. And that's only if something big doesn't come sniffing around to find her first."

"Then leave Karskie with her. He's got a gun."

Neels laughed at the suggestion. Karskie ignored the insult and shook his head even more vigorously when the sergeant implored him.

Promise strode their way. Neels's mouth dried as she approached. She stopped short, letting her voice cover the last of the distance.

"Let me go with you."

The American opened his mouth to reply. Neels cut him off, pushing in front of him to speak directly to the girl. The sergeant was short and bluff and did not move easily.

"Here's why you're not going. You're done. You know that. I'll see to it. There's one place left for you, girl, in the whole world. You want us to take you into Mozambique, to your uncle Juma. So you can run to him."

"I won't. I swear."

"You swear. Kak. What have you sworn? Tell me."

"To kill the man who shot Wophule."

Neels inched closer to the girl, inside arm's reach. He could strike her, she knew it, but she held her ground. He leaned in, his nose a hand's breadth from hers.

Could she do it? Kill a man? The rhino she'd taken down had been a great beast, a bull, dropped by a machete. He kept his voice low.

"Will you, now?"

She whispered, "Yes."

"What would you do if you were me? Tell me the truth, girl."

"I'm a poacher. Wophule is dead."

"Ja."

"I'd shoot me."

"That's right. But the Yanks over there won't let me. So now what?"

Promise extended her hand in the small space between them, for Neels to take it.

"I won't run."

"And what about your great-uncle Juma? You going to stop me from killing him?"

The girl could have been carved, so rigid was her expression and motionless her hand. Her black eyes, close to Neels, seemed to lose focus only for a moment, then softened on him. He'd seen this look in the Selous Scouts, in Angola and the Kruger, on the faces of the dying and the killers, a hardness that leavened into acceptance, always among the ones who sensed death was coming.

"No."

Neels gripped her small hand in a forceful, private bargain.

He turned to the short sergeant.

"She goes."

• • •

They waited for the captain to finish his satellite call. The rangy officer walked a small circle, lapping several times; he worked his free hand before him as if to brush away cobwebs. He seemed unhappy with the person on the line and could not sway the conversation. He did not glance back at Neels or his sergeant.

Promise sat beside Wophule, tending the boy's rock pile before leaving it behind. She filled in gaps where Neels had disturbed it with more sand and stone. The girl would never see her partner again, nor the Kruger, not from jail or her own grave, wherever today led her.

Karskie returned to the hedge, the place where he'd slept the night. He lay down again under the thorns.

The stocky sergeant could not stand quietly on his own. He fidgeted, checked the fuses in the dynamite, examined the Belgian rifle, ate more PowerBars. He watched his captain go round and round on the phone. He sweated badly, mopping and cursing. Neels had been like that once, impatient for the next bit of action, popping like water on a hot pan. Neels had been young and eager, proving himself. Years of reading the spoor of men and creatures had taught him to pace himself; there could be no impatient trackers. But this sergeant was not a young man. What was he proving?

The sergeant caught Neels looking at him. He walked over, as if Neels was the last item left to distract him. The man seemed uncomfortable, as did his captain, both out of place in the bush. Or perhaps their awkwardness came from being in military camouflage without any insignia at all, like a dress-up game.

The sergeant appraised Neels with a confidence Neels read as false.

"You look like you served."

"A while ago. The Border War."

"You married? Got a family?"

This would have felt intrusive if it had not been rote, this stumpy sergeant tossing off routine questions between strangers. Neels was expected to answer yes or no, then ask, "What about you, friend?" Or maybe explain that his wife had left him, then they might bond over shared miseries, planning out the beers they'd blather over later. Neels measured the American for a punch and imagined how nice it might feel to do it with no explanation. He crammed his lips together to shut his own mouth, listen to his own breath whistling in his nostrils. Neels walked away. The American wisely said nothing behind him.

Chapter 24

LB threw rocks as far as he could into the bush. He had to do something, move; everyone was occupied but him. Promise hunkered beside the grave, pouring grit on it. Wally argued on the sat phone with Torres, big Karskie had gone back to sleep, and old ranger Neels stalked around, seething at something in his head. LB aimed a stone at a gnarled tree to see if he could scare something out of it, a monkey or whatever, but got nothing. The sun rose fast here in Africa, and the scrubby Kruger, as far as he could see, was going to offer very little today, not shade or water, just dust, brush, and thorns.

The gray drone balanced on its nose and one wing, dull in the rising light, strapped to dynamite and condemned. LB threw another rock at the tree and thought about throwing one at the drone just to shake everybody up. He imagined lighting the fuses but not waking Karskie, just to see how high the fat boy would jump from sleep when the drone blew. Wally showed no signs of winding up his discussion with Torres, the ranger girl looked lost, and Neels snarled into the air, conducting some angry one-sided conversation. LB picked Karskie.

He moseyed over and sat close, waking the boy. Karskie snorted, then wiped his knuckles in his eyes as he came upright.

"We ready?"

LB shook this off.

"Wally's still working out our orders. Tell me something."

"If I can."

"What's going on?"

"Specifically?"

"With rhino horn. All this killing and money. I mean, in a word, fuck."

Karskie chewed on his thoughts, waking, considering where to begin. Right off, LB saw he'd asked a bigger question than he'd realized.

"First, understand that for a thousand years, traditional healers all over South Asia have said that horn would give energy, strength, that sort of thing."

"Supposed to be some kind of aphrodisiac."

"That was the big myth for a long time. Powdered and drank with water. No one believes it anymore. Now the healers just use it for hangovers."

"Tell me it doesn't work."

"Of course it doesn't work. A horn's nothing but keratinized fiber. Hair, like a horse's hoof. It's got zero medical properties."

"How bad is it? How many rhinos are you losing?"

"Over a thousand a year, and that's just in the Kruger. In the world, there's maybe five thousand wild black rhinos left, twenty thousand white rhinos. Both have already been declared extinct."

"Extinct? Come on."

"The deaths are greater than the birthrate. If we can't get a handle on the poachers soon, yeah. Extinct."

"This isn't about hangovers."

"No."

"Who's buying it?"

"Most of the horn goes to Vietnam. Then China, Korea, Indonesia."

"What the hell for?"

"There's a lot of money in Asia these days. The economies in China and Vietnam especially have gotten red-hot. That's made a rising class of rich, called the new dragons. They spoil their kids with horn, make it a graduation present. They mix it with Cialis and Viagra and Red Bull. They hang horns in their houses to show off their money. It's a prestige thing, like a Lamborghini or a Rolex. A sign of untouchability. China and Vietnam don't have rhinos of their own. Why would they care about someone else's?"

At least a car and a watch, even at obscene prices, did something useful. But to slaughter a rhino, decimate a species, for a worthless energy drink or a trinket was brutally senseless and selfish. LB had never seen a real rhino, not even in a zoo, and now he very much wanted to, particularly if they might be gone in a few years. He scanned the bush that stretched away in sere, ropey shapes, hoping for a hulking, prehistoric, horned beast prancing in the distance. Far off, a few heads popped above a line of trees, just grazing giraffes. LB considered asking Karskie what the chances of seeing a rhino were but didn't want to sound like a child or a tourist. He closed his mouth but kept open the hope.

He reached into Karskie's pack for a water bottle, partly to wash away the imagined bitter taste of powdered horn. Near the drone, Neels stared off into the plains with hands balled at his hips, quieter than he'd been, as if watching something disappear. Promise hid her face in her dark hands. Wally had begun to nod into the sat phone, finally hearing words he could agree with. LB wanted to know more from Karskie about the kind of men—and women, like sad Promise—they were about to go after.

"Tell me about poachers."

Karskie knew plenty.

Poachers crossed in waves into the Kruger, hundreds per week, all from bleak lives, equipped with machetes, sacks, and hunting rifles stolen from farmhouses. Most of them snuck over the porous border with Mozambique, while the rest came from neighboring townships inside South Africa. The poachers didn't work independently; large-mammal poaching was an organized crime, backed by international syndicates and big, illicit money.

A typical ring was set up in vertical tiers. It started at the bottom with a triggerman and his team. These were poor villagers who killed the rhino, then cut the horns off whole, with flesh attached to show the horns were fresh. To get the entire horn, including the root below the skin, the poachers had to hack deep into the rhinos' nasal cavities. If the rhino was still alive when they started cutting, this finished it.

LB gestured to Promise.

"That what she did?"

"Yeah."

"Geez."

Karskie continued. The shooter and his team hand delivered the horns to the next level up. This was their only connection to the syndicate, the transporter, the one who recruited them in their villages and was responsible for paying them. The transporter disguised the horn in legitimate shipments to Hong Kong, Hanoi, Jakarta, any number of Asian ports. Sometimes, cargo ships even waited offshore from Maputo, Cape Town, or Port Elizabeth to trade the transporter a load of drugs or diamonds directly for the horns.

LB said, "That's this guy Juma."

"He's the second tier in this syndicate, yeah."

"Who's the third?"

"The financiers. These are the big dogs. Transporters are hard enough to catch, but a level three is almost impossible to nail. This guy moves the money. He lives in Jo'burg or Cape Town. He's got offshore accounts in Dubai and Switzerland."

The money disappeared into a maze of businesses. It came out as dividends and capital gains, clean and laundered.

The last tier, level four, were the murky figures who received the shipments in Asia, the black marketers. In their hands, the horn was chopped into slabs or powdered, whatever the local market demanded, then sold to the end users. For the past decade, the street price for horn had outpaced pure cocaine, doubled gold, and risen as rhinos became scarcer.

Public campaigns had been mounted all over Asia, trying to raise awareness that their folly was destroying the world's greatest wild animals. The result was that the number of rhinos and elephants killed each year had exploded.

Karskie spit in the dirt.

"The cost of horn's gotten so high, even private wildlife reserves have been caught poaching their own rhinos."

Some greedy private-reserve owners pretended to discover the carcasses on their fenced-in grounds, then beat their breasts over how they'd been violated and held fundraisers for anti-poaching charities. They'd buy a replacement rhino from a breeder or another reserve for twenty thousand American dollars.

Some private owners had begun to dehorn their rhinos themselves, disfiguring the animals but protecting them. They registered the horns with the state, then locked them away for the day when selling horn became legal, a movement gaining steam in South Africa. A few speculators had cropped up, breeders raising rhinos not for display or preservation but to harvest the horn, which, if taken carefully, grew back. This was potentially a billion-dollar industry, which would increase the supply of horn and lower the price, pulling the rug out from under the poachers. But Karskie, who'd seen a few carcasses, agreed with the wildlife-preservation community that legalizing horn was a surrender to the poachers and an insult to the beast itself, reducing the rhino to the status of a chicken or a pig. LB saw both sides and said so, a mistake.

Karskie began to squirm, uncomfortable on the ground, his face registering disgust.

"Whatever it is, something's got to change. You need to understand, the rhino's just the marquee animal. If we lose them, the same syndicates will wipe out the elephant next."

Karskie described an awful event a few years ago, in Zimbabwe's Hwange National Park. Poachers laced water holes with cyanide, poisoning four hundred elephants at one time for their tusks. The boy tossed more terrible numbers at LB, how Africa was losing four elephants every hour, three rhinos per day.

"Here's the clincher. After the rhinos and the elephants are finished, the lion will be next, for lion-bone wine. Then the tigers for bone tea, sharks and great tortoises for soup, abalone for their shells. Did you know you can buy an ashtray made out of a gorilla's hand?"

Karskie had gotten passionate. LB was about to put his hands over his ears to signal he'd heard enough. Just then, finally, Wally stuffed the sat phone into his vest and headed their way. Karskie ratcheted up his intensity, getting in his last licks before Wally arrived.

"There's a shit ton of money in horn, and frankly, not much risk. The Kruger's basically a shopping mall for poachers. We should have two thousand rangers on the ground, but we've got four hundred. Less than half are on patrol at any time. When we find a carcass, our response is to track them. That's it, in the twenty-first century. That's the extent of our technology. Yeah, we have a few shot towers to catch the sounds of gunfire, we fly a drone here and there. But essentially, we catch poachers because men like Neels bloody track them down. When we do manage to catch poachers inside the park, all we can do is prosecute the poor bastards or shoot them. Either way, their families get paid off by the syndicate. There's no shortage of villagers who can fire a gun or swing a panga. In the end, there's not a lot of disincentive to poaching."

Neels had finished his agitated reverie and fallen in behind Wally. Promise, without being called, got to her feet. With dusty hands, she drifted away from her partner's rock pile.

LB aimed his chin at the girl.

"What's going to happen to her?"

"Jail, for a long time. Poaching. Accessory to murder."

"And what's his deal?"

"That man there? He's gone *bossies*, I'll give you that. Crazy. He's got rhino fever. Seen too much, been in the bush too long. But he understands this is a war. Neels is the disincentive."

Promise shuffled behind Neels, bowed and shamed. She was a plucky and clever girl, even pretty. If this was a war the way Karskie described it, no wonder Neels wanted to shoot her. She wore the same uniform as he did, a Kruger ranger, and had defiled it.

Still energized, Karskie hopped to his feet. The big boy had worked himself into a state and looked like he was raring to go. Wally walked past, curling a finger for LB to follow. LB took only one stride before Neels hooked a hand inside his elbow to drag him to a stop.

"Where you going?"

Wally answered while LB yanked his arm free.

"I'm going to brief my sergeant. If you don't mind."

"I do mind. Let me tell you a little something."

Wally's shining shades flattened his features when he turned to LB, who could only shrug. The two of them were helpless without Neels and had no power to compel him. Neels would gun Promise down before letting her out of his sight. Karskie was brainy but sure to be useless from this point forward.

Neels tapped his own breast.

"You see, lads, I'm going to Macandezulo whether you come or not. Me and the girl, even Karskie, we've got authority to cross the border in pursuit of poachers. I'm in pursuit of Juma. And Promise there? She'll have a word with the moer who shot Wophule."

Neels sauntered closer, pointing east to the Mozambican border, where he knew the way.

"I don't give a fok about your missile. That's your problem. So understand. I'm not going with you. You're going with me. And that's only if I say so."

Neels took a last stride, stepping between LB and Wally. He lapped heavy arms across their shoulders as if in a huddle. He volleyed a happy glance between them.

"See, if you two do tag along, you know my mission, but I don't know yours. Doesn't seem fair, ja? Or smart. So tell me what I need to know right now. Then let's light the fuses and get to it. Or good luck to you."

Neels did not pull down his arms until Wally and LB pushed them off. The old ranger folded his arms across his chest. Something out in the bush hooted; it was easy for LB to hear it as a laugh.

"Your call, Wally."

Neels waited only moments in Wally's reflecting glare before turning on his heels, heading for Macandezulo as he'd warned. Wally spoke to his back.

"There's a self-destruct charge on the missile."

Neels pivoted with a curious expression.

"I thought that was just in the movies."

"Not this time. It's so they could blow the drone over the ocean."

"Makes sense, since one of your missiles was on a South African drone. Why was that?"

"That I can't tell you. But use your imagination."

"I already have, lad. I've done a few covert missions in my time."

"Then you can figure out why we can't leave it with Juma."

"No, you can't." Neels liked this. "What's the range on the charge?"

"Fifteen miles line of sight. Ground to ground, I don't know. Depends on the terrain."

"Why not just walk a few more miles east? Macandezulo's not that far past the border. Blow it up. Kill the bastard for me."

Wally pursed his lips. He didn't answer Neels quick enough, so LB jumped in.

"It's not what we do. We're rescue. We don't endanger civilians, even at our own risk."

Neels swept the back of his hand at LB, dismissive.

"Civilians? Juma's no civilian."

"The people around him might be."

"Anybody with Juma is a fokken criminal. Period. Blow it."

Wally said nothing but seemed to replay something in his head. What that was struck LB. He whirled on Wally.

"That's what you were arguing with Torres over. That's what she wants you to do. Blow the missile from a distance. Don't go after it. She wants you safe."

"Yeah."

"What did you tell her?"

Wally lifted his chin off his chest.

"What you just said. It's not what we do."

This was no small thing. How could Wally put himself in harm's way, how could Torres send him there, if they were involved, if they were to be married? The complexities of this threatened to draw focus away from their present dilemma. LB patted Wally's shoulder to say he was sorry and he was proud that Wally had argued with her.

"What's our move?"

Neels and Karskie sensed nothing of the tug-of-war inside Wally. Promise gazed at him sadly, but her heart was gone, so the sadness was likely for herself.

Wally pointed at Neels, giving him the order, taking command.

"Light it."

• • •

The drone blew apart with a thunderclap and a concussion in the ground. No pieces sailed above the gouts of dust, at least none that LB could see, too pulverized were they by the twenty sticks of dynamite. A fireball of scorched black and shades of orange unfurled, feeding on the drone's fuel. The boom dissolved across the plains, plainly heard for miles in every direction. The bush was not startled by the blast but took the jolt into its vastness and reasserted silence and heat even while the red dirt rained and the fire burned out.

Neels didn't turn for the border until the cloud settled. Little remained of the drone or LB and Wally's parachutes, only a blackened crater and bits that the wind and rains would soon comb into the ground. Neels said nothing but clapped a hand on Promise's shoulder, pushing the girl east for Mozambique. He made her walk in front, to either shame her or keep a better eye on her. The girl was the only one of their company without a weapon. Next came Karskie, not so fierce behind the trudging girl; his was the first rifle in line should they meet something, or if the girl broke her word and bolted. Neels did this just to screw with Karskie, knowing he'd do nothing.

Neels strode in the middle. He told them not to worry about their tracks; his Shingwedzi extended patrol was certainly hurrying to the explosion, but they wouldn't follow any footprints away from the site. The Kruger boys would do as Neels had trained them, what Promise did not: call in the irregularity in their sector and wait. They'd stay with the body of their fellow ranger.

At the rear, LB and Wally walked side by side. Promise kept to the game trails, wending past weather-beaten shrubs, dense spiny hedges, and twiggy trees, many of them knocked crooked. Dung of every size and shape made their path a slalom. They dodged oblong beads, ebony balls, and green-tinted loafs. A smoldering pile of elephant dung burst into flame right in front of LB, ignited by gasses and the African sun. Neels turned back to stomp it out without comment; Karskie brightened and thought this marvelous. Promise kept walking. The old ranger shouted for her to stop until they could catch up.

Wally set the back of his hand against LB's gut to signal they should hang back, slow their gait so they could talk.

When Neels was far enough away, Wally checked his watch. "We got ten hours."

For what? Was the tritonol charge inside the Hellfire on a timer? That made no sense. Wally raised a finger for LB to let him explain without questions.

"The White House got a call this morning."

Wally had to be kidding. Had the stolen missile gone that far up the chain?

"Somehow, the president of Zimbabwe's gotten involved."

LB kicked at pieces of crap on the trail that looked like brown pickles.

"This gets more fucked up by the minute."

"LB, let me get it out."

Without clarification or reason, the president of Zimbabwe, neighbor to both South Africa and Mozambique, had informed the White House that he'd been asked by an anonymous party to broker a negotiation over a South African drone and an American Hellfire that had gone missing in Kruger National Park. The Zimbabwean asked for no explanations and offered none about how or why he'd been brought in. He said only that in good faith he wished to inform his counterpart, the American president, that this potentially embarrassing matter would be made to go away for a payment of $200 million paid in secret by midnight tonight.

Yesterday, on the plane, LB and Wally hadn't been able to contain their laughter at the outrageousness of this mission's machinations. Neither man cracked a smile now. Once the CIA's Pandora's box of plots was thrown open, no one could predict what craziness would fly out.

Rhino poachers had linked up with the president of Zimbabwe. Together they were actually blackmailing the United States. And the whole unlikely comedy of errors had landed in LB's and Wally's laps.

The official credo of the Guardian Angels was "That others may live." But the unofficial motto, grumbled among the GAs at times like this, was "You fuck up, we clean up." LB ran both hands through his crew cut.

"Who the hell is running this syndicate, Al Capone?"

"Torres says all we have to do is get close enough. She gave me the freq and the key code. Cover story is the poachers screwed up and blew themselves to pieces. Done. No one's expecting anything else from us."

"That's not our ROE. She knows it."

The rules of engagement governed the Guardian Angels' response to hostiles. These were made clear before every mission. Usually they were to evade, and engage only as a last measure. Regardless of what Torres or anyone three thousand miles away from the Kruger, the drone, dead Wophule, bat-shit Neels, broken Promise, Mozambique, Juma, and the stolen Hellfire said, every GA—including Wally and LB—had sworn to lay down his own life before endangering innocents.

"Why don't they just pay it? Two hundred million's lunch money."

Wally didn't answer, and LB didn't expect him to. The United States couldn't finance blackmailers, poachers, and crime syndicates, especially one that had already shown itself to be powerful and connected.

Also, unknown to the blackmailers or the president of Zimbabwe, the American president knew where the missile was.

LB had no issue with getting rid of bad guys. The challenge on this mission was making sure no one else got hurt. The danger was that only LB and Wally seemed to care.

Walking ahead of them, Neels glanced over his shoulder. He seemed displeased to be left out of the conversation but strode on, staring backward at them.

"We'll need eyes on."

Wally agreed with a nod. LB stepped around a fresh dung heap reeking a grassy odor.

"How do you figure to do it?"

Wally gazed far ahead, past scowling Neels and soft Karskie. "The girl."

Chapter 25

Promise knew the way east to the border. She could lead them across to Macandezulo, too, but Karskie said he would find the village. He'd told her this while walking at her back. He said he knew it from looking at maps for hours every day. Karskie needed a role, and Promise had no reason to take it from him.

She wasn't leading the Americans and Neels to Mozambique. Not yet. She headed northward, but trended east so Neels wouldn't notice and stop her.

The first sign had been a midden; lumps had been kicked around and busted open, releasing the scent. Soon after, snapped branches showed in the heavy brush where only a thick-hided thing could go, followed by the aroma of wild sage and rosemary from broken leaves. Then, where the game trail joined another, two fat, new prints crossed her path.

Promise glanced behind her. Karskie followed closely, as if he were in charge of her. He smiled. What was this large, wobbly boy doing here? Why did he smile? Didn't he know she was to be despised? Twenty strides behind him, Neels had tugged down the brim of his hat against the climbing sun. Promise could be gone in a flicker, into the acacia thorns again, and then run all the way. There she'd wait for Neels, who would quickly catch up. But why risk running? Neels was paying more attention to the Americans than the ground; he'd missed the rhino's tracks. He hadn't noticed that Promise was not leading them to the border. She could walk, and they would follow, to the water hole.

White balls of dung on the path told Promise the first beast she would meet was a hyena. Promise found her in a clearing beside the trail. The hyena reclined in a hole she'd scooped out to have her pups. Promise stopped at a distance when the spotted creature showed her teeth. The hyena was patience, she did not judge, she was the eater of death. Karskie came beside Promise and muttered in amazement. Neels and the Americans stopped, too. Neels told them a story about the time he'd seen a hyena snare red-hot cans of beans out of a campfire and bite them in half.

Neels told Promise, "Go around." Then, lightly, he shoved her. She did not check the Americans' faces for sympathy but walked on, heading more northward than before.

Promise crossed an open field where the earth ticked with heat. The stringy branches of grazed-out trees gave little shade to the grassy ground. The sapphire sky was an open eye on her. The stench of a days-old kill hinted a carcass was near the trail. She found it beneath a bush where a lion or cheetah had dragged it, the skull and horns of an impala and an empty, sun-leathered hide.

The second beast was an elephant far across the plain, a medium male out on his own. Strolling, he flapped his great ears. The elephant was wisdom. He knew the day he would die.

Drawing closer to the water hole, the grassland gave way to fever trees and a cooler breeze. A family of baboons gathered on a fat branch, hiding in the leaves. The baboon was the cheater and trickster. Promise opened her mouth wide to them, a sign of submission. A young one dropped to the ground, curling fingers at her, begging. The rest of the baboons scratched blandly and watched her pass.

Two hundred meters from the water hole, still unseen behind the brush, a warm dampness sifted into the air with the smell of mud. Neels stomped past Karskie.

"What the hell are you doing?"

This time Neels pushed Promise to the ground.

"You got an ambush in mind, girl? Uncle Juma out there waiting for us?"

The Americans ran up. Karskie stayed back from trouble. Neels raged over her. Promise stayed in the dust.

The captain and LB hurried in front of Neels, walling him off. She scooted on her backside, retreating enough to climb to her feet. LB turned on her.

"What's up?"

Neels growled before she could answer.

"She's taking us the wrong way." He jammed a hand southeast. "Macandezulo's there. Karskie?"

The big boy nodded. "I think he's right."

LB offered open hands to Promise, showing he had nothing to defend her.

"What do you want me to do? Where you taking us?"

"To the water hole."

"Why?"

Neels barked. "A fokken trap."

The captain lowered his sunglasses, looking at her above the rims. His blue eyes were set in crinkles, like bird eggs on straw.

"Talk to us."

"This is Shingwedzi. My sector."

Neels almost choked on something indecipherable.

Promise walked on, leaving it to the Americans to control Neels. Why should she explain herself? Nothing she could say would matter. She pushed straight into the thick hedge, turning her shoulders and hips, taking more cuts on her bare arms and knees. She did this to make them follow and hurt themselves or dash around the scrub to catch her.

Promise exited the hedge, alone for the moment. Neels dashed the long way, old and heavy legged, making a ruckus with his curses and gun. The Americans and Karskie ran with him.

She headed straight for the water hole, incautious about her approach or the direction of the wind. Three female lions lounging near the water's edge reacted first, yawning pink tongues and long teeth. They were power and courage. Promise lengthened her strides, unsure how long she had before she'd be taken away. Five zebras and six small springbok lifted their mingling heads. Cunning and speed.

Neels shouted, gaining ground on her. The animals shivered at the harshness of his voice, but none ran away. The rhino she'd tracked to the water hole lay in the shallows on its belly, resting on wet, folded legs. A young male cooling himself, he slowly turned his horned head and golden, lashed eyes to Promise. She sped to reach the water.

It was not the Americans but Karskie who intercepted Neels. The boy, lumpy and ungainly, put himself in front of the old ranger, arms out. He told Neels there was plenty of time, the village was not so far away. Let her say good-bye. She's fucked.

Promise didn't acknowledge this—again, nothing she could say, even thank you, would change anything—but eased her gait while nearing the water's edge. Every animal watched her step to the spot where days ago she'd buried her bloody clothes. She stood on her sin. Everything she cared about was here around her, the bush, the creatures, everything but Gogo and Khulu. She could not tell her grandparents, so she spoke to their old gods.

She lowered herself to her knees, sinking into the mud. She said to the young rhino, "Forgive me."

Promise searched herself to say more, but this was enough. The zebras bobbed their heads as if they understood. The lions spread themselves in the sun, satisfied. The dim-sighted rhino did not turn away but pricked up its ears at LB sloshing forward to stand close to Promise.

"I've never seen one before."

Promise wanted no company. The rhino, too, was alone. He was strength and endurance. He was ancient, surviving in his primitive form. The sergeant folded his arms and stayed quiet, admiring.

Promise made to stand. LB, who'd come to fetch her, touched her shoulder.

"Take a minute. It's okay."

Promise, despite herself, patted the American's muddy boot beside her.

Chapter 26

Late in the morning, some of Juma's girls tidied up the bottles and cans in front of the blockhouse. Allyn didn't speak to them, though they did things to allure him. He caught only glimpses of Juma shuttling in and out of the blockhouse. Left alone in the rumble of the generator, Allyn began drinking again in the lawn chair.

He sat for hours as the day warmed. Juma ran out of beers too quickly, before Allyn could get drunk. He didn't seek shade but let himself perspire in his clothes. Allyn couldn't recall the last time he'd lain on a beach or relaxed by a pool with Eva. Even on the deck behind his mansion beside the lake, he stayed under an umbrella, concerned the sun would age him. In sparse Macandezulo, the sunlight glowed ruby through his closed eyelids, the color of a blood orange. Sweat dribbled down his back and throat into his already-moist shirt. The flesh of his cheeks and arms tingled and reddened. Allyn sought these sensations, he wanted the change.

During the morning call with the president of Zimbabwe, Juma had beamed with pride at Allyn, his old protégé. The president decried the duplicity of America over this affair of the missile and the drone; he sympathized as if Allyn were acting out of civic duty. The president agreed to negotiate the deal and set the price at two hundred million dollars. The president would keep a 50 percent broker's fee.

Juma could barely contain himself, he'd not imagined this kind of sum. Allyn hushed him. The president ended the call by saying the deadline for the ransom should be midnight tonight. Allyn challenged this as too fast to arrange that amount; the old politician and crook called the number a pittance. The time must be short, to leave America no chance of finding the missile and sending a team of assassins.

When Juma heard this, he emptied Macandezulo of all but the women, his four guards, and Allyn. He opened his basement arsenal and distributed rifles and unlocked the ammo cabinet. In teams of two, he sent his poachers, drug dealers, and whoremongers, even the cooks, to the perimeter of the abandoned village, with orders to stay on guard until tomorrow morning. That was why there wasn't enough beer left for Allyn. In one of Juma's hurried passes, he propped a loaded rifle against Allyn's lawn chair. It stood there, like Allyn, untouched and heating in the daylight.

There was nothing to do but wait and sun. He could toy with the women, but the thought of grappling in the heat and salty sweat lacked appeal; he'd save that for the darker, cooler hours spent on the straw mattress waiting for word of the payment. Allyn let the women slide by when they walked from the blockhouse to the well or to the alley to relieve themselves. Their shadows crossed him, fingers slipped across the top of his head; many times he did not open his eyes. Allyn silenced his cell phone when the mine rang him twice. He checked his watch, an expensive item. Any of the men in Macandezulo would have knocked him senseless for it on a dark Jo'burg street but not here, not where he was one of them.

Just after noon, Juma returned to the blockhouse. He disappeared inside long enough to emerge with a steel canister from the basement. The big man stepped up onto the bed of the bakkie; his weight pressed it down to the tires. Deftly, he loaded an ammunition belt into the mounted machine gun, then eased his great frame down. The worn truck springs sighed.

Juma joined Allyn in the lawn chairs. Despite stomping around the village for hours, he'd not sweat at all. Juma beheld his old friend with a shaking head.

"We should move you inside, shamwari. You look to be frying."

"I'm fine."

"Perhaps I should throw a bucket of water on you."

"You can throw a bucket of champagne on me tomorrow."

"Fifty million dollars each. It's quite a thought."

The two had no beers, and the cooks were on patrol. There was nothing to watch in the emptied village, and little breeze. More sweat drizzled into Allyn's clothes. He thought he might take them off and sit nude in the sun, like a steam bath. Who would see him but Juma and the whores?

"Is it always like this?"

"Is what always like this?"

"Crime."

The expanse of Juma's chest jiggled. He knit his fingers.

"It's a game of hide and seek. The one who hides has little to do after he's in his hiding place. The seekers make all the effort. We've done what we did. Now we wait. They look."

"Will they find us, Juma?"

"No." Juma shook his head with closed eyes and a pursed lower lip. "No."

"What about your contact? The one you left alive."

Juma considered this, tapping his belly.

"You ask about crime, yes?"

"Yes."

"A criminal must know human nature. His life and freedom depend on knowing how to turn a person away from what they thought was right. My contact in the Kruger is poor and needs my money. He is gifted but very unappreciated. And I have had a ranger killed at his feet."

Juma meant that he did not trust his contact so much as owned him. He and Allyn were safe. But Juma did not say these things. Juma had put twenty guns around Macandezulo, and his big machine gun was loaded. To say they were completely safe would have been a lie.

Allyn wanted to be in this place, but he wanted a drink, too, to leave it a little.

Juma got to his feet.

"I have more to do. You'll be alright here?"

"Fine."

Moving behind him, Juma lifted the rifle to lay it across Allyn's lap. The metal and wood were warm on Allyn's legs, as if the gun had already been fired.

Chapter 27

Neels made it clear to the girl that another misstep or lie would be at the cost of her life. He told her to head to the border, nowhere else. Neels moved Karskie to the middle of the line and stationed himself behind Promise, rifle in hand.

In the last several years, he'd not spent enough time in Shingwedzi. He'd tried to let the younger men have it, had trained them to act in his stead. He'd tried to have a wife and a house, to leave the bush to others. But the animals continued to die without him, and the roars late at night were only his own and his wife's. A desk was not the veld, a lamp was not the sun. Neels did not cheer up on the trail, for he had no faith he could even spot the traces of cheerfulness in his life anymore. He clamped his teeth and pushed on toward violence, knowing he was just.

Promise led them at a confident pace. She never looked over her shoulder, as if she were walking alone. She snagged leaves from a giant jade and chewed them for the water and vitamins. Passing the plant, Neels did the same.

Behind Neels, Karskie held his own. The big boy seemed lost in his thoughts, like Promise. Only the Americans talked quietly to each other.

The game trails dissipated as they neared the border. Promise entered a patch of hip-high grass where pods hitchhiked on their legs. The grasses bled into a dry streambed, a moonscape of stones and amber dust where the fence had fallen to the spring rains long ago and had not been repaired.

On the verge of the border, Neels called a halt. Karskie sought out a shrub to sit beneath its shade. Promise waited, dark and quiet as a well. Neels addressed the Americans.

"Macandezulo is four more miles, east along this ravine. We've got a few choices."

The captain spoke.

"They are?"

"You hit a button and blow the damn thing right from here. Or we wait until dark."

The tall man turned his sunglasses skyward, checking the sun.

"Another eight hours. Can't wait that long."

Neels extended an arm at Karskie.

"Hey. Karskie."

The big boy stopped guzzling water.

"What?"

"Is Juma stupid?"

"Likely not."

Neels brought the arm around, as if handing Karskie's observation to the captain.

"Juma's not stupid. If he's got an operation in Macandezulo, he'll have guards out. We can't just stroll in. So, if you don't want to wait until nightfall, the choice is made. Blow it now."

"What if Juma's nowhere near the missile? I thought you were so hot to kill him yourself."

"Oh, have no doubt, Captain. Your rocket might take care of him. That's fine with me. If it doesn't, it'll at least wreck something of his. But I know who the bastard is now. Where he is. Juma's dead by your hand, or later by mine."

"We need to get closer."

"How close?"

"Enough to see it."

What was this mad Yank saying? Was he going to fight his way into Macandezulo in broad daylight? Impossible with just the three of them, plus a woman and a boy who'd shoot off his own foot. Neels explained again that they were here at his consent, and he wasn't going to trade bullets with Juma's boys at high noon like an American cowboy.

"I'm telling you to blow it. Either that or I turn you around. Choose."

The tall captain dug into his web vest for a handheld radio. The thing wasn't much bigger than a delicatessen sandwich with an antenna. He held it between them.

"See this? It's a low-wattage radio. Made for team communications only, not much power. The destruct charge on that missile is wired to an air-to-air frequency. Its range is based on line of sight, with nothing in the way. My radio on that high-end frequency isn't strong enough for long range, not used ground to ground. Even if I wanted to detonate it from here, I probably can't. There's vegetation, terrain, maybe buildings between me and it. I need line of sight. I need to be close."

"How close?"

"I don't know, not until we figure out where Juma's holding the missile."

The captain tucked the radio away. The stocky sergeant stepped beside him. In unison, both Americans took their weapons—the ones Neels had brought them—into their hands.

"Now let me be clear. We've got orders, and they don't include waiting until dark. We're going to Macandezulo now. Promise, can you get us there?"

The girl's dim pulse barely seemed to quicken. She looked at Neels without defiance or temper.

"Yes."

"Where's the border?"

She pointed east along the dry ravine.

"Right there."

The sergeant hooked the girl by the arm and pulled her behind him. The captain kept talking; he was the sort of man Neels had followed in the Scouts. Grim, and like he'd said, clear.

"You do what you have to, Neels. Come or stay."

Shouldering the strap of his own rifle, Neels almost called the man sir.

"Macandezulo in the middle of the afternoon?"

"That's right."

"You got a plan?"

"I do."

Beside the captain, the sergeant jerked as though a shock had gone off in his feet. He opened his mouth but shut it after catching a faceful of the captain's shining sunglasses.

Neels spread his hands.

"Let's hear it."

The captain gestured to Karskie, who was on his arse, listening intently from under the shrub.

"Mr. Karskie?"

The boy reared at his name the way a big-eared kudu would at the first sound of danger.

"What?"

"I need you, son."

Chapter 28

Wally took charge. He left Promise in the front of the line but put LB behind her, Karskie in the middle, then himself. Neels trailed. The old ranger had struck up another of his one-sided arguments with the air. LB was losing confidence that Neels was bolted together tightly enough.

With guilty determination, Promise trudged over the border into Mozambique, like she was going to the gallows. She had every reason to break into a dead run and not look back. She could rush ahead to warn Juma that Americans were coming, that the missile he was holding for ransom was rigged. Juma could throw it in a truck and hightail it out of Macandezulo, way beyond the reach of Wally's little radio. She could go into hiding with Juma, save her own life along with his. If he did manage to pull off this massive blackmail, he was going to be rich past LB's ability to imagine. Promise would be in line for some gratitude. She could buy her grandparents a house from afar, then hide forever from Neels and his justice.

But the girl crossed the downed fence without a word or glance up from her boots. She continued over the amber dirt of the ravine under a noon sun that had grown tiresome. LB had nothing to console Promise, and he wanted to, for taking him to the water hole, the wild marvels he saw there: lions, zebras, antelope, and the young rhino that had looked at him almost drunkenly. The big beast had stood graven in the water, heavily sure of itself, armed with long horns and a ton of muscle, unaware of its own danger and everything Karskie had said, as if the bush were not being overrun with long rifles and machetes. LB had been moved at the sight, he was moved now, but he could not step beside Promise to thank her. He'd knelt beside fighting men, hopeless and dying men, and had never once been unable to comfort them somehow. LB had never seen anyone as alone as Promise. He followed her into Mozambique.

Behind them, a hundred feet of steel fence lay on its face, tangled wires and rusted posts, neglected and useless. On this side of the border, the earth turned stony, unnourished and untrammeled, the plants sparse and ugly, every tree scraggly and spooky. While the Kruger had not been welcoming, Mozambique shouted, "Go away."

For three and a half miles in the dry creek, they saw no creatures, not a bird, nothing scurried out of their way. At the back of the line, Neels stopped mumbling. Karskie drained his water bottle and asked for more. That was it for talking.

When Promise finally stopped walking, LB almost bumped into her, mesmerized by the sameness of the bleached terrain. Karskie lumbered up and agreed they were a half mile west of Macandezulo. This was where Wally had said they would split up. This was the moment LB had been waiting for to argue with him.

Neels completed the circle. He surveyed their surroundings, seemed calmer and more focused.

"Captain."

"What?"

"I go."

"We talked about this. I need you in reserve. I got it."

Before Neels could repeat himself, LB jumped in.

"Look. This sounds weird because he just said the same thing, but you need to stay behind."

"No."

LB retreated, gesturing for Wally to follow him so they could have a private debate. Neels wagged a finger, insistent.

"Enough of that. You two talk in front of us. We're all in this."

Wally held his ground. LB had no choice.

"Alright, fine. I'm saying let me and the kid handle it. You hang back with Neels. Something goes wrong, you figure out the next plan. Tactics is what you do. Call Torres. She'll tell you the same thing."

"Is this about Torres?"

"It's about a lot of things. Mostly it's about us taking two good shots at this if we need to."

"That's what we're doing. Me and Karskie first. Then you and Neels."

"It's got to be me."

"Why you?"

LB grabbed Wally's arm to tow him away in the ravine. Neels objected. LB whirled on him.

"Fuck you. Shut up."

When he'd dragged Wally far enough, LB dropped his voice.

"You're the captain. You're my oldest friend. And, yeah, you're getting married. None of that matters right now. Listen, if we do need backup, you really think that obsessive asshole over there won't do something nutso? I don't know what to do with the guy. You stay with him, he respects you. If me and Karskie don't pull it off, the two of you can get it done. Me? I'll shoot Neels if you make me stay back with him. I swear. Five minutes in, I'll shoot him."

Wally worked his jaw while training his shades on the old ranger. LB tapped his own chest.

"You've sent me in a hundred times. I always come back, don't I?"

Wally made a thirsty, smacking noise. He took a swallow from the canteen on his hip, then offered it to LB, who accepted.

"Give me your radio," Wally said.

LB took a draft, returned the canteen, then gave Wally the handheld from his vest.

"The missile's on two hundred sixty-one point one."

Wally dialed the frequency knob.

"The code is five-four-three-one-zero. Don't be standing there when you hit zero."

Wally set the radio in LB's palm.

"I want a really good wedding present."

"I'll stay sober at the reception."

"Done."

"Wally."

"Now what?"

"How about the girl?"

"You trust her?"

LB glanced at Promise, who stood separate from Neels and the big boy. She'd crossed her hands in front of her, hanging her head as if in prayer.

"I don't know. If she wanted to take off, she'd have done it by now. Keep an eye on her. Keep Neels off her."

"I'll try."

LB and Wally rejoined the others. Karskie left his rifle with Neels; LB refused to be unarmed. Karskie mopped his brow on his bare arm. LB stepped up to him, a fist on the boy's sloping chest.

"You good?"

Neels spoke for him.

"He's good."

This brought a pinched smile to Karskie's lips.

"I suppose I'm good, then. Shall we?"

Karskie took the first steps. LB joined him.

Like an automaton, Promise fell in behind them. Neels stabbed a finger at the girl, but he aimed his surprise at Wally.

"What the fok is this?"

Wally told Promise to stay back. She shook her head.

"Juma won't believe you. He will believe me."

Neels lunged for her.

"You're going nowhere, you little *lafaard*."

Before LB could move, Promise dodged Neels's grasp. She skipped around him, looking ready to box, on her toes, nimble and resurgent. She spit her words.

"Touch me again, old man."

LB grabbed her by the back of her tunic. He tugged her off balance, away from Neels, who looked ready to slug her. Wally jumped between them. Karskie flapped his long arms, already frightened, now flustered.

LB swung Promise toward Macandezulo; she stumbled when he let her go. How could he leave her behind with Neels and that amount of hatred? If LB did wind up needing Wally, he'd need the old ranger, too, and fast. Better to separate Neels from the girl, if for no other reason than to keep him quiet.

Besides, she might be right about Juma. LB stomped close. She balled and unballed her hands, leaning as if she might charge Neels, fired up and fed up.

"Stop it."

Promise throttled her tension back enough for LB to speak in a normal tone.

"You know we're putting our lives in your hands. Yeah?"

"Yes."

"And?"

"My word is not worthless."

"You've broken your word. Recently."

This slapped Promise, as LB intended. More of the girl's truculence drained away.

"I know."

"But now you're telling me you'll keep it. That right?"

Promise's eyes flexed; something behind them snapped into place, hard.

"I will. To Wophule."

LB eased his own challenging stance.

"What did that mean? What he called you. Lafaard."

"Coward."

"He's not even close. How do you say dickhead?"

"Pielkop."

"I'll hang onto that one. Listen to me. This is serious. Juma's not going to be glad to see you."

"I know."

"You keep it together. Follow my lead. Nothing else. Can you do that?"

"I can."

"We're there to get rid of that missile. Anything else will have to wait. I know you're pissed. But I got a mission, and nothing, not me, not you, not Wophule, comes before that. I mean it. Understood?"

"Yes."

"And let me give you some advice. You got enough to worry about. Don't make it worse thinking about killing somebody. It'll take care of itself if he's that big a creep."

"I won't interfere."

"That as good as I'm going to get?"

"Yes."

"I guess it'll have to do. Walk."

Promise joined Karskie, facing east along the dry creek to Macandezulo. LB left his pack behind and shouldered the rifle. He tossed Wally a thumbs-up. Neels had turned his back.

• • •

LB didn't believe in signs, but buzzards wheeled in the blue distance. What could have died, since he'd seen no animals since crossing the border? LB had been in shit holes before, rescue missions in desert wastes and high, airless buttes; dead salt basins; and frothing oceans. But vacant, sun-warped Mozambique took a spot near the top of the list of forbidding places LB would try to avoid in the future.

He slogged on between Promise and Karskie. The girl spoke first.

"You should not have brought your weapon."

LB answered, his eyes on the buzzards.

"I disagree."

"I've seen Juma's men. They're bushmen. We won't know when they are close. They may shoot first."

Again, the girl had a point.

"Karskie."

"What?"

"What color underwear do you have on?"

"Beg pardon?"

• • •

When Promise refused to carry the long stick, she smiled for the first time since dawn. LB couldn't do it, either, he needed both hands ready. With a hefty sigh, Karskie accepted the added indignity.

The big boy hoisted the branch high into the hot day, his white boxer shorts attached to the end. Advancing through the ravine, Karskie waved the stick back and forth more than necessary. LB focused on the bush and hoped Juma's men would arrive soon. Karskie muttered a series of poor jokes at his own expense, then hushed. The meager bush sizzled, and their boots kicked red puffs of dust.

LB could not have told how they snuck up on him. Beneath the buzzards and the undershorts, his attention might have waned. But the clack of a bolt sliding a round into a long barrel was unmistakable. LB sensed the crosshairs finding him. He raised his hands before the voice reached out.

"Drop your gun."

Karskie turned his boxers in the direction of the voice, waving furiously. LB pushed the boy's arms down.

"That's enough. Lower it. Jesus."

Before dropping the stick, Karskie tugged his underpants off the end. Clutching them, he lifted his own hands, oblivious and scared. Promise didn't raise her arms but keyed in on the exact place where the poachers emerged. Two dark men appeared behind a large rock, stepping out of the heat ripples above it. Far off, the buzzards circled behind their heads.

One man was small, burdened with an AK-47 that looked too heavy for him. The other, his dark limbs like dead branches, came with a hunting rifle up at his oleo-colored eyes, finger on the trigger. He wore a leopard-pelt poncho.

Beside LB, Promise muttered, "Thank you."

"Who're you thanking?"

"The old gods."

LB had no time to consider this. The leopard-skin shooter advanced quickly, insisting with both his voice and gun that LB drop his own rifle. The little one with the AK-47 seemed to brighten as he approached, smiling at Promise.

With hands still high, LB whispered, "You know these guys?"

"Yes. The tall one, Good Luck, he will die."

So this was the poacher who'd shot her partner.

Without lowering the hunting rifle from his cheek, the shooter stopped ten strides away. He looked to know how to use it, and his barrel did not waver from LB's chest.

"Promise. I did not think to see you again."

Good Luck spoke with a lisp, without front teeth.

"Tell your friend to put his gun on the ground, or I will kill him. Friend, listen to her. She knows."

Keeping his palms facing out, LB eased down his hands.

"I'm Master Sergeant DiNardo. United States Air Force."

"If this is true, why do you have nothing on your uniform? No flags, no patches."

"It's a secret that I'm here."

"Whoever you are, I tell you a last time. Put your gun down."

The only thing that could make Mozambique worse was being weaponless. LB hesitated too long. Good Luck stuck out his tongue.

Promise moved in front of LB, making a beeline to the shooter. She stopped with her breast inches from his muzzle.

"Juma will bury you with your head between your legs if I tell him so. This American has come to see the missile. Take us to Juma. Now."

Behind the hunting rifle, the poacher's smile was black. The animal skin over his shoulders and his fanged grin gave him the look of a big, wicked cat.

"Juma will not know you were here if I bury you, Promise. And your secret Americans."

"Not an American." Karskie waggled his underwear to get attention. "South African. Thank you."

Neither Promise nor the hunting rifle gave way. Good Luck appeared to despise Promise as much as she loathed him. Next to them, the little one, not much more than a child, seemed unable to lift his Kalashnikov to enter the fray on either side. This was no stalemate. It was about to get worse.

LB waved his own hands.

"Okay, okay. Here, look."

He shed the strap of the ranger R-1 from around his neck to set the gun down. Good Luck sent the small one to snatch it up. The boy did this, blinking relieved eyes up at LB. He struggled to haul the gun away.

The shooter lowered his hunting rifle, satisfied.

"I've never met an American."

"Well?"

"You look fat. Who is this?"

Karskie spoke for himself. "Donald Karskie, SANParks."

"Are you here for the missile, too?"

"Yes."

"Lower your hands. Are those underpants?"

"Oh, for fuck's sake. Yes."

"Put them on or throw them away. You look foolish."

Karskie snorted. "I suppose a leopard skin is the rage in your village."

The lanky shooter gaped, flaring his red gums first at LB, then Promise, looking for someone to tell the big boy to shut up and do as he was told. LB poked Karskie.

"One of us is going to shoot you. Do it."

Karskie made Promise turn her back before dropping his pants. LB looked away, too. Good Luck's little helper covered his mouth to giggle politely.

When Karskie was dressed again, the shooter instructed the little one to search the three of them. Karskie dwarfed the boy while his pockets were being patted. Promise let herself be touched. The boy seemed in awe of LB, who barely felt the boy's touch on his legs.

When he was finished, Good Luck turned them east. The little one almost dragged the two rifles through the dust. Promise spoke to him gently and followed, then Karskie and LB, who walked the ravine unarmed and unidentified, a murderer at his back. On the way to Macandezulo, he saw the buzzards, gone from the sky, had clustered in a gloomy, leafless tree.

• • •

Several times the poacher Good Luck barked at Karskie to be quiet. The big boy talked to calm himself, and when he could not he seemed out of kilter. LB worried that Karskie would trip himself and fall, then Good Luck would simply plug him and leave him. Promise slowed to walk beside the big boy, even laying a hand on his back. LB imagined her doing this for an animal, consoling it; she seemed a natural empath. Killing a rhino with a machete didn't fit this girl.

The little poacher looked to be the epitome of African poverty, a thin and willing boy, probably smart. He wore threadbare clothes, with plastic sandals under cracked, calloused heels. Unlike the shooter who marched them at gunpoint, this boy seemed caught up, snared into poaching and guns, with few choices to escape his poverty. This didn't make him innocent, only sad and ordinary. Promise called him Hard Life.

The short distance to the village remained lifeless; other than the buzzards, nothing stirred in the bush. The land looked like a bone picked clean, pale and brittle. To live here, to have anything on your back, in your belly, or over your head, you'd need to scrabble every day. You could wind up like Good Luck, kill for money, wear an animal's skin, and hate. Or like Hard Life, and serve.

LB looked for ways to keep his silent tension from mounting on the walk to Macandezulo. Typically, waiting in copters or Humvees before jumps, rescues, even combat, he and the rest of his GA team slept or listened to headphones. They marshaled themselves. But with Good Luck's gun at his back, jittery Karskie relying on him, Promise so unpredictable, and a bleak landscape, LB had little to distract himself. He envisioned how annoying Neels was being to Wally right now. That helped a little.

They entered the outskirts of the village. Good Luck shouted "Juma!" just as LB became aware of the first structures. The gray scrub obscured the remnants of a few abandoned hovels that had caved in to the elements. Broken window glass glinted, tin roofs canted awkwardly, pastel walls rotted. The dirt of the bush gave way to a dirt street. At the far end, the rusty hulk of a pickup truck sprouted a mounted machine gun from its back. The muted tapping of a generator made the only reply to Good Luck's call.

LB fingered the radio tucked in his vest. He might be in range now. He could try to blow the Hellfire. Somewhere in the ruins of Macandezulo, the blast would be terrific. In the street, LB would win a tussle with Good Luck; the little poacher boy was no threat. Juma would go to hell, or not. LB, Karskie, and Promise could scoot out of the village, back down the ravine to Neels and Wally, then over the border to the Kruger and safety. Mission accomplished.

Just punch in five numbers. Five-four-three-one-zero. Done.

LB's first sight of Macandezulo attested to what Neels had said. Everybody with Juma was a criminal. The village was wrecked, filthy, overgrown, fit for nothing but a hideout. Who'd live here if he or she wasn't part of Juma's operation? LB thought back to the water hole, the slow-eyed majesty of the rhino. This village was home to the sons of bitches who would kill it.

Five numbers, then run. Why not? To save who?

LB slowed to shorten the distance to Good Luck behind him. The toothless poacher gave him a shove, urging him along the seedy road. Twenty years of risking his own life had brought LB to hot Mozambique and Macandezulo to do it again. He stopped walking, inviting another push from Good Luck. For the first time in uniform, ever, LB was unsure for what, or for whom, he was putting himself at risk.

He didn't know if the disheveled and shoeless white man walking toward him from one of the huts was an answer.

LB left his fingers on the radio.

Chapter 29

The sun finally drove Allyn indoors. One of the women wanted to follow, but he waved her off. He left behind the gun Juma had given him and went to his paltry mattress in the shade for a nap.

He did not drift off in the sweltering afternoon. A new kind of loneliness settled on him like a blanket, adding to the heat, stealing his rest. The hours to midnight seemed too many, like the years he had left in his life, to do what with? He believed this was the first time since her death a month ago that he missed more than Eva's presence, missed her company. Her conversation, often insipid or natively wise, never featured Allyn, his business or worries, money or influence, but always her own inanities, her bridge club and gardening, a trip she wanted, a piece of art, a new friend, a fresh slight from an old friend. Allyn listened and did not, was concerned and was not, loved and did not. Though she was shallow in his life, she had breadth, she touched a great amount of his time. Now he'd been left by himself, with only time for company. He missed sharing time with his wife, cutting it into portions, bearing it more easily.

At the call for Juma in the street, he jumped up from the mattress. Allyn did not think to straighten himself up, nothing else in Macandezulo was. Untucked and barefoot, he stepped from the hut into the dirt road.

Two of Juma's armed men escorted three remarkable people into the village. Juma had warned of this, someone would come for the missile. But these didn't look like assassins, not at all. The first was a large, loosely knit young man in hiking clothes, who glanced about in plain fright at the rubble of the poachers' village. The second was a wiry black woman who wore the green khakis of a Kruger ranger. She barely registered Macandezulo or Allyn's approach, she seemed somehow beyond her surroundings. The third was another white man but in military camouflage and boots, a formidable tank of a fellow kitted out in a web vest, unarmed but with his hand on a radio.

Allyn let them come to him. The little poacher in front smiled as he passed. The tall one in the rear was the same evil-looking chap with a long rifle who'd been in the back of the pickup when Juma came to collect Allyn from the chopper ride out of Jo'burg. The man wore a leopard pelt that lent fierceness to his gap-toothed mouth and red, peeking tongue. He gave no order for his hostages to stop walking. On her own, the ranger girl paused in front of Allyn. The two whites halted with her. The tall poacher seemed unsure of Allyn's authority, knowing only that Allyn was closely aligned with Juma. So he stood by.

The girl addressed Allyn.

"Where is Juma?"

The stout soldier nudged her aside, she did not speak for him. Allyn wanted to laugh; these three were such a curious result of his worries and waiting, drinking and loneliness.

The soldier eyed Allyn head to toe. He did not extend a hand to shake.

"I'm Master Sergeant DiNardo. United States Air Force."

"An American. Good. Do you have any identification, Sergeant?"

"No, sir."

Allyn knew little about the military beyond what the movies told him, but it did seem odd that America would send one man with no insignia, no papers, and apparently no gun. If he was, in fact, a killer, he kept strange companions and had been rather easily nabbed in broad daylight.

The sergeant jabbed a thumb over his shoulder.

"These two will vouch for me."

The large white man, young and flaccid, reached into a pocket. That movement drew the end of the poacher's rifle into his back. The big boy reacted as if it were a cattle prod, arching away, whirling.

"It's my wallet. Do you fucking mind?"

He handed a green ID card to Allyn. *Donald Karskie, Information Specialist, SANParks.* Karskie began to explain that he'd been assigned to accompany the sergeant into the Kruger. The American cut him off, moving him aside less gently than he'd done the girl. He motioned to her.

"This is Promise. She's a Kruger ranger."

"I can see that." Allyn inclined his head. Promise was a striking young thing, muscular and dusky. Her hands were veined and strong, but her features carried the disdain of those beyond reach. Allyn had seen those same wandering eyes, jaws set against cheap talk with a dismissive tilt of the head, on the powerful and wealthy. Allyn said her name, wanting to remember it.

She asked, as if she had a right to, "Who are you?"

"You can call me Lush Life."

The American looked skeptical.

"Seriously."

"If you like. However, I find the less I take seriously, the better I tolerate it."

The American had a bright look to his eye and seemed on the edge of banter. The ranger girl broke ranks and hurried away.

Followed by his four gun-toting guards, Juma ambled up the street.

"Ah. There's your man."

Juma motioned for his protectors to let Promise through. He met the girl with open arms. They walked while embracing, talking quietly. But when they reached Allyn, great Juma put the girl back in line beside the sergeant and Karskie under the poacher's long gun. She seemed confounded. Juma did not explain himself.

"I am Juma."

The American and Karskie reintroduced themselves. Karskie offered his identification card. Promise nodded as her way of adding validation. Again, no one shook hands.

"Promise says you've come to inspect the missile."

The sergeant flattened his palm in the direction Juma had come.

"Lead the way."

"Sergeant, forgive me. This is a bit irregular."

"How so?"

"You ask me to believe that you've been sent by the United States with these two to verify that I do, indeed, have your rocket. One sergeant in an unmarked uniform."

Juma gestured to his small poacher boy carrying the two rifles and asked him a question in a different tongue. Allyn spoke enough Bantu to interpret the question Juma asked: Was the American carrying that rifle when you found him? The boy rattled one of the guns, nodding. Juma returned to English, and the sergeant.

"An American sergeant carrying a Dutch FN, the weapon of the Kruger rangers. That is odd, surely. Why would you be found with that instead of an American weapon? Accompanied by a female ranger, whom I suspect, by now, you know is of dubious character. And a low-level parks employee sent to vouch for you by way of his plastic ID card."

Juma rubbed his chin.

"Are you a spy, Mr. Karskie?"

"Do I look like a spy?"

The poacher in the leopard pelt spoke up, also in Bantu. The lisp from his missing teeth spoiled several words; Allyn made out only "underpants on a stick." That had to be a mistake, but Juma's chuckle jiggled his girth.

"Frankly, Sergeant, this is not the delegation I expected."

"What did you expect, exactly?"

"Something a bit more, what can I say? Dangerous? A death squad, perhaps. A stealth bomber. Something more impressive. Something American."

"How's this for impressive? You called the president of Zimbabwe. He called the president of the United States. He called me."

Juma made a mistake. He cut his eyes at Allyn.

The sergeant caught it.

"You boys have a midnight deadline for two hundred million dollars. Right?"

Allyn wanted to walk away, right now. Or drool and stutter, play Lush Life the drunken fool, distance himself from this plot. But it was too late. The American shot him a piercing glance, the kind that records. The sergeant didn't know Allyn's name, but he unraveled instantly that Juma, the giant poacher king of this village of shambles, was not the one who called the president of Zimbabwe.

The sun hammered on the earthen street. Juma's bodyguards fidgeted, wanting out of the light, waiting for someone to speak. Allyn dropped all pretense.

"Juma. A word."

On his bare feet, Allyn turned away. Juma followed far enough for them to speak privately. Juma was so large Allyn could not see around him to the American, the South African, and the girl ranger.

"Who is the girl?"

"My sister's granddaughter."

"Was she your contact inside the park?"

"Yes."

"We can assume, then, that she's told them who you are and what you do here."

"Yes."

"She doesn't know who I am, does she?"

"No."

"How did they find her?"

Juma looked over his meaty shoulder. Allyn gazed up into the fat bottom of his chin, the brown folds of Juma's prosperity.

"I think it more likely she found them. I will get the truth, shamwari. It is difficult to believe anything they say. But she brought them here. That I know."

Allyn curled a small hand over Juma's forearm. The big man's skin felt cool against the heat of the day. The fire, the burning will of their youth in the mines to become men of stature, had become banked in Juma. Juma had done the easy things since those years, stolen, bullied, and murdered his way to wealth. Though they'd sworn loyalty to each other and had kept it, Allyn read much that scared him in Juma's glare at the girl.

"Listen to me. It doesn't matter how they found her, or who they are. What matters is who sent them. Only that."

Allyn tugged on his old friend.

"Juma."

"Yes. Yes."

"Leave your men around the village tonight."

"This should not have happened. The Americans weren't supposed to know where the missile is."

"They know now. Let's focus on that."

"What will it mean?"

Funny that Juma, the criminal, asked Allyn what the likely outcome of their crime would be. In the end, everything was business.

Juma prodded.

"Do you think an attack? A bomb, another drone?"

"I don't think so. We left them very little time. Besides, two hundred million isn't much to America. It makes sense for them to pay. It's cheaper than coming after us. Much cheaper than explaining themselves tomorrow. They've been caught playing nasty. They'll take their medicine. I would."

"I believe you." Juma's belief appeared to buck him up. "Look who they sent us. A soft boy, an unarmed soldier."

"We're alright for now. Listen to me. We'll take the sergeant to see the missile. That's all we can do. We'll wait until midnight. Then . . ."

"Then what, shamwari?"

"Then you and I are done, my friend. We can never talk, never see each other again. You have to leave this place. Leave Mozambique. I may disappear myself for a while. They may pay us, but they will not forgive us."

"What if the money does not come?"

"That changes nothing. We took a chance. But it will come."

Juma took a moment before nodding. Again, Juma's gaze fixed on the girl.

"Juma. She's your family."

"She's a traitor before anything else."

Allyn did nothing to halt Juma's pivot away from him. A fuse that burned beyond his reach had been lit in his old friend.

Chapter 30

Juma kept his back to Promise as they moved up the street. He left her to walk with LB and Karskie, surrounded by four guards and Good Luck. The little boy Hard Life was sent ahead, dragging two rifles in the road. Old, white Lush Life strode without shoes beside Juma. The man was short, hard used, and mismatched to Juma and Macandezulo. Promise asked LB who he was.

Good Luck hissed at her to be quiet.

Promise whipped toward the shooter, but LB dug a hand inside the band of her shorts, hauling her backward down the street until she spun to face forward.

"Easy, girl. Eyes open. Mouth shut."

Karskie stepped up to bracket Promise, with LB on the other side. She walked like this, blocked in by men. She thought of Wophule. If he were here, would he be so angry, would he want killer Good Luck's throat in his hands? Perhaps not. Wophule had been gentler. The animals saw this. Treasure would have seen it, too, given time. Promise had stolen that time from her and Wophule, left his body lost, his spirit closed in by rocks. Promise did as LB demanded, shut her mouth, walked on, and watched. She sensed the spoor of judgment and payment in the dust of this road, in the unstinting light of the day, in the broad backside of Juma in front of her.

They moved into the village through sour human smells, past haphazard huts and peeling buildings. The bush was not patient with Macandezulo, blistering, choking, swallowing the place. Juma was not the power here, he was just rubbish and the sputter of one generator.

They stopped before the largest structure in the village, a two-story house of gray block. Hard Life waited in one of two lawn chairs outside. Juma told Hard Life to go inside and head upstairs. Somewhat automatically and emotionlessly, the little boy left his guns behind and disappeared through the door, up the flight of stairs. Juma ordered his guards and Good Luck to stay outside. He pointed to the emptied lawn chair.

"Mr. Karskie. Wait here with Good Luck and my men."

Karskie's reluctance to stay behind was met by a raised finger from LB. The big boy collapsed into the lawn chair. Good Luck folded into the chair opposite him, the long rifle across his lap. Juma's four guards backed into the street. They slung their weapons and reached for dagga cigarettes. Juma hefted the two rifles Hard Life had lugged into the village, a Kalashnikov and the ranger rifle taken from LB. Juma headed for the door. Promise called to his back.

"Juma."

Her great-uncle acted as if he'd not heard. Lush Life touched Juma to make him turn. Who was this white man that he could do this? Coming around, Juma sighed.

"What, child?"

"I want to come, too."

Juma filled the doorway, owlish and slow. He slumped, saddened, and Promise saw how old Juma was. Older than Gogo, older than Lush Life beside him.

"Why?"

Because she had slaughtered a rhino. She'd called Juma to the missile. She'd betrayed the Kruger rangers, her partner, and the animals. She'd brought the American here. She was betraying Juma even now. She was as bad as him.

And what if LB, with his fingers on his radio, were to explode the missile while he stood over it? She didn't think him crazy or a zealot, but he had said nothing was to get in the way of his mission. Not her. Not him. He might do it. Would she want to survive that? Be left to Juma's guards, to Good Luck?

"I've earned it."

Only the corner of Juma's mouth moved, a tiny twitch on a giant's face.

"Yes, you have. Come, then."

Chapter 31

Juma took none of his guards into the blockhouse. He led the way, carrying the little poacher boy's Kalashnikov and LB's FN rifle. Juma ducked under the door frame, followed by Lush Life, LB, and Promise.

They descended a stairwell to a metal door. Juma undid the padlock. LB didn't need to see the missile to know Wally couldn't have detonated it from a half mile away, maybe not even from the edge of town. The air-to-air freq and his weak radio couldn't have reached the missile down here behind concrete walls. Juma pushed open the door and, without looking back, entered an armory.

Juma was clearly a significant dealer in illicit arms. LB could barely step into the room for the stacks of rifles in uncountable calibers and international makes and the handguns spilling out of crates, a thousand guns to fuel poachers, militants, bad guys of every stripe. Juma yanked the magazines out of the FN and the AK, then tossed the rifles onto a pile. He left himself unarmed. Was this trust or contempt? Juma was a mountain of a man, maybe he figured he was in no danger. LB took this as a small insult.

Juma's cache of guns was big but sloppy, as if he'd shoveled them in the basement door. Every hard bit of it seemed humbled, bowing before the battered table in the center of the room where the Hellfire lay.

Now that he'd seen the rocket, LB could blow it. He wasn't sure from how far away. He inched closer until he stood between massive Juma and the secretive, little white man. Promise crept up, too. Juma and Lush Life looked at the missile like it was a pile of money, with lip-licking avarice and a tinge of worry that they might not collect. Promise stared in openmouthed awe, which alarmed LB.

Then she nodded to him.

LB clapped loudly, just to fuck with them all. They jumped.

"We're good. Let's go."

Moving for the door, LB played out tactics in his head. Before leaving the village, he'd assure Juma that all was in good order. Yes, that was his country's missing Hellfire on that table; he'd report it that way. He'd walk Karskie and Promise straight down the dirt road. At fifty yards, just far enough to endure the blast, hopefully close enough to activate the tritonol charge, LB would punch in the five numbers, and the three of them would hit the ground.

Boom. Under the shock and surprise of the explosion, they'd run like hell.

If there was no blast, LB would send Karskie and the girl on. He'd turn around. Act like he'd forgotten something. Wave to Juma. Hey, buddy, one more thing. Keep dialing.

Five-four-three-one-zero.

Then boom. Maybe.

Maybe not. Keep walking. Dialing.

At some point, the damn thing would go off. The question remained: At what point? The Hellfire's warhead was going to blow this building to smithereens; the shock and flying concrete were going to crush anything within twenty, thirty yards. The heaps of ammo would cook off, too. Juma had complained he wanted something impressive: too bad he wouldn't get to see the crater. Bye-bye, Juma, his guards, his illegal weapons. And mysterious little Lush Life, who had a bigger hand in all this than he let on. They'd be collateral damage to LB's mission. But no one in South Africa, Mozambique, or the United States was going to weep for poachers, arms dealers, and blackmailers.

Assuming LB wasn't in small pieces himself, he'd catch up to Promise and Karskie. The girl knew the bush like the alphabet. She could hide them, move them until they made it back to the ravine, Wally, and Neels. Then they'd scurry over the border. A debrief would be next, some beers with the team in Jo'burg, then home.

That was what was going to happen: simple, straightforward, and the only plan LB had come up with.

Outside in the sun, Juma's guards squatted on their haunches, puffing. Karskie stood from the lawn chair, expectant. Mean-looking Good Luck and his rifle stayed seated.

Lush Life rubbed his hands like a man finished with a meal. "Well, Sergeant?"

"I'll radio it in."

Lush Life seemed satisfied. Juma asserted his immense hand for a shake. LB left it hanging.

"Sergeant?"

"No thanks."

"Where are your manners? This is business. Nothing else."

LB's immediate thought was at this moment it would have been better to send Wally.

"I said no thanks. We'll be leaving."

"On an insult?"

"I got a few better ones, if you want to push it."

Lush Life raised hands, refereeing, but Juma did not lower his own mitt. No blood dripped off it, so LB splashed some on him.

"Pal, I know who you are. You killed this girl's partner right in front of her. I saw a rhino today, and my heart almost jumped out of my mouth. You would've cut it into pieces. You're blackmailing my country. And, by the way, you think you got enough guns down there? How many more people and animals you plan on wiping out for business? You're a piece of shit."

LB turned on Lush Life.

"And I don't know who the fuck you are. Let's leave it that way."

Before he could turn, Juma pressed his great hand over LB's shoulder. The weight of the man's touch, the strength, was powerful and woeful. LB would've had to fight hard to knock it off. He pitied Promise for being under it. He stood still while Juma leaned in. In the street, Juma's guards straightened up and rattled their weapons into their hands.

"Those are angry words from an unarmed man."

"A man who needs to walk out of here for you to get your money."

Lush Life agreed and tried again to soften Juma, telling him the sergeant needed to go about his business. Juma nodded, withdrawing his paw.

"True, shamwari."

Wordlessly, LB gave Juma one last grave digger's glance. LB had killed men before. Years ago as a Ranger captain, he'd spent a decade doing it in jungles and dunes. After that, as a pararescueman, he'd killed only to accomplish his rescue missions. They were never his choice, the killings, but the choices of others. While a Ranger, he'd followed orders. In the Guardian Angels, he sometimes had to battle his way in, or out, to rescue downed and isolated warriors. Not once in twenty years had LB looked forward to a killing, and never did he fail to remember every taken life. He had a memory full of bodies; he thought of them as his cemetery. When LB had run out of room, when the graves crowded his sleep, he'd become a PJ, so he could put himself on the line to preserve lives instead of end them. To make some space in his graveyard.

But Juma. There was room for him.

LB's feet itched to walk away. His fingers played over the radio. He jerked his head at Promise and Karskie.

"Let's go."

Juma lifted a palm like a stop sign in front of Karskie.

"I don't see why everyone has to leave."

The big boy reacted before LB could speak.

"No. Look, no." Karskie raised his own hand against Juma's and staggered backward as if he might somehow slip away. "I'm not that important. Really."

Juma motioned to the lawn chair.

"Have a seat, Mr. Karskie."

Good Luck, already seated, pointed at the lawn chair across from him.

He lisped, "Sit."

Karskie shot LB a pleading look. *Get me out of this.*

The boy was as good as dead if he stayed, if LB blew the missile. Karskie hadn't signed on for that. LB had.

LB said the words fast, so they were out before he could hesitate. It was like jumping from a plane, once he stepped, all he could do was fall.

"I'll stay."

Lush Life was crumpled, a little bleary, and needed a shave. Up close, he smelled stale. He had a stupid, fake name. But Juma didn't talk whenever he did.

"Sergeant."

"What?"

"Who is Mr. Karskie? Really?"

"A parks employee. Like his ID says."

"Why did you bring him here?"

"To verify who I am."

"Why do you have no papers? No patches on your fatigues. Not even your name."

"This is supposed to be a covert mission."

"So if you're found dead, you would be unknown. Is that right?"

"Right."

"That takes courage."

"I don't think about it."

"Then Mr. Karskie is as he says. Unimportant."

"He's not much of a bargaining chip, no."

"I believe . . ." Lush Life tapped the side of his nose twice, then pushed his fingertip into LB's vest. "I believe he will be for you."

Karskie flapped his arms.

LB and Lush Life were close to the same height. LB outweighed him by seventy pounds. The white-haired old man didn't blink. He had some steel in him. Or, just as likely, he was missing something. LB pushed Lush Life's finger down from his chest.

"Let him go."

"You prove me correct, Sergeant. Tell me something else."

"If I have to."

"Why did you bring the girl? She could've stayed outside the village. Why bring her in here? To anger my mate Juma?"

Promise started forward, tipping to her toes, arming her answer. LB silenced her with a raised hand. He did this to answer for her, just as he had for Karskie. The only way to keep them both safe was to show Juma and Lush Life that they didn't matter.

"She wanted to come."

"Why?"

"Why do you care?"

Juma shifted beside Lush Life. Side by side the two couldn't have been more different. A massive black man, nattily dressed, next to a short, spotty old Englishman with flyaway hair wearing slept-in clothes. But something about them had been paired long ago, and though they were crooked as lightning, they were friends.

"I don't expect you to understand, Sergeant."

"Try me."

"We had a saying in the mines. 'I am well if my friend is well.'"

LB had seen all this before. Honor killings in Afghanistan. Tribute murders in Honduras. Stonings to salvage a family name in Iraq. People who used force instead of real human dignity to get ahead, people who made the rules to fit themselves. LB imagined these two had it tough early in their lives and decided to survive together, screw the cost to others. They were loyal and believed that made them respectable. It made them little more than mobsters.

LB tugged the small radio from his web vest to show it.

"I stay. As soon as Karskie and Promise are safe out of here, I'll call it in. Then we'll wait for payment together. You, me, Juma."

LB indicated the seated Good Luck.

"And handsome here. That's my deal. There isn't another one."

Karskie shook his head in tight, tiny tremors. LB couldn't tell if he was shivering or saying no. Promise plainly shook her head no.

Again, the destination. LB had been here before in his thoughts, many times. The intense training of every pararescueman forced all GAs to wrestle this notion to the ground, to imagine that defining moment when one's own life may become forfeit. LB had been here in the field, too, on combat missions and rescues, facing enemies and long odds. Each man and woman who went into battle knew his or her life might be the price. But only the Guardian Angels wore a patch that said so. "That others may live." LB didn't mind coming to this lonely place again without the patch on his sleeve. He'd worn it a long time.

Time slowed. Every moment was a large fraction of what he had left to him. LB drew a deep breath, allowed himself a long blink to smell the world and hear it, too. He had no regrets for things left undone and only some for the unsaid. He was sad to go but thankful to choose this fate of a Guardian Angel, instead of a later, different, sadder, hollow death he would not pick.

To Promise and Karskie, he repeated himself.

"There's no other deal."

Lush Life paused, stymied, while LB held out the radio. Good Luck didn't care, and the four guards appeared disconnected and a little high.

Big Juma wagged a sausage-sized finger.

"Sergeant, no. This is Macandezulo. My Macandezulo. You do not dictate terms here."

The great finger shifted to Karskie.

"He will stay."

LB puffed out his chest, swelling before confronting Juma.

"I said no."

"And that is precisely why I say he will."

Again, Lush Life interceded, this time taking big Juma by the arm to walk him several steps away. The two conferred quietly in a language LB had never heard before. When they returned, Lush Life spread his hands accommodatingly. The little man had pull with Juma.

"Sergeant. You may stay."

As he'd learned before when doing the hardest things, LB acted quickly, faster than his heart. He told Promise and Karskie to go.

Neither moved.

A titter, then a cough tumbled through the doorway of the blockhouse. The sounds were followed by shuffling bare feet scuffing the stairs, descending from the second floor.

Into the sunlight stepped eight women. Each wore white, their loose garb stained in some places, torn in others, but pale against ebony flesh, without undergarments. They filed between LB and Juma like geese, honking in a gaggle, oblivious to what they interrupted. They were glib, giggling, dully touching the guards as they passed. One cupped Karskie's dropped chin. Another stroked Promise's khaki shorts before walking on.

Karskie regained himself before LB could speak. He pointed after the girls. None of them strolled a straight line.

"What is it, Juma? Meth?"

"Yes."

"You got your own lab?"

Juma tipped his brow at a shanty close to the blockhouse. LB figured it to be within the blast range. Karskie bounced his gaze back and forth to the hut, measuring; he might have been thinking the same.

On the radio, LB's thumb settled over the first number, five, but did not push it.

"Sex slaves, Juma?" LB asked.

"Sex workers. And, Sergeant, you and I are not explaining ourselves to each other."

Juma aimed his thick finger at the chair Karskie had vacated.

"Sit."

LB did not. He wasn't of a mind to take orders. Instead, he indicated the blockhouse.

"Is that all the women?"

"Yes. Why? Didn't you see one you liked?"

The women had already tottered thirty yards up the street and were headed farther. They were not geese or slaves but safe at that distance.

LB took Promise by the arm. Pulling her close, he returned the soft, small nod she'd given him down in the armory.

"Go. Go right now."

LB had spent a dark night in the Kruger. Promise's eyes were darker.

She spoke past him.

"Juma."

"What?"

"Let me stay."

She tried to free her arm from LB. He resisted until Juma asked him to let her go.

Moving to her great-uncle, Promise flattened both hands against his wide belly. She pressed her cheek to his chest. She seemed to be listening through a wall.

"I'm in trouble with the rangers. They know what I did for you. That's why I came with the American. So I could ask you to let me stay. Juma, I'll go to jail. They might kill me."

Gently, Juma enveloped her wrists.

"Nomawethu. You are my family."

"Yes."

"I will give you one more gift."

He eased her hands away from him, pushed her back a step, then set her loose. Juma spread his arms wide. Like this, he was immense.

"Do what the sergeant says and go now. Or you have my word you will die where you stand."

"Juma."

His eyes did not break from hers. Leaving his arms out, Juma retreated, some ceremony of departure and damnation.

"Good Luck, the next word she says, shoot her."

The toothless poacher didn't stand from the lawn chair when he shifted the rifle off his knees. Lush Life seemed appalled, wanting to say something. But he only appraised his mountainous friend and found him unmovable. The old white man put an arm around Promise's waist to nudge her away from Juma. He backed her beside Karskie, muttering, "Sorry, dear," and left her.

Karskie put his back to Promise and LB. He faced the dirt road of Macandezulo. The boy's shoulders rose and fell. One more time, Karskie's hands flapped against his pockets.

He pirouetted, quickly if not nimbly, and caved into the lawn chair opposite Good Luck. Juma dropped his arms. LB lowered the radio he'd been holding out.

"What are you doing?"

"It's not your fight, LB. I wish it was, trust me. But it's not."

"Yes, it is."

"The missile's yours, but not the rest of it. You've seen one rhino. I've been here a month and already seen a hundred, all dead. Tell my father I said that. It's good."

The whores up the street had gathered behind a hovel. Some squatted inside their skirts, one worked a well pump, the rest splashed in the spilling water.

"Get up, Karskie."

"It's alright. I got this."

"No, you don't."

"It's sitting in a chair. My skill set."

"Get up."

"You save people, right? That's what you do."

"It is."

"Then you should keep doing it. You know. Me next. Because I'm scared shitless."

"You don't have to do this."

"No, I don't. Tell my father that, too. And Neels."

LB couldn't insist further, couldn't argue without tipping his hand to Juma and Lush Life that whoever sat in this lawn chair had a strong chance of never leaving Macandezulo.

The first of the women began to filter back toward the blockhouse. They'd bathed in their clothes, their cotton gowns clung and turned translucent. The women became geese again, cackling, wet and dumb to their own danger.

"Will they pay, LB? If you tell them to?" Karskie asked.

LB nodded. Karskie shrugged, extending an empty palm to him. The gesture said, *Then I leave it to you.*

The big boy sat back against the flimsy chair. Good Luck glowered in his leopard pelt, returning the rifle across his lap.

Karskie folded his hands.

"Chess?"

Good Luck showed his tongue and gums.

Karskie pretended LB was not standing there. He watched the whores come.

This was not the first time LB's fate had taken a hard turn. For twenty years, as a Ranger and a PJ, whenever he thought he'd bought the farm, he'd been wrong. Those times, he'd been left standing in the smoke or panting on the ground, but alive, wondering how the hell he'd been spared, and why? He never could figure out how, just the fog and fortunes of war. But the why, LB always knew. He was meant to live for the next time. And each of them, like this one, felt like the end until LB found it wasn't.

He didn't move until Promise tugged on him.

"We have to go."

Juma snapped his fingers at his four armed guards. The men shook off the laziness that had settled over them. They formed a picket in front of Juma, Lush Life, and their hostage, Karskie. Above them, Juma inclined his head at LB.

"Midnight, Sergeant."

Without a glance at Promise, the big man squeezed through the blockhouse doorway and vanished.

In the sun, Lush Life focused on his bare feet.

LB asked, "You're a smart guy. How'd you get caught up in this?"

Lush Life made a smacking, regretful noise.

"It's only been minutes since I've been caught up in anything. It all seemed quite simple before you."

Lush Life flicked a finger at Promise.

"And her."

Lush Life tipped his brow at Promise in parting. Turning on his bare feet, he spoke across his shoulder.

"Midnight, Sergeant."

Lush Life did not join Juma in the blockhouse but strode up the street. He passed through the returning flock of women, hands in his wrinkled pockets. The man couldn't have been more different from the women, all of them black, young, and sloppily sensual. But as they flowed around the old white man, LB noted a kind of bond between them, a kinship of despair, the taint of a cage. All their feet dragged, none of their heads were up, and even as some of the women traced their hands over Lush Life, the touches meant nothing to him or any of them.

Looking old, Lush Life stepped up on the tilting porch of a pink house, one of the few with four straight walls. From there, he watched the whores return to the blockhouse above the missile. He sat on the house's rotten steps while LB and Promise walked out of the village.

Chapter 32

At the edge of Macandezulo, Promise put a hand to LB's back. She meant it as empathy, knowing he was torn. LB misinterpreted the gesture, thinking she was asking him to act now. He shook his head.

"I can't do it."

He considered Promise for long moments. She expected him to ask if she could. But he did not. LB wasn't a man to seek approval.

She would have pressed every button. And like LB, she would not have asked what anyone else thought.

Promise told him that Karskie was right, he wasn't important. But none of them were, or they wouldn't be out here. That got a rise from LB. When the hard muscles in his back quaked from a quiet laugh, she dropped her hand.

With the sun well past noon, they reentered the bush. Fever trees, fat jades, and spiky acacias made their path roundabout, but Promise soon guided LB to the rusty soil of the creek bed. Along the way they walked side by side but exchanged no looks or words. The buzzards circled again in the distant crystal sky.

LB broke the long silence.

"Did you mean it, when you told Juma you wanted to stay?"

"Yes."

"Because you're in trouble?"

"I haven't much purpose left."

"What if I'd blown the building?"

"I would have kept Good Luck near it."

Their boots had fallen into the same cadence in the red dust. They walked back to Neels and whatever awaited there.

"We have things in common, LB."

"That so?"

"You and I both considered dying in Macandezulo. I think we both have less purpose than we would wish for."

"You don't know me, lady."

With their steps in rhythm over the dry ravine, Promise told him a quick story. Two months ago, she and Wophule reported a rhino that had a thorn in its eye. They guided a vet into Shingwedzi. When they found the sick rhino, it was in the company of two others, both bulls. Wophule darted the beast with the bad eye. It fell, and while it was down the vet pulled the thorn and disinfected the eye. The other two rhinos backed off fifty meters and stood, still as boulders.

"They did not move. They would not be frightened away. They could do nothing else but safeguard their comrade. I have seen you, LB. Your kind of beast. In the bush, many times."

"So I'm a rhino."

"If you wish. I can grant that."

Again, Promise rested her hand along LB's spine. She left it there over many strides, and he did nothing to make her remove it.

She had thought to die in Macandezulo. But not like LB, not to protect someone, but to find a way to avenge Wophule. What sort of man was this under her hand? What would he be like to know? A man who would lay his life down for a stranger, a mission, a missile. What kind of life could LB build if every day he was willing to spend it? Like a house you might leave at any time, how could you settle in, how could you make it a home for yourself or anyone else? How could you love?

Promise and LB had both been sent away from their deaths, she by Juma, LB by Karskie and Lush Life. Both walked on, joined by that, by the silent bush, and her hand bridging to his back.

She pitied him along with herself. She spoke without voice, uttering only the breath of the words so they would enter the world but LB would not hear. "Uxholo, umnunzan." (I am sorry, sir.)

Chapter 33

Neels pulled off his bush hat. The sun ironed his tunic against his shoulders, but he did not sweat. He ran a hand over his scalp. His skin felt cool. He could stand like this for hours, had done it in his youth and refused to believe he could not now. Only one hour had passed. Macandezulo had not blown up. In the open, in the red ravine, he watched and listened to the east.

The American captain did not stand near Neels in the mean light of Mozambique but waited on his own. The captain sat some, paced a little, and spoke on his satellite phone, explaining himself, arguing a bit. He ignored Neels and seemed to ignore his sergeant who was off doing the job. Neels would not look anywhere but east until Macandezulo exploded.

He didn't worry for the sergeant, not only because he didn't like him but because the sergeant was a military man and they didn't always return. Karskie shouldn't have been asked to go, but the captain had said someone from SANParks added to their cover story. Without Karskie, LB would have been just a solitary *fokkol* soldier strolling into the village with no identification. He probably would have been shot before he opened his mouth. In truth, the little bastard's chances of being shot would get worse *after* he opened his mouth. But Neels hoped to see Karskie again.

And Promise. The girl had turned her back on everything Neels valued. Why should she get away with it? She was his ranger, a traitor in his sector. Promise was a blunder, an embarrassment and a pain. She had to come back to pay.

In the distance, buzzards ringed high above something dead elsewhere. Neels wondered what it could be. The animals of the Kruger rarely crossed the border; they knew it to be fatal for them in Mozambique. Probably a human. Some poacher or lost migrant, somebody miserable the buzzards could barely pick. The veld was harder than a man. To die here was no surprise.

Neels kicked a pebble. It skittered a long way. Without him, without his boot's toe, the stone might have lay in place for a thousand more years. It took him coming along to move it. Long ago his farmer father and teacher mother had quoted one Sunday's church sermon at supper. The meek shall inherit the earth. Neels had asked: Inherit from whom? They didn't know, but he did, and he told them. The ones who act, that's who. His parents said he was cheeky. Ten years later the proof came. After Neels left for the Scouts, their family's lands in Rhodesia were nationalized and given to the local people who had no idea how to work the soil that Neels's grandfathers had settled. Not long after, both his parents died meekly, a factory worker and a teacher in Durban.

Why had Neels been punished for not standing aside like his parents, like the Bible said? What should he have done? Quit his job, let someone else do the tough work because he had a wife with no stomach for it?

He should have carried her into Shingwedzi, pushed her close to a rhino freshly dead by a poacher's hand, gutted by the bush. See that? A murdered animal, a shot poacher, a Cuban corpse, a dead Angolan rebel, a rotting ape tied to a fence. Look what I have done. My acts.

Who was she to tell Neels who he was? What would have made her happy? The kind of man she needed was not inside him, that man would not do what he was about to. Aloud, Neels said good-bye, but did not believe she heard.

Macandezulo had not blown up. Juma was not dead. A hundred meters out, the sergeant and Promise pushed toward him along the ravine. They walked on their own warped reflections, shimmering heat ghosts. Where was Karskie?

The American captain, yakking on his satellite phone, hadn't seen them yet. He waved an arm to whomever he was talking to, but he seemed incapable of saying the right things. Neels had two rifles across his back. He dropped one of them into his hands.

"Hang it up."

The captain shifted only a piece of his focus to Neels. He kept talking.

"They're back."

Neels pointed up the ravine. The sergeant and the girl had trod out of their mirages, only dust clouded their strides.

The captain rang off and stowed his phone. He turned to greet Promise and the sergeant.

Neels spun the rifle around. He raised it high and clubbed the captain in the back of the head.

Chapter 34

LB broke into a run at Neels, with the girl on his heels. When LB was ten strides from barreling into him, the old ranger jammed a boot into the middle of Wally's back. He dropped the muzzle of his rifle to the rear of Wally's head, then commanded LB and Promise to stop. Both skidded to a halt.

Wally lay facedown in the ravine. Neels loomed over him, one foot between his shoulder blades. Wally groaned and clutched at the dirt. Neels held his rifle one-handed, standing it on end in the cleft beneath Wally's skull. Neels's finger curled over the trigger.

"I didn't hear anything blow up, Sergeant."

LB had nothing, no gun or blade, not a rock to throw. Neels wasn't wearing his bush hat. He looked to be baking, red faced.

"Wally, you alright?"

Neels's foot stopped Wally from turning his head to answer. He spoke facing away from LB, lips in the dust. His sunglasses had been knocked off.

"Not really."

Promise inched forward. LB held her back. He held an open hand to Neels.

"What are you doing, man?"

Neels licked his lips. He looked thirsty. He held out his free arm to LB, seeking answers. Neels looked frustrated, like he'd been forced to do this.

"Where's the boy?"

"They kept Karskie."

"Did you see the missile?"

"It's in a basement."

"Is Juma close?"

"He's in the same building."

"Is Karskie why you didn't blow it?"

"He is. And there's women. Eight of them."

"You mean whores."

"I mean women."

Promise stepped back from LB, circling away from him. Out of his reach, she approached Neels. He cocked his head at her.

"Far enough."

Promise crossed her hands over her breast.

"This is all my fault. You're mad at me. Don't do this."

Neels laughed, a bit hyper.

"I don't give a fok about you, girl."

With Neels's attention on Promise, LB stole inches closer. He stopped when Neels's eyes slashed like knives across him. LB held out both palms, placating.

"Okay. What's this about?"

Neels shifted the rifle barrel from the back of Wally's head to Wally's shoulder. He raised all his weight onto one boot over Wally's spine, and pulled the trigger.

The report was muffled by the meat of Wally's shoulder. Wally howled and rippled like a carpet with wind under it. Neels's boot pinned him to the red dirt.

With a fuming glare, Neels dared LB to move toward him again. Promise barred her mouth with one hand, her heart with the other.

The old ranger slid the barrel back where it had been, under Wally's skull. Wally's ruined left arm lay bent next to his head with trembling fingers.

"Turn around, Sergeant. Go back to the village. Make sure Juma's inside that building. Then blow up your missile and go home. I should hurry, your captain's bleeding."

Neels stabbed a hand back toward Macandezulo.

"Do what I tell you. Turn around, or I kill your captain. Then I'll tell you again."

LB worked his jaw, desperate for something to say. Nothing came, not a word to find a way out of this. His jaw hung while his fists balled, useless as his tongue. Any move he made, any word he uttered, was going to cost lives.

Neels answered LB's silence by tapping his finger on the trigger.

"I'll shoot him, Sergeant. Then the girl. Then you, if I have to. I'll claim you were all done in by poachers. I barely got away with my life. Trust me, I'll be believed. The buzzards will do for you. The sun and wind will finish the rest. You'll stay unidentified a bit longer."

The hole in Wally's shoulder bled into a rusty mud. Above him, Neels wobbled. Wally groaned when Neels balanced himself on the rifle like a cane. Neels thrust a pale finger at LB.

"You come to the Kruger to fix some cock-up your country made. You stay for a few hours, and you tell me, you tell *me*, who lives and dies."

Neels ground his boot into Wally's ribs. Wally gasped into his own blood.

"See your captain here? He's doing what I've done for forty years. Bleeding into Africa. You want to save Karskie? You don't know Karskie. The boy wants to be a ranger. Good for him. I'm going to let him."

Neels swung his finger at Promise.

"He'll be a hero like Wophule. Remember him, jou poes?"

Neels mopped his white brow with the back of his hand. He found it dry, noted this, and carried on.

"Juma's women? Their lives are shit. You want to save eight. I say there's eight hundred we save."

Neels teetered again. He had heatstroke, LB was sure of it. He'd seen it in the Kush and the hot plains of Iraq. Dizzy, ashen, disoriented, no sweat, cool skin.

LB lifted his own palm against Neels's accusations, wanting to tell him he needed to get out of the sun. Everything could be figured out if they all stayed calm.

This angered Neels even more, the idea that LB might have something to say. He stomped on Wally's back, squeezing out an agonized curse.

LB did everything in his power to root his boots to the ravine and keep from bull-rushing the man. Neels ignored him.

"Poachers take twelve hundred rhinos a year. More. The beast will be gone before the decade's over. You don't have rhinos in America, why the fok should you care? Don't tell me Juma lives. Don't you fall out of a plane, spend one night in my park, then come tell me Juma lives today for Karskie and eight whores. No."

Neels shook his extended hand, panning for LB's radio.

"Give it to me. With the code. I'll do it."

LB traced fingers over the radio stuck in his vest. He'd been ready to die in Macandezulo. But that was with Juma, not instead of him.

In agony beneath Neels's boot, Wally managed to turn his head. Dust clung to his lips and chin.

"Don't do it." Wally couldn't lift his eyes, only his voice. "LB. Don't."

Neels dropped his appeal for the radio, placing both hands on the rifle.

"Sergeant."

Neels's features, already colorless from the heat, went blank. His hands firmed on the rifle and trigger. Standing over Wally, he seemed like a clock ticking seconds.

Again, Wally spoke into the red dirt.

"Don't."

LB plucked the radio from his pocket, to do something, anything to string out a few more moments. Neels reached for it, easing his weight off Wally. LB hefted the radio. What a small thing it was, small as the time left to him.

What was next? Tuck the radio back in his vest, or give it to Neels? Either brought terrible consequences. If LB kept the radio, Neels would pull the trigger. The old bastard was crazed and sun sick, but zeal convinced him he was right, and sacrifice told him he was justified. Wally wouldn't survive him, no doubt.

If Neels shot Wally, LB would charge him. Too much rage, LB would do it. The mission would fail, with one murdered GA, two dead rangers, and an unexploded Hellfire. Juma and Lush Life would walk away scot-free with two hundred million dollars.

If LB gave Neels the radio and the code, the cost to take out Juma would be Karskie and eight blameless, sad women. How many rhinos would that save? How many lives would be saved by ridding the world of Juma's weapons, poaching, drug- and human-trafficking operations?

Neels was right.

What would Karskie say? Would he make that trade? Neels didn't speak for him. And the women, would they throw their lives on the fire to stop Juma? Would they die today to defend other unknown women on another day? Did Neels speak for them?

Neels was wrong.

Wally lay under the muzzle of Neels's gun. Wally had made the decision for himself. He'd made the brave and right choice of a Guardian Angel.

What would Torres say? Did Wally speak for her?

Could LB?

Neels spit in the dirt. LB had taken too long holding the radio.

Time was up.

"I'm sorry, Captain. Your sergeant prefers Juma."

LB tensed to speak, leap, something! What a fucking awful thing for Wally to hear, to be told that LB would let him die. A lie, a lie that would stand. He couldn't get to Neels fast enough.

Promise—LB had forgotten her—threw out her arms.

"Wait. There's someone else."

Neels hesitated. LB hugged the radio to his chest, not putting it away, not offering it, just clutching it. Wally exhaled what was almost his last breath. Neels tipped his head toward the girl.

"Who, Promise? Who else is there?"

"An old man. In the village. A white man."

"A white?"

Neels looked to LB, as if for some reason this might be his department.

"Who is he?"

Again, as in Macandezulo, LB couldn't keep up with the careening of his fate and emotions. Seconds ago, he was prepared to kill or die trying, to either see Wally executed or sentence Karskie and Juma's women to death. Neels asked questions coldly, fact-finding, as though all of them did not stand on the edge of many unmarked graves. LB was in no frame of mind to answer Neels while he sorted out what to do.

"Promise, shut up."

Neels tutted, detached and mercurial. He turned to Promise for answers.

"Who is the white man?"

"A friend of Juma's."

"A friend. What's his name?"

"He called himself Lush Life."

"Really? What did he look like? How was he dressed?"

"His clothes were dirty. But they were from the city. Expensive."

"Odd. Sergeant, isn't that odd?"

Under Neels's boot, Wally was fading, blanching. Judging by the puddle of blood, the bullet had gone all the way through his shoulder. It might have hit a vessel. Another ticking clock.

"Sergeant."

"Yeah. Odd."

"How did he behave? Who is he?"

"He's Juma's partner. It was fucking obvious."

Neels's face lit up as if the sun had flared on it. His mouth opened, eyes lifted from LB to the sky, fathoming something and thankful.

LB edged one boot closer. He leaned on his toes.

Neels had the instincts of the bush. His attention flashed back to LB.

"Sergeant."

"What?"

"I might shoot you first."

LB shifted his weight back to his heels.

Neels stepped down. He lowered the rifle to his waist and retreated. Out of range, he squatted on his haunches, weapon across his knees, ready.

"Do you have a first aid kit?"

"In my pack."

"Take care of your captain."

LB hustled to his pack. He tore into it for the small med kit from the plane. Promise rushed to help Wally roll onto his back. She set to unbuttoning his tunic. By the time LB had alcohol, gauze, and antibiotic ready, she'd stripped Wally's shoulder bare. He sat upright, woozy, gritting his teeth.

His shoulder was a scarlet mess, but the wound cleaned up well. Both entry and exit holes were neat. Fired at close range and high velocity, the round was a through and through, in and out; it hadn't bounced off a bone into a lung or anything vicious. LB moved his face close to Wally's to check him for shock.

"Hey."

Wally's cheeks had gone pallid, but his eyes focused.

"Don't worry."

LB scooted behind him to patch the entry wound. A red ring, the imprint of Neels's gun, showed just below Wally's hairline. While LB stuffed gauze into the open wound, Wally stiffened with a deep, pained grunt.

LB spoke to the back of his head.

"Worry about what?"

"I know."

Behind him, where Wally could not see, LB nodded. A lot welled up in him that he could not name or separate into categories or years, just a lot. LB swiped away a tear so he could do his work.

"Man, I'm sorry."

"I said I know."

Promise knelt to hold Wally up. LB skidded around to deal with the exit wound. Wally blinked with every touch, sucking in his cheeks, until LB wrapped his arm to his chest with an elastic bandage. When LB finished, Wally closed his eyelids to rest for moments. His blood loss had weakened him, but he was clear-headed. Ten yards away, Neels hunkered, waiting and observing like one of the buzzards.

"Captain."

Wally opened his eyes. He didn't answer right off but stared back, drawn and tired. Under Neels's gun he'd made his decision, just as LB had in the village. Everything else about being alive seemed faraway and temporary.

"What?"

LB took a knee beside Wally. The girl remained standing, always ready to bolt.

Neels patted the rifle in his lap.

"I want you to understand. I need your radio and the code to the missile."

"You've made that clear."

"This white man, Lush Life, has to die. He has to. More than Juma."

"Why?"

"Because he's a tier three. A financier. These are the right bastards. They drive all this, the poaching, organized crime. For money, Captain. Lives are nothing to them. Nothing. Just things to steal and sell. We never see them. They kill and spoil and do it all from inside corporations and bank accounts. But this one. Lush Life. I don't care why or how, but he's come out where we can see him. And he's one kilometer away from me. You're going to let me kill him. Or I will shoot all three of you. By God, I will."

The sun had soared well past its peak. Neels's shadow in the ravine crept at LB and Wally. Its outline was sharp in the bright, unbroken light. Neels wavered. He put a hand in the dirt to steady himself.

"Captain. Juma and this white man are blackmailing your country. They've ruined the girl there. Your own lives are at risk. You've got reasons to see them dead, too."

Wally seemed to want to collapse. Like Neels, he dropped a hand to the dirt for balance.

"What did they do to you, Neels?"

The old ranger was staggered by either the question or the heat. He rocked forward onto his knees, the rifle tumbling out of his lap. He didn't reach for it but ran a hand across his mouth, a tremble in his fingers. Neels's lips parted as if to give some answer. His posture went slack. On his knees he looked to be a man in surrender.

Wally said nothing more. The bullet from Neels's gun seemed to link them, he wobbled, too. But he did not lie back down.

Wally drew his legs under him, propped himself on his good arm, and struggled to rise. Promise rushed to support him. LB did nothing, amazed.

Wally got to his feet. Time had run out. He did not rush at Neels but walked.

Neels watched him come for two, three strides. Slowly, but fast enough, Neels gathered the rifle off the ground and leveled it at his waist. At this range, with an automatic weapon, there was no need to aim. Just fire.

Wally didn't stop.

Neels shook his head, not at Wally but elsewhere.

LB shot to his feet.

"Alright."

He snatched the radio from his vest. LB held it out like a lantern against the dark gun and Neels's shadow under Wally's boots.

"Here, take it. Go."

Neels's gun and the prospect of dying in front of it did not stop Wally. LB's words did. Wally reeled to a halt.

"What?"

"Let him have it."

"No."

LB stood, still holding out the radio.

"I'm not letting you die today."

As if another bullet had struck him, Wally winced, then staggered.

"That's not your call."

"I'm making it anyway."

"And Karskie? The women? You making it for them?"

"This isn't our country. It isn't our fight. Like he said."

Wally shot his good arm at Neels.

"Like he said? *Him*? He's out of his fucking mind."

"I can hear you, Captain."

Wally spun on Neels.

"You are. You know that?"

"I don't rule it out. It changes nothing. Sergeant, the radio. And the code."

Wally pivoted between the two, off balance.

"No."

LB approached Wally, coming close enough to whisper.

"It's our missile. We've got orders to blow it up. Let's do it and go home. Okay?"

Without his sunglasses, Wally's eyes questioned, confounded.

"Go home?"

"Yeah. Home. To Torres. To your life."

Wally gazed down at the radio in LB's mitt. When he raised his face, he seemed dazed.

"This is my life."

His voice cracked, as if those were the last words he would ever speak to LB, as if he were speaking from a deathbed.

Wally sat where he stood. He cradled his wounded arm, the pain welling up.

LB would have taken a bullet for Wally over their dozen years of bickering, competing, and quiet admiration at any time. But this was not that day. To save Wally under the unblinking sun of Mozambique, today LB would take shame instead.

Neels followed him with the rifle as LB handed over the radio. Behind him, Promise came to Wally's side.

"The missile's in the blockhouse at the end of the main road. It's in the basement, so get close."

"The code?"

"Five-four-three-one-zero."

"Back away now."

LB retreated several steps. Neels got to his feet, keeping his weapon trained on LB.

"Promise will lead you back across the border."

LB spit in the dirt that had soaked up Wally's blood. And Wophule's blood, and soon Karskie's and the women's, Juma's and Lush Life's, the blood of poachers and rhinos. Tragedy flocked to Neels like flies.

"Hey. Pielkop."

The old ranger appeared light-headed. He ignored LB's curse.

"Sergeant."

"Make sure I never lay eyes on you again."

"Bluster, Sergeant. And my advice to you. Leave the bush as quickly as you can. You don't fit. This is a place for Promise and Juma and me. For lions and jackals. For killers. There is no mercy. Nothing is rescued here. Go home."

Neels tucked the radio inside his belt. He backed away behind his rifle, with the other gun strapped across his back. At the rim of the ravine, before he turned to face Macandezulo, he called to LB.

"Don't follow me."

Neels walked away along the creek bed.

Then he stumbled.

Chapter 35

Neels lay in the red dust. He'd rolled onto his rear, pointing his rifle back at the Americans should they try to take advantage now. After frantic and scrabbling moments, he lay still. Only his head bobbed up and down, on guard and exposed.

Promise stepped to LB.

"Give me water."

The sergeant started to speak, stopped, and began again.

"What? For him?"

Neels, in his khakis, could have been a shrub low to the ground. He could have been a rock. But left to lie in the open like that, in the beating sun without mercy just as he'd said, the buzzards would know within hours that he was flesh and dead.

"Yes. For him. Is that who you are now? Will you let him die, too, to solve your problems?"

The wounded, sitting captain unclipped his canteen. He handed it up to Promise without looking at her.

Promise snagged the water. She cupped LB's elbow.

"Take care of Neels. Wait here."

LB reversed the grip, laying his hand inside her arm.

"Whoa, whoa. What are you doing?"

"I'm a tracker. I follow trails."

She shifted out of LB's hand, away from his reach.

"I pray you find yours. Follow it."

She had nothing to say to the captain, did not know him save for his courage. Promise jogged away.

Neels tried to sit up at the sound of her boots. The rifle had flagged between his legs, and he could not raise it. He managed only to come to his elbows. She slowed to approach him at a walk. Already Neels looked like a corpse, linen white and puffy.

"Stay where you are, girl."

He tried to muster some threat in his voice, but his hands were empty. Promise showed the canteen. She eased beside him and knelt, soothing.

"Where is your hat, Neels?"

"In my back pocket."

"Let me get it out."

Promise plucked the crushed cloth hat from beneath him. She poured water over it and screwed it onto his simmering pate.

"Drink."

Neels worked to free one arm off the ground to take the canteen. She helped him hold it to his lips; he guzzled, spilling too much. Promise took the canteen away. She closed it and laid it in his lap.

"You won't make it."

"Yes, I will."

"You'll faint, or you'll get caught."

"What do you want, Promise? Why not let me die? You'll be free."

Promise glanced back to LB standing at the rim of the ravine, watching. The Americans knew what she'd done. Even without them, Promise knew. She laughed, a short, mirthless burst she did not explain to Neels. Without all of them, even herself, the bush knew what she'd done.

How could she come home to it? The bull rhino dead, the aardvark dead, Wophule dead, Neels dead, Karskie dead. Where would she be welcome? In Hazy View, in Gogo's hovel that Promise could not lift her out of? Gogo's brother dead? Promise was more blighted and stained than she could ever match or wipe away by being sorry.

"Is there a bounty on Juma?"

Neels attempted to sit straight up, but he was done in by the heat and stayed on his elbows. Droplets from the soaked hat dripped onto his bloodless cheeks.

"No."

The world in that moment was very large for Promise. If she just walked away, she might live. She knew how to disappear. She could do it even under such a sun, then let the concerns of the Americans perish in the bush with Neels. She could let others die for her and be free.

"Give me the radio."

Neels clamped a hand over it at his waist.

"No."

"I'll do it."

"You're a liar and a poacher. You'll warn Juma."

"I don't need the radio for that. And I would have warned him already."

Promise could snatch it from his belt, but Neels had to give it to her. She needed a promise from him.

"Give it to me. Wait an hour. If you hear nothing, the Americans have another radio. Come do it yourself. Five-four-three-one-zero."

"I want Juma and Lush Life."

"Yes."

Promise opened her palm and waited. An animal could not be forced to trust. It must decide.

"Understand me, girl. You've still done what you've done."

"I know. As have you."

"Why do this?"

"Why do you fight with the air?"

The question gave its own answer. Because they were both trackers who had lost their paths. Promise had found hers again;

she could not say it to LB because he would have tried to stop her, but it led one way, one narrow trail to Macandezulo. Where Neels's path led, only he knew.

Neels tugged out the radio. He laid it in her hand.

"Go."

"I want something from you."

"What have I got that you want?"

"Your word."

Neels chortled at his own body, lying drained and weak in the hot dust of Mozambique.

"I haven't lost that yet. For what?"

"Swear to me my grandparents will get a house. Swear you'll help them."

Neels peered into the shimmering, heated distance.

"Open the water."

Promise unscrewed the canteen. She held it to Neels's lips. He shook it off.

"You."

Promise took a short draft, enough, then closed the cap. Neels extended a hand.

"Help me up."

She pulled hard to put him on his feet, he was a big man and weak-kneed. Standing, Neels rubbed his damp face. She returned the canteen. He surveyed the way east to the village.

He offered the ranger R-1 on his back.

"Take this."

"No. Give me your knife."

Neels bent toward the sheath tucked in his boot but lost a bit of balance. He straightened. Promise took the knife herself.

"LB is a medic."

"I won't let the bastard touch me."

"If that's your wish."

Promise did not offer her hand for a shake, Neels would not take it. She took one backward step and instead fixed her gaze on his eyes to bond him. Neels said nothing until she turned away.

"That's what all this is about? A fokken house for your grandparents?"

Promise did not stop to answer, on her path, but called across her shoulder.

"Yes."

Neels raised one open palm, not in farewell but in oath.

"My word."

• • •

Promise left the ravine to dart among the thorny acacias and flowering hedges. She ducked under low branches denuded by drought and dashed from trunk to shrub, waited and listened, scanning for Juma's guardians on the outskirts. She hurried inside her hour. She needed a third of it to approach Macandezulo unseen.

She stayed careful of the sun and the wind, for Good Luck was a man of the bush, too. But when Promise finally saw him from a distance, he still wore his leopard muti and had his long rifle across his lap in a picnic chair. He sat across from Karskie, doing what he'd been told. Good Luck was not wary, not thinking Promise would keep her vow and come for him.

She slipped into the village, creeping near the hovels. Moving through clutches of weeds, she was a shadow unstaked from the ground. Promise sped and crawled from wall to wall, until she'd maneuvered ten meters behind Good Luck. As she hid behind the last structure, the generator purred loudly enough that Promise could not hear the *shuss* of Neels's long knife sliding out of its sheath at her waist. She tucked the radio into the small of her back. Promise thanked the old gods, asked for strength and silence, and pressed a finger to her lips. She stepped into the open.

Immediately, Karskie saw her. Keeping the finger to her mouth, she waggled the knife, showing her intent and pleading with him to say and do nothing. The big boy blinked as if Promise had cast chips into his eyes. She stopped sneaking and spread her hands wide: *What are you doing*? Karskie got control of himself, then did something clever and cold-blooded.

He leaned in front of his chair for a water bottle.

"Here."

Karskie tossed it into Good Luck's leopard-skin lap. With short strides, Promise tiptoed closer.

Good Luck was slow to take up the bottle. Promise could not see his features, but he was a hateful man, and she pictured his tongue poking out at Karskie for throwing the bottle at him. She stood at arm's length behind him, ready. Karskie kept his eyes off her, locked on Good Luck. The big boy fidgeted, and to occupy himself, he grabbed another bottle off the ground. He uncapped it and drank, tipping it high. Now Good Luck did the same.

Promise flashed. She reached her empty hand around Good Luck's head, knocking the bottle aside. Water gushed over his face. Before the shooter could yelp or spit, she clamped her hand tight across his mouth. Widening her stance, Promise plunged Neels's long blade into the rear of the lawn chair, through the leopard pelt, stabbing with every bit of her strength, which had been enough to down a rhino, and with Wophule's spirit, which had lingered for this moment. She stopped Good Luck's mouth, muffled his cries while he strained, flailed, and kicked to leap away from the dagger and Promise's suffocating hand. She held on and shoved hard. Good Luck coughed bloody water against her palm, exploding against her hand, backward into her face. She leaned close to Good Luck's shaking, gagging head, bracing against him, but she whispered nothing in his ear that the blade did not say better in his back. The fight in Good Luck lasted long, because he was evil and he had muti. But as he gurgled and faded, Promise twisted the knife so the shooter's ghost would feel a final pain before it fled.

Karskie did not take his hands from his own mouth, stifling himself, staring in shock, until Good Luck shuddered and went limp.

Promise pulled her wet, crimson hands off him. She walked around to face Good Luck. He'd died with his mouth gaping, like Wophule. Promise threw a handful of dirt onto the dead snake of his tongue.

With his vengeance done, Wophule's spirit followed his path, away. Promise bid him good-bye and asked forgiveness.

Karskie climbed to his feet, stammering and hissing.

"Holy shit. Promise."

"They're waiting for you in the ravine. Go."

The killing and the corpse, the blood spattered over Promise's face and the leopard skin, the suddenness of it all baffled Karskie.

"Wait. What?"

Promise tugged the radio from her back.

"I'm going to blow the missile."

"But I thought the Americans . . ."

Promise placed her hands on Karskie before he could finish. She spun him and pushed to make him leave. Karskie lurched a few steps before he saw that Promise hung back.

"What about you?"

"Ask Neels. He knows."

Karskie had no idea what to do with his large, soft hands. He offered them to Promise, as if to hold her or carry her away, something unsure but a deed, as if he were a ranger and brave.

"I should stay with you."

"You're a good man. Go, right now. Don't run, walk out of the village. West into the sun. You'll find the ravine."

"Promise."

She turned her back to make Karskie go. She hauled Good Luck out of the lawn chair; the shooter was not a heavy man, lighter without his spirit. His cracked heels dragged in the dust. Promise kept her back to the road, and when she had stashed the body in the weeds behind the blockhouse, Karskie was gone from Macandezulo. She folded the sliced lawn chair and tossed it, the long rifle, and the knife on top of Good Luck. With the water left in the half-drunk bottle, Promise washed the blood off her cheeks and hands.

She walked down the center of the dirt road. The village dozed in the late afternoon. All of Juma's guards slouched somewhere shady. Juma could be laying with some of his women, or even with Hard Life. The generator prattled behind Promise, insects in the overgrowth sang while hiding.

With the radio in hand, she stopped in the center of Macandezulo. The blockhouse stood thirty meters away, with the missile asleep in its belly. Promise ran her thumb over the face of LB's radio, and the five numerals that would wake the missile.

She closed her eyes in the street. Promise told the sun on her eyelids and the old gods behind them that she was done. She was grateful to have been brought this far, and if they found her redeemed, she asked them to use the time that might have been hers to watch over the ones she loved. Promise had regrets but did not dwell on them because, truly, no one cared about that but her.

She climbed the steps of a tilting porch, into a pink house with four straight walls.

Chapter 36

The sun beat on the roof like rain, keeping Allyn inside.

He lay on the mattress tick gazing up at the bare rafters. A clever vine wound about one beam to reach for another. In a few months this small house would be claimed and green, in another year melted into the bush. Allyn wondered where he would be then. Today he lay unclaimed, quiet as the heat.

A water jug stood untouched near the mattress. Eight hours remained until midnight. Allyn figured to wait here for most of that time, and the water would allow that, so he marshaled it. The cell phone sat on the tick beside him. He thought to call Zimbabwe to check on the negotiations, the progress of the money, but he chalked that up to nerves.

He'd loosed his belt before lying down. Restless, Allyn slid his hand inside his pants. He marveled at the urge, how, like the bush, it seemed so insistent, even at his age. Would it ever stop, or was this his companion to the end? He began to stiffen and thought of having a woman.

He conjured images of Juma's whores. They walked past again, enfolding him in linen and black flesh. This time they didn't drift by, headed for the alley, but stopped in a circle, Allyn in the center. They hiked their dresses and squatted to urinate. He smelled them, urine and sweat, the sour rawness of their loins. The vision surprised Allyn, as he didn't believe he'd bidden it, but his stroking hand sped. Inside the imagined ring he pivoted to select a whore. This pleased him, as they all wanted him. Allyn spotted the one he'd lain with last night, she was shaved and looked very young inside her thighs. He almost picked her.

But why must he take a whore? They didn't want him truly, they were addled. They'd been given to him by Juma, they were his property. This felt like charity. Allyn wasn't desperate, he was rich.

His thoughts banked toward Eva. She appeared in the circle, squatting, pissing with the whores. He didn't want her there, but his arousal could not stop it, his hand insisted on it. She was his bride, blond and supple, adoring, the path between her spread legs was his path to everything. Then, just as quickly, Eva in his vision became Eva his wife, aging and simple. Allyn regretted summoning her. He decoupled from the image completely. This left him stroking himself emptily. He stopped.

But the want of a woman was not thwarted. Allyn could invoke no one in particular, just the presence of a nameless, faceless female here on his mattress. Not for sex particularly, just someone to lie in the heat with, sweat next to, make himself real to. He didn't enjoy his own company, and that's what Eva had left him with, the cause of his grudge against her. The money would fix this. Allyn concocted new fantasies around the great wealth that waited like a jack-in-the-box inside the coming night, how it would spring and change everything.

He almost did not hear the light tread on the floorboards. Thoughts of money and foreign lovers and the renewed motion of his hand had shut his eyes and swelled his senses. His first thought was that this was one of Juma's girls sneaking in and he might keep her a little while. Allyn craned his neck without sitting up.

The ranger girl stood at the foot of his tick.

Allyn yanked his hand out of his pants. Pushing himself to a sitting position, he surveyed her quickly. No gun, nothing to hurt him. He considered being embarrassed that Juma's young relative had caught him playing with himself, but the girl had invaded his privacy.

"Promise, is it?"

"Yes."

"What are you doing here?"

"I have nowhere else to go."

Allyn glanced behind her.

"Are you alone?"

"Yes."

"You might have knocked."

"There's no door."

"Don't be cheeky, girl. You might have announced yourself."

"Sorry."

"What do you want?"

The girl was coal skinned and glistening from her walk back to the village. The bare legs between her shorts and socks showed muscle, her arms lithe and veined. She had a tribal face of angles and ovals, short, wiry hair. Like many black Africans, the girl's teeth seemed unnaturally white and inviting.

She reached behind her back. A weapon? Needles of alarm bit inside Allyn's lungs. He pushed backward on the tick, raising a hand against whatever she was doing.

Promise produced a small radio. She held it out for him to see, harmless.

The prickles in Allyn's chest needed moments to ease. He cleared his throat while taking hold of his breathing. He laughed to release his nerves.

"Look at me. I apologize."

Allyn gathered himself, brushing the raised hand through his hair to fill the pause.

But was this life in the bush? He looked at himself even as he said the words to Promise. He'd spent just one night and day in Macandezulo, and already he had become a creature of suspicion, instinct, lust, boldness. It amazed him. The mines had been like this. He'd been young in the mines, but it hadn't been his youth that made the days breathtaking; he'd been young in the city, too. After he left the tunnels for fancy offices and big houses, he lost the thrill of living and dying and the fortunes that could come in the mines from a flame, a rock, a shovel, the commonest of things.

Just now, he'd been so frightened he'd recoiled from a young woman reaching behind her back. The relief that she held only a radio made him laugh. The sight, the smell of her, gave him a sudden pang for her.

He knew his want. He asked again for hers.

"What are you doing here? In my room specifically."

"The American gave me this radio to bring to Juma. So they can communicate about the money. To be certain there are no problems."

"Are there problems, Promise?"

"Perhaps."

"What are they?"

"I've killed Good Luck. Karskie is gone."

Allyn jumped to his bare feet, standing on the tick should he need to run or fight. He was uncertain how effectively he could do either against this woman. He sensed no threat. Promise made no move toward him except to show the radio. But she had come to him after killing a man. He had no idea what might be next.

"Did the American send you to do that?"

"No. Good Luck murdered my partner."

The bush again, asserting itself. Like the vine in the rafters, the heat on the roof.

"Tell me what you want. Or please leave."

"I need your help."

"For what?"

"You can sit."

"I'll do as I see fit."

Where had that come from? Apparently, Promise approved of his snippiness, for she showed her white teeth and sat on the edge of the tick. Allyn folded himself in the center of the mattress, warily, for she was a killer.

"What sort of help?"

"I want you to tell Juma to let me stay. I can't go back to the rangers."

"Juma's already made up his mind. He sent you away."

"He'll listen to you."

"How do you know that?"

"I could see it. He always has. Juma is big. But you are the bull."

"After tonight, Juma and I will leave Macandezulo."

"Ask him to take me with him."

"He won't."

"Then take me with you."

She sat only a meter away. Allyn searched her hands, her clothes, for blood. He found no evidence of a killing.

"Why should I do anything for you? Why trust you?"

"Because I can help you."

"With what?"

The girl leaned to him. She made a cup of her free palm and reached between his crossed legs.

"With this."

Allyn watched her black eyes. She did not pull them from his even while she rubbed him. Her stare was hungry, and something of the mines was there, too, a sparkle, like a fuse. Her gaze held him as much as her hand as she stood from the bed.

"Come with me, Lush Life."

She guided Allyn off the tick, past the water jug, and out the door. Allyn followed, as if the girl carried all of him in her palm. She trailed her fingertips away from his crotch only after they'd stepped down the splintered porch into the dirt road.

He hurried behind Promise, admiring and wanting. Allyn thought of nothing past having her, no time but the time until that happened, no light but that which died on her ebon skin, only the blood pooling in his loins.

Halfway to the blockhouse, in the murmur of the generator, Promise turned around fully, as though to see that he was still there. She walked backward in the street, drawing him with her feral smile.

Still backpedaling, Promise brought up the radio she'd not let loose since she entered his hovel. When she brought her face up, her eyes were rimmed with tears. One broke down her cheek and shone like a river.

Allyn wanted to reach for it because it was intimate, he would lick this woman's salt tear off his thumb.

"What are you crying for?"

"My grandmother."

"Is something wrong?"

Through more falling tears the girl tried to laugh. She failed and seemed to fight for breath. Still backing down the street, Promise bit her lower lip. She stopped in the shadow of Juma's blockhouse. There, she regained her voice.

"Everything is well." Promise held the radio high, then punched in several numbers. She paused before the last digit, then, staring deeply at Allyn, hit it.

Her next backward step tripped her. The girl almost toppled, had to wave her arms to keep her balance. Ungainly, surprised to still be on her feet, she spun to stare at the blockhouse.

From behind, Allyn put a hand to her shoulder. She startled, as if his touch were electric.

"Are you alright?"

"Yes."

"What were you doing with the radio?"

Promise gazed up at the hard, gray building where Juma slept, the women lived, the guns were stored. The structure stood between her and the sun.

"The American. He gave me a code. To tell him everything is good."

"So he knows you're here now. And safe."

"Yes."

"Fine."

The girl seemed transfixed. She held her ground, reluctant to move closer to the blockhouse. But just as she'd said, the toothless shooter in the leopard skin was missing from the place at the front door where Juma had stationed him. So was the hostage, Karskie, and one of the lawn chairs.

This was where she'd killed Good Luck minutes ago. That was why she hesitated. Juma would be furious.

"Where's the body?"

Promise recovered herself, her steadfastness, with her answer. "Behind the building. Go see, if you want."

She'd actually done it, naked violence. First a rhino, then a man. What else might she do?

"I believe you. Are you frightened?"

Again the girl made a halting, struggling laugh.

"Very."

Allyn imagined her hands on him. Promise was powerful and dangerous. But as much as he wanted her, she needed him. So not all the power was hers. Allyn grew impatient.

"I'll speak to Juma."

They took a step in tandem. Then she ran away from him.

The little poacher boy, Hard Life, had come down the stairs and emerged from the blockhouse. He looked groggy, knuckling his eyes as if the sunlight dazzled him. Or he, too, had been crying. Promise dashed the short distance to him.

She grabbed Hard Life by the collar and hissed something into his small face, urgent and beyond Allyn's hearing. She pushed Hard Life into the street as if he were a cart she wanted to roll away. The boy didn't seem to understand and backed off several steps, but ran out of momentum and stopped. Promise aimed a hand up the road, beseeching. The boy, probably stupid, took a few more shuffling strides away.

Allyn passed the boy and brushed a hand across the top of his head as if he were a tyke. But he wasn't. Hard Life was a teenager, stunted by Africa. He pushed Allyn's hand away.

Promise would not go inside the blockhouse until she'd watched Hard Life amble farther up the dirt road. Allyn slipped his hand inside the crook of her elbow, as if she wore a dress, as if to escort her somewhere nice.

"How do you know him?"

"I killed his partner."

"What did you tell him?"

"To leave Macandezulo. That Juma was leaving."

She patted Allyn's hand on her arm. The tears had not dried in Promise's eyes. Her black pupils seemed to be set in diamonds.

"And you are going, too."

Clutching the radio, she watched the boy walk off. When he'd gone as far as the pink shanty, Promise took Allyn's hand. It was not a murderer's strength in her touch but a woman's. Allyn lifted the back of her hand to his lips.

Promise beamed and snatched a breath. She sniffed and seemed contented, comforted by his peck on the back of her hand.

"No one has ever kissed me there."

"Then I'm glad. You were right, Juma will listen to me. Stay out here. I won't be long."

Before he could release her, Promise closed her hand around his fingers.

"I want to go to the basement."

Her request was curious, but what was not curious about this girl? Again and again, she was like the bush to him, a place where things hid.

"What is your name?" she asked.

"Allyn."

"Take me downstairs, Allyn."

"It's better if you wait out here."

"I don't want to wait."

The girl rested his hand on the ledge of her hip, as if to dance. And that was what Allyn desired, to dance in the wild.

The guard who should have been sitting outside the blockhouse lay dead around back. With Promise in tow, Allyn pushed open Juma's door without knocking.

Chapter 37

Promise unlaced her boots, then peeled off her tall socks. Her ranger's blouse went next. She unbuttoned it, not facing Allyn but the missile. Allyn asked her to turn around, believing she was disrobing for him. She let the tunic molt from her arms and puddle on the hard floor. Last, Promise stepped out of her shorts and underpants. These she tossed away. They fell on a pile of weapons; where else could they land in this room?

Promise stood before the missile as bare as a beast. Her tears were finished, her hands did not quake when she lifted the radio off the table.

"Promise."

She pronounced the name she wanted no more of. She discarded it on the heaps of steel around her, tossed it off like her clothing to go onward without it.

Behind her, old, white Allyn edged closer. His small warmth lay against her spine. She'd not noticed, but he had doffed his own shirt.

"Yes. I promise."

She decided these last minutes were madness.

Promise filled her lungs, naked and ready. Holding her breath made her think of wishes, like a birthday cake. She wished to feel the breeze on the hill where Gogo would live. And for Juma and Allyn to be dead.

She tapped a fingertip on the radio's keypad.

Five. Four. Three.

Behind her, Allyn withdrew.

Promise pitched forward, slammed in the back as if gored. A great pain struck her shoulder. The room spun. She collapsed forward onto the table, bumping the missile that had not exploded. Her own cry became lost beneath a shocking, sharp roar.

Her tumble stopped on the cool floor. She fought for focus, struggling to peer out through her agony. She had no feeling in her left arm. Looking at her dead, hanging hand, she saw the radio was gone.

Promise gripped a table leg to hold herself upright. In her life, she'd never felt this much pain. It threatened to close around her like jaws. She crawled under the table and curled in her knees, cowering, a primal urge.

The bullet had hit high in her back, below her neck. Promise clung tight to a table leg, scanning the concrete floor. The act of turning her head almost cost her senses. There was too much, the jumble of guns, the drops of her own blood, the feet of Lush Life backing away, her dropped clothes. Panic licked at her. Where was the radio?

Not on the floor. Where had it spilled from her hand?

On the tabletop, with the missile.

From beyond the mounds of guns, where she could not see him, Juma bellowed.

The white man's feet continued to retreat. She gathered her left arm into her lap.

Juma screamed again.

"Promise!"

That was not her name. She was Nomawethu. *With my ancestors.*

The last boundary was not time nor life. She'd chosen death. Only pain held her back, and it was mighty, weighty.

She held tight to the table leg, panting, bleeding, sliding down. She had no way forward, no track to follow. No grave to lie in.

An unbidden warmth flowed over her. Not her blood, not a man, but the breath to blow out a candle.

Like mist, her spirit slipped away from her body. With surprise and relief, shedding all hurt, she stepped free.

Promise rose from beneath the table.

In the doorway stood Juma, a pistol at the end of his thick arm. He strode into the basement. White Allyn backed away until he had moved behind Juma.

For the last time, Promise turned away from them. On the tabletop, under a fin of the missile, lay the radio.

With her one working arm, she slid the radio to her. Without lifting it, she pressed the number one.

Before her fingertip could touch the final key, a tiny, black hand flashed under hers and snatched the radio away.

With her good hand, she caught herself as she buckled. Her body and spirit, cut loose from each other moments ago, rejoined. There was more to do here, and only a little life left to do it.

The pain returned, and with it, the madness.

Chapter 38

The girl struggled up from under the table. The bullet hole bled one red wing down her back. Allyn lurched backward from her, horrified.

The gray room shivered from the pistol shot. Juma advanced, pistol up, shouting. The little poacher, Hard Life, ran through the maze of weapons and snagged the radio off the table, out of Promise's reach. Allyn didn't stop backpedaling until he'd gotten behind Juma.

The girl faced the table, leaning on her good arm. Crimson drizzled down her back, over her buttocks, to her heels. The boy, Hard Life, dashed with the radio past Juma and Allyn, out of the armory into the stairwell. Juma muttered, "Good child."

Juma stopped closing in. He snarled.

"You want to die?"

Still turned to the table, Promise bowed her head to the missile.

Allyn wanted to fetch his shirt, but it sat on the concrete too close to the girl. He stayed behind Juma.

"What's happened?"

Big Juma ignored him but lowered the gun. Anger worked on Juma's lips and tongue, trying to contain itself in words. He addressed Promise's bleeding back.

"Tell me, girl. Now, or I'll kill you. Will the American come to blow up the missile?"

Allyn crossed his hands over his waist. He was shirtless, a reminder that he'd been caught down here with this naked girl.

"Is that what she was doing with the radio? Juma?"

"Yes, shamwari. With the radio."

"She was going to kill me?"

"Both of us."

"Shoot her."

The words were out before Allyn thought them. They were the end of his journey from Johannesburg, from Eva and the mines. He'd arrived here, where he'd demanded a murder. He stood shirtless in a basement in Mozambique with a live missile, where his life had been one second from being snuffed. Allyn held his hands out from his sides, like a man dripping with something.

"I'm done, Juma. I want to go home."

Before Juma could answer, the girl whirled on them, shrieking.

Her black eyes darted, eyes that Allyn had almost wandered into. Juma raised the pistol again. Allyn stepped back. Every muscle in the girl tensed, she coiled for some move. Her fingers worked for something to clutch.

Juma waved the pistol, barking her name. Promise paid no attention. She had one bullet in her. The girl was wounded and dreadful; how much could she fear one bullet more?

She lunged at a pile of rifles. Juma followed with the pistol but did not squeeze the trigger. The girl picked the gun up, not by the wooden stock but the barrel. She raised it high, two-handed, like a club.

Promise glared at Juma from under her brows, with her head dipped as if she might charge. Instead, she smashed the heavy gun down on the tip of the missile.

She was trying to set off the warhead.

Juma yelled for her to stop. Allyn rocked to his heels, bile in his throat, needing escape.

Promise hammered the rifle down on the warhead again.

Juma fired.

This round sent Promise sprawling over the table. The rifle dropped from her hands, clattering to the concrete. Remarkably, in the shreds of the pistol's echo, the girl pushed herself erect, away from the rocket she'd only managed to dent.

Allyn staggered backward until he found himself in the doorway.

Juma advanced to stand an arm's length from the girl, his family. He'd killed her, surely, with the two bullets. He lowered the gun, unafraid. Juma no longer shouted.

"Is the American coming back to blow up the missile? Are the Americans not going to pay?"

Promise wavered on her feet. A red trickle seeped from her nostrils, over her lips. She wrapped her arms around her small breasts as though cold.

Nothing moved in the armory but a purl of gun smoke against the ceiling. Juma and Promise had reached some understanding in the silence that coiled between them. She was going to die in the next seconds, and all that remained was the quality of that death.

Allyn had no urge to see it. He felt no more greed for the money and the plot. Juma had warned him that he wasn't suited for this. Allyn should have listened while they sat on his veranda beside the lake. He intended to walk out of Macandezulo. He slunk backward into the stairwell. The boy, Hard Life, stood there, clutching the radio.

From above, a commotion rumbled. The steps clogged with a cascade of fair dresses and ebony skin, hurrying feet, and the dense smells of perspiration and oils. Juma's women flooded down, pushing Allyn and the poacher boy back into the armory, crowding in behind them.

Promise and Juma had not moved. They stood on blood in a field of weapons.

One of Juma's women, the drunkard Allyn had lain with last night, shouldered forward as if she were the leader. She looked Allyn up and down for a fool. She bore him no ardor now, only contempt. The others gabbled to know what was happening: Why was there shooting? Was this naked girl the ranger? Was that a rocket? Where did all these guns come from?

"Quiet!"

Juma's voice came as loud as another gunshot. The women snapped into silence.

At the front, Hard Life stood beside Allyn. With black eyes too large for his face, the boy gazed up, wanting Allyn to do something, to make this stop. Allyn's only reply was to slide one foot behind the other, to fade into the skirts and skin behind him.

Promise saw him sliding away. She tried to lift an arm to him but failed. Why? To say good-bye? To stop him?

Promise called out, not to Allyn but to the boy beside him. Her voice quavered with the effort of staying alive.

"Hard Life. You will not get your fortune."

The little poacher shook his head, disagreeing.

"I will."

"No. Juma will keep it. Allyn will keep it. You'll die in the Kruger. A thousand more like you will die. Ten thousand animals. Hard Life. Save them."

Juma shoved the pistol between Promise's breasts, point-blank. She didn't look down.

"You women. How many of you will die?"

The one who had lain with Allyn answered.

"A great many."

"Press the button. Zero."

Juma fired.

Promise catapulted backward onto an iron mound of guns. Her head lolled, and both arms fell motionless down the heap. Her legs worked against the concrete floor, kicking at spilled weapons. The soles of her feet were stained red. Arched, on her back, Promise seemed to run, only a few steps in some unseen country, until she stopped, knees bent. A pale wisp curled from her chest.

Allyn pressed into the women at his rear, making them part.

In the center of the room, Juma swung the pistol. He spoke to Allyn down the length of his arm, over his great fist, across the small, dark tunnel of the gun.

"We are partners, shamwari. Stay."

"I want to go."

"And you will. After midnight."

Juma shifted his aim to the little poacher.

"Give me the radio, boy."

Hard Life recoiled into the skirt of the woman behind him, the leader. She crossed her arms over his chest, protecting him. Juma, massive and towering, jabbed the gun at her face. He took one stride closer.

She snatched the radio from Hard Life.

Ignoring the pistol, she asked the boy in her arms, "Is this for the missile?"

Hard Life bobbed his head against her white dress.

Juma inched the gun closer.

The woman glanced at the stolen women around her. The boy, Hard Life, pressed against her skirt. Promise lay dead across a pile of guns. Allyn saw everything she saw and wanted to run from it. He begged the whore.

"Please. Let me go."

"Why?"

"I didn't intend any of this."

She smiled with a tribal face, merry and toothy, and Allyn hoped he might yet get away. But her laugh was as dark as Juma's.

The jest was short-lived, throttled by the tang of smoke and blood. The woman moved her thumb across the radio's pad, over the digit zero.

Juma strode closer. She extended the radio like a talisman, her muti, to stop him. His leather shoes creaked. Three of the women laid hands on Allyn to hold him in place. Perhaps he could have fought them off, but Juma would have shot him if he'd tried to escape, or the woman would have pressed the button. Someone would kill him. His best chance was to let Juma handle this. The man was huge, ruthless. They were whores.

Allyn thought of Eva, that he wanted to see her again, then recalled she was dead.

Juma lowered the pistol. He begged, too, which Allyn would not have believed he could do.

"Please. Don't."

"Why not?"

"You'll kill us all."

The woman hugged the boy close. He looked like a child against her. This seemed a wish of hers. Hard Life embraced her hips.

Allyn pushed at the dark hands holding him, trying to break free.

A tear flowed down the woman's cheek. It hung on her chin.

"And if I don't"—she pointed with the radio, first at Juma, then Allyn—"you will."

Chapter 39

Neels did not stand when the boom and a dust plume arose in the east. He stayed huddled against a low bush, in a small patch of shade.

He checked his watch. The girl had done it in thirty-five minutes, well inside the deadline. This saved Neels from forcing the second radio from the Americans.

Neels nodded to the east, a simple testament that Promise had kept her word. But what had she done? Who was dead? At what cost?

The stocky sergeant jumped to his feet. He peered at the cloud. Since Neels had come back from the ravine, he and the Americans had sat separately, silently. Neels had shot one, been threatened by the other. What was there to talk about?

The sergeant stomped toward him.

Before the American could speak, Neels readied one of the rifles.

"How's your captain?"

"He needs a doctor soon. Like you give a shit."

"I would have done exactly the same if I did give a shit."

The sergeant thrust his hands to his hips, unarmed but puffed up and bellicose. Animals did this, swelled themselves, screeched and pawed the earth to look fierce in the face of a stronger beast. Neels tapped the stock of the rifle across his knees.

"Yes?"

"What happens now?"

"Your mission's accomplished. Go home, Sergeant."

"Just like that. Go home."

Neels hooked a thumb over his shoulder, west along the creek bed.

"It's that way."

The sergeant looked away as if for guidance from some invisible counsel. His boots shuffled. Neels did not stop tattooing the rifle in his lap.

"Yes?" Neels asked.

"You have no idea how much it pains me to ask this."

"Alright."

"What are you going to do?"

"Wait here a bit."

"And do what?"

"See."

"See what?"

"What happens."

Neels's clipped answers had the desired effect, making the sergeant go back to his captain, who sat in the slanting sunlight. The officer was a tough man, but he'd lost some color with the blood. The sergeant knelt beside him to confer. Both glowered at Neels, who sensed his own strength returning with the rest and the shade and the explosion.

He was impressed with the two American rescuers. They didn't rise and walk off, cursing Neels with something suitably unoriginal as they passed. They didn't rescue themselves immediately after their job was over but chose to stay in place, near Neels, to make sure he got off the field, too. And Promise, and Karskie. Neels thought to tell the Americans they had guts, but that would do nothing to change the dynamics and the facts, so he kept his counsel.

From his canteen, Neels swished water in his mouth. He wet his kerchief, then tied it around his neck. In the distance, the detonation had scared away the buzzards, so the settling pillar above Macandezulo was the only mark on the horizon. Neels blinked into the sky, gladdened at its barrenness, sensing nothing of his wife or his own heart in it, just untroubled blue and the cloud of dust.

He drew in his legs, testing them as he stood. They held. The dizziness had gone.

Neels raised one rifle. Both Americans jumped when he fired into the air so Karskie, several hundred meters off, would come this way. The boy, tiny in the distance, moving alone against the stillness of the Limpopo bush, waved excitedly and began to jog for the ravine.

Neels approached the Americans. The sergeant stood. Neels handed him one of the rifles. The American seemed surprised, confused about what to do with it.

"Karskie's coming."

The captain reached up a hand to his sergeant to be helped to his feet. The pain of rising wracked his features. He did need a doctor.

"The girl?" asked the captain.

"I didn't see her."

Neels put his canteen in the captain's good hand. Gently, he patted the officer on his wounded, wrapped shoulder.

"Sorry, lad."

To the sergeant, Neels extended a hand. Blank faced, the sergeant shook it.

"Karskie will see you back to the Kruger. You'll get there by sundown."

The sergeant looked at the ghost of the explosion wafting away. Neels let go of his hand.

"No, Sergeant. Do not consider coming with me. Get your captain home safe."

Neels turned to head toward Karskie. Behind him, the sergeant called.

"Hey."

Neels walked on, waving away the invitation for one more comment, some parting bon mot, a bad trait out of American movies.

In the open, Karskie slowed to a tired slog; the big boy had run as far as he could. Winded and hot, Karskie halted with his hands on his knees. Neels met him with arms out and straightened him.

"Catch your breath. Then tell me what happened."

Karskie heaved in and out, head tipped back. He took longer than Neels thought was needed.

"Alright. Come on then."

"Promise. She killed the guard. What's his name? She knifed him in the bloody back."

The one she swore she would kill. Good for her.

"And you got away."

"Yeah."

"Then?"

"Then I don't fucking know, Neels. She said she was going to blow the missile. You heard the blast."

"Yes."

"She said you'd explain what she was doing."

"I will. Not right now."

"Why not?"

Neels pointed into the bush, toward the sun.

"The Americans are that way. Can you get them back to the Kruger?"

Too many questions garbled Karskie's reply. He began several at once.

"Why? What? Where?"

"Stop that. Can you?"

The boy centered himself enough to nod.

"Good. One more thing. You got money, yeah?"

Karskie continued bobbing his head. Neels poked him in the chest to pin home the point.

"Promise wants a house for her grandparents. See to it."

Before Karskie locked up in another gush of questions, Neels patted him on the arm, then pushed the boy onward to the creek bed. The Americans would explain as much as they could. If he came back from Macandezulo, Neels would tell the rest.

With Karskie making for the ravine, Neels stopped to pluck a smooth, sun-warmed pebble off the ground. He slid it under his tongue.

• • •

Neels moved down the center of the dirt road. The village smelled of human waste. Trash gathered between the abandoned hovels, weeds grew in windows, painted walls of shanties rotted, yielding to the bush. The air smelled fusty with the last floating dust from the blast. The deeper Neels entered Macandezulo, the stronger the murky odors of soot and fire became.

Halfway down the street, every structure bore marks of the explosion, a powdery coating of concrete, gray fragments on the roofs. Closer to the blast site, several shanties were crushed, caved in by the concussion and debris. A pickup truck lay flipped on its back.

A sturdy building had stood at the end of the street, made of block and cement, now rubble. Approaching the crater, Neels picked through the debris, everything loose and sliding under his boots. He peered into a great scorched hole. The missile had razed the building to its foundation, busted it sky-high into bits that had rained into a jumbled, jagged ring. Metal rods and construction mesh sharpened the wreckage. Black iron peppered the ruins, the remains of hundreds of twisted, melted, or intact guns. Neels bent for a barely scratched pistol. He spun it back into the crater.

The gun skidded down into the hollow, past a tatter of white cloth. This might have been a curtain. Or a dress.

A long time ago, in a different war, these were the things Neels had done. He brought demolition and death to the enemies he was sent against. He'd borne no intention for those enemies to survive. Innocents and comrades died, too. Neels made no apologies then and saw little reason to do so now.

He shouted into the crater.

"Juma!"

Neels cupped his hands and turned to call out into the village.

"Juma!"

Three men, rifles up, walked up the dirt road toward him. All were thin, wearing loose, mismatched clothes and plastic sandals. These were dark and hesitant men, poachers with guns trained on Neels.

He did not lift his own rifle, only an empty hand.

"Stop there."

Two did stop, and the third, seeing he'd gone past his pals, scurried back in line.

"I'm not here for you, boys. Only for Juma."

The three didn't lower their guns. Neels imagined them firing but not the tingle of being hit. He pointed behind him into the crater.

"See this? I'll kill the three of you. Then I'll kill your villages. I'm a Kruger ranger."

One by one, the poachers eased their rifle barrels to the ground. They kept their distance.

"Where's Juma? Have you seen him?"

The trio was slow to consult each other. One called back.

"No."

Neels turned his back to the poachers. He surveyed the debris and scattered guns, another shred of cloth, a flame gnawing at a chunk of wood, a dusky severed arm.

"Juma!"

The destruction was too complete to make an echo.

"Promise!"

Neels called once more for Juma and a last time for Promise. Nothing came from the canyon but the throb of lingering flame and the old reek of war. Neels was not satisfied or the victor, only alone and tired and aware that he was not among the dead. The rewards of war, any war, were scant.

He strode straight at the poachers. Neels didn't angle away but made them step aside to avoid him. The poachers stank, too.

Neels wheeled on one, it didn't matter which, and shoved him to the ground. The poacher dropped his rifle. The other two backed away.

"You."

Neels included all three with a sweep of his arm.

"You stay the fok out of my park."

He walked on. The sun in his face forced Neels's eyes down while the road and village faded into the bush.

Chapter 40

Wally slowed them down, but they did not stop until they reached the border at sundown.

Karskie brought them to a spot where the fence still stood. The three trudged south under the bruising dusk. A starry hour later, in full darkness, they found a fallen patch of fence and stepped through to the greeting calls of the Kruger's monkeys and beasts.

Wally ran out of steam only a hundred yards into the park. He found a rock large enough to sit on. LB took his first sip from the canteen, saving the rest for Wally and Karskie. The big boy had done well, uncomplaining.

LB took Wally's pulse and checked his bandages. Wally was fatigued but in no peril; the wound wasn't weeping, his color was fine. Fumbling one-handed with his vest, Wally asked LB and Karskie for some time to himself. LB left him the canteen.

The moon hadn't risen yet, and the Milky Way was so bright it almost hummed above the bush. Karskie and LB hadn't talked much on their exit from Mozambique, they'd focused on keeping Wally moving. LB had kept an eye and ear over his shoulder for pursuers.

"I don't think he can go any farther. Not tonight."

Karskie took a seat on the open ground.

"Me neither."

"Can you call somebody to come get us? A car, a chopper?"

"Our copters don't fly in the park at night. And we don't drive off the paved road."

"Why the hell not?"

"The Kruger belongs to the animals. We take that seriously."

"So we're stuck out here again."

LB turned a circle. The bush lay unchanging in every direction, stretching into the hills beyond the fence and the South African plains west. The land was little different from the night sky, a dark world above and below. The bush was going to be a hard place for him to shirk. LB knew that, he felt the seed of it as he pivoted in place. He'd left things here, and they would stay here forever.

"What's on the menu tonight? Ants? Bees?"

Karskie shrugged his big, soft shoulders.

"I'm not a ranger. I don't know."

LB could have told Karskie that he was a ranger, but it would have been a lie. Karskie wasn't cut out for it. A man could only be what his nature dictated, what his talents allowed. Everything else, he was not, and would not be.

LB dropped the rifle into his hands.

"I could fire off a few rounds. See if that clandestine patrol finds us."

"Don't do that. They will find us, and they won't know who we are or why you were shooting. We're near the border. Keep in mind, Neels trained them. Best leave them alone. We'll get out in the morning."

Karskie gazed out into the bush with LB, and he seemed less afraid. This was not the same boy who'd crept up on the drone last night.

Who else had changed, and how much? Promise, Juma, Lush Life, the women?

"Where's Neels, do you think?"

"Dead or out here somewhere."

Karskie made it sound like they were the same.

"What's going to happen to him?"

"For shooting your captain?"

"Yes."

"Nothing. No one's going to prosecute him, especially if Juma's dead. Neels is a ranger. He was in Mozambique legally, doing his job. Frankly, doing yours. He'll claim one thing, you'll claim another, and there you have it."

"What'll you claim?"

"No one will ask. As I said, I'm not a ranger."

The boy was right. No one was going to ask him, or LB and Wally. This was a covert mission, and it was going to stay that way. LB wasn't going to be allowed to push this. He'd be forced to just bury it.

"What about you?"

The boy laughed. The bush, vast and teeming, seemed to answer. Far away, or maybe close, a creature howled. Karskie's smile was starlit.

"Apparently, I'm buying a house."

LB left him sitting with the night. The boy didn't look like he would move for hours, listening to his park, at ease.

Wally beckoned LB over. He held up the sat phone, dials glowing in the dark.

"Torres wants to talk to you."

LB took the phone.

"Major."

"LB. I'm on a plane inside the hour. I'll be there by sunup."

"Wally'll be glad to see you. He's going to have a long night."

"I'll escort you both back to Lemonnier. We'll start the debrief."

"Yes, ma'am."

"Your cover story is you were on a survival course in the Kruger. Ran into some poachers. Wally got shot."

Karskie's prediction about this mission disappearing took no time at all to come true.

"LB."

"Ma'am."

"I just want to say."

"Don't."

"I want to say thank you."

"Just a sec."

LB walked away with the sat phone, moving far enough from Wally to not be heard.

"Major."

Torres gave him no chance to speak first.

"You saved his life, LB. He said so. Straight up. You saved him."

"Major, you need to stop talking."

This flummoxed Torres. LB wedged his voice in.

"Saving him wasn't my job. And it wasn't his. Wally knew it. He tried, and I stopped him. That's what happened."

The satellite line hovered silent. LB walked farther from Wally into the bush, what felt like a long way, until Torres spoke.

"You did the right thing."

"Did Wally say that? Or is that you?"

"It's me."

"Okay. I need you to do me a favor."

"If I can do it. Anything."

"Send me home. To Nellis. I got six months left on my contract. Get me a job in logistics. I want to drive a truck. Then I'm done."

Above the bush one shooting star coursed and blinked out. Tonight would be hungry, but they'd eat bugs and leaves and drink dirty water, and they'd see tomorrow.

LB crossed one arm over his chest, lapping his hand across the sleeve where the Guardian Angel's patch, "That others may live," had been for so long, and would not be again.

Acknowledgments

I am the creator of this book only in the sense that I'm at the center of a great many creators. Each individual thanked below told me one stunning story or another, and all I did was make furious notes, then later, at my keyboard, choose the parts that fit the whole.

How do you thank a person for something as singular as his or her life's story or the wisdom and recollections of his or her life's work? Appreciation pales if the finished product, the full novel, doesn't hold. So, in no small part because I'm deeply indebted to so many, I wrote this novel hard, with an intensity born out of fear that my treatment of their lives would fall short of the original versions.

I start with retired USAF Maj. Scott Williams, the real LB, who hosted me in Port Elizabeth and let me grow close to his great wife and kids. Scott, a former USAF pilot, loves the Guardian Angels as much as anyone and is mainly responsible for bringing me into the pararescue community. A lot of Wally and LB grew out of him. I can't repay Scott, but I can do my job as well as he demands.

Scott introduced me to Brian Bailey, who then linked me to his father, Don. The Baileys own a lot of stuff in South Africa, and all of it was made available to me, including marvelous time spent with these two gentlemen. The core of Kruger Ranger Promise comes from Brian's work with a township orphanage and his own experience as a wildlife ranger. Much of Allyn's character comes from late-night cigar and brandy sessions with Don on his veranda in Plettenberg Bay, where he told me of his past with courage and candor. Don showed me penguins, Finagolo (the pidgin language of the Zimbabwean mines), the joys of cricket, and an unmatched English elegance. I received from the Baileys more kindness and gifts of the heart than any traveler could hope for. I trust I have made lifelong friends.

Lt. Col. John McElroy, former combat-rescue officer with the GAs, claims that I write no more or less than what he dictates. I call him a liar publicly and privately acknowledge the truth of that. I've made my peace, Mac. These are your stories. Mac makes up the largest slice of Wally. He is cheerful, a beautiful athlete, brave, and loyal. The image on the cover of *The Devil's Waters*, a skydiver in scuba gear, is based on Mac.

My first cousin Bob Bigman served in an unnamed US government agency as a cybersecurity chief for thirty-one years. The craziest plot twists in these GA novels, the head-scratchers, are Bob's. He winks and grins when he tells me, "I didn't say we did that. I only said we could."

USAF Capt. Chris Baker of the GAs never fails to take my calls, get me back on the proper track, and make me laugh. Chris knows almost as much as McElroy. That ought to be worth a few more hours of debate on my sailboat.

Will Fowlds is a world-renowned veterinarian and warrior in the rhino-conservancy battle. He took me into the bush to dart a rhino at the Amakhala Game Reserve and spent hours teaching me the intricacies and horrors of poaching. Also at Amakhala, Simon Allen, a naturalist, let me come on long walks in the veld and showed me how to track, what to eat (ants!), and how to survive on foot among creatures that might have different notions. With both Allen and Will, I saw true marvels.

Marius Roos paved the way for my time in the Kruger. Because of him, I was able to travel over the same ground as the poachers, see their terrible spoor, and learn firsthand the hatefulness of their works. Also, because of Marius, I rekindled my dislike for rum and Coke.

Big Willem Geel took much time with me in the Kruger, though he claimed to never warm up to me. Chopper pilot Ian DeBeer showed me not only rhino carcasses so awful as to be netherworldly but also many splendors of the bush. Imagine being charged by a black rhino while sitting in a helicopter, or buzzing a herd of eland to make them stampede. Good times.

Gen. Johan Jooste, the man in charge of the entire Kruger National Park, gave me an unforgettable hour of advice and quotes. Ansi Venter, special prosecutor with the Organized Crime Unit of the Office of Public Prosecutions (she's in charge of prosecuting South Africa's racketeers, including poachers) told me enough to fill five legal pad pages and scare me about the current state of poaching in South Africa. Ansi convinced me that the poachers are stoppable, but that will require more than the resources available in her country.

Johan Brits of the Directorate of Priority Crime Investigation, Organized Crime Unit, coined the beautiful phrase "children of the bush," speaking of the rhinos. He, too, gave me unfettered time and advice.

Driver Glenn Batcheller-Adams is an example of the sublime being handed to the writer who listens well. In his van, headed to the airport, he told me of his time in the Angolan Civil War as a member of the Selous Scouts. Glenn regaled me with stories of fierce training, shocking combat, and a dead baboon nailed to a fence with a cigarette in its mouth.

Likewise in the serendipity department, Trecy Kent III sat next to me on a flight to LA. Turns out Trecy was an armorer in the USAF for a dozen years. There I was, writing a book involving a USAF missile. Trecy went far beyond the expected bounds of a well-met stranger on a plane and has become a friend and go-to adviser.

Kruger Chief Ranger Maj. Jack Greeff avoided me for a week, until I plugged a practice target between the eyes from seventy-five meters with his rifle. Jack took me seriously after I repeated the feat and gave me a seminar on policing the bush. He's hunted poachers in the Kruger for thirty years, knows every poaching trick, and seethes at the thought of them. Jack became the bedrock of Neels.

Lastly, the most blatant theft of character I committed for this novel is from my good comrade David Barske; I barely bothered to cover up his name. David is shameless and brilliant, a big, likeable kid with a crazy streak as broad as his toothy grin. Together, we chased bushpigs over the Skukuza golf course, drank from boots and cans, listened to lions roar and rangers brag and bitch. David gave me priceless time, documents, advice, and insights into the hunt for the Kruger's poachers. David is a brave young man on the front lines of the dire fight to save the rhino from extinction. He's one of many.

On the business side of this book, I thank first, and again, my agent, Luke Janklow of Janklow Nesbit. Luke and his assistant, Claire Dippel, are my irreplaceable teammates. I actually look forward to having something to complain about so I can talk with them. I sometimes make things up.

The reason I have to pretend things are wrong is Alan Turkus of Thomas & Mercer. Alan treats my work with respect as art, and value as a product. He's a gentleman, and he runs a classy outfit, Thomas & Mercer, which has never failed to regard me with friendliness and a professional level of courtesy. I've been published by quite a few houses, and never by such competent, collegial people who believe their writers are customers and act accordingly.

David L. Robbins
Richmond, VA

About the Author

David L. Robbins currently teaches advanced creative writing at VCU Honors College. A *New York Times* bestselling author, he has written twelve action-packed novels, including the pararescue novels *The Devil's Waters* and *The Empty Quarter*, as well as *War of the Rats*, *Broken Jewel*, *The Assassins Gallery*, and *Scorched Earth*. An award-winning essayist and screenwriter, he has also had two stage plays successfully produced. In his hometown of Richmond, Virginia, where he lives, Robbins founded the James River Writers, an organization dedicated to supporting professional and aspiring writers. He also cofounded the Podium Foundation, which encourages and supports artistic expression in Richmond's public high schools. His latest nonprofit effort is as creator of the Mighty Pen Project, a veterans writing program in partnership with the Virginia War Memorial. Robbins extends his creative scope beyond fiction as an accomplished guitarist and student of jazz, pop, and Latin classical music. When he's not writing or teaching, he's often found sailing, shooting sporting clays, weight lifting, and traveling the world for his research.